The Antenatal Group

Amy Bratley lives in Dorset with her
husband and two children.

Also by Amy Bratley

The Girls' Guide to Homemaking

The Saturday Supper Club

The Antenatal Group

AMY BRATLEY

PAN BOOKS

First published 2013 by Pan Books
an imprint of Pan Macmillan, a division of Macmillan Publishers Limited
Pan Macmillan, 20 New Wharf Road, London N1 9RR
Basingstoke and Oxford
Associated companies throughout the world
www.panmacmillan.com

ISBN 978-1-4472-1838-8

1 3 5 7 9 8 6 4 2

A CIP catalogue record for this book is available from
the British Library.

Typeset by Ellipsis Digital Limited, Glasgow
Printed and bound by CPI Group (UK) Ltd, Croydon, CR0 4YY

Visit **www.panmacmillan.com** to read more about all our books
and to buy them. You will also find features, author interviews and
news of any author events, and you can sign up for e-newsletters
so that you're always first to hear about our new releases.

For Sonny and Audrey, my sprogs.

Acknowledgements

For their support and encouragement, my sincere thanks to Veronique Baxter and Laura West. Many thanks to Macmillan's Jenny Geras for her great ideas and editorial insight.

In writing this book I consulted my well-thumbed and much-loved copy of *The Rough Guide to Pregnancy* by Kaz Cooke. I watched the Birthwise Antenatal DVD, read *Afterbirth* edited by Dani Klein Modisett and read information provided by the National Childbirth Trust, babycentre.co.uk and mumsnet. I also made use, with permission, of anecdotes provided by friends, including Isabel Cook, Charmaine Parkin and Melissa Four. Whilst I have tried to make each character's pregnancy and birth realistic, it's worth remembering they are my own interpretations based on my personal knowledge and experience of having babies. Thanks to my family, in particular my mum, Anne Cook, who always knows best. Love, as always, to my husband, Jimmy, and children, Sonny and Audrey. Thanks to my best pals and the great mum friends I've made over the years – I couldn't do it without you lot! Finally, love to the memory of my father, Donald Bratley. One of a kind.

Chapter One

'I'm so sorry,' said Leo, almost inaudibly. 'But I can't have this baby.'

Leo was, at least, polite when breaking up with Mel. There was nothing sordid for her to deal with. She didn't have to find a blonde bombshell in bed with her fiancé, long, slim legs wrapped around his torso, a silk thong wedged down the side of the sofa or an explicit text message not meant for her eyes. There was no unseemly catfight or slapped faces to contend with. No, it was Leo's timing that was just the *tiniest* bit off kilter. Standing on the stone steps outside Birth & Baby, a centre for antenatal classes in Brighton, Mel was nearly eight months pregnant with their first baby when Leo decided now would be a good moment to split.

'I just can't go through with it,' he muttered to the back of Mel's head.

Leo was standing behind Mel while she fished around in her enormous tote bag, searching for something she'd lost. He watched and waited while she lifted out a bruised banana, knitting needles, balls of wool, a make-up bag, a water bottle, a battered copy of *The Rough Guide to Pregnancy*, a half-eaten bar of chocolate and a book of baby names, before repeating himself with more volume.

'What?' Mel said, frowning down into the depths of her bag and screwing up her nose, having not heard a word. 'I can't see my pregnancy notes. I definitely put them in here, I'm sure I did. Do you think they fell out on the bus? You have to take them *everywhere* with you. The midwife is going to think I'm completely hopeless—'

Mel sifted through the bag again, gave up with a frustrated sigh then began to unbutton her coat – a bulky maternity one she hated – and, struggling with the sleeves, knocked into a pregnant woman carrying a yoga mat.

'Oh, I'm sorry,' she said to the woman, pulling a panicked face. 'I've no spatial awareness these days.'

The woman smiled forgivingly, in a sisterly manner, and Mel smiled in return, once again warmed by how nice pregnant women were to one another, then continued to extract her body from her voluminous maternity coat. For mid-February, it was a ridiculously warm morning. The sky was the brightest blue and people were walking around in T-shirt sleeves, while she was overheating in her outfit, made worse by her sturdy maternity underwear and leopard-print maternity tights. The tights had felt like a good idea at the time, when she was only a few weeks pregnant and on a hormonal spending frenzy in Top Shop, but now they stretched over her bump in inky blue splodges and cut into her skin just under her hammock of a bra, making her feel like a melon squeezed into a sausage skin. She breathed out and glanced around the busy car park, at a queue of cars waiting to find spaces. Seagulls screeched noisily above and Mel began to wish she lived in a tiny village in the Swiss Alps, where she could gaze out over glacial valleys and listen to the gentle tinkle of cowbells instead.

'What were you saying, Leo?' she asked, pushing her fringe back and wiping sweat from her forehead. 'I didn't hear you for all this noise. Do I look red in the face again? I didn't know it was possible to emit this much heat. I could stand in elderly people's homes as a cheaper option to fuel. What do you think?'

Leo closed his eyes for a moment, then looked nervously towards the busy main road, where a police car edged its way through traffic and off into Brighton somewhere, siren blazing. He sighed deeply and rested his hand on Mel's arm in an odd, almost sympathetic way.

'Mel,' he said, even more clearly this time, looking at her pink, glowing face, which was framed by a black, angular bob. 'I'm really sorry. I know what kind of bloke this makes me, but I can't do this. I just can't come to this antenatal group.'

Mel leaned against the handrail and took the weight from her left foot, which was constantly swollen all the way past her ankle. Her ballet pump had given up trying to be a shoe and barely covered her toes. She'd definitely gone up a shoe size. The days when Mel wore heels felt like decades ago. Out the corner of her eye she glimpsed a very pregnant-but-slim-everywhere-else woman with oodles of blonde curls and watched her happily link arms with her partner as they walked towards the steps. He had her pregnancy notes tucked under his arm like a newspaper. Both were grinning from ear to ear. Leo, on the other hand, was looking deadly serious. Mel gave him a hard stare, but felt her stomach flip nervously.

'What do you mean, you can't come in?' she asked crossly. 'Didn't you get the morning off work?'

Leo, dark-haired but pale-skinned, a long, thin scar running along his chin, was dressed in dark-grey trousers, a black jumper and a sheepskin coat with a tartan scarf knotted around his neck. He suited the winter. Mel had met him in December, two years ago, at a friend's house party in Hove. They'd both nipped outside the basement flat to smoke roll-ups in the courtyard garden and Mel had been struck by how good-looking he was, in his dark jumper and with a beanie hat pulled low over his ears. Curls of smoke lingered around his pink lips as if reluctant to leave his mouth. Someone in a neighbouring house had let off fireworks, and Mel and Leo had 'ooh'ed and 'aah'ed at them together like small children, hesitantly finding each other's hands, then mouths. Now, on the steps, waiting for him to answer, she felt nostalgic for that first kiss, when her heart had exploded like a firecracker in her chest.

'No,' he said, leaving a long pause. 'It's not that. I'm sorry, but I've been thinking about this for weeks, but been trying to do the right thing. I can't have a baby, I don't want my life to be over already when I'm barely twenty-seven years old and my career has only just got off the ground and—'

'You can't have a baby?' interrupted Mel, her eyes wide open. She pointed at her belly. 'Leo, I'm thirty-five weeks pregnant. There's only five weeks to go. '

For some reason, all Mel could think about was the tiny pair of baby booties Leo had bought for their unborn baby when she had been only nine weeks pregnant. They'd had a row about leaving the lid off the butter and he'd gone out and returned with the white booties from Baby Gap, holding them on outstretched palms as a peace offering. Mel had gasped with a mixture of joy and terror. How could anything with feet so tiny be her responsibility? *Mel* – untidy, disorganized, impulsive Mel – taking care of a tiny, mewling baby who could do nothing for itself and would be completely dependent on her for years. Could she do it? Could she be a good mother? Could she raise her baby to be confident and energetic, compassionate and wise? The question seemed bigger than her. She had clung on to Leo that evening as if her life depended on it. He would help: calm, dependable, capable Leo would be a good dad. There was no need to panic. The boots were in her top drawer, still wrapped in tissue paper, though she often took them out, to sit and stare and dream of what was to come. Now, she raised her eyes to Leo, trying to fathom if he was serious, but he lifted his hands in the air, as if asking for mercy. He shook his head.

'I know,' he said. 'But, Mel, you never even asked me if I wanted all this.'

'Never asked you?' she asked, incredulous. 'Leo, we both got pregnant, not just me. Isn't it a bit late to be backtracking like this? '

'Yes, of course it is, but I didn't want a baby, still don't,' he garbled. 'You bulldozed me into thinking I did, but now that it's a reality, I just don't know. It's complicated. Look, we shouldn't do this here. Let's go. Let's go and get a coffee and talk.'

Bulldozed? Mel was so shocked she stopped breathing. She swallowed. In her head, she begged: *Please don't be saying this, Leo*. She watched his mouth move a little more but couldn't make sense of what was coming out. It was as if he was talking another language entirely. The baby kicked hard inside her and she gasped. Don't leave me, Leo. Don't leave *us*. She forced herself to speak.

'I don't drink coffee' was all she could think to say, her scalp prickling and her throat burning with the need to cry. She took a deep breath. 'I'm going to the antenatal class. Come with me. You're just nervous. It happens.'

Mel held out her hand towards Leo and smiled bravely, blinking away the moisture in her eyes. But Leo shook his head sadly and jammed his hands under his armpits as if he didn't trust himself not to take her hand, not to do the right thing after all. He looked again towards the road and Mel wondered with a sickening shudder if there was someone – some other woman – waiting for him in her car with the engine running, wearing red lipstick and leather driving gloves and revving the accelerator, ready to steal him away. With her heart bumping, she followed his gaze but saw only random strangers making their way to work, snaking across the streets as if this were a perfectly ordinary day.

'You're having an affair,' she said flatly, losing grip of the bag handle, so her bottle of water rolled on to the steps. 'Are you in love with someone who isn't me?'

Leo picked up the bottle, looked at her with a lack of comprehension, pushed the bottle angrily into her bag and shook his head emphatically. He moved closer to her and put his hands on her shoulders, fixing her with a troubled stare. Mel saw that his eyes were filling with tears, and this made her stomach sink more than anything he'd actually said. She'd only ever seen him cry once before.

'Absolutely not,' he said. 'I swear there's no one else. This is about me. About whether I can be a decent father to the baby and partner to you. I don't think I can. I'm not the right person. I have my reasons. Don't hate me, Mel. I wouldn't do this unless I had to.'

Mel felt all the energy and fight seep out of her. She thought back over the last few days and weeks. Had she missed something? There had been no clue that this was going to happen. Nothing at all. Was it her fault? Had she been too moody and hormonal? Yes, probably. When had they last had sex? Two weeks ago. He'd seemed content afterwards. Quiet, maybe. Had she been too obsessive about her pregnancy? Maybe. She'd been incredibly excitable at times, and grumpy at others, especially about the profound tiredness she felt, as if she'd been hit over the head with a frying pan. She was a subscriber to babycentre.co.uk and checked in most days to chat online with other mums due in March, but she rarely recounted the conversations unless it was about something *really* important, like whether she could have one or two tins of dolphin-friendly tuna per week. She knew how boring some of her friends had been about their pregnancies and didn't want to fall into that trap. Bewildered, Mel shook her head. Feeling that the steps were melting under her feet, she eased herself down on to the edge of one, clutching the handles of her bag, suddenly feeling terribly cold.

'Don't hate me, Mel,' he said again, quietly.

But I don't hate you, she thought, I love you. Loved you. Still love you. You don't snap your fingers and hate someone, especially when you're having a child together. Not when you've mapped out a future together. She had the unhinged urge to laugh and so held one hand over her face. This was something she had done in childhood – giggled intensely and uncontrollably at completely inappropriate times, like when her mum broke the news that her dad was not coming back from hospital. Mel had thought her mum might slap her for laughing, but instead she had understood, pulling Mel into her chest and holding her there as tightly as you can hold a person, unconditionally loving her.

'I'm sorry,' Leo said, choked. 'Sorry. I'll call you later. I'll stay with Nick for a while. Good luck with the class.'

'Good luck with the class' sounded to Mel like *Have a nice life then. Byeee!* Then, without even looking back at her, Leo paced across the car park, leaving Mel sitting on the steps, an overwhelming surge of nausea swimming through her, worse than any morning sickness she'd known. Feeling utterly numb, she watched his figure grow distant until he seemed to evaporate, her urge to laugh replaced by the urge to scream at the top of her lungs. She stared into her bag again and saw her notes, pressed up against the side, her twelve-week-scan picture of the baby, black and white and swirly, poking out of the folder. Her eyes filled with tears. There was no way she could go to an antenatal group now. She would just go home. Call her boss and take the afternoon off work. Call her mum. Think. All at once overcome with overpowering tiredness, she wondered if there was anywhere she could lie down and close her eyes.

'Are you all right sitting out here on the steps?' came a well-spoken voice from behind her. 'Are you here for the antenatal class?'

Mel looked up to see the curly-haired blonde woman she'd

seen earlier smiling down at her. Mel nodded but didn't speak, pushing her fingers to the corners of her eyes to wipe at the tears.

'Let me help you up,' said the woman, offering Mel her hand. 'I'm Katy. My husband, Alan, is just inside, finding out where we need to go. Was that your partner? Couldn't he stay?'

Mel took Katy's outstretched hand and lifted herself to standing, a rush of blood from her head making fizzy dots appear in front of her eyes. She shook her head, muttered something about Leo 'having an important meeting at work' and followed Katy in through the revolving doors, a burning sensation in her throat. It was hot inside, really hot. She started to tremble and sweat at the same time, recognizing the need to throw up.

'Oh no, I'm . . . I—' Mel gasped to Katy, dropping her bag and coat in the reception area and rapidly pushing open the door of the Ladies' toilet. 'I think I'm going to be sick.'

Chapter Two

Poor woman, thought Katy, watching the dark-haired girl wearing a pink flower in her hair and leopard-print tights rush into the Ladies', apparently to be sick. She looked awful. Katy had heard that some women suffered morning sickness even this far into pregnancy. How horrible. She'd never had morning sickness, hardly ever felt nauseous. Thank God. In fact, her entire pregnancy had been plain sailing, right from the word go, when she'd got pregnant the first time she and Alan had tried. Well, she sighed inwardly, opening a small Tupperware pot containing neatly sliced carrot, cucumber and celery sticks to nibble on, unless she counted the effect it had had on her relationship with her business partner, Anita.

Nightmare, mused Katy, thinking of Anita, who was probably sticking pins in a Katy doll right this minute, as Katy bit into a carrot stick, ambient rainforest music softly playing from speakers above her seat in reception. Pushing Anita from her thoughts, she ran her eyes over the rust-coloured walls, strung with tasteful abstract images of pregnant women's bodies, sensuous and lovely. Someone had designed this place perfectly, like a womb. Tucking her blonde hair behind her ears, she thought of her own body and how radically it had changed in pregnancy. Her breasts had grown from an A to a D cup, her belly protruded in a neat bump and a dark line ran from her belly button to her pubic bone. By eating carefully, she hadn't put on any unnecessary weight. Pushing the lid back on the Tupperware pot of vegetable crudités, Katy brushed her fingers over a hardback book on a side table entitled *Positive Birthing: Water Babies*. It was one of many pregnancy and birth books she had at home and had read cover to cover. What was that Guides' motto she'd had shoved down her throat when she was a child? *Be prepared*. It was part of Katy's DNA.

'Oh, bloody hell,' she muttered as her phone beeped with a text message from Anita. She read the capitalized message: I need you in the office!

Straightening herself in the chair, Katy felt a stress headache gripping her. She massaged the back of her neck with one hand, rested her mobile on her knee with the other and took a deep breath. Perhaps Anita was right, maybe I shouldn't have come to antenatal group. Maybe I *should* be at work, she thought, panicked. They *were* almost drowning in work. They'd never had so many requests for filming and events locations before, and it was Katy's job to find suitable places, be it the grounds of a stately home or an art deco house on the beach, with swimming pool. Images of her office flashed into her mind: emails mounting, missed calls, Anita's Post-it notes all over her desk, covered with red-ink scrawl as if she'd written them in blood.

'Katy,' her husband Alan said from beside the water cooler.

He grinned at her and pressed a plastic cup under the tap. 'Do you want water? It's good and cold, angel.'

A little startled, Katy looked up at him appreciatively. He was dapper, Alan, with his salt-and-pepper hair and multi-striped Paul Smith shirt. Only he could call her angel and get away with it. He seemed a little out of place against this nurturing and holistic backdrop. He better suited French antique interior design and looked great reclining on the Louis XV-style chaise longue in his office. He worked in the fine-food business and had fine tastes himself: drank only the best grape, loved oysters, wore a gold vintage Rolex and drove a midnight-blue BMW. It was only his Antipodean accent that gave him away as anything other than the English gent he looked to be.

'Yes, please,' she said, standing and smiling sweetly when Alan kissed her cheek, his hand finding the small of her back and stroking it, sending a pleasing shiver up her spine. As she took the water, she registered a couple arriving through the revolving door who must have been in their teens, or only just out of them. The girl was Asian, with light-brown skin, long, glossy, black hair tied in a loose knot on top of her head, enormous dark-brown eyes and a tiny gold dot in her nose. Her baby would be beautiful. She had a fabulous figure, which suited pregnancy. She wore a chunky cardigan over a generous cleavage and pair of harem pants with a crotch that ended up just above the knee, and battered white plimsolls. Charity-shop chic, thought Katy. I could never pull that off. Designer: yes; charity shop; no.

'Hi, I'm Rebecca Harris. I'm here for antenatal classes with Ginny,' she heard the girl say to the receptionist. 'This is Lenny.'

Lenny sniffed the orchid on the reception desk.

'That's me,' said Lenny. 'Howdy.'

Katy ran her eyes over Lenny as discreetly as she could. He was carrying a guitar and yawning ostentatiously. She stole a look at Alan and they exchanged exasperated expressions. Surely no more than nineteen, Lenny wore shirtsleeves rolled to the elbow, a waistcoat, brown trousers that nipped in a little at the bottom and a hat over his wavy golden-brown hair. Underneath the hat, he had a handsome wide-open face and a cheeky grin, which, she realized, he was aiming in her direction. She felt suddenly naked under his gaze. He looked like he was on the pull. What a nerve! But there was something about him she felt instantly drawn to. He was confident and self-assured – admirable qualities. She gave him a brief smile in return, feeling flustered. She never quite knew how to behave around handsome male teenagers. She sighed. A part of her still felt as though she was twenty-one and welcomed the appreciative smile Lenny was giving her. It was deserved. She'd earned it. Another part of her reminded herself that she was actually twenty-nine and soon to be a mother. From her bag, her phone beeped again. She picked it up and, seeing another furious message from Anita, tossed it back in and groaned.

'Anita's on my back again,' she said under her breath to Alan, rolling her eyes.

'Oh, for God's sake,' he said, shaking his head. 'Tell her to go jump. You're having a baby!'

Katy flashed him a smile but, inside, she felt saddened. Not so long ago, Anita and Katy had been best friends. They'd had a brilliant working partnership when they'd launched their company, Spotted. Not any more.

I'll be in soon, she texted, her fingernails clicking on the keypad.

Turning her head towards the door, Katy saw another couple enter. The woman was frowning and she wore a green coat. The man, equally serious, skin pale as milk, followed behind. At the same time, the midwife, Ginny, who was running the antenatal class, opened the door of the classroom and let out a gentle peal of laughter at nothing in particular. Katy blinked. Ginny, marmalade-dyed hair whipped into an incredible beehive, her eyes accentuated by eyeliner that winged out in cat-eye style, wore a navy-blue wiggle dress, white belt and navy-blue wedges. On her wrist she wore an oversized charm bracelet that jangled as she moved, and a necklace to match, which she fiddled with as she spoke. Katy didn't have a clue how old she was. She looked to be in her mid-twenties – but hadn't the blurb said she had four kids and years of midwifery experience?

'Wow,' she whispered to Alan. 'I was *not* expecting her to look like that. Hardly an earth mother, is she?'

Katy caught Rebecca's eye. They smiled at one another. She was obviously thinking the same thing about Ginny. Weren't midwives supposed to be dumpling-shaped women who wore flat, rubber-soled shoes and blue smocks and had humbugs in their pockets? Apparently not.

'Okay, mums and dads to be,' Ginny said with a warm smile. 'You all look absolutely lovely. We'll make a start in five minutes.'

Katy pointed towards the toilet and whispered to Alan, who was gawping at Ginny.

'I think I should check on that girl quickly,' she said. 'She's been in there a while.'

Chapter Three

'Anywhere here will do,' Lexi said to the cab driver, as they pulled into the Birth & Baby car park. 'Bollocks. I'm going to arrive late. I'm never late for anything.'

'Language!' grinned the cabbie, shouting over his blaring heavy-metal music and catching her eye in the rear-view mirror. 'You know, your baby can hear everything you say.'

'I think he has his hands over his ears right now,' muttered Lexi, grinning at the cabbie in return in the mirror.

She called her baby 'him', but she didn't know what she was expecting. Either would be amazing. Lexi caught sight of her reflection and did a double take. Christ, does that big, puffy face belong to me? She sucked in her cheeks and raised her chin. She'd let herself go *way* too early. In her experience, most women waited at least until the baby had been born. Then exhaustion flattened any vague desire to look nice. But pregnancy had ruled Lexi's appetite. The baby had made her hungry for white bread. Since a few weeks into her pregnancy, she could eat a farmhouse loaf a day, if she allowed herself, spread thickly with butter. Plain if it was warm and fresh from the bakery near work. Now she felt she resembled three big lumps of uncooked dough, belly and two breasts, only just kept in check by the swathes of material in her red maternity wrap dress. Not that she minded. Apart from the heartburn and the water retention, she had never felt so feminine, with hillocks all over. But what was with her hair? It had thickened up so much she could barely get a comb through it; mad topiary came to mind. Every cloud had a silver lining, though. Maybe the extra weight had inflated the wrinkles on her face, but her skin was incredible. Airbrushed amazing. She might have put on three stone already and have a hairstyle more suited to something on an Alan Titchmarsh show, but her skin was iridescent. She wondered if that was why the cabbie kept staring at her in the mirror. She hoped it wasn't because she'd slept with him in a former life.

'Okay, love,' he said, hitting the brakes much too hard and making Lexi lurch forward. She slammed her hands against the back of the passenger seat, to protect her bump. The cabbie gasped and whipped round, his face screwed up into an apologetic wince.

'Jesus!' Lexi said cheerfully. 'The baby nearly came out of my mouth!'

'Shit,' he said. 'Sorry. Bit heavy-footed on the brakes there. It's these new boots, I can't feel the pedals.'

'That's reassuring,' said Lexi, fumbling in her purse for cash. Mercifully, the driver clicked off his Guns N' Roses album, which had been playing on a loop. He turned to face her and she saw that he had a gold tooth halfway down the right side of his mouth and his hair was longish and straggly and held back by a headband. On his forearm he had a winged-heart tattoo with a space for a name, which had been filled in with black ink. Love hurts.

'Is this your first baby?' he asked.

'Yep,' said Lexi. 'My first and probably my last.'

The cabbie nodded and Lexi warmed to him, for at least pretending to be interested. The expression on most of her male colleagues' faces when she talked about her pregnancy could be described as that of wholehearted uninterest.

'How are you feeling?' he said. 'Are you enjoying it?'

'Am I enjoying it?' asked Lexi, stopping to think. 'There's a question I don't know how to answer.'

She gazed into the middle distance. In all seriousness, it was difficult to put her feelings into words. The magnitude of what she was doing, as a single woman, never left her, but having a baby was something she just *had* to do. She'd always wanted to be a mother. She had so much love to give and wanted to prove to the world (and herself) that not every Mason woman was as mean-spirited as her own mother. She knew she could do a better job. She had to do a better job. And, since she'd turned thirty-five, she had felt almost hypnotized by the biological, primeval need to be pregnant. It had got to the point where she could hardly look at a pregnant woman without jealousy carving her up. And when she heard a baby cry, she felt hollow. All she'd needed was a sperm – one kindly, liberal-minded, intelligent, handsome sperm to get it together with one of her eggs. But, without being in a relationship, this was a tall order. So, single and babyless, she'd had to take action. Now, thirty-six weeks pregnant and only a few weeks from becoming a mother, a role presumed to be instinctive yet clearly so complex, a role she just *had* to get right, she thought she'd feel a constant tremor of panic at the prospect. Instead, she felt oddly serene.

'Yes,' she said decisively. 'I've enjoyed eating for two, at least. Bread. I can't get enough bread. Funnily enough, I never used to like it much before.'

Lexi was well practised at being flippant about her pregnancy. It was easier than all the explaining she had to do. It didn't need an award-winning psychologist to deduce that she wanted to deflect people's attention. The driver laughed and she gave him a smile.

'Okay, I'm getting that pleasantries aren't your style,' he said. 'Do you want me to pick you up afterwards to take you back to the office?'

Lexi groaned. A social worker on the children's team for the local authority, she had a mountain of work left to do before she went off on maternity leave in a week's time. Though she loved her job, she wasn't going to miss the long hours, high stress and excessive workload she had to cope with on a daily basis. She'd worked until midnight every night the previous week trying to deal with new referrals, dragging herself to bed, only to wake up once she'd gone to sleep to write lists of things that needed to be done before she left. It was a 24/7 job.

'No, thanks,' she said. 'I'm not going back in today. Anyway, here is your money. I'd better get inside.'

'No problem,' he said. 'So what is it that you do, Mrs—?'

Lexi laughed.

'Ms Mason, but I prefer Lexi,' she said. 'Are you always this interested in your customers? I'm a social worker. I work mostly with children and young people.'

The cab driver looked impressed.

'Can't be easy work when you're that pregnant?' he said.

Lexi thought about her job. It was hard work at any time, no matter that she was pregnant. But, yes, the driver had a point. Sometimes, when she'd trekked across half of Brighton to visit a family who needed support – and they had deliberately avoided her, or were hostile towards her – she felt more pissed off now than she would have done before. Her caseload was ridiculous. There wasn't enough time in the day to devote all the energy each young person required. Working with children who had massive problems in their lives just wasn't a job you could drop at five p.m.

'I'm only interested because I'm writing a script,' blushed the driver. 'It's about a cabbie and the women he meets in the back of his cab.'

'Thriller?' Lexi said, her eyebrows raised. 'Does one of the women end up dead in the boot? The pregnant one?'

He snorted.

'Romance,' he said. 'Happy ever after. Tin cans tied to the bumper at the back of the cab rattling along the pavement as the sweethearts drive off into the sunset.'

'Fantasy then,' Lexi said, not missing a beat.

He laughed again, and Lexi, deciding she liked him, gave him a tip.

'Good luck with the baby,' he said, giving her a look that lasted just a few seconds too long to be meaningless. Lexi wondered if he'd sussed her out already. No – she dismissed the thought. Impossible. It must be her breasts. They had inflated into hot-air balloons.

'My name is Gary. Here's my card. If you need a cab to take

you to hospital, I've got plastic sheets I can put down, just in case it all kicks off en route, flashing lights – the lot. Expect your other half has thought of that, though . . . has he?'

Lexi accepted the card and sighed. Other half. What other half? Why was the world obsessed with measuring people in terms of their relationship? Halves, singles, couples, three-somes – it was one of society's preoccupations. Maybe she should have SINGLE tattooed on her forehead just to get it out the way, or wear a placard with a list of FAQs on it.

'Thank you, I'll keep that in mind,' she said as she climbed out of the cab. She slammed the door and waved, watching the cabbie leave and clocking his hand extended out of the window, saluting as if he were an old friend. Turning towards Birth & Baby, she caught sight of another pregnant woman, with shoulder-length auburn hair contrasting beautifully against her long apple-green coat, waiting just outside, her partner taking her hand in his. The sight of them made Lexi's heart skip a little faster, and a rush of acid shot into her throat. She swallowed uncomfortably, closed her eyes and counted to fifteen. Ten was never enough. That rule could be applied to most things in life, especially hot, sugary doughnuts from the pier. She often grabbed a bag on the way home from work, for a carbohydrate boost.

'Right,' she said, speaking to her bump. 'Here we are at antenatal class.'

Reaching into her bag, she pulled out a bottle. Unscrewing the lid and tipping the contents of the bottle into her mouth, she winced as the liquid hit the back of her throat. Resting one hand on her bump, she took another big sip and sighed.

'Gaviscon,' she said, looking at the almost empty bottle

of indigestion remedy. 'I'd be lost without you. Right, let's go inside.'

Moving toward the Sixties-style building, which looked as if it had recently been renovated, Lexi felt her baby kick reassuringly in her belly. She had been here several times during her career as a social worker, accompanying pregnant teenagers who needed extra support in the community. But this time, she was here for herself, which made her feel excessively excited but surprisingly nervous. As she approached, the woman with the auburn hair glanced at her, a solemn expression on her face. They exchanged hellos then, pushing open the door into Birth & Baby, Lexi glanced around the waiting room at the pregnant women and their partners already there, noticing an attractive young couple, and a blonde woman coming out of the toilet with a dark-haired woman. Moving to the reception desk, she stopped dead on hearing a voice she couldn't fail to recognize and took a sharp intake of breath. The distinct Australian tones of Alan Nicholls. A blast from the past. No, Alan Nicholls was more like a *bomb* from the past. 'Blast' made her think of a gust of wind, or a record turned up too high . . . She sucked in her breath and looked in the direction of the voice. There, in a colourful striped shirt, looking the spit of Colin Firth as Darcy, she saw him. *Him*. The blood drained from her face and she felt sick.

'Shit,' she muttered. 'Oh fuck. Fuck. Fuck!'

She stood stock still, her feet apparently glued to the floor, her stomach flipping and her heart leaping, breathless. Come on, Lexi, she told herself. You're tough. You're a social worker. You've picked yourself up and brushed yourself down on countless occasions. Don't let a man you slept with once – well, lots of times during one night – reduce you to a quivering wreck. Not knowing whether to run or stay, she almost fainted when he turned and looked at her. Their eyes locked. She lifted the corners of her mouth into a smile while her face glowed with heat and her legs wobbled. Broken images ran through her mind: his hairy torso, empty bottles of wine, a wild-mushroom omelette, her heart being squished by his big toe like a cigarette butt in gravel.

'Hi,' he said, his eyes widening then breaking out into a smile. 'Lexi?'

She watched him gulp, like a stork swallowing a whole fish, then take a step towards her, before changing his mind and standing still. He raised his hand in a wave then dropped it down.

'Lexi Mason,' he said. 'How the hell are you?'

Lexi had thought about this moment, oh, about one million times. After everything he'd told her about his life, about his deepest feelings, after every X-rated position he'd seen her in, after the tears he'd spilled on her shoulders, she'd expected more. More *action*. More *emotion*. More *guilt*.

'Hi, Alan,' she said, trying to sound calm and collected, though inside she was praying for a meteorite to plummet through the roof and wipe her out.

'Wow!' said Alan, grabbing a slim curly-haired woman by the elbow and swinging her at Lexi in a *Strictly Come Dancing* manoeuvre. 'Katy, meet Lexi Mason. Lexi's an old friend of mine. Lexi, this is Katy. My wife. My pregnant wife! How are you, Lexi?'

Old friend. Ha! Old friend whose pink lace lingerie you removed with your teeth. Old friend who unashamedly cried with joy when his head was wedged between these here breasts! Katy smiled politely at Lexi, ran her eyes over her from top to bottom, then registered Alan's flushed cheeks. She raised her eyebrows.

'Wow, your bump is *far* more impressive than mine,' Katy said, all innocently, a lock of blonde hair falling perfectly over her enormous eyes. 'But I know some women retain tons more water than others, don't they? Do you know what you're having?'

'A baby hippo perhaps?' said Lexi with a forced laugh, though she felt deflated.

'Hope not, for your sake,' said Katy with a false smile.

For all the abuse she took as a social worker from disgruntled parents and teenagers or overworked colleagues, at this moment her thick skin had well and truly disintegrated. She felt twelve years old again, crushed by the pretty girl. Thanks, Goldilocks, she thought, rallying, briefly imagining herself snipping off those golden ringlets with her kitchen scissors. At this point all she could do was fiddle with the card the cab driver had given her. She pulled out her mobile phone and pregnancy notes and wafted both vaguely in the air.

'Er,' she said, 'excuse me, but I have to make a call and book a cab, I have a midwife appointment later, and it's on the other side of town—'

What was she saying? Lexi's hands were clammy, and the pregnancy notes slid out of her fingers and dropped on to the floor, the contents landing in a fan of paper across the carpet. She caught sight of her most private details and blushed boiling red.

'Shit,' she said, lowering herself down to kneeling position, hoping Alan wasn't reading her medical history.

'Let me help,' he said, suddenly so close to her she could smell his cologne and feel the heat from his body. Her body felt charged with electricity. If he touched her, she would surely die. Did he feel it too? She couldn't look at him, hating him for reducing her to melting butter. She felt herself turning taramasalata-pink.

'No,' said Lexi firmly, sweeping up the papers in one determined armful. 'I'll cope alone, thank you.'

I'll cope alone. Lexi's mantra. The philosophy she'd pledged allegiance to since the age of seven, in the bath with her My Little Pony collection, her miserable mother slumped in bed, crying into her unwashed, flat-as-a-pancake pillow. Alan flinched and moved away, back to Katy. Lexi longed for him to come back. Wedge his head between her breasts and weep.

Chapter Four

He *can't* leave me, thought Mel as she shuffled into the ante-natal classroom, accepting a sticky-label name-tag and slapping it on her chest as she went. I won't let him leave me.

Swallowing down the rising acid taste in her mouth, her heart beating too quickly, cheeks throbbing from crying, she scanned the seating options. Two sofas and several single chairs were set out in a crescent shape in front of Ginny Croft, the bee-hived, truly amazing-looking midwife taking the class, who was perched on the edge of a table, smiling broadly and gently swinging her legs back and forth. Next to her was what looked like the skeleton of a small mammal, a few plastic dolls, a jigsaw puzzle of the female anatomy, a stack of information leaflets and a freestanding TV and DVD-player which reminded Mel of being at school. Everyone found seats and Mel eyed their sticky label name-tags. Katy and Alan, designer clad, were holding hands. They emanated success and should probably have been in a London boardroom, sealing deals and talking shop. There was a young couple, Rebecca and Lenny, who could be on the books of a modelling agency. Mel thought their baby had to have been the result of high jinks, just like her own. And then a slightly older couple, Erin and Edward, who had kind, intelligent faces but were quiet and stiff as lamp posts in their chairs. And Lexi, with pink cheeks and painted lips, sitting with her arms folded above her bump, was a shiny glacé cherry in her red maternity dress.

'Make yourselves comfortable,' said Ginny, beaming. 'Then we'll begin. We've got a lot of information to cover today about understanding the signs that labour is near, plus the different stages of labour and birth.'

Mel's heart sank. She didn't want to be there. She couldn't go through with this. All she wanted to do was go home, crawl under the duvet, get on the phone to her mum and eat a bag of Kettle Chips. She could tell she was nothing like any of the other women – and how could she possibly act normally after the bombshell Leo had just dropped? She just felt like bawling and banging the floor with her fists.

'Here you all are, ready to embark on a very exciting journey,' continued Ginny as the group quietened. 'You might be feeling completely terrified or really excited about the birth. Maybe you feel a mixture of both. But whatever you feel now, it'll all change again when you actually meet your baby and become a parent.'

Everyone in the class stared intently at Ginny, smiling a little but saying nothing.

'Having a baby is a lot about sacrifice – giving up on sleep and your social life for a while – but it's also about learning. Having a baby is the most natural thing on earth, but it's also the most confusing. That's why you're all here today. When your contractions hit at three a.m. or your waters break over your shoes in the supermarket, it's good to know what the hell is going on. Hopefully, my sessions will help you on your way.'

'Knowledge is power,' said Alan, grinning like the Hoff.

'Absolutely right,' said Ginny, crossing and uncrossing her legs and laughing her low-key laugh. 'So, you're all fairly close to the end of your pregnancies and that's why you've chosen this four-week intensive course. This week we'll talk about the different stages of labour; next time we'll discuss pain management, in session three we'll talk about breastfeeding; and then, finally, in the last session, how to care for your newborn at home. Do any of you know whether you're having a girl or boy?'

Mel shook her head. She and Leo had decided against knowing what sex the baby was, though she felt sure she'd seen something distinctly penis-shaped on the scan. Leo insisted it was the umbilical cord. He had been so nervous that day. Oh, Leo. He had to come back. They were having a baby, for heaven's sake. No one walks out on a baby, do they?

'We've decided not to find out,' said Erin, with a small, cautious smile, and Lexi nodded along with her.

'Me, too,' she said. 'I want a surprise.'

'We're having a boy,' said Katy proudly. 'I like to be prepared for everything in life. I have a name, too, but I'm not telling a soul before he's born. I don't want anyone stealing it!'

Rebecca grinned at Katy then glanced at Lenny. 'We're having a boy, too,' she said. 'A mini-Lenny.'

'Lucky world,' said Lenny, beaming. 'Another one of me.'

Ginny laughed and neatly slipped off the edge of the table on to her feet.

'So, every woman's labour is different and, for first-time mums, labour usually takes between ten and twenty hours, though it can last longer or be over much more quickly,' she continued, holding her head to one side. 'How are you all feeling about the actual birth?'

'Like I want to move to Mongolia,' muttered Lenny in a low voice. He gave everyone a waspish grin when they laughed, letting his gaze linger on Ginny, who seemed to blush a little every time she looked in his direction.

'Lexi?' said Ginny.

Lexi pointed to the massive blue birthing ball at the side of the room.

'My baby is quite big, so I'm wondering how it will actually get out,' said Lexi. 'I think I'm giving birth to one of those balls.'

Everyone laughed.

'Thank you, Lexi, but you'd be surprised by how women's bodies can stretch,' said Ginny. 'Some tiny women have big babies as easily as if they're squeezing out a peanut. How about you, Katy? How do you feel about it?'

Katy's mobile phone beeped on her lap. She checked the message and flushed before composing her answer.

'Calm,' she said, nodding determinedly, with Alan's big hand now resting protectively on the back of her neck. 'Calm about the labour, but stressed up to my eyeballs about work. Back-to-back meetings at the moment. Maybe if I didn't have a busy job I'd be more worried about the labour, but I'm feeling good about it. It might actually be a rest.'

Ginny nodded slowly, trying to conceal the 'Yeah, right' part of her smile but failing miserably. Mel sighed. Katy was one of those dynamic women who did everything, wasn't she? Mel couldn't help feeling a bit annoyed by her. Behind Ginny was a window, with a view of the hospital where Mel would have her baby. She felt hot and cold at the same time, not wanting to speak, knowing she could cry at any moment. This was supposed to be a happy day, but Mel felt self-conscious and bemused. Why had Leo said he didn't want the baby? Inside her, the baby's feet were pressed up against her diaphragm, making her feeling slightly breathless. She moved, trying to make herself more comfortable.

'Erin?' said Ginny. 'What about you?'

'I'm having an elective caesarean at thirty-nine weeks, so it's going to be different for me,' said Erin quietly. 'I'm desperate to meet the baby. These last few weeks are going so slowly, I feel like the days keep on rewinding themselves, just to aggravate me.'

Mel looked at the clock on the wall. They'd only been in there for five minutes. She willed the time to hurry up, so she could get out and call Leo.

'Most women find the last few weeks tough, but it's supposed to give you time to prepare for what's to come,' said Ginny. 'Anyone else? Rebecca and Lenny? Mel?'

Mel glanced over at Rebecca, who smiled at her kindly. Mel tried to return the smile.

'I don't know what to expect,' said Rebecca. 'I'm slightly concerned I'll moo during labour.'

Lenny burst out laughing, and Rebecca smiled again.

'Everyone moos,' said Ginny, waving her hand through her hair. 'It's normal. When you moo, you know you're nearly done. Mooing is good.'

Katy cleared her throat, lifted a bottle of perfume out of her bag and sprayed three squirts on her wrists and neck. Pregnancy had given Mel a super-sensitive sense of smell, and now, the air cloying with an expensive, pungent fragrance, she could hardly breathe. Lexi coughed and heaved herself out of her seat. She opened a window with a thump and a cool breeze sliced into the room.

'I'm seriously scared,' said Lenny. 'All that blood and guts and pain and screaming. Have you seen that programme *One Born Every Minute*? Jesus, I can't watch it. As soon as it's on, Rebecca's in tears and I'm hiding under a cushion . . . Did you see it last week? There were about twenty people in the room trying to get the baby out of that woman, pulling it about like a farm animal. It was like a bloody horror film!'

The women gasped.

'Lenny!' Ginny said. 'That was enlightening.'

'Sssshh,' said Rebecca, nudging him. 'Stop talking rubbish.'

Rebecca smiled apologetically to the group while Lenny put his hand over his mouth and jokingly widened his eyes. A few nervous, half-hearted laughs ensued, then all eyes shifted to Mel.

'Mel,' said Ginny. 'Shall we hear from you?'

'I'm nervous.' Mel shrugged, her eyes moving to the closed door, praying Leo would burst in. Tell her he'd made a terrible mistake. Say that he was just stressed out at work or something. Yes, that was it. His job as a website designer was full on. And there she was banging on about pregnancy like a woman possessed. She'd neglected him, hadn't she? Why hadn't she recognized it before now?

'All these feelings are to be expected,' Ginny said kindly, 'and are absolutely normal.'

Mel tuned out of Ginny's talking, pulled out her mobile phone and compiled a text: Hi Leo. Is this about your job? I understand how hard you're working. Maybe I haven't been supportive enough? Come back, Mx.

Before she could think any more about it, she sent it, then stared at the screen, waiting for an immediate response. None came. Her scalp started to prickle with dread. Who was she kidding? Leo wasn't the type of man to make a decision lightly; he must have been thinking about it for weeks. Months. And he loved his job. Even when he had to work at the weekend, he rarely complained. Her stomach plunged into her boots. *Especially* when he had to work at the weekend? Did he actually enjoy being away from her? No, it wasn't that bad, was it?

'If you're wondering,' said Ginny, holding up the skeleton that looked like it came from a small mammal, 'this is a model of a pelvic bone, the area your baby will travel through in labour. Here's an information sheet, with diagrams explaining how the baby moves through your birth canal, and of various birth positions, which we will discuss next week.'

Ginny handed out the leaflets. Mel's eyes rested on an illustration of a woman on all fours, a baby's head poking out of her vagina like a hotdog sausage sticking out the end of a bread roll. She felt slightly revolted.

'I'm glad you said that was a pelvic bone,' said Alan to Ginny. 'I thought someone had lost their dog.'

More tittered laughter – especially loud from Lexi. Mel frowned. Alan seemed somehow out of place in the classroom. He was too hairy, too action-hero *male*, as if his watch might double up as a pistol. Mel wished that he'd go and Leo would come back. Leo was far more suited to this environment, much more gentle. Ginny carried on talking about pelvic bones and Mel withdrew into her thoughts. *Would* he come back? She tried to envisage herself as a lone parent. Her mum had been a lone parent after her dad had died, and life had been horribly quiet without him. Her mum had tried to make it look easy, but she knew it had been hard for her on her own. Could she cope without Leo? Her mind filled with a sad little picture of her and the baby in the future, perched on a beach towel together sucking ice lollies, pretending to enjoy themselves but wishing Leo was there.

'Okay, everyone,' said Ginny. 'Now, can anyone tell me how you know that labour is near?'

'Does your bump kind of drop down further?' began Rebecca.

As Rebecca spoke, Mel zoned out again and thought back to the day she'd told Leo she was pregnant. She'd been throwing up – morning sickness – when he'd come into the bathroom to see how she was. She mumbled something incomprehensible and pointed at the home pregnancy kit she'd secretly done, the blue line bold as a strike. Leo hadn't said anything either, just pulled her to him and kissed her head. She'd felt his tears in her hair and held on to him. She remembered what she'd said to him.

'I've always wanted a big family like yours,' she'd said. 'After my dad died, I vowed that one day I'd have a big, noisy family, with kids running around in the garden, or with everyone sitting round the kitchen table talking at each other. I felt I owed it to my mum as well, you know? And now this has happened, *we* can be a family. We can get started. Leo, you do want to be a family, don't you?'

It had been a saccharine speech for Mel, who rarely talked about family like that. She was too realistic to indulge in childhood fantasies of re-creating the Waltons. She knew life threw a lot of shit at you, but, in her innermost desires, she wanted a chance to belong to more people and have more people belong to her. With Leo, she thought she'd been in with a chance. Was it such an outrageous expectation?

'It's a surprise,' he'd said. 'A big surprise.'

That was all. No objection. No crisis talks. No smashed coffee cup. No debate. Just quiet acceptance. How could he say she'd bulldozed him into having the baby? Aware of voices in the room growing quiet, Mel felt all eyes on her again. She flushed with heat.

'Mel?' said Ginny. 'Do you know of any other signs?'

At the same moment, the phone in Mel's hand beeped. She glanced down at the text from Leo: It's not about work. It's about me. I'm sorry. With sweat pricking her forehead and disappointment making her arms ache, Mel opened her mouth to speak, but nothing more than a croak came out.

'I'm . . . I'm—' she struggled, swallowing. 'I think ... I'm sorry, I—'

Mel swiped at a tear rolling down her cheek.

'Are you okay?' asked Ginny, frowning in concern. 'You're bound to feel emotional. Don't forget, your hormones are all over the place.'

Everyone nodded and murmured in agreement, then they fell silent again, waiting for Mel to speak, waiting for her to agree that, yes, it was just hormones making her cry. Her stomach churning, Mel lifted a hand to her cheeks and shook her head, pulling at her bag for a tissue. Typically, she couldn't find one.

'Here,' said Lexi gently from beside her, handing her a bundle of tissues. 'Have one of mine. Have lots of them.'

Mel thanked Lexi, took the tissues and held them to her leaking eyes.

'Sorry,' she said, in a tiny, high voice. 'I've just had some bad news. I shouldn't have come in, but I didn't know what to do. I don't want to miss this class – and . . . outside, just before we came in, my boyfriend Leo, well, he . . . he . . . he—'

Mortified that she couldn't hold it together, that she was about to tell these strangers everything, that her tears were beyond her control, Mel broke down into sobs. Why couldn't she be more like Katy over there? Cucumber-cool.

'Oh dear,' said Ginny, moving to kneel down in front of Mel and take hold of her hands. 'Whatever it is, don't get yourself too worked up. You're going to be just fine.'

Don't be kind, thought Mel, blushing. If you're kind you'll make it worse. Tell me to shut up. Shut up and pull myself together. Slap me.

'Oh,' she croaked in between sobs, pushing her knuckles against her head, 'what am I like?'

All she could do was shake her head and push the tissue against her nose, which was streaming with snot and tears. The information sheet was soggy and damp on her lap, the woman on all fours disintegrating before her eyes.

'Leo, my boyfriend, has just left me,' she said, hiccupping now. 'He's left us, me and the baby. He says he doesn't want a baby. I lost my dad when I was six. I can't do this on my own. God, I'm so sorry, I just can't stop—'

There was a communal gasp from the women in the room. The men looked as if they wanted to teleport themselves to the moon.

'He told you just now?' said Lexi from beside her, her hand on Mel's back. 'You poor thing.'

'Yes,' said Mel. 'Just now.'

'That's terrible,' said Rebecca, from the other side of the room.

'Awful,' said Erin, shaking her head sadly. 'Awful for you.'

'Oh no, sweetheart,' said Ginny, her voice full of sympathy. 'No wonder you're upset.'

Mel managed a small smile, buoyed up slightly by the women's reactions, before warily raising her eyes to the group. They were all staring at her with wide, sympathetic eyes. Even though she knew nobody in the room, she felt the women's warmth like a duvet and, for a second, was grateful to them.

'I'll happily kill him for you,' said Alan's cheery voice, from beside Katy. 'What a jerk.'

There was a ripple of comments and a peal of laughter from Lenny at Alan's threat. Mel tried to raise a smile, but she couldn't. Sudden, unexpected anger rose in her. Not about Leo leaving, she told herself, but because of what Alan had said. *The rude bastard!* She instinctively wanted to defend Leo. *He's not a jerk!* He was one of life's good, honest people, with moral fibre and backbone. He was talented, too. Brilliant at all that technical stuff he did, and musical. He always carried Mel's suitcase when he met her at the station, back from visiting her mum in Edinburgh, achy and tired. Last week, she'd watched him physically restrain an irate customer in the Co-op who had been about to punch the manager, while everyone else pretended nothing was happening. He rubbed her back almost every night. The first of her birthdays they'd been together he'd bought her twenty-four little presents for every year of birthdays he hadn't known her. He told her she was his one and only. He opened the window every morning, so they could smell the sea air while they lay in bed. Leo wasn't a jerk. He couldn't be. She loved him. He was the father of her child.

'Perhaps its nerves,' said Katy to the group, raising her eyebrows as if in question. 'Perhaps he thinks he can't cope with the pressure of being a father. Some men can't face the whole fatherhood responsibility issue. Do you think it could be that?'

Ginny, who was pouring Mel a glass of water, nodded in agreement.

'Some men should be strung up and de-balled,' said Lexi. 'That might help iron out those responsibility issues. I see so many men get their girlfriends pregnant then disappear into thin air it makes me question the male species.'

Alan had a coughing fit.

'Quite,' said Katy, smiling politely at Lexi, while Mel shrugged hopelessly. She felt a flicker of annoyance. Mel needed to pull herself together and take control. Her eyes skimmed over Mel's open bag, which was like a bomb site, with old banana skins – and was that a knitting needle and ball of wool tangled up with a hairbrush? That made sense. Mel looked like one of those craft-mad women, with that flower in her hair, those leopard-print tights and her oversized jewellery. She was probably knitting her baby clothes – unlike Katy, who didn't have the time or inclination to knit, sew or bake. What was the point when the world was full of lovely shops to buy gorgeous things from? But that handbag! It was all she could do to stop herself from pouring it all out on to the floor and sorting it out.

'Could be that,' said Mel in a small voice, with a sniff. 'I've no idea what's going on in his head.'

Katy suddenly thought of Anita's husband, Giovanni, who had cheated on Anita more than once. Anita had been thrown off course when she found out – as if it weren't completely obvious just by looking at him that he was a snake, him with his slicked-back hair and roaming eyes. Couldn't you just tell when a man was going to turn out to be a shit? Katy had known enough of them before she got wise and looked for an older, wealthy man who wanted a younger wife. In other words: Alan.

'Could there be another woman involved?' asked Lexi, glimpsing at Alan, for some reason. 'I've seen that a lot, too. I'm not saying Leo's being unfaithful, I just mean an old flame in the wings or something?'

Mel looked completely distraught and violently shook her head. Katy frowned, knowing that she knew Lexi from somewhere, but finding it hard to place her. Perhaps she'd been into Spotted for an interview with Anita on their latest recruitment drive? Thinking of work, Katy checked her watch. She had a really important meeting with the National Trust about a filming location just after lunch which she couldn't miss. She might have to leave early if all this crying went on too much longer. Crying got you nowhere in life – Katy had learned that years ago. Growing up in a poor family with parents who worked two, three jobs at a time to make ends meet, no one had time for tears. It was nose to the grindstone, and that work ethic had stuck. Most women would be on maternity leave by now, but Katy was working until the end. Not that she'd told Alan. He had encouraged her to take more time away from the office to nurture herself in these last few weeks, but the agency was just as much of a priority as the baby. Anita was making sure she didn't forget that.

'Hang on a minute,' said Alan. 'Despite what I said about wanting to kill your boyfriend, I have to protect my species. We're not all unfaithful deserters! Personally, I would crawl to the ends of the earth to make sure Katy was happy and healthy while – and after – she carries our child. I don't know your story, Mel, and I'm sorry you're so upset today, but the guy may have issues he's not being honest about. I've seen men do strange things when their wives get pregnant. He's probably feeling confused about his role – that kind of thing. It's difficult for men, too. I have to admit to confusion myself, over what having a baby means for me. Give him time.'

'I don't think it should be about the man at all,' said Rebecca, holding her hair up from her neck. 'The man gets to carry on with his life once the baby is born. Even though men and women are supposed to be more equal now, you just have to look around to see it's still women who look after the babies and children. It's a female domain. I've seen it in the school opposite our house. The gates open at home time, and who's there to meet the kids? The mums. Same with the nursery I helped at when I moved here. On the whole, it's the mums who do the childcare. So why should *he* be so fearful? It's the woman whose life changes, isn't it?'

'That's true,' said Ginny. 'But the man's life is very affected, too. You have to be careful not to pit the sexes against one another.'

'That won't happen to us,' said Alan, a steady smile on his lips. 'Katy has a successful business and is going to carry on working, so I'm going to be looking after the baby part-time when she goes back. I can do a lot of my work from home, so I'll do that. This attitude that men don't pull their weight really grates with me. We do, don't we, Lenny and Edward? Back me up here.'

'I'll be leaving the whole thing to Becs, mate,' said Lenny, 'while I stick to wine, women and song.'

Katy threw Lenny a disapproving glance and watched Rebecca sigh then tuck a loose tendril of hair behind her ear. Katy was taken aback by how beautiful she was. There was something feline about her eyes, her nose was delicate and her lips curled up at the edges in a constant smile. When she did truly smile, she was radiant. Katy glanced at Alan, who, let's face it, was probably imagining what it would be like to have sex with Rebecca. Erin's husband, Edward, probably was too. Clearing her throat, she rested a protective hand on Alan's knee.

'It's an economic decision, isn't it?' said Edward. 'There are families who can afford for one partner to stay at home, and families who can't. Often, the woman breastfeeds and so it works out that the woman takes time away from her job. I think it's different for everyone.'

'I *want* to look after the baby,' said Erin. 'I can't wait.'

'I want to, too,' said Rebecca. 'But I was trying to say

that Leo, Mel's boyfriend, shouldn't be the one panicking about his life changing. It's Mel's life that's going to change the most.'

'A baby's a big deal,' said Alan. 'And Leo's probably scared by the responsibility of it all. You might be physically having the baby, Mel, but his life is going to change too. That's what I'm saying.'

'I know,' Mel sniffed. 'But I just don't get it. He seemed happy—'

Katy watched Mel closely, her eyes and nose bright red from crying, balls of tissues scrunched up on her lap, and, though she felt sorry for her, she also felt slightly embarrassed and wished she would pull herself together. It was a similar feeling to when she had meetings with people who were excruciatingly bad at presenting themselves in a positive light. Though she had to be polite and patient while they stuttered and shook, sometimes she wished she could press a button to open a trapdoor and put everyone out of their misery. What was it with people like Mel? Yes, she'd just had a horrible shock, but everyone in the room was a stranger. Shouldn't she wait to share this news with friends or relatives after the class? She picked up a pen and scribbled 'unplanned baby' on the corner of the handout Ginny had given her, shielding it so only Alan could see. He shrugged at her noncommittally and mouthed, So what? Katy sighed. Alan could never be persuaded to say anything remotely negative. She had just been trying to say that might be why Leo had left so abruptly. Maybe they had never planned to have the baby. Maybe he had never even wanted a baby. Not the sort of question you could ask of a stranger.

'Pregnancy and birth can cause all kinds of problems within couples,' said Ginny. 'I've seen it myself, running these classes. There was once a spectacular bust-up when a couple disagreed about whether the husband should be at the birth! But if you talk to each other, I'm sure you can work it out. The worst thing to do is not to talk.'

'The pregnancy wasn't planned,' said Mel apologetically, as if reading Katy's mind. 'But I didn't see any reason why we shouldn't go ahead. Obviously, it was a shock, but Leo had never said he didn't want a baby and I always knew I definitely did. I'm an only child and it's always been a bit of a dream of mine to have a big family—'

She started to cry again, her hair sticking to her pink cheeks. Lexi put her hand on her back and rubbed it gently and Mel looked up, half laughing, half crying.

'I've got to shut up,' she said, with a great big sigh. 'You must think I'm nuts. Sorry, everyone.'

Ginny, leaning forward slightly, had her arms folded across her middle. Katy silently urged her to take charge and get on with the antenatal class before it turned into an Oprah Winfrey show. Thankfully, she did.

'Mel,' Ginny said, 'whatever happens with Leo – and I hope it works out – you need to stay positive and empowered, for the birth. This is an amazing journey, with or without your partner in tow.'

Ginny handed Mel the glass of water and started to talk about the other signs that indicated labour was near: the appearance of the mucus plug, an upset stomach, waters breaking, contractions. Mel leaned back in her spot of the sofa, listening, holding the water in both hands, and fell quiet, deciding she had said enough. Katy felt relieved that the drama was over. Emotional outbursts had never been her strong point.

'Right,' said Ginny. 'Anything else anyone wants to share at this point before we move on?'

'For what it's worth, our pregnancy was unplanned, too,' said Rebecca, holding up her hand and looking at Mel. 'I probably would have waited another ten years, so I could get on with my own thing. I wanted to go travelling and do voluntary work overseas, but you can't plan life out like that, can you? We decided it was fate and to go with the flow, have the baby and see what happens.'

Katy smiled and nodded, but she was baulking. She couldn't disagree more with what Rebecca had said. Of course you can plan. She resisted the temptation to point out that the pill had been made available on the NHS in the sixties exactly so that women *could* plan and have rewarding careers doing something they loved. Where was Rebecca's drive? There was no way Katy would have got pregnant aged twenty. After witnessing what having a baby too young did to the lives of some of the girls on the estate she grew up on, Katy had been crystal clear about what she wanted from life: a career as a businesswoman, a financially independent husband, money in the bank. Then – and only then – a baby.

'Okay, thank you for that, Rebecca. It's always interesting to hear everyone's stories, and I'm sure you'll all become friends,' said Ginny. 'Building a network is extremely important for new parents. Might be an idea to swap numbers after the class. I still know the women from my antenatal classes. One became my best friend. So, on to where you plan to give birth. If I remember right, Rebecca, you're having a home birth, while

Erin, Mel, Lexi and Katy plan to have a hospital birth. It's worth remembering at this point that normal pregnancies can last from anywhere between thirty-seven and forty-two weeks, and only 5 per cent of babies are born on their due date, so don't get hung up on the date you've been given. It will probably come and go without a murmur.'

Everyone nodded and murmured.

'By now you'll probably be seeing your midwife every week,' Ginny said, holding up her pelvic-bone model. 'And she should be able to tell you which way your baby is lying. Your baby will still move, sometimes right up until he or she is born, but the best position for your baby to be in for birth is head down, with her back against your belly, facing your back, so she can fit through your pelvis.'

'My baby is lying back to back,' sniffed Mel, 'so I'm trying to get it to move.'

'Right,' said Ginny. 'You can use a birthing ball to encourage the baby to shift position, or get down on all fours, and swimming is good, too. Try to avoid sitting for too long. But there's plenty of time for the baby to get into position for labour. Okay, so let's split up into groups, so we can talk about your expectations about labour. Mel, if you and Rebecca and Lenny group with Lexi; then, Erin and Edward, you put together a list of your hopes and fears with Katy and Alan. We'll take five minutes to do that, then watch a birth on film and talk through the stages of labour.'

There were a few moments of movement in the classroom while Ginny bobbed around with her marmalade beehive. She gave Katy a whiteboard. Katy pulled a whiteboard pen out of her bag, whipped off the lid and felt instantly at ease. She loved lists most of all. She wrote down the title – Birth: Hopes and Fears – and waited, pen poised, for someone to speak.

'My hope is that a baby pops out within half an hour,' said Alan, trying to break the tension. 'Just a pretty pink baby in a clean nappy making gurgling noises and wanting her daddy.'

Erin and Edward said nothing at all but looked as serious as ever.

'I'm no comedian,' muttered Alan, 'but surely that deserved a smile?'

'Oh, sorry,' Erin said, 'I'm miles away. I have a lot on my mind.'

'Of course,' said Alan, clearing his throat awkwardly. 'Of course.'

'Mel,' Lexi said, focusing all her attention on her, 'do you have anyone else who can step in? A mum? A sister? What about your best friend? You know, sometimes it's better to have a woman as a birth partner. I read all this research done by a top gynaecologist who said that men shouldn't be at the birth of their child because they make the whole thing more stressful. Might be bollocks, you know, but could be a grain of truth in it—'

Lexi knew she was gabbling and probably irritating Mel, but she couldn't stop. When nerves hit, her tongue had a life of its own. Useful sometimes, but not today. Even though she was trying with all her might not to look at Alan, he was a magnet for her eyes and she repeatedly turned around to see if he was still there. Alan Nicholls. The only man she'd ever had an orgasm with. Alan Nicholls, the man who no other man in the last five years, or in the whole of her life prior to their meeting, had lived up to. Alan Nicholls, the man who had, for a brief moment in her confusing life, made her believe she had a soulmate. What a joke that was. Ha bloody ha.

'My mum lives up north,' said Mel. 'But I think I'll have to ask her to come down if Leo doesn't . . . doesn't . . . My best friend could help, but she's up in Manchester for a new job. I'm not sure who else I'd ask—'

Lexi nodded and murmured her response, but was only half listening to Mel. Her mind had cast itself back to the day she had met Alan. They had been on the same bus in central Brighton when one of the passengers, a man, had had a heart attack and collapsed. Lexi, dressed like Bettie Page for a fancy-dress party, was trained in CPR and so she gave the man mouth-to-mouth resuscitation. Alan, also trained in CPR, took over briefly, when she took a moment to breathe. When the ambulance arrived, the man had regained consciousness and the passengers had given Alan and Lexi a standing ovation. They had, between them, saved the man's life.

'If anyone was going to save my life,' Alan had said when they got off the bus, running his eyes up and down Lexi's curvy body, 'I would choose you. Amazingly cool woman. Let me buy you a drink. I'm Alan—'

And that had been it. Alan hadn't realized Lexi was in fancy dress as a vixen until her wig came off in a gust of wind, but that had broken the ice and he had said, being a gentleman, that he preferred blondes. She told him that this was the more glamorous end of social work. They walked, elated from saving a man's life, adrenalin pumping, to a bar, where, in a red leather booth, they drank half a pint together. The half-pint led to a bottle of wine and a bowl of pistachios, unshelled, which Lexi was grateful for, because it gave her something to do with her hands. Otherwise, she wouldn't have been able to resist reaching over the table, grabbing his trousers and ripping them down. After a long stretch of alcohol, Alan suggested he should walk Lexi home. They both knew what was going to happen. When Alan touched Lexi – with trembling hands, she noted – she knew it was different this time. That here, finally, was the man she'd been waiting for. The couple made love repeatedly that night, stopping only to talk and drink, then for an omelette, cooked by Alan. Lexi didn't know what it was about her, but she thought she must have been born with a sign above her head saying 'Tell me everything.' Many, many people had confessed their innermost secrets to her over the years, and Alan was no exception. He had told her everything about his life. The difference with Alan was that he had wanted to know about her, too. For the first time ever with a man, she'd opened up, properly, about her mum. By the morning, they were exhausted, and slept, entangled, in a room full of sunshine, until the late afternoon. When they woke, Lexi knew she was in love. Utterly, desperately, in love. Or so she thought. She had held her breath, waiting to hear that Alan felt the same. 'Do you—?' she'd asked, clutching the bed-sheet around her, unable to conceal the hope in her voice. His protracted silence spoke volumes. He didn't. Alan, after much sighing, admitted to being at the very beginning of a relationship with the love of his life, Katy, and, though he liked Lexi, he didn't want to lose Katy. In other words: not on your life. He left her on the doorstep with a scratchy, hot kiss on her lips, wearing a silk dressing gown so shockingly short that it barely covered her bottom, her hair wild as brambles. When the door closed, Lexi refused to cry. She wondered whether the night had happened at all. She decided to pretend to herself it hadn't. She washed the bed-sheets and did some casework on the computer. It was easier that way, to stare at somebody else's hideous problems than to think of her own, to admit to the crushing disappointment standing on her chest in heavy black boots. It was easier to cope alone.

Two weeks later, she'd received a note-card decorated with a sketch of Bettie Page from Alan. He'd written that the man they'd saved had phoned to thank him and that he would never forget the night they'd spent together. *I make love to you sometimes, in my mind*, he'd written. Fat lot of good that did her, him making love to her in his mind. But she kept the card. Now, Lexi wondered, as she surreptitiously glanced at Alan once again across the classroom, whether she was still in his mind. Somehow, she doubted it. He seemed very un-affected by the sight of her there, eight months pregnant. Could have been yours, Alan, she thought, could have been yours. With a big sigh, she tried to concentrate on the rest of her group. Rebecca was drawing columns on the whiteboard, the sun shining through the window and bouncing off her jet-black hair, almost giving her a halo. Just below her right shoulder, Lexi could see a small tattoo of Lenny's name. The cabbie, with his blacked-out love-heart, popped into her head. When she'd called him to say she'd changed her mind and she did want to book a ride for after the class, he'd said he'd known she would call. What was he on? He'd given her his card. She'd called the number. The End.

'So,' said Rebecca, smiling sweetly. 'What should I write down?'

Lexi opened her mouth, but Lenny got in there first.

'Like I said, I'm worried about the baby coming out,' said Lenny. 'I have a problem with blood, like, a big problem with it. So, basically, I could pass out during labour. In some ways, I'm more worried and nervous than you, Becs, aren't I?'

Nobody in their group said anything, though Lexi and Mel privately shared a look of exasperation. Lexi felt sure that she, Mel – and possibly even Rebecca, who was writing something completely different to what Lenny had said on the white-board – were thinking the same, not very polite, thing about Lenny. What an arse! Why did men have to try to stake a claim on the ultimate female experience? Wasn't there even a pregnancy-imitation pillow that men could buy and wear to know what the woman was going through? Why? There's no way she would want to dangle a fake penis from her nether regions in an attempt to find out what it was like to be a man. Anyway, after kissing way too many frogs in a quest to find Mr Right, she pretty much knew what went on in men's skulls by now: white noise. Maybe the occasional toot of a dog whistle. No – she stopped herself: it's not Lenny's fault men had let her down so badly. Her son, if she had one, wouldn't be like those men. Her son was going to be everything most men were not. Gracious. Generous. Honest. Open. *Hers.*

'Becs wants a home birth,' continued Lenny, 'which is fair enough. She's that kind of girl, you know, but it makes me nervous.'

'Hello?' said Rebecca, waving her hand around. 'I *am* here, you know, Lenny.'

'Oh yeah!' said Lenny, giving her a cursory look. 'But I really don't know whether I want to see you writhing around in pain at home when you could be in hospital surrounded by doctors who can help out if something goes wrong. If you were speaking to your mum, she could come and help, since she's a doctor. But that's not going to happen, is it, babe?'

Lexi, watching Rebecca stop writing to listen to Lenny, her expression unreadable, thought she must have the patience of a saint to put up with Lenny, who seemed to love the sound of his own voice. Lexi felt her head turning towards Alan again, but forced herself to resist. If you look at him again, she threatened herself, you are weaker than I thought. She started playing a game with herself. If you look at him again, you'll have a long labour. If you look at him again, you'll get even fatter. She started to feel miserable, raised her feet, which were swelling to elephantine proportions, rotated her ankles and turned her head to gawp at him.

'We've talked about this,' said Rebecca. 'We both wanted a home birth because it's more relaxed for all of us, remember? The midwife will know if we need to get to hospital, and we're hardly far away, are we?'

'What if the Beetle packs up?' Lenny said. 'I guess I've got my Chopper.'

Rebecca opened her mouth to reply when Ginny interrupted.

'Okay, everyone,' she said. 'Do you want to finish up those lists, then we'll grab a cup of tea.'

The women all stood up and moved towards the kettle, smoothing their hands appreciatively over their bumps, as if they were brand-new car bonnets in a showroom, while Ginny turned the whiteboards round to face the centre of the room. Lexi lagged behind, her heart hammering, so she could get a good view of Alan and Katy. Katy's beautician had been working overtime on her eyebrows, that was for sure. And it looked as if Katy hadn't paid attention to the advice about not dying your hair while pregnant. No one was that platinum blonde. Katy was pretty much everything Lexi wasn't: attractive, very slim, perfectly proportioned, fashion conscious even in pregnancy, now speaking about her birth plan in that authorial tone that comes with supreme self-confidence and partial disdain of those around you. Speaking to Alan so only he could hear, she turned to leave the room, probably to do pelvic-floor exercises in private. Even more aware of Alan now Katy had left the room, Lexi deliberately turned her back on him. Waddling towards Ginny to ask her a question, she felt a tap on her shoulder. She turned round to find him facing her.

'Lexi the life-saver,' Alan said in a soft voice. 'I'm amazed to see you again. In reception I was a bit shocked – you know? I often think about the day we met. Do you remember—'

He stopped speaking and smiled at her, eyes gleaming. Lexi blushed and smiled back, enchanted.

'No,' she said, deadpan. 'I don't remember a thing. Who are you again?'

Alan laughed. He lifted his hand, to shake hers.

'I'm Alan,' he said, taking her hand in his then lowering his voice. 'I seem to remember liking your pink underwear.'

'Right,' blushed Lexi, meaning to pull her hand away, but she left it there, a moment too long. Just long enough for Katy to walk back into the room and notice.

'Alan?' she said, suddenly by Lexi's shoulder. She turned to Lexi. 'I've been thinking I recognize you from somewhere. Have you ever come into Spotted, my locations company?'

Lexi turned round to face Katy, beaming from ear to ear, praying that she couldn't possibly recognize her from the time she'd waited outside Alan's office building a few weeks after their meeting, like a proper bunny-boiler. When Alan had come out of the office holding a woman's hand – Katy's, she realized – Lexi had thrown herself on to the floor behind a wall, pressing her nose into a discarded box of KFC to hide herself. Not her proudest moment.

'No,' she said, 'I'm a social worker, so I'm out and about in Brighton quite a bit. We may have seen one another, though I normally have my ear glued to the phone, so I'm not really aware of what's going on around me.'

'Where's your other half?' said Alan. 'Is he coming?'

Here we go. Lexi sighed and chewed her bottom lip. However positive she felt about her decision to have a baby on her own, if she told Alan about it, she felt as if she'd be admitting to him that he'd been right to reject her. That all men had rejected her. That she was not worth loving. She was tempted, for a second, to make something up. *Billy, my husband, is overseas on business. Roger died in a mountaineering accident. Quentin is out riding his horse.*

What am I thinking? she chastised herself. There was no man. No one had ever come close to winning her heart – except Alan. Being single was just fine. She was going to be a mother. She didn't need a man. Even so, it wasn't an easy thing to tell people. Taking a deep breath in and composing herself, she told the truth.

'Oh,' she said. 'There is no other half. I'm kind of going solo on this.'

'Going solo?' Katy repeated, in a louder than necessary voice, her narrow eyebrows wiggling around. 'I see – so you're single?'

Lexi smiled uneasily. She knew everyone in earshot had their ears pricked up, despite pretending to be absorbed in each other's conversation. Okay, she thought. I can handle this. I handle far more tense situations on a daily basis. I've developed trusting relationships with dangerous, abusive people in order to try to heal their broken lives. I've talked a suicidal teenager down from the top of a building. I've convinced an alcoholic mother with mental-health issues to hand over her child so she would be kept safe. I'm a centred, tough person. I don't judge anyone else – why should I care whether these people judge me? I don't. There was nothing to be ashamed of, nothing to be embarrassed about. The decision to have a baby alone had been a brave, independent woman's choice. Brighton was a forward-thinking town. Many female couples had gone down a similar route to have children. But, somehow, standing here, in the company of Alan, whom she had held on a pedestal as the kind of dreamy man she'd like to father her children, Lexi was reminded of how she had felt in the school playground: different, wishing she could be like everyone else, scrabbling for a story to tell or a wisecrack to make or a hairstyle to try to divert attention from people looking too closely at the real her, asking too many questions.

'Perhaps it's none of my business,' said Katy apologetically. 'Sorry if I've asked the wrong thing.'

Lexi shook her head, dismissing Katy's apology.

'I used a sperm bank,' Lexi said softly to Katy and Alan, watching them trying not to look shocked. She steeled herself. Now would come the interrogation. She thought she'd heard all the questions by now. How much did she pay? Few hundred per vial. Did she know the donor? Not personally, but she had his details. Would she have any others? Undecided. Was she giving the child a fair chance? She believed so. Was she worried about HIV? No, the donor is screened and the sperm is washed.

'Are you gay?' came Katy's reply.

'No,' said Alan.

Katy glared at him. 'How would you know?' she snapped.

'I mean, no, you shouldn't assume that,' he said. 'It's not 1982.'

'What's the significance of 1982?' said Katy.

Alan shrugged. 'I'm not sure,' he said, flustered.

Lexi smiled and rocked on her heels to get their attention.

'I'm not gay,' she said. 'I'm single and thirty-six years old. I guess I'm worried that I'm not going to meet anyone in time to have a baby with them and I wanted to take control of the situation, not be sitting around waiting for a man to swan in. The sperm came in the post from a company in Denmark,' she added unnecessarily. 'It cost a few hundred pounds. From what I know of the father, the donor, he speaks four different languages, has a degree in social education, plays the piano and looks very Scandinavian, with bright blue eyes and blond hair. I never found my Mr Right, so this was another option . . .'

Lexi let her words trail off, feeling relieved to have told the truth. Ginny, who had been half listening in, gave her a warm smile.

'Good on you,' said Katy. 'You've made it happen, which is more than I can say for a lot of women, who moan on about not finding a man to have children with. Like most things in life, sometimes you need to take action to get what you want, not sit around waiting.'

'Absolutely,' Ginny said. 'I admire you, doll.'

'Thanks,' said Lexi, genuinely surprised. 'Thank you. I wasn't expecting that response.'

'I mean it,' Katy said. 'I'm seriously impressed. Aren't you, Alan?"

Katy shot Alan a sharp look, but he didn't seem to notice.

'Yes,' he said, staring right at her, his expression unreadable. 'Lexi, you're obviously a very cool woman.'

'You'll probably find your Mr Right now,' said Katy, screwing up her nose. 'Sod's law.'

Lexi looked anywhere but at Alan, forcing out a polite laugh.

'No,' she said. 'He's been and gone already.'

'Perhaps he'll come back,' Katy said. 'Never say never.'

Chapter Five

While the group finished their tea, Ginny showed a short film of a woman in active labour. Everyone sat in stunned silence, unable to believe that they were just weeks away from experiencing the same ordeal. Ginny handed round a big bag of Maltesers and, during the musical interludes, talked the group through the different stages. Erin kept her eyes closed almost the entire time, catching only the final moments, when a grey, rabbit-like baby slipped out of the woman's vagina and into a midwife's waiting hands. She turned to look at Edward, whose eyes were cloudy and his fists tightly clenched. She reached out to touch his arm then let her hand drop.

Why haven't I said anything? she thought, as she sat there straight-backed, listening to Ginny explain 'transition', which was when the cervix completely dilates to let the baby's head fit through, like the parting of the Red Sea. Why don't I tell them the truth? That I already know all this.

Erin knew what the other women thought of her already. That she was quiet and reserved. Not passionate and vivacious like the stereotypical redhead. She hadn't been quiet before, though. Three years ago, Erin had been as loud as Lexi and as self-assured as Katy. She'd been *someone*. Everyone on the performing-arts scene in Norwich had known her. Now that she'd moved to Brighton, she was totally anonymous. Moving had not been easy. The plan had been to put the past behind them and move on, literally. But Erin's mind had sabotaged that plan. The past was always in her thoughts and was somehow made even more vivid by being in new, unfamiliar surroundings. The past was where she retreated, not for comfort – on the contrary – but as a subconscious reminder of why she was in Brighton, of why she should make more effort here, in her new life. It was even harder than she had expected.

'Did you hear what Lexi said before?' Katy leaned over to whisper to Erin when the film finished, and Ginny pushed the DVD-player to the side of the room. Erin shook her head. She had, but pretended she had not. She didn't want to come across as a gossip.

'No,' she replied. 'I was in a world of my own.'

'Lexi's baby is a donor-sperm baby,' said Katy, raising her eyebrows. 'Big decision that, isn't it?'

Erin thought about this for a moment. She looked at Lexi, who was smiling and laughing at something Rebecca was saying and realized she had been too quick to judge her. She'd put her down as a carefree, jolly woman, who probably enjoyed a pint and a stint on the karaoke, but how could she be carefree when she'd made the decision to have a child all by herself?

'I suppose your biological clock starts ticking really loudly when you get into your mid-thirties,' said Katy. 'I expect she wants to be with a man really. It's hardly the dream, is it? Starting off where most women fear ending up.'

Erin chewed her lip. The discovery that Lexi's baby was from donor sperm was something of a revelation. Of course, she knew that people didn't have easy lives, but, somehow, lately, she'd got into the habit of thinking it was only herself and Edward who'd had a difficult time. Perhaps Lexi was a potential friend. Perhaps they could share stories.

'Dreams rarely turn out quite how you expect, do they?' she said, staring past Katy's head and into the middle distance.

'When I say "dreams", I'm really talking about ambitions,' said Katy, correcting herself. 'I'm a big believer in making things happen for yourself. So, Erin, what do you do for a living?'

'I used to be a dance teacher,' said Erin, thinking of her old life, which seemed to have happened to someone else entirely. 'I helped run a dance studio in Norwich, but then . . . then —'

Erin paused. She looked at her hands and sighed, knowing that she wasn't going to say anything meaningful about her past. Although she'd made the conscious decision to stay quiet today, it depressed her. Part of her wanted to blurt out the truth.

'Oh well, things happened, and we moved to Brighton a few months back,' she said instead, wondering for a moment if she appeared to Katy as mysterious as she felt she was being.

'Hmmm,' said Katy, apparently unconcerned or uninterested in whatever it was that Erin was hiding. Then Ginny clapped her hands together.

'Now you've seen a normal labour,' said Ginny, 'let's talk about your expectations for your own birth. How about your group first, Katy?'

'Yes' Katy said, glancing at Erin. 'Hopes are, of course, for a natural, uncomplicated labour and, for Erin, a calm C-section. Personally, I want to do it all by myself. No pain relief, no intervention. If things go wrong, then that changes, but Alan will step up then and take control.'

Erin watched Alan, who lifted his hand as if to acknowledge his role. They were a dynamic couple, the sort of people who earned pots of money and went on city breaks all around Europe.

'Nothing's going to go wrong,' he said. 'But yes, I'm there.'

He was exactly the sort of man you'd find in a magazine list of Britain's Top 50 Most Eligible Men. Handsome, but not overly, he oozed capability. With his Rolex watch slipping slightly on his wrist and his winter suntan, there was something terribly charming about him. He wasn't showy. The way he held himself, too, was appealing. Erin thought he'd be a good dancer.

'I'm going to be taking the gas and air,' he said. 'I've got my own birth plan. What do you think, Edward? Are you up for the gas and air?'

Erin tensed as she waited for Edward to respond. She'd almost forgotten he was there, silently sitting by her side. She pulled her cardigan around her.

'Indeed,' said Edward, with an awkward laugh. 'But I don't think that will be necessary in our case.'

'Okay,' said Ginny, 'we'll be discussing pain management next time. And what about something from the other group?'

'Mel talked about her fears over whether the baby will be born healthy,' said Lexi. 'A fear we all share.'

'Yes.' Ginny nodded. 'Everyone worries about that.'

'Sometimes I think you can know too much,' said Mel weakly. 'At my anomaly scan, the sonographer found these little white marks on my baby's heart. She called them echogenic foci, I think. Well, I *know*, since I've been googling it ever since. There are whole threads on chat forums devoted to it. Anyway, they usually just go away, or they can be a marker for Down's Syndrome. I've decided to think they will just go away, but if that's the case, did I need to know they're there?'

'Did you have the nuchal-fold test?' asked Ginny. Mel nodded.

'Yes,' she said. 'It showed low odds for having a baby with chromosomal abnormalities, but I think the extra anxiety from the anomaly test is awful.'

'I didn't have the test for Down's,' Rebecca said. 'Because I want to love the baby no matter how it turns out.'

'I had it,' said Katy, 'because I'd rather be pre-warned, whatever the issue might be. Make a choice based on information.'

'It's all a very personal experience, but, often, you don't know how you're going to feel until it happens,' asked Ginny. 'So, let's hear from someone else. Erin, are there any concerns about your C-section birth you'd like to flag up?'

Erin felt the blood rush to her scalp. She tucked her hands between her knees and rubbed her lips together, as if in thought.

'Nothing much,' she started. 'Actually, that's not true.'

She glanced at Edward, who was staring back at her, his eyes dark and shiny as beetles.

'I worry about—' she said, feeling her heart beat in her chest.

Everyone was looking at Erin expectantly. They were her audience. Now was her chance to tell everyone what was really going on in her head and in her heart. Fleetingly, she imagined standing on a chair and announcing herself to the crowd, telling her secret to them all. 'Hello, I'm Erin. I'm thirty-six years old, and two years ago, I—' No, she told herself. None of them would understand. They would judge her. Think ill of her. Pity her. This was a secret she would keep buried deep, a secret she would have to keep tightly wrapped at the very core of her heart.

'I worry about—' she said, blinking slowly. 'I worry about—'

Edward grabbed Erin's hand and squeezed it. Everyone was looking at her.

'I worry about how long it will take me to recover from the operation,' she said flatly.

Edward's shoulders dropped. He looked away, and Erin felt drained of all energy. She could have told the truth. Instead, it was still all her burden, locked up in her heart. While Ginny addressed her question, Erin disappeared again into her thoughts. For the rest of the session, while Ginny talked, through a haze of memories, Erin listened, though she knew it all. Every last piece of information was already imprinted on her mind. She said nothing else. There were no words.

Chapter Six

Walking – or waddling, to be accurate – to her flat on the corner of Bedford Street after the antenatal group had finished, past the blancmange-pink-painted shopfront of Brighton Flea Market on Upper St James's Street, with its pink neon sign in the window throwing light over a collection of old-fashioned biscuit tins and an art deco vase, Mel automatically looked up to the large sash window of her living room, expecting to see Leo. Ordinarily, when she came home from work, he would be waiting by the window, only to wave then disappear when he saw her, to open the front door and give her a welcome hug. The thought made her gulp. Leo was a romantic, thoughtful person. He'd previously told her he'd sometimes stay twenty minutes by the window waiting for her to appear. Why then had he said he didn't want the baby?

'I don't get it,' she mumbled, feeling her legs throb and ache after the hours of sitting down at the antenatal class. She blushed, remembering her tears, wishing she'd been able to hold on to them until she'd been alone.

What must those women think of me, crying like that? she thought, shaking her head. What a mess.

It was a perennial problem. She'd never been able to swallow tears. Ever since she was a small girl, if she wasn't laughing inappropriately, she was crying too easily. It was as if her emotional-response gauge had been wrongly wired. It was only recently that she'd been able to convey anger without crying. Too many times in her life she'd been furiously angry, only to feel her lip quiver uncontrollably and the balance of power tip in her opponent's direction when the first tear slid helplessly down her cheek. It had been one of last year's resolutions: have an argument without getting emotional; talk about a serious subject without laughing. Not that she'd achieved either: when the sonographer had told her there were white marks on her baby's heart she'd chewed her lips until they bled to stop herself laughing. No wonder Leo had left. She was clearly nuts. Fumbling around in her bag for her key, wishing it was yesterday and that Leo would be there to open the door and smile and steer her towards their warm double bed, she heard Mrs Lelani, in the ground-floor flat, moving around behind the door.

'Mrs Lelani,' Mel called through the letterbox, 'could you let me in, please? I can't find my keys.'

As she waited for Mrs Lelani, a lady in her sixties who had lived in the flat for thirty years and had introduced Mel and Leo to Brighton gems, she looked past the neighbouring white houses, many with 'To Let' signs outside them, and, taking a deep breath of air, towards the seafront, to the Brighton Wheel. Yesterday, she hadn't realized how lucky she was. She'd had a family in the making – something she'd always privately considered the ultimate accolade – the sea on their doorstep, a lovely flat with big old windows and high ceilings and proper floorboards, hope in her heart. What had gone wrong?

'Melissa?' Mrs Lelani said, peering out from behind the safety chain before releasing the door. 'Melissa, what's going on? I saw Leo with a suitcase and a cardboard box this morning. He said he was moving out. He was so agitated with the box – I think it was giving way at the bottom – he barely gave me the time of day. I've never seen him like that. He was so rude! Melissa, are you moving out? Why didn't you tell me? I've been in crisis about it all day. I thought I was going to see you bring home the baby. I thought I was going to be able to hold the baby. I've bought him a sleepsuit with frogs all over it! I'm an old lady, I get excited about these things – oh, and there was a French woman here for you. I don't know who she was, probably a saleswoman, but she said she'd come again—'

The news that Leo had been back to the flat and taken a suitcase and box silenced Mel. She didn't understand his haste or his reasons why. Up until now she'd been hoping that he'd been in a bad mood, or felt nervous, or *something* easy to explain. She'd thought that he'd probably come home after he'd finished the day at work and say he didn't know what he had been thinking of. She stepped in through the communal front door and on to the red Persian carpet runner that climbed the wooden stairs up to her own flat. Catching sight of her reflection in the enormous gilt mirror that hung ostentatiously in the dark corridor, Mel clocked that her eyes were red and her skin much too pale. Realizing that Mrs Lelani had stopped talking and was watching her, waiting for a reply, she blinked.

'You're not old,' Mel said, softly, a little stunned. 'And I'm not moving out. Leo . . . Leo . . . Leo . . . Leo is . . . he . . . Leo has—'

'Spit it out then, dear!' said Mrs Lelani. 'Leo is what?'

'Oh, Mrs Lelani,' Mel said. 'I've had a horrible morning.'

Mrs Lelani looked deeply concerned and flung open the door to her flat, indicating that Mel should go inside. Always dressed in deep-coloured velvets or ornate brocade, jewellery and high heels, hair dyed black and pinned up, face made up with pale powder and red lips, Mrs Lelani seemed highly sophisticated, despite the slightly shabby furnishings of her home.

'Good grief, just come in, will you?' she said. 'I've had an awful morning, too. First, Leo with his silly box. Then I had to make an appointment for a colonoscopy, which I'm dreading. I'll be asking for pethidine. Will you be having pethidine? Take whatever you can get. Then I had to phone my ex-husband, and we arranged to meet for coffee but he didn't show up! I waited forty minutes before I left a message on his phone telling him never to bother me again. Now I'm worried he's dead in a gutter somewhere. And that couple in the top-floor flat? Good grief, they're going to bring this house to its knees. What on earth do they do up there?'

'Zumba,' Mel said. 'They both teach it.'

'Is that some kind of fetish thing? Good heavens. But, honestly, Mel, sometimes I wonder what it would be like to have a normal life. Boring, probably, but even so, I'd love to give it a try. What happened with your morning then, dear child?'

Mrs Lelani's Maine Coon cat, Marie Antoinette, barged past

Mel's legs as she was ushered into the flat. Mel felt instantly boiling: the heating was always turned up full blast and a pot of soup or stew was continually simmering in an orange Le Creuset pan. The hob gave off fragrant smells of nutmeg and cinnamon which permeated through the ceiling and Mel's floorboards and into her flat. Marie Antoinette, now sitting on the living-room rug, proceeded to kick up one of her legs and unselfconsciously lick the fur around her bottom.

'Marie Antoinette, please! I do not know where to look! Mel, you must ignore her bad manners. Sit down, dear,' Mrs Lelani said, pointing to the couch, an old red leather Chesterfield nestled into the bay window. 'Let me get you a drink. I could do with a vodka, personally, but it's only midday and I'm a slave to etiquette. *You* mustn't, of course. Peppermint tea?'

Mel sat down on the Chesterfield and felt the silvery sun warm her back. She rested her hands on her bump, rubbing it slightly and feeling what she thought must be an elbow or a knee jutting out. Mrs Lelani handed her the tea in a porcelain teacup and saucer decorated with tiny blue flowers and offered her a plate of lemon-curd tarts. Mel, realizing she hadn't eaten since breakfast, took two of them and ate ravenously.

'We were on our way to my antenatal group this morning,' she began, in between bites, 'when Leo decided he didn't want to come in with me and that he, in fact, didn't want to have a baby at all.'

Mel raised her eyebrows to emphasize horror and Mrs Lelani swallowed noisily. She put down her teacup so heavily, Mel worried it would crack.

'What tosh,' she said without missing a beat. 'So is that why he's gone off clutching his suitcase like Paddington Bear? With you almost eight months pregnant? Good heavens! What did you say to him?'

Mel shrugged and shifted in her seat so she could raise her legs up a little.

'I didn't really say anything,' she replied. 'I was completely taken aback. He said he wasn't the right person to be a dad.'

Mrs Lelani threw her head back and laughed. 'He's obviously scared,' she said. 'He's scared he'll be hopeless.'

Mel shook her head and leaned forward in her seat.

'I can't see why he'd be scared. It's not as if he's going to look after the baby anyway. I'm the one giving up work, while he carries on.'

'Do you think there's another woman involved then?' said Mrs Lelani matter-of-factly.

'You're the second person to say that today,' said Mel, hugging the cushion, running through all the females he knew. She couldn't see him going for any of them. 'He says not. But I guess I don't know anything for sure.'

Mrs Lelani reached down, picked up Marie Antoinette and placed her on her lap. 'In my husband's case, there was another man involved, by the way. Don't rule that out,' she said, stroking the cat so firmly its long and lustrous fur went completely flat. 'Yes, that *was* interesting.'

Mel communicated her sympathy with an upside-down smile. She'd heard the story of Mr Lelani, who had decided five years into their marriage that he was gay but wanted to stay living as husband and wife. Mrs Lelani declined that offer but had seen him every week for coffee because she still loved him and he still loved her.

'You know, a friend of mine, Ellen, came home to find her husband trying on her silk underwear,' Mrs Lelani whispered. 'She was terribly understanding about it all, but, quite frankly, I don't know how she didn't fall about the place laughing. Hugh is a mountain of a man! Over six foot tall and at least sixteen stone, bald as a coot but with a great big Captain Birdseye beard.'

Marie Antoinette, now looking like a seal, fled her lap and ran out through the cat flap.

'Look,' said Mrs Lelani, unperturbed. 'You can always rely on me to help you while Leo does his growing up. And you have lots of friends, don't you? How about those women at the antenatal group? My mum friends became my absolute best friends, I have to say.'

Mel nodded, and tears slipped into her eyes. She didn't want to think of a future without Leo in it.

'They were fine,' she said, wiping the moisture away. 'But I was too busy crying to really notice. They seemed friendly. Oh, God, that's my mobile ringing. Jesus, what's the time? I should be at work by now.'

'No,' said Mrs Lelani. 'You're in no mood for the office. You should stay here and watch a film. *It's a Wonderful Life* always cheers me up. I could make some soup and we could watch it together. There's a box of peppermint creams needs eating up, too. I'm sure your baby would love them.'

Mel smiled and fumbled at her bag until she located her iPhone. Realizing the number was her office number, she answered it quickly, cringing when she heard her boss's irate voice demanding to know where she was and why she wasn't at her desk working on a logo design for a sports-shoe client they were presenting to at five p.m.

'You're the star of this agency,' her boss said. 'I'm relying on you, Mel.'

Talk about a guilt trip. Mel thought about her job. It was true that she was probably the best designer at the agency; she'd recently won them a mobile phone poster series commission that would bring in thousands of pounds. They'd already hinted that they didn't want her to take too much maternity leave. Her childless boss had even said he thought twelve weeks should be enough. Mel had remained silent, having no real idea of how she would feel afterwards. And what now, with no Leo on the scene? She could hardly leave the baby to fend for itself.

'I'll be there in fifteen minutes,' she said.

Mrs Lelani put another lemon-curd tart on Mel's plate and pantomimed that she should tell her boss she couldn't come in. Smiling gratefully at her, Mel put her phone back in her bag and told her that she had better get to work.

'I'll leave the peppermint creams outside your front door,' Mrs Lelani said.

Mel laughed and accepted a hug from her landlady, who smelled of expensive perfume mixed with soup and lemon.

'You don't have to worry about the rent if it becomes difficult – if Leo doesn't come back,' Mrs Lelani said kindly. 'You're more of a daughter to me sometimes than my own daughter, out there on the other side of the world working as a cowgirl, of all the things to do with your life. Why did I kill myself taking her to ballet lessons all those years? People are born a certain way, aren't they? Anyway, if Leo doesn't come home soon and you find yourself alone, you're absolutely *not* alone. I'm here in body and spirit. Try not to worry.'

'Thanks,' said Mel, her voice quivering. 'What would I do without you?'

Chapter Seven

Friday was usually the biggest and booziest night for Lenny, Rebecca and their friends. It had originally been a Thursday, but when Lenny started to put on a regular night at the Pig and Whistle for local bands and DJs to play, everyone saved their cash and waited until Friday to get lashed. It had been a Friday when Lenny and Rebecca had first got together and a Friday, Rebecca had worked out, when they had been reckless with contraception and conceived. Stupid not to have been careful. But Lenny had seemed so exciting, so lawless, compared to her strict family that she had been carried away by the thrill of it all. Where she came from, a tiny village on the Welsh and Herefordshire border, kissing a boy at a bus stop and experimenting with a puff of cannabis had earned her a reputation as a disreputable whore. Everywhere she went in the village, there was a tut waiting to sting her. She didn't much care what those conservative, narrow-minded tutters thought of her, but her parents, both doctors, wanted the family to be highly regarded in the community and so insisted Rebecca behave like a nun. Coming to

Brighton had been like being released from a convent. Here, even in their small top-floor flat, she felt free. She could be exactly who she wanted to be – get her nose pierced, wear clothes her mother would hate, listen to loud, shouty music, even stick her bare bottom out of the window if she wished. No one in Brighton gave two hoots that she was pregnant by but not married to a boy who played guitar in a band, took drugs, told her he wanted to fuck her on the pier, worked in a vintage-clothes shop and said he would rather die than get an office job. Nobody cared if he licked pistachio ice cream off her nipples with the curtains wide open. She had never felt so alive.

'That was gold,' Lenny said after they'd made love on the futon in their flat, in the spoons position. 'Your breasts are amazing now you're pregnant.'

Rebecca moved to sitting and lifted her long black hair off her shoulders and into a loose knot on the top of her head. She felt Lenny's appreciative eyes all over her and felt like a giant peach, all pregnant and ripe and delicious.

'I'm sure there's a compliment in there somewhere.' She laughed, and held her satisfyingly full breasts in her hands. 'I hope they stay like this. They feel like water bombs. Do you remember those?'

'Except those ones are full of milk,' said Lenny. 'Are you going to start wearing those weird pads in your bra soon?'

'Yeah,' said Rebecca. 'Doesn't put you off me, though, does it?'

'No way, babe,' said Lenny. 'You are hot.'

Since getting pregnant, Rebecca's breasts and Fridays had changed somewhat. She couldn't handle how embarrassingly

71

and boringly drunk all her friends got on the Friday blow-out, so she stayed in while Lenny – not wanting to let down his devoted fans – partied until the early hours. Before he left, they always made love, and Rebecca, having done a course in massage when she moved to Brighton, would rub Lenny's shoulders and back afterwards.

'Hey,' she said now, as he turned on to his stomach and pointed over his shoulder to his back, indicating he wanted his massage, 'how come I'm giving you a massage? I'm the one who's going to need it when the contractions start.'

'You know you love it,' he said, closing his eyes while she worked her hands up and down his muscles. 'I'm like a wrestler before a fight. When I'm going on stage, I need one of your massages. It's especially important tonight because there are going to be some A&R people there from London. Maybe I'll get an album deal.'

She kissed his back, straddled him and continued to massage him, pressing as hard as she thought he could bear. In her head she prayed that he would get an album deal one day soon. He'd already had a single released, but an album was what he wanted, and she feared that, if he didn't get one, he would be pretty hard to live with. Outside, the sky had gone dark and Rebecca paused to turn on a lamp, which threw an amber glow over the room.

'What do you think about names?' she said. 'What do you like?'

'Clarence,' Lenny said. 'After Clarence White, the best blue-grass guitarist in the world.'

Rebecca burst out laughing. 'Clarence?' she said. 'No way. I was thinking about River or Wind or something.'

Now it was Lenny who burst out laughing. Rebecca grinned.

'What are you on?' he said. 'Wind? That's no name for the future Elvis. Hey – cool. What about Elvis?'

She gave him a look. 'Nope,' she said. 'Not Elvis. Hey, Lenny, will you get paid tonight? We have to pay our rent next week. I should offer to massage some of those women in the antenatal group. They're probably all loaded.'

Lenny grunted, and Rebecca wasn't sure what he meant by it, but he seemed annoyed.

'That Alan bloke pissed me off,' said Lenny, out of nowhere. 'Did you hear him going on about how much stuff they had for the baby? Mamas & Papas cot, a nursery decked out with furniture, the entire Bugaboo range, designer Babygros, top-of-the-range monitors that tell the room temperature as well. I mean, for fuck's sake, talk about ramming his wealth down your throat.'

Lenny turned over and Rebecca climbed off him. He stood up, naked except for his socks, and pulled on his trousers. No pants. Rebecca thought about Alan and what he'd said. Unlike Lenny, she'd thought Alan was making fun of himself and Katy, about how excessive they'd been, not showing off. Typical that Lenny would see him in competitive terms, even though the two men couldn't be more different.

'We, on the other hand,' said Rebecca, 'have nothing, except for the Moses basket I found in Help the Aged. I'm not bothered, though, are you? We don't need all that stuff.'

'I don't know,' Lenny said. 'Why should our kid be the one with nothing? Maybe I should get a real job now, instead of holding out for an album deal. I mean, we have a single out, so we might well get an album deal, but is what you really want for me to go out to work? Buy a suit from Top Man and get a desk job?'

Lenny sat on the edge of the bed and angrily laced his shoes, as if she'd answered yes, that's definitely what she wanted. He ran his hand through his hair and turned back to face her, his eyes gleaming. Rebecca was struck by his looks. He was incredibly good-looking. Film-star good-looking. No wonder his female fans went hysterical when he took his shirt off on stage. What he had said bothered her, though. They'd always agreed that material possessions were meaningless as long as they had each other and did something they were passionate about. That was one of the reasons she loved him so: he didn't want to conform. The last thing she wanted was for him to get a proper job. She loved his freedom, his refusal to play the game. Secretly, she feared he would quite quickly lose his appeal if he was sitting behind a desk selling insurance.

'No, Lenny, I don't want that,' she said. 'You've got to stick to music. You said you couldn't live without it. You said you never wanted to be average. Somehow, I can't see you in an office. We'll cope. The baby doesn't have to cost a fortune. I can strap him or her to my back in a bit of fabric. We don't need a Bugaboo. We can use cloth nappies, I'll breastfeed and still do massage to earn a few quid. One of the other mums might babysit sometimes. We'll be fine. Once you've got your album recorded you'll get more gigs, but I think we should stick to what we've always wanted.'

Rebecca stroked her tummy, realizing that the baby wasn't at all what *she'd* wanted when she'd moved to Brighton. A grass-roots job with a non-governmental organization was what she'd been aiming for, campaigning for something she believed in – something controversial, though she wasn't sure what. She'd been so long without a voice, she knew she could shout really loud on behalf of someone else's good cause. Oh well, there was plenty of time for shouting. And then there was travelling. She desperately wanted to travel the world and see the places she'd read about: Goa, Brazil, the Great Wall of China, Angel Falls, India.

'And when the baby's old enough I want to go travelling,' she said. 'There's a whole world out there, Lenny. We have to go travelling. There's no way I'm giving up on that dream. I looked in the Trailfinders window, and round-the-world tickets are less than a grand. There's loads for us to do, and the baby is going to be part of that. It's not about prams and Babygros.'

'You're right, babe,' said Lenny, looking pleased with Rebecca's little speech. 'That bloke Alan just did my head in. His wife did, too. Bit snooty, wasn't she? '

He stretched out and stood up. He went to the window, leaned both hands on the windowsill, lifted up the net curtain and looked out over the impressive listed buildings and grounds of Brighton College, a prestigious independent school which, despite being just over the road, seemed to Lenny to belong to a different universe. Rebecca hadn't admitted that she'd been to a similar school, with croquet and crochet on the curriculum. Or that her family were very well-off and had, up until a few months ago, when she cut off contact, given her a decent monthly allowance.

'I felt sorry for Mel,' said Rebecca. 'How can her boyfriend have left her?'

'It's not all black and white, though, is it?' said Lenny. 'It's tough being a bloke sometimes. Whatever you do, you can't win. Maybe he thinks he's done the right thing by her, if he doesn't love her. Maybe she's a pain in the arse. She seemed it, to be fair. I know if I left you, you'd cope. You're one of those resilient, strong people, which is why I love you, babe.'

He continued to look out of the window, speaking in the direction of the college. Rebecca felt suddenly cold. An image of herself clutching the baby, standing on the doorstep of her parent's house, flashed into her mind. She would never let that happen. Besides, they'd probably disown her. She pulled on a cardigan.

'Am I strong?' she said. 'You're not planning on leaving, are you?'

'No,' he said, glancing at her, before gazing again through the window. 'Course not! But I'm just saying, if I did what this Leo has done, you'd just get on with it. You're strong like that. Determined. I knew that when we first met. After all that crap you put up with when you were at home, your belly is full of fire. You're not possessive or dependent on me. You'd be fine as a single mum. That's a compliment.'

Rebecca's perfectly circular eyes bored like infrared lasers into Lenny's back. Sensing her stare, he rolled his shoulders, turned and grinned at her.

'Right,' he said, rubbing his palms together and pushing his hair away from his face. 'Show time.'

Rebecca, alone now, looked around the flat, wondering what to do. She ought to use this time to relax and catch up on sleep, because, thanks to her restless legs and constant need to pee, her nights were interrupted. But it wasn't even seven p.m. yet. She thought about trying to make the flat more homely. Since they'd moved in three months ago, they hadn't really done anything, even though the landlord said they could. Most of their books were still in boxes. Now, she felt an urge to give the flat a fresh coat of paint, get the books out, put pictures up and make it feel like a home. She had already collected quite a few bits of furniture from Brighton's Recycling Centre. Lenny reckoned that the guy there fancied her because he saved all the best stuff for her to look at first. Rebecca didn't think so, but she went there a lot, just so Lenny would act a bit jealous. Not that she'd admit it to anyone in the world, but she liked him to be jealous. It shifted his focus from himself and on to her. She liked the power his pout gave her.

She dug her fingers into her lower back and rubbed in small, circular motions. Her back had begun to ache.

The record Lenny had put on had stopped long ago and flat was too quiet. All her friends would be out by now. She thought about her friend Ella, who had gone travelling. She'd put loads of pictures up on Facebook yesterday of Australia. Rebecca had been transfixed. Here, the fridge hummed and the tap dripped. Was this how it was going to be from now on, Lenny out playing gigs while she stayed at home with the baby? Before getting pregnant, she'd never even thought about what it would be like to have a baby. She had been too busy enjoying her freedom. And though she'd vowed to herself time and time again that it wouldn't change their lives, she'd already noticed a change in people's reactions to her. Some of her friends talked to her only about the pregnancy now, even though she'd told them that the baby didn't *define* her. Walking across the open-plan living room, she felt dizzy and knew she needed to eat, but, because of how the baby was sitting, she couldn't fit much into her stomach without feeling uncomfortable. She ate a banana and drank a glass of milk, staring at the Moses basket, trying to imagine how it would feel when she looked inside and saw her baby's legs and arms waving around. Feeling the baby somersault inside her, she wondered whether his eyes were open or closed and whether he knew what she was thinking. She thought he probably did.

'I'll have to tell Mum soon,' she said, patting her tummy and feeling her cheeks burn with shame. Seven and a half months pregnant and she still hadn't told her parents she was expecting. But she was going to have to *see* them soon so had no choice but to admit the truth. It was pathetic, she decided, that she hadn't already done so. To begin with, not telling them had felt like a rebellion – just as not giving them her new address had felt like defiance. Now, it felt frightening. She couldn't imagine how they'd react. Her mum would definitely freak out. Her dad would let her mum do the talking and look painfully awkward, and probably retreat to his study to work out his passive aggression on his computer keyboard. They were the sort of people who did things the right way: marriage, careers, house-buying and then children.

Moving to the sink, she tossed in the plates they'd used earlier in the day and started to run the tap. In her mind rolled pictures of Lenny on stage, of the appreciative gazes of all the females in the audience, the huffy stances of their boyfriends, dipping their noses into their beer. 'Lenny's lady' was how she had become known; she felt a glimmer of pride, despite being a feminist. She started to wash up.

'This is too boring,' Rebecca said after two minutes, peeling off her Marigolds and throwing them on the washboard. Feeling crowded in the flat and desperate for a breath of sea air, she put on her parka. She pulled out her phone and thought about Mel. She lived close by, and seemed like she might like company. Texting her, Rebecca asked if she needed a pregnant friend? Yes, please! came the almost immediate reply.

Chapter Eight

'We weren't supposed to hear that, were we?' said Erin. 'About Lexi having a donor baby on her own, I mean.'

Erin and Edward sat side by side in their king-sized bed. Edward was reading the *Telegraph* and Erin was wiggling her fingers around to ward off yet another attack of pregnancy-related pins and needles. Though in their bedroom the only sound was the clock striking nine o'clock, in the distance came the sounds of a band playing at the Pig and Whistle. The crowd was going mad for whoever was singing. The noise of all those people clapping struck a chord in Erin's heart. When she thought about when she was on tour with *Chicago*, it seemed like another life entirely. There was nothing like energetic applause at the end of a show. Performers would receive it breathlessly, waiting to see if it would fade out, or whether they would encore. God, it was fabulous. She watched Edward's reflection in the mirror on the mahogany wardrobe a couple of feet away from the bottom of the bed. The spotlights in the ceiling highlighted his receding hairline and made him look older than forty. Erin made a mental note to move the dressing screen along slightly, to obscure the view.

'I don't know,' said Edward. 'She was talking in a pretty loud voice for someone who wanted to keep it secret. But I guess she was having a conversation with Katy and Alan. I don't suppose it's any of our business.'

Erin looked at the wallpaper and decided she would peel it off tomorrow and re-decorate.

'I can understand why she's done it,' Erin said. 'I think I would have used donor sperm, if I didn't have you.'

Edward hummed. She knew he didn't really agree, or probably felt somehow offended by her comment but was unlikely to tell her exactly what he felt.

'Doesn't make a man feel like he has many uses,' he said.

'Oh,' said Erin, 'don't be daft. You know I didn't mean it like that. I'm just saying that women have a biological clock, don't they? And if you've not met a man, then why not have a baby by other means? I heard her say the sperm came from Denmark. I think I read somewhere that there's a shortage here. I bet loads of women go there. You have to applaud them.'

Edward rustled his paper. Erin noticed how tightly he was gripping on to the pages. Silently, she accused him of turning into his own dad, an uptight naval officer, then felt immediately guilty. She knew she was pushing him, but she couldn't help it.

'Isn't it a bit selfish?' Edward said thoughtfully. 'It's all about Lexi. What about the baby? Doesn't he or she need a mum *and* a dad? A stable home?'

Erin folded her arms across her chest. The baby was doing acrobatics inside her.

'How many people do you know who have a perfect nuclear family?' she said, as patiently as she could. 'And what about so-called "normal" couples who decide to have children? It's hardly an unselfish act, is it? I mean, *we're* not having this baby because we want to give society another good person, or because we want to give the baby the gift of life, are we? Aren't we having this baby for purely selfish reasons? Because we, more than anything, need one to complete us?'

Erin stared at he. He stayed perfectly still. He didn't like it when she raised her voice, didn't respond well to being criticized or attacked. Who did? But Edward in particular hated confrontation or being forced to react without having time to think. That was why teaching at Brighton College was perfect for him. He could plan every lesson from beginning to end and work from his meticulous notes. He was always in control, and those pupils were angelic; they rarely surprised him by being outspoken. She watched his pulse thumping in his neck, like the beak of a woodpecker knocking against wood and wondered if, one day, it would burst right out of his skin.

'I wouldn't say that,' he said, resting his newspaper on the duvet. 'Erin? Why are you so angry?'

'I'm not angry!' she said, pushing back the duvet, swinging her legs out of the bed and pushing her feet into her slippers. There was another burst of applause from the pub. 'I just feel like our life has frozen up! I feel like I'm in the deep freeze! Where's our life, our friends, my studio? Where's the old us? We go to bed at nine o'clock. We're living like hermits! Aren't you ever tempted to kiss me? Do you think this is fun for me, feeling like a big, fat lump?'

Edward paled. He took off his glasses and put them on the

bedside table next to his glass of water and alarm clock. He turned to face her.

'How do you mean "frozen"? We're not frozen,' he said soothingly. 'We've wanted this baby more than anything, and we moved here to make a fresh start, didn't we? We're nearly through the pregnancy, and then we can get on with our lives. You can start dancing again and you'll soon make friends. You're just feeling tense. We go to bed early because we think it's best for the baby that you're well rested, don't we?'

She hated that he said 'we' when it was only her who was going through the pregnancy, only her who had given up her life so completely to come to Brighton. Only her who really knew the feeling of responsibility of having another being growing inside her. Only her who felt that each day of the pregnancy took a year to pass. He patted the bed and left his elegant, pale hand resting there.

'Come back to bed,' he said, patting again. 'Come here.'

Erin tightened the belt of her dressing gown, moved her hair off her shoulders and glared at Edward.

'I'm not a bloody cat,' she said, 'I'm a bloody woman. Treat me like one, will you? You used to think I was like Ginger Rogers, not a bloody ginger tomcat.'

Edward's jaw dropped, but he said nothing. He looked hurt and utterly bemused.

'Oh, for God's sake, Edward,' she said. 'At least allow yourself to get angry with me. Go wild for once, why don't you!'

Sweeping out of the bedroom and letting the door slam behind her, Erin closed her eyes, shaking, and furious with herself for being so awful to Edward.

'Write it down,' the midwife had said to her when she'd told her about her horrendous mood swings and the molten anger she felt glowing inside her at the most irrational times. 'Write down what's bothering you. It'll help.'

She marched down the stairs, one hand, still numb with pins and needles, on the banister. Pen. I need a pen and some paper. The windows of the house were huge, and the moon, shining almost in a perfect circle, was bright enough to light up the living room. She didn't bother to turn on a lamp. The moon seemed to shine like a torch on a painting Edward had recently bought of children dressed in Victorian-style sailor suits fishing from a rock. Erin glanced out at the sea and had a mean thought: Edward belonged in that painting, in the Victorian era. He wasn't remotely a modern man. Not like Lenny. Not like Alan. Walking directly to the bureau, she unlocked it and pulled out a pad and pen, then the blue jewellery box she kept all her most important treasures in, ever since she was a young girl. Carrying them to the table, she pulled up a chair and started to write:

I know he loves me. Every day I long to thank him for loving me, but he's like a wooden soldier and instead I push him away. I want him to grab me in his arms and tell me he wants me, like he used to. But he treats me like I'm one of his antique vases. Look, but don't touch. Why does he put up with me when I'm so horrible? That in itself makes me resent him. I know I'm taking it all out on him. Poor Edward. What is wrong with me? Feel like I'm cracking up. Hormones, the midwife says. Anxiety, the counsellor says. I think it's impatience. I want this baby to come out. I want to see her face and study her features and hold her to me and listen to her breath, and I want to be returned to the woman I once was. I want to be me again. Not screwed up tight like a clenched fist, but laughing and open and affectionate. I want to dance. I haven't danced since. I wonder if I've forgotten how. I want to feel her breath on my face. In my dreams the breath doesn't come. I cannot stand the wait.

Erin didn't hear Edward's footsteps on the stairs as she opened the jewellery box and pulled out the tiny white hospital wristband she had kept more safely than any of her jewels. She read the name: Baby Josiah Newman. Tears filled her eyes. She tried to blink them away, but they kept on coming. Holding the band in her hand, the tears dripped on to the paper, blurring the ink of her words.

'Erin?' Edward said softly, coming into the room behind her. He had enough sense not to turn on the lamp. Resting his hand on her shoulder, she felt his warmth travel through her body. They both looked out towards the sea. She grabbed his hand and gave it a squeeze.

'I know I can be distant,' he said with difficulty. 'I should tell you every day that I love you.'

Erin's cheeks glowed at Edward's words, but her heart thawed. She chastised herself for giving him such a hard time.

'I'm fine,' she said, too shrilly, tightening her fist over the band. 'I'll be up. You go.'

Edward let his hand drop from her shoulder then wrapped his arms around Erin from behind, pushing his face into her neck. Twisting round, she found his mouth and lips. They kissed, briefly but warmly.

'Erin,' he said, his voice quavering as he noticed the band in her hand. 'Oh, Erin. Tell me.'

The room was silent, but all Erin heard was a deafening sound of rushing in her eardrums.

'Erin?' he said again. 'Say it.'

'I . . . I . . . miss him,' she managed to choke out before breaking down into heavy sobs.

She turned around and stuffed her hot face into his chest. For a while they held one another, until she pulled away, feeling the words bubbling in her chest, vying to get out. She'd kept them in for this long, for seven and a half months, out of respect for both of them, to keep them going, not to indulge those dormant fears, not to make it all worse. Now they rose up in her throat, like burning paper, and she had no choice but to voice them. She covered her eyes.

'What if it happens again?' she said into her palms. 'What if this baby dies, too?'

A cloud passed over the moon and, for a moment, the room was completely dark.

'It won't happen again,' Edward said, smoothing down her hair, tears rolling down his cheeks now. 'I promise you, it won't happen again.'

Mums. They knew everything. How did that happen? How did you transform from being a person meandering her way through life, not knowing if she was making the right decision over buying skimmed milk or semi-skimmed, to becoming a mother and knowing exactly what her daughter should do at every turn? With her ear still burning from her earlier phone conversation with her mum, which had lasted the fifteen-minute journey home from work, up the stairs and into her flat, Mel moved over to the window and saw Rebecca crossing the road, her bump neatly zipped into her parka. Mel's mum's exclamations ran through her mind. 'Phone Leo and talk to him right now! Find out what's going on! You're about to have his baby, for heaven's sake! He can't just walk off! He can't just decide he doesn't want a baby!' Thanks, Mum. As if I didn't know all that already. But her mum simply loved her. Mostly, she'd been rational and helpful, offering to come straight down on the train that night. And she was right, too. Mel did need to speak to Leo, to get some answers, but, since he'd left that morning, indignation had kicked in – and exhaustion. The kind of tiredness she felt now she was heavily pregnant was a non-negotiable tiredness, like the cable being pulled out of the back of the telly. The doorbell rang.

'Hi, come in,' she said to Rebecca, opening the door. 'How are you doing?'

Mel showed Rebecca into the flat and gestured that she could hang her coat up on the coat-stand. Rebecca had changed into a grey jersey dress and had left her hair down. She looked stunning. Mel felt a wreck in contrast, wearing Leo's old track-suit pants and a striped maternity top she had slept in the previous night.

'Good, thanks,' Rebecca said. 'Lenny's out playing a gig, and pregnant girlfriends are not permitted. I was at home about to tackle the washing-up, then I thought, I'm twenty years old, I'm going to have a newborn soon, what the hell am I doing? I thought you might need some moral support, though I guess you have lots of friends rallying round.'

Amy Bratley

Mel nodded, but realized that she hadn't yet told any of her friends that Leo had left her – hoping, perhaps, that he'd be back before she had to make it public knowledge. Bizarrely, just as she'd felt in the antenatal group when Alan had slated Leo, she didn't want all her friends to start hating him. She knew from previous boyfriends' misdemeanours that her group of friends were harsh judges. Once they got their teeth into Leo, they'd gnaw on his bones indefinitely.

'You know what,' she admitted to Rebecca, 'I haven't told them yet. I'm hoping we can sort it out. Otherwise . . . I'm not sure what I'll do. I can't face thinking about it.'

Mel felt tears prick her eyes, but she blinked them away. She'd done enough crying for one day. Instead, she let out a bark of laughter.

'I understand,' Rebecca said. 'Maybe you both need a bit of space. Pregnancy can be pretty intense, can't it? I have to keep reminding myself there's a reward at the end, in the shape of a baby boy hopefully.'

'I know what you mean. I've missed my wardrobe and my heels, but having said that, until Leo walked out, I've really loved being pregnant,' Mel said. 'I was so excited at the beginning I told people way before twelve weeks had passed. Leo was pissed off with me for that, but having this little being inside amazes me. It's so weird, growing another creature like this, isn't it? I know millions of women have done it time and time again, but I've loved the glowing feeling you get, as if all of us pregnant women are a bit special. Blokes stand up for you on the bus and people treat you nicely—'

'Or squeeze your body in the supermarket like they're testing mangoes,' said Rebecca, pulling a face. 'I think that's gross!

When else would you lunge in and grope a complete stranger and not get arrested for harassment? Never.'

'Thankfully, that hasn't happened to me,' said Mel. 'But you never know what treats are waiting around the corner! I didn't think Leo would ever do this—'

'He'll come back,' said Rebecca, touching Mel's arm. 'How long have you been together?'

'Just over two years,' Mel replied. 'We met at a party in Hove. We got talking and found out we both work in design. Well, I'm a designer and he's a website designer. We just clicked. Anyway, I thought we'd probably never see each other again, and I wasn't that bothered because I was happy single, but he kept calling me and asking me on dates, so we started going out. He wasn't like other men I've been out with. He really makes me laugh. He doesn't even really need to do anything and I laugh. He's kind of random. Like he'll buy me a bunch of flowers but stick them in the window box so I'll see them when I open the window. Or he'll phone me at work and pretend to be a police officer. Doesn't sound funny when I say it to you, but there was no macho crap. There *is* no macho crap.'

'So, is it really unlike Leo to go off like this then?' said Rebecca. 'Or had you been having a hard time?'

Mel screwed up her face, thinking about her answer.

'Not really,' she said. 'We've never argued much, only over small things like whose toenail cuttings are behind the sofa. Nothing major. Since I got pregnant, he's been normal. I guess he hasn't been as loving as usual in some respects, and I know he gets pissed off with me because I'm so tired the whole time, but only because I fall asleep when he's talking. He sees a lot of his brother, who has the worst kids you can possibly imagine. Honestly, they're horrendous little monsters. I think even their mother wants to kill them! Maybe it's something to do with that . . . Whatever it is, he needs to tell me. If he's stopped loving me, I need to know. It's going to hurt, but I guess I'll survive.'

Mel's lip wobbled, and she sighed in exasperation at herself. 'Anyway, would you like a cup of tea? I promise I won't cry tears into it. Or I've got wine if you want a little glass? It's supposed to be all right to have a glass now we're this far gone. My mother was just telling me she had a Guinness every day when she was pregnant with me. Probably explains my stunted growth.'

Rebecca laughed. 'I like the idea of wine,' she said, 'but I'll have tea, please. Peppermint, if you've got it. And do you have any crisps or anything salty? I'm suddenly starving, and I didn't bring anything with me.'

While Mel was in the kitchen boiling the kettle and emptying bags of crisps and pretzels into bowls, she called through to Rebecca. 'What about you and Lenny?' she asked. 'You're the Brad and Angelina of the antenatal group. How did you meet?'

Rebecca laughed again. Through the door, Mel saw her picking up various things – the cardigan she was knitting for the baby and the folder of information from the antenatal course, a picture of Leo and Mel together. She put the picture down really carefully and straightened it up, a gesture that made Mel like her.

'At one of Lenny's gigs,' Rebecca answered. 'I was one of many girls gawping at him from the wings, but I didn't let him know how I felt at first. He has a bit of an ego, as you might have guessed. I knew he liked me, since I'd seen him gawping back, but, as you can probably tell from meeting Lenny, I knew it would take a lot to win him for keeps. I reckon he's had lots of girlfriends before me, whereas I've not had a lot of experience. So, my friends advised me to play it cool – ha! Cool? I was hopeless. Every time I saw him I couldn't speak properly and legged it as quickly as possible. I think he interpreted that as nonchalance because, after we'd met a few times, he made a play for me. He got down on one knee and asked me to have dinner with him, followed by sex on the pier.'

'Subtle!' Mel said.

'Subtle's not Lenny's thing,' said Rebecca. 'But I've always loved that about him. He isn't like anyone else I'd ever met. He's the opposite of my family. He's so exaggerated, a real show-off. Like, last week, he got fed up with a game of cards he was losing at the pub and threw the whole pack on the fire.'

'Really?' Mel laughed. 'That's one way of losing.'

'He's got another side, too,' said Rebecca. 'When he's just woken up, he's all quiet and sleepy and cuddly. That's when he tells me all his insecurities and, it's bad to say it, but I like it when he does that. It makes me feel like we're more equal. We're so different really. He's from this wild, hippy family that had no rules. I'm from the most straight-laced family you can ever imagine.'

'Opposites attract?' asked Mel, bringing Rebecca her peppermint tea.

'Maybe,' Rebecca said. 'Though sometimes, especially now

I'm pregnant, I worry that we'll begin to clash. When he's out all the time with his band, I feel neglected. I can just see what the future will be like. I'll be looking after the baby while he goes out as normal. On the other hand, it could bring us closer together.'

'I expect so,' said Mel. 'I'm pretty scared about those first few weeks with the baby. I'm not sure what kind of mum I'm going to be. I'll probably be a helicopter parent, obsessed with every tiny thing the baby does.'

Especially if I'm on my own, she thought. But even though he'd left the flat, Mel couldn't believe that Leo would stay away for long. Surely this was just a blip.

'I can't get my head around being a mum,' said Rebecca. 'I feel too much like a child.'

Mel yawned. The tiredness was coming over her like a blanket. Putting her tea down, then sitting on the sofa next to Rebecca, she felt her eyelids drooping. 'Me, too,' she said, straining to keep her eyes open. 'What did you think of the other women in the group?'

Rebecca put her tea on the table in front of them and took a handful of crisps from a bowl.

'Erin seems really quiet,' said Rebecca. 'Lexi's quite full on and Katy reminds me of my mum in some ways. They're really different, but both total control freaks. What about you, what did—'

'Sorry, I—' began Mel, before she leaned her head on the cushion and closed her eyes and *bang!* she was asleep, landing in her dreams with a thump.

*

Rebecca carefully shook Mel, poked her arm gently, then called out her name quite loudly, but she wouldn't wake up. Rebecca was amazed how deeply she slept and wondered if it was dangerous somehow to leave her there, in the sitting-up position. Putting a cover over her and leaving a note at her feet explaining that she'd gone home, Rebecca closed the front door and let herself out of the flats. As she passed the ground-floor flat, she smelled a strong, lovely smell of cinnamon and orange. Not yet tired, she decided to walk home past the Pig and Whistle. From a street away, she could hear the DJ's set, laughter and the sounds of empty bottles being emptied into an outside dustbin. Lenny would be hitting the Jack Daniels now, soaking up the compliments about the gig with Mack. Standing outside the pub, she looked in through the window and saw Lenny holding court at one of the tables. While he spoke, the other people at the table leaned in to him, apparently transfixed by his words. She wondered what he was talking about. Her? Doubtful. She tried to catch his attention by waving, but, when he didn't see her, she felt embarrassed. She thought about going in. Just then, an older woman approached Lenny, whispering into his ear and resting one of her hands on his shoulder. He threw his head back, laughing, and the older woman smiled, running her finger around the rim of her glass. Rebecca didn't like the feeling in her stomach, so she pushed open the door and walked inside, feeling her heart beat faster. Immediately, she felt out of place and, by the way people were staring at her, as if she'd fallen out of space.

'Lenny,' she said, approaching him. When he didn't hear

her, someone else nudged him and pointed at her. He rubbed his nose with his hand and walked towards her, grinning. The woman who had been whispering into his ear glimpsed Rebecca then evaporated into the crowd.

'Babe,' he said. 'What's up?'

'Who was that woman?' Rebecca asked, feeling annoyed. 'What were you talking about?'

Not missing a beat, Lenny tapped his nose, took her by the elbow, grabbed his coat and led her outside. 'It's a surprise,' he said, wrapping his arms around her. 'You'll soon find out. Look, do you want to get home? I don't mind leaving now. The gig was good, but I can't be arsed with everyone tonight. Let's go home.'

Holding hands, they walked down the road towards their flat, opposite the looming buildings of Brighton College. Lenny took off his scarf and draped it around Rebecca, kissing her cheek.

'When you say "surprise",' said Rebecca, as they walked in the darkness hand in hand, 'I only like good ones, understand?'

Lenny shout-laughed, threw his arm over her shoulders and leaned his body into hers. 'I heard you,' he said, then, leaning down to talk into her bump. 'Calling Elvis . . . did you hear that, little man?'

Chapter Nine

A week later, Lexi arrived at the Birth & Baby centre for the second antenatal class dressed in her favourite maternity outfit. Not for Alan, you understand. She had spent ages deliberating between ensembles, for *herself*. Just before the class began, she felt her nose itch. Knowing she was about to sneeze, at the same time she registered that her bladder was full to bursting point. She'd drunk two big mugs of tea that morning, trying to finish up at work under the hawk eyes of the regional director, Beverly Swain, who wasn't as sweet-natured as you might hope from a woman at the top of the caring profession.

'Oh, God, I'm going to—' she muttered, pushing open the doors at the same time as letting out an enormous sneeze. Following the sneeze came the feeling of a trickle of warm pee soaking into her underwear and out on to her trousers. Just then, Alan arrived in reception, looking at her, his sensual lips just open enough to trigger a memory of the high-pitched sounds she'd previously emitted in his company. Orgasms had historically eluded Lexi (she'd half-heartedly faked them out of politeness) and, like buses, they had all arrived at once with

Alan, leaving her feeling totally besotted and the neighbours reaching for their earplugs. What was it about his penis? Was it shaped differently to that of every other man she'd dated? And was that a normal thought to be having about another woman's partner when nearly eight months pregnant with sperm from a Danish man who would certainly never make her orgasm? Or smile. Or an omelette.

'Oh, God,' she said again, realizing that the pee hadn't stopped coming. Darting shame-facedly into the Ladies', she pushed past Katy, who was at the mirror, filling it with blonde curls and blue eyes while at the same time energetically talking into her iPhone. Lexi quickly sat on the loo, yanking down her trousers to find that an embarrassingly huge wet patch had soaked through her silk trousers.

'Oh no,' she groaned, resting her head in her hands. In a few minutes she was going to be sitting in the classroom with Alan talking about pain control in labour. This wasn't exactly the impression she wanted to give. She listened to Katy end her telephone conversation, and presumed she was still admiring herself in the mirror, because all had gone silent. She wondered how she could blow-dry her trousers and pants with the hand-drier without anyone noticing. She groaned again. Katy tapped on the door.

'Lexi?' You're not sick, are you?'

Lexi rolled her eyes. She rubbed the top of her pregnant belly, where something sharp was protruding. Must be an elbow, a knee or a foot. Or an umbrella. Were babies born complete with umbrellas? She patted it, and it moved, which made her smile, despite everything.

'No!' said Lexi brightly, pulling up her trousers and flushing the loo. She looked at her backside. Her entire bottom and the tops of her legs were wet. How could she explain that away? 'Everything's just brilliant in here.'

After a few more minutes of standing in the cubicle, it was clear that Katy was waiting for Lexi to emerge. Lexi wondered if Katy could read her mind and detect that she had been having lewd thoughts about Alan. She pulled a guilty face and shook her head. This had to stop. Really, it had to stop. Alan was a virtual stranger. Katy was his wife. They were having a baby. *She* was having a baby. Lexi pinched herself hard and then felt sad. Pinching herself was what she used to do when she was a child and getting carried away in a daydream that made her giggle in class and everyone else stare at her. She sighed. If her boss knew what went on in her head, she'd probably be the one recommended as needing support in the community! Gingerly, she came out of the door, and, after trying and failing to tie her coat around her hips, stood with her back against the wall, her face glowing red, and forced a smile.

'Katy,' she said, 'would you mind standing guard for me outside the Ladies', please? My underwear is all twisted, I must have put it on all wrong this morning and the cubicles are too small for me to change in and I really can't sit through another class feeling this uncomfortable, so if you—'

Katy had a smile on her face, and her nostrils were widening then narrowing like billows. Her eyes slipped to Lexi's trousers and Lexi felt how she had at school, when the pretty, popular girl trapped her in the toilets, inspected her uniform and told her it was from a charity shop. Back then, charity shops hadn't been remotely cool, so when the popular girl called her a tramp, she hadn't been able to pass it off as vintage chic, or think of a decent comeback other than to kick the girl in the ankle.

'Did you have an accident?' Katy broke out into a grin. She put her perfectly manicured hand on Lexi's arm and began to laugh. Lexi breathed out hard, disliking Katy immensely. Katy would tell Alan this stupid, silly fact about her, she knew it. 'Oh, Lexi, it happens to me, too! I do hundreds of pelvic-floor exercises every day, yet still I leak like an old lady. I have to wear those awful pads! It happened to me when I was in the gym. I was buddying with this muscle man I know and I quickly had to run to the showers.'

Lexi's lips twitched. She momentarily forgot about Alan and laughed along with Katy. Her eyes widened.

'Katy, did you just say you go to the gym?' she asked, incredulous.

'Yes,' Katy said. 'Every day. I'm a little bit obsessed, but I'm like that with everything. I can't do anything by halves. Anyway, I was just on the phone booking up for Pramaerobics for two weeks after the baby's born. It's on Tuesdays, starting from the new pier. You should try it. It's better than sitting around drinking coffee all day. Fancy it?'

You should try it. Was Katy having a dig? Lexi frowned. Perhaps it was all in her head.

'I don't think so,' she said. 'I'm not very good at moving unnecessarily, unless it's to the fridge. And *I'm* a *coffee* addict, especially if you throw a pain au chocolat in. Oozing with chocolate.'

'That's not how the French make them, you know,' came Katy's retort. 'In Paris, the chocolate is just a taste; here, the pastry is stuffed with it.'

'Which is exactly how I like them,' Lexi said. 'Anyway, would you mind if I used the hand-drier?'

They stood looking at one another for a moment, after this uneasy sparring, then Katy laughed awkwardly and gave Lexi a weak smile before walking out of the door. Lexi felt exhausted. She propped herself up on the sink.

'Everyone's going in,' Katy said, swinging open the door. 'Better be quick.'

Shut the bloody door then, Goldilocks! Lexi mouthed silently, pulling down her leggings and jutting her bottom out under the drier, trying to aim the air at the patch of pee.

'Okay,' she called. 'Thanks!'

Just then, the door swung open again, and in walked Erin, who looked aghast when she saw her.

'Gosh, sorry, Lexi,' she said, turning quickly into a cubicle and locking the door behind her. 'You're not in labour, are you?'

Lexi's face turned luminous red. She felt so ridiculous, she burst out laughing.

'Katy was supposed to stop anyone from coming in,' she explained. 'I'm so sorry. I was just trying to dry my under-wear.'

'Oh, God,' said Erin. 'Did you sneeze? That happens to me, too.'

'Really?' laughed Lexi. 'Katy just said the same thing. This is like some kind of sisterhood.'

'That'll be pregnancy for you,' said Erin, from behind the toilet door. 'The ultimate sisterhood.'

In the class, Ginny, dressed today in a strawberry-print skirt, wide belt and low-cut white top, was taking them through pain-management options. She asked the women about their ideal births, and Rebecca was talking about the birth she fantasized about (outside, under an oak tree, at sunset – but she'd settle for a home birth in a birthing pool), the tiny gold dot in her nose glinting in the sunlight as she spoke. Katy thought that, for an earth-mother type, she was a sweet girl. Incredibly beautiful, dreadfully naïve and sweet. She felt a little bit sorry for her today, with Lenny by her side looking like a rogue, with his pen between his teeth as if it were a cigarette, clearly listening to music through one earpiece. Why else would his foot tap so rhythmically? She narrowed her eyes at him, but he was oblivious.

'As I said last week,' said Katy, when her turn came, 'I think it's better to experience labour without any pain relief. If I had the time, I would have hypnosis. But work is madly busy. Basically, though, my birth plan is to refuse any pain relief at all. I know it's each to their own, but I personally feel I'd be selling out if I had even a puff of gas and air.'

There was a sharp intake of breath from the other women. Katy knew what she'd said would ruffle their feathers, but so be it. It was what she believed.

'You've got to take it easy with work,' said Alan. 'You've got to put yourself first.'

Katy tried to hide her irritation. Alan really wasn't helping matters by telling her to slow down the whole time. Right now, she needed to speed up. Lately, Spotted had taken more calls than ever before from clients looking for various locations for summer events, and she needed to be at the office, or out on location organizing, or they would lose business. Alan seemed to think her pregnancy was disabling and that she needed rest. Yes, she was knackered, but she was successful and knackered.

'How do you feel about popping a paracetamol, Katy?' said Lexi. 'Or is that selling out, too?'

Katy shook her curls and frowned. What was the problem with that woman? Ever since she'd met Lexi there had been a certain brittleness between them. She wondered if Lexi regretted telling her and Alan about the donor sperm last week. But both of them had been fully supportive. She just didn't get it. Jealousy, she thought. She's probably jealous of her having Alan, just like most women were. She shot Alan a look and could perfectly understand why women admired him so. There was something very alpha about her husband, but not in a macho way. You just felt, should you need help of any description, you could call him up and he'd be there at the drop of a hat. Even when he was miles away on business, he would get things sorted out by people he knew. Well connected, was Alan. He had his weak points, too, of course. But she could count them on one hand.

'Strong pain relief sounds great to me,' chirped up Lenny. 'Bring out the class As.' He burst out laughing at his own joke. Rebecca whacked him with her pregnancy notes.

'Yes,' said Ginny, jangling her bangles up her arm with an indulgent smile. 'This is usually the bit that the men enjoy the most. So, when your labour begins, you might have contractions but not be in unbearable pain. This is where you could use the TENS machine, which you can hire from most chemists. Or does anyone else have any ideas about what might help?'

'Moving helps me when I have period pains,' said Rebecca. 'Or keeping a hot-water bottle on my lower back. I work as a masseur, and I can imagine that would help – if someone would do it for me . . . Lenny, for instance.'

Katy noticed Alan's knee start manically bobbing up and down when Rebecca said she did massage. She placed her hand firmly on his leg.

'Yes,' said Ginny. 'Massage is great, and warm baths might work, too. You could be in the early stages of labour for a long time.'

Katy looked at her watch. She couldn't be out of the office too long. Though she'd worked a sixty-hour week last week, eating dinner at her desk each night, Anita had made her feel as though she wasn't taking the agency seriously enough. She didn't understand what had got into her.

'And at what point do you go into hospital?' asked Lexi. 'I'm bothered about this, because I'm probably going to be on my own, although I did contact a doula this week. Do the midwives object to doulas?'

Ginny shook her head and sat up on the table in front of the group.

'No,' she said, 'not at all. In fact, the more people there are to help, the better. And, as for your other question, you should hold off as long as you can before going into hospital, but let the midwives know they'll see you soon. If you go too early, you may well be turned away. So does anybody know what the other pain-management options are?'

Katy glanced at her watch again, wondering whether, if she started speaking, she could get this part of the class moving on. Everyone looked so bloody relaxed! Probably they were all on maternity leave by now. That was just not going to happen for Katy. She'd be working up until the moment her waters broke.

'Pethidine,' she said. 'Which makes the babies very drowsy. Then there's the epidural, which too many women end up having.'

Mel, who hadn't said anything up to now, cleared her throat. 'Why do so many women have an epidural?' she asked. 'I've assumed I'll probably have one. I don't think I can cope with the pain.'

Katy inwardly despaired of Mel. She didn't seem to have improved since last week. The poor thing seemed to be one of life's victims. Katy couldn't help feel impatient with her.

'Mostly, because first-time labours are getting really long,' said Ginny. 'We need to be active during birth and, more often than not, women are lying on their backs. If you see the size of the pelvic bone and what happens to it, when you're standing or lying down, you can see that's going to slow labour down. Women get exhausted, frightened and don't feel in control, then out comes the epidural. I'm not against it. I think it's very helpful in some cases, when women are exhausted.'

'I want everything,' said Lexi. 'I'm going to get in there and say, "Give me that epidural now!" I don't see the point in putting yourself through hell when you don't have to.'

Mel put her hand up. 'Me, too,' she said.

'It is painful,' said Ginny. 'But it's a satisfying pain. It's nothing you can't deal with. I've done it four times and loved every minute.'

Nothing you can't deal with. Loved every minute. Katy liked the sound of that. She took in a deep breath, imagining herself in birth. It was her body. Her baby. Birth wasn't going to be a problem for her. She was determined that her labour would go smoothly. She, like always, no matter how hard it got, was going to be in control. Right now, though, she really should get back to work.

Rebecca wasn't fearful of the pain of labour, as such. It was more that she didn't know what to expect afterwards. There was going to be a seismic shift in her life with Lenny and she wasn't sure how they would fare. She knew labour *would* be painful, but it was only for a few hours of her life, a bit like running a marathon. Experiencing it was something she wanted to go through as a rite of passage, a personal achievement that would make her feel more like a woman and less like a girl. She looked around at the others. Katy seemed to know even more than Ginny, so she'd be fine, and Erin was having an elective C-section, but the rest of them were equally apprehensive about the pain side of things. In a way, she wished she hadn't started to come to these classes, but just dealt with it on the day, instinctively. Then maybe she wouldn't have started to worry about Lenny as well. What would he be like in labour? Would he be able to cope with all the attention being on Rebecca? Her stomach tightened. She began to doubt whether it was a good idea for him to be in there with her at all. What if she did a poo while she was pushing? What if there was blood everywhere? He would probably faint. Her mum, Harriet, would be an amazing birth partner. She was a doctor, completely calm in a crisis. Rebecca felt suddenly homesick, then chastised herself. It wasn't as if her mum hadn't *tried* to contact Rebecca. Just lately, she'd left several messages on her phone, begging her to get in touch. And Rebecca had almost dialled her back, but, at the last second, fear of how her mother was going to react stopped her from going through with it. She'd sent a text instead, telling her that everything was okay. Rebecca sighed, just catching the end of Ginny's sentence.

'—very rarely things go wrong in labour. A baby can have difficulties, or be poorly, and need extra care. Occasionally, babies are stillborn. I'm sorry to have to bring it up, but I must tell you about every possibility and, sadly, it does sometimes happen. One of my ladies in a class I had last year lost her baby in this way. She wrote to me asking that I talk about it in future groups, because she had no idea it could happen. There's often no clear reason why it does, it's just one of those tragic mysteries in life.'

The room fell silent and Rebecca watched the dust particles shine in the sunlight, her throat throbbing with tears. The women glanced at each other sympathetically, all except for Erin, who was searching through her handbag for something. Rebecca frowned. She didn't seem to be listening, which must have been annoying Edward, because his expression was black.

'There are many organizations that can help you deal with this,' she said. 'And they're all in the list of support groups at the back of the pack I gave you this morning.'

Erin stood up, her bag on her shoulder.

'Excuse me for a moment,' she said, her voice almost a whisper. She didn't make eye contact with anyone before pushing open the classroom door and letting it swing shut. Edward stayed stock still, clasping his hands together, just staring ahead at Ginny. Rebecca looked at him, and he caught her eye, which seemed to startle him. Ginny, smiling now, clearly felt the tension in the air.

'Is Erin okay, Edward?' she asked.

Edward nodded, still wringing his hands.

'She's nervous about the whole thing,' he said. 'We've wanted a baby for a long time.'

Ginny nodded kindly and smiled.

'It's not long now,' she said. 'And, really, there's nothing to be nervous about. It's simply my job to make you all aware of some of the very rare things that could happen. Almost always, the baby pops out perfectly healthy and all is well. Does anyone else have any questions they want to ask at this point?'

'What do you recommend taking to hospital with you?' asked Lexi. 'There's a list as long as my arm in the pregnancy book I'm reading, but do you really need disposable pants and a bottle of water spray?'

'I've already packed my hospital bag,' said Katy. 'I was saying to Mel that you can order a pack online, if you can't be bothered to do it yourself.'

'It's not that I can't be bothered,' said Lexi. 'I'm just asking what is essential and what is superfluous.'

'One thing to remember is that there are never enough pillows in hospital,' Ginny said. 'And you need to bring your own towels. It's not a hotel, it's a hospital. Disposable pants are useful for after the birth, when you lose quite a lot of blood, but you can use any old pants, if you prefer. Your birth outfit is worth giving a thought to, as well. You need something you can move around in but can take off easily.'

'I've had a special labour outfit designed,' said Katy. 'Alan's sister is a lingerie designer and she has a boutique in Auckland. I sketched something I thought would be good and she has made it for me. It's very cute. A bikini bra top and a little floaty skirt.'

Rebecca and Mel shared a look. Rebecca smiled, and Mel chewed her lip.

'I wasn't planning on wearing anything,' said Lexi.

'You don't have to,' said Ginny. 'But, as well as the midwives who are in the labour room with you, there can be students calling in, plus, a doctor might come in and check up on you, or even the person bringing round sandwiches, should your labour be around lunchtime.'

'Surely there's no time for a sandwich?' said Mel.

'You'll want to drink a lot,' said Ginny. 'So you have to make sure you empty your bladder every couple of hours. That's the job of the birth partner, to make sure you go to the toilet, during your labour. Got that, men?'

'Yes,' said Alan. 'Loud and clear.'

'Fuck!' said Lenny, suddenly standing up. 'I've got to go. We're doing a soundcheck in an hour. Sorry, babe.'

He turned to a surprised-looking Rebecca and kissed her on the top of the head. At the same moment, Erin came back into the room, looking even paler than usual, the darkness around her eyes more pronounced. She smiled a small, distracted smile at nobody in particular and sat back down in her seat, pulling her fluffy grey cardigan closer to her body. Edward put his hand on her forearm for a moment, but she discreetly shook him off. Rebecca wondered if she was feeling ill or was in pain – there was something going on, but Erin didn't look as if she wanted to talk about it.

'I'll see you later,' Lenny said. 'Sorry, girls, got to shoot.'

He pulled his jacket from the back of the chair and swung it on to his shoulders so energetically the contents of his pockets flew on to the floor. As well as his empty-as-usual wallet, something gold and tiny spun through the air, almost in slow motion, glinting in the sun. It landed on the floorboards in the middle of the room, bounced with a pinging sound – once, twice and three times – before spinning on the spot, rolling towards a wide crack between the floorboards and disappearing. Rebecca gasped. Was that a ring?

'Shit!' Lenny said, falling to the floor and scrambling to catch it before it slipped into the crack. 'No!'

Rebecca stood up and kneeled down beside him. 'Lenny,' she said, 'was that a ring?'

He ran his hands through his hair, his face like thunder.

'Sixty quid that cost!' he said. 'I'm going to have to get that out of there.'

'What was it for?' asked Rebecca quietly. By now, Katy and Alan had joined them on the floor, trying to look through the cracks in the floorboards. Rebecca's face was burning.

'*You!*' he said. 'I was going to ask you to marry me tonight, babe! Now I've lost the ring!'

Rebecca was stunned into silence. She started to laugh. 'Really?' she said. 'Lenny, was this the surprise?'

'Yes!' he said. 'Now the surprise is under the floorboards. What am I going to do?'

The other women were making excited noises and beaming at Rebecca and Lenny.

'So,' said Lexi. 'What's your answer, Rebecca?'

'I didn't think you wanted to get married,' Rebecca said. 'What's changed your mind?'

'I don't know,' said Lenny. 'I just want to do the right thing for once. I don't have any money, I'm a bit of an arse, I just wanted you to know I'm sorry for that and that I love you.'

'Ahh,' everyone said. Mel started to clap. While this was going on, Alan had found a coat-hanger, slowly lifted the ring out of the crack and passed it to Lenny. It was a small ring with a red stone on it.

'Might as well do this properly,' said Lenny, going down on one knee in the middle of the crescent of chairs. 'Will you marry me?'

Rebecca cracked up. Everyone started clapping, Lenny was in his element. Then he checked his watch, stood up again and brushed off his jeans. He kissed Rebecca on the lips then left the room before she had a chance to reply.

'He didn't even wait for me to say yes!' she said, half laughing, leaning back in her seat and trying on the ring, which fitted perfectly.

'How sweet,' said Ginny. 'Congratulations, Rebecca! Okay, so when everyone's ready, we're moving on to birth positions. If you'd like to look at the illustrations on the handout I gave you—'

Rebecca smiled absent-mindedly while Ginny talked through the different ways to give birth, demonstrating squatting, leaning against a wall and being on all fours with the ease of a true professional who didn't care what her bottom looked like. After another hour had passed, Ginny wound up the session, reminding the group that, next time, she had invited a new mum to demonstrate breastfeeding to the group.

'Shall we go for a cup of tea?' said Lexi afterwards. 'To celebrate Lenny's proposal?'

'I've got to get back to work,' said Katy.

'Oh, go on,' said Alan. 'You need to get to know each other. Just take fifteen minutes, hey, angel?'

'I'll have a very quick one,' said Katy. 'Shall we go?'

'Christ!' said Lexi. 'Let me pick my bag up.'

Rebecca, grinning, invited Erin. 'Do you have time to come for a tea?' she asked. Erin shook her head.

'Erin?' said Edward. 'I can walk around Brighton for a while if you'd like to go?'

'No, Edward,' she snapped. 'Thank you, girls, but I have something to do. Congratulations, though, Rebecca.'

'Okay then, I think we can go now?' said Katy, checking her watch.

Rebecca smiled kindly, but Erin's smile was cursory. Rebecca sensed that Erin didn't like her and wondered if she'd said or done anything to offend her. Maybe she found Lenny annoying; he couldn't be more different to Edward. She wanted to ask what was wrong and why she was acting so strangely, but Erin had left the room. She exchanged a look with Mel.

'Don't mind her,' said Lexi softly. 'I think she has stuff going on. Let's go before Katy hyperventilates.'

Chapter Ten

The Metrodeco tea salon, a Thirties Parisian-style café, was buzzing. When Mel, Lexi, Rebecca and Katy arrived outside and looked in through the window, two different people leapt out of their seats to open the door for them. Walking inside, Mel breathed in the delicious fragrance of the twenty or more teas on the menu. Before pregnancy, she'd been a coffee guzzler, but now, tea was her thing. Finding a table tucked into the corner of the space by an enormous mirror that reflected the bright blue sky and an old-fashioned street lamp that stood in the centre of the salon, the women lowered themselves into the seats, their bumps flush with the table's edges.

'Here we are,' said Lexi cheerfully, 'the pregnant brigade.'

The sun shone through the tall windows and filled the room with an apricot light. Teaspoons tinkled against saucers and Mel felt a sudden lift in her mood. Leo might have walked out, but she had joy in her heart about what she, Katy, Lexi and Rebecca – all such different women – were about to experience. Ever present was an ache for Leo, but she was relieved that, if only fleetingly, her excitement about her pregnancy had returned. Whatever Leo was doing or feeling, she was ultimately responsible for bringing a new life into the world, and she would take up the challenge with all her energy. If her mum could be a parent on her own, she could do it, too.

'Apparently, there's art deco furniture for sale upstairs,' said Katy, reading the back of the menu. 'Epstein, Eames and Wegner. Right, shall we order?'

At that moment, the door opened and a woman carrying a baby – probably about six months old – in a sling entered. The woman, with black hair twisted up on her head and completely clear skin, looked radiant. Mel glanced at Lexi, Katy and Rebecca. All of them were fixated on the baby, beaming unselfconsciously at the woman, their hands resting on their bumps.

'Your baby is gorgeous,' said Rebecca to her. 'How is it, being a mum?'

The woman sighed and widened her eyes. 'I haven't had a night's sleep in seven months,' she said, her eyes welling up. 'I'm exhausted! Nobody told me I'd feel like this! My house is a heap, my career's over, there's baby sick all over my clothes, my friends think I'm boring and my marriage is a mess.'

The women's eyes couldn't be any wider. Their smiles diminished.

'But, listen, don't let me put you off,' said the woman hurriedly. 'It's really worth it. I've fallen in love all over again. With my baby. Not my husband. He's a pain in the arse – ha!'

They all laughed nervously, then Mel tried to comprehend what it must be like not to sleep for seven months. She loved sleeping. And, as quickly as the optimism about motherhood had arrived, it disappeared. The energy drained out of her.

She didn't want to do it alone. She wanted to be with Leo. How would she cope alone with months of interrupted sleep? What if Leo didn't want anything to do with the baby? What if being apart, as they had been for a week now, was a permanent arrangement? Mel gulped, telling herself not to think about it. Picking up the menu, she scanned the teas on offer and ordered a Graham Greene & Chocolate tea and a pastry.

'There's probably a tea we can drink if we go overdue,' Lexi said. 'What's that tea Ginny mentioned that's supposed to soften up the cervix?'

'Raspberry-leaf tea,' said Katy. 'I've got a box already. So,' she continued, turning to Rebecca, 'how do you feel about the proposal?'

'It was very spontaneous,' said Lexi. 'He's definitely a showman. Did you know Lenny was planning that?'

Rebecca shook her head. She held her ring finger and stared, confused, at the shiny gold band and red stone as if it belonged to someone else entirely.

'Not at all,' she said. 'I didn't think Lenny would ever propose. To be honest, it makes me slightly suspicious of his motives.'

The waitress brought over their order and laid it out on the table.

'Ha! I know what you mean,' Lexi said. 'Girl after my own heart.'

'Oh, Rebecca,' said Katy, pulling a disappointed expression. 'You shouldn't be so cynical. Not all men are bad. Lenny clearly loves you and wants to do the right thing by you and the baby. I think that's honourable.'

'Yes, I know what you mean,' said Rebecca. 'It just doesn't

sit well with what I know of Lenny. He's always been against marriage, and we're both kind of relaxed about the whole thing. It was a surprise. I'm just shocked.'

Mel, pulling her knitting from her tote bag, started working on the baby cardigan she had started. Katy sighed and looked out the window.

'Better than doing it all on your own,' said Mel. 'Which is what it's looking like for me.'

'Oh, Mel,' Rebecca said. 'I was wondering about Leo. Have you found out what's wrong with him?'

Mel shook her head. Since he'd left, they'd spoken only once, when Leo rang to ask how she was and how the baby was. They'd agreed to give each other complete space for a few days. Now, Mel was secretly waiting for him to take the initiative and get in touch. She didn't want to grovel.

'I just hope he comes back,' she said. 'I can't face being a single mum.'

'I'm sure he will,' said Rebecca. 'You know how weird men can be.'

'You should speak to Lexi about being a single mum, shouldn't she, Lexi?' said Katy, nodding towards Lexi. 'You seem pretty cool about it.'

'I didn't realize,' said Mel. 'Are you single?'

Lexi nodded. 'Yes,' she said. 'I'm having a baby by donor sperm.'

Mel's eyes widened. She instantly felt full of admiration for Lexi and felt guilty for bemoaning her luck with Leo.

'Really?' Mel asked. 'Wow. That's brave. What made you decide to do that?'

*

Brave. People were always telling Lexi she was brave for buying donor sperm. She didn't really feel brave. Battle-worn – yes, that was more like it. After seeing her doctor and being told the waiting list for donor sperm on the NHS was years long, she decided to go private. Her initial Internet research almost put her off the whole idea. First up was a whole load of unregulated websites where women were seeking free sperm from unregulated, unscreened donors. Just one look at the kind of responses those women were getting from prospective donors (would you like a cuddle, too? I'm up for it if you are) made Lexi feel sick. Then there were online forums where sperm donors were competing over how many kids they'd conceived. None of them could even spell! Yikes. One woman she'd found in a chat room had bought unregulated sperm from an online donor which had arrived in the post in a leaking plastic bottle. Grotesque. Pity the poor postman.

'That's what you get if you go budget,' her friend Catherine said. 'You'll have to go first class.'

Lexi had tried the UK first, but, apart from the waiting list, it didn't seem as straightforward as if she looked abroad. Because of changes in the law, British sperm donors had lost the right to anonymity so, some people suggested, there were fewer men donating sperm, making it more expensive and less available. Catherine said she knew a woman who had been to Denmark to be inseminated, where donors still had anonymity and lots of fit twenty-somethings donated sperm, and so Lexi found a well-respected Danish sperm bank that shipped donor sperm to more than sixty-five countries, including the UK, which held detailed records of all its donors so she could choose the best sperm for her ('You don't want any old wanker's sperm,' said Catherine).

'I turned thirty-five,' explained Lexi to the women. 'I wanted a baby but was short of the XY chromosomes necessary. In other words, I wasn't in a relationship. I've never had any luck with men, but I started dating, insanely. I joined every dating website there is: Gorgeous Get-togethers, Match, Love Me, Single and Sad. Ha!'

'Bet that last one didn't have too many subscribers,' said Rebecca.

'You'd be surprised,' said Lexi. 'I once read a quote by Anita Roddick saying, if she could find a cure for loneliness, she'd be the richest woman on earth. Anyway, it was a fruitless search. I got to the point where I thought, if I want a baby, I'm going to have to sort it out myself. I gave it a lot of thought and, to cut a long story short, I ended up buying sperm from Denmark, where there's a booming industry, because they're a lot more open-minded about the whole thing. A lot of British women are going there, apparently.'

There was a hush around the table and Lexi guessed they were probably feeling uncomfortable. She didn't blame them. Ordering a baby online wasn't very romantic. But neither was being denied your most important ambition in life.

'Was it hard to choose a donor?' asked Mel. 'Did you have a choice?'

Lexi thought of the catalogue of donors she'd scrolled through, with Catherine sitting on one side, a glass of wine on the other. It had felt far less demoralizing than standing on the edge of a nightclub dance floor waiting for some bloke to offer her Sex on the Beach.

'It's an odd thing, buying sperm online,' she said, aware that the couple on the next table had stopped speaking to listen in. 'You choose from various donors – hair colour, eye colour, etc. – who are happy to be identified. The guy I used did this video of himself, naming all his hobbies, interests and beliefs, so that was good. Almost like going on a date!'

Mel and Rebecca smiled. Katy frowned.

'I'm joking,' said Lexi.

'What about the practicality of having a baby on your own?' Mel asked. 'Do you feel daunted by that?'

Lexi thought about her life to date. She'd pretty much done the entire thing on her own, give or take a few helping hands. Her dad had worked in the military and was away, almost always. Lexi had imagined he was a hero, but her mum had set her straight; the bastard had deserted the forces and them for his other wife and daughter in Weymouth. But who could blame him? Her mum was eternally depressed and alternated between being dependent on uppers and dependent on downers. Lexi became good at looking after herself.

Her mobile began buzzing on the table, jerking her into the present. It was her mother calling from Spain.

'Excuse me for a minute,' she said to the group. She pressed her phone to her ear. 'Hi, Mum. I can't really talk. Can I call you back?'

'No,' her mother drawled. 'I need to speak to someone. You're the only one I've got left.'

She started crying. Lexi's shoulders drooped. Resigned, she looked down at her lap while the others talked. 'What's wrong?' she asked. Her mother sniffed.

'You're what's wrong,' she said. 'Everyone I know thinks it's awful that you've bought your baby on the Web. Imagine how it makes me feel to think you can't get a man. Is it because you've put on weight? Couldn't you just have gone jogging ?'

Lexi closed her eyes and counted to three.

'No, Mum,' she said firmly. 'It's not because of my weight. It's because I can't find anyone I want to spend my life with, and I'm running out of time. I work all hours and I don't want to spend the next few years trying to find a mate just so I can have a baby. If you don't like telling your friends, then don't. I'd rather you didn't go blurting it out to everyone.'

'Why?' said her mother. 'Are you ashamed? Because I am, Lexi. You're making me feel worse about life than I already do. And what about the poor child? How the heck is she going to feel when she finds out you paid for her with a credit card?'

Lexi channelled the baby in her womb. *Don't listen*, she told it. *Don't listen to her. I'm nothing like her, I promise you. I love you.*

'No, I'm not ashamed,' said Lexi wearily. 'I'm proud of what I'm doing and I'd shout that from the rooftops, too.'

She didn't mean that literally; she just wanted to shock her mother into silence.

'Good grief, you never cease to amaze me,' she said, and hung up before Lexi had the chance.

Her throat burning with an acid taste, her temples throbbing, Lexi sighed and placed the phone in the top of her bag. Rubbing the bottom of her bump, she exhaled, deflated.

'Are you all right?' asked Rebecca, concerned. 'It sounded like you were getting an earful.'

'Yeah,' Lexi sighed. 'Just my mother calling to give me a

hard time. She's not a very happy person. She doesn't approve of what I'm doing. She's never been a big fan of mine.'

As soon as she said it, she wished she hadn't. This was way too much information. Why was she giving away such secrets to women she hardly knew?

'Oh no,' said Mel, resting her hand on Lexi's forearm. 'That's awful. Well, we're all big fans. We think you're great.'

'Thanks,' said Lexi. 'Anyway, forget that. Where was I?'

'We were just asking if you were daunted by the prospect of being a single mum?' reminded Mel. 'But probably you don't feel like talking about that now.'

Lexi flicked her eyes up to the ceiling. She hadn't felt daunted ten minutes ago, but now, after speaking to her mother, her mood was low.

'Oh, I don't know, not really,' she said. 'If there are big decisions to make about the baby, I suppose I will miss the chance to talk to someone, but, ultimately, no. Most of my friends have children, so I can talk to them.'

'And will you still look for a relationship with a man in the future?' Mel asked, pausing in her knitting. 'Because I think Leo is free.'

Everyone laughed.

'I'm not actively looking,' said Lexi. 'But if I meet someone in the future then that will be a bonus.'

Katy screwed up her nose. 'But have you thought about whether you'd have a baby with him, if you did meet someone?' she asked. 'I'm a person who likes to plan everything out, as you may have noticed. I detest uncertainty.'

Lexi reined in her irritation at Katy's words. She hadn't been the only person to ask such a personal question. For some reason, people seemed to think they had the right to pry.

'I've no idea what I'll do until it happens,' said Lexi, suddenly feeling exhausted. 'I probably wouldn't have a baby with him, as I only want one child. How about you, Katy? Are you planning on a brood? I can't really see you in an apron with scores of children hanging off your snake hips.'

Katy gave her a rueful grin. 'Just one for me,' she replied. 'I want to get back to work quite quickly. Luckily, Alan wants to help out. But he's like that. Very thoughtful and attentive. I'm very fortunate to have him, I realize that. He's always putting my needs and interests first.'

How bloody marvellous for you, thought Lexi. I've just told you I can't find a man and my mum's a bitch, but all's well in your world. Whoop de do! Angry at Katy's smugness, she opened her mouth before she could stop herself.

'Yes,' said Lexi. 'I thought Alan was quite a catch when we first met. You did well for yourself there. I'm sure there was plenty of competition.'

Katy gave her a quizzical look. Lexi's face turned pink. What *was* she playing at? She looked away. Picking up on the tension, everyone fell silent.

'So,' said Rebecca finally, 'what do you think of Erin? I don't think she likes me and Lenny.'

'She's strange,' said Katy, quickly. 'But I think there's something going on with her. Edward hardly says a word, does he? Still, he said they've wanted the baby for a long time. Maybe they've been trying for years. I fell pregnant the first time we tried, but I can imagine it's awful to have to wait.'

'You were very lucky then weren't you?' said Lexi, feeling like throwing her cup of tea at Katy.

'So,' said Katy, fixing Lexi with a stare, 'how are you going to get through the labour on your own? Do you have a birth partner in mind? It must be difficult without a partner sometimes.'

Lexi's scalp prickled. Katy knew exactly what buttons to press to wind Lexi up, yet she pretended she was completely innocent.

'Not really,' said Lexi. 'You can't pretend that relationships are going to work out when you have a baby even if you do have a partner. It's a decision, as a woman, you have to make knowing that you could cope on your own.'

Katy's face darkened. 'That's so cynical!' she said. 'That's not how I look at it at all. This baby is mine and Alan's. It's a shared experience. As long as you communicate with one another, you're fine. We've always been completely honest with each other about everything.'

Lexi pursed her lips, but her inner devil stuck out his horrible forked tongue before she could stop herself. 'Everything?' she echoed, before putting her hand over her mouth. She just wanted to score a point against smug Katy. Lexi was sick of people like Katy thinking that they were superior to her. She was sick of her mum. She was sick of Alan.

'Yes,' said Katy. 'Everything.'

'He must have told you about me then?' Lexi asked, her eyebrows raised. 'About when we met? I didn't know if he would. I hope you're cool with it?'

'What do you mean by that?' Katy said quietly.

'Oh, just some fun we once had,' said Lexi, her shoulders sinking.

Mel poured everyone more tea. Lexi immediately felt guilty and exhaled loudly. Petty and pointless, that's what she was being. Not so unlike her mother.

'Sorry,' Lexi said. 'That was uncalled for. I shouldn't have said that.'

Katy, sipping her tea, was now silently fuming. Everyone fell silent.

'Lexi,' said Katy, rallying a little, 'Alan had many meaningless flings with women before meeting me. He is not a schoolboy, hence his decision not to tell me about your "fun". Please, let's keep the past where it belongs, shall we?' She gave Lexi a short, sharp smile then turned her attention to Rebecca.

'*Anyway*,' said Rebecca, 'do you think you'll all come to my wedding? I'll probably have a humanist ceremony on the beach in the summer. When I've got my figure back. It's all going to be very budget.'

'Yes, of course!' Mel said. 'I can design your invites if you like.'

'That'd be amazing,' said Rebecca. 'I've got to save on everything I can. I'll give you a pregnancy massage in return if you like.'

'Ooh, yes,' said Mel. 'Leo rubbed my feet, so with him gone—'

'I'll step in and help out,' Rebecca said. 'Until he comes home.'

Mel smiled gratefully.

'That applies to all of you,' said Rebecca. 'If you need a massage, just call me.'

'Sounds lovely, Rebecca,' said Lexi, sheepish now. 'Thank you.'

'I might be able to look out a cheap location for you,' said Katy to Rebecca, now completely recovered. 'If it's a last-minute thing, some places on our books, like town houses and their gardens in Brighton, can go for a bargain.'

'Wow,' said Rebecca. 'That's amazing! Thank you all. I'm really looking forward to it now! My parents won't be pleased, though.'

'Why's that?' Lexi asked, relieved at the change in topic. Her heart was beating too fast in her chest. Katy was now blanking her, unsurprisingly, and had just been really sweet to offer her help to Rebecca. Lexi felt like a mean bitch. She wanted to go home.

'They won't approve of Lenny,' Rebecca said. 'They're pretty conservative people.'

'What about the baby?' Katy said. 'They must be happy about the baby. Everyone's always happy about a baby.'

Rebecca's eyes dropped to her teacup. She sighed. Lexi could tell she was struggling. 'They don't know about the baby,' she mumbled. 'I haven't told them yet.'

Chapter Eleven

Erin hardly spoke as they walked towards the centre of Brighton. She knew it wasn't fair to take her irrational feelings of anger out on Edward, but if it wasn't him who bore the brunt, how would she vent her emotions? Throw a brick through a shop window? Slash a tyre with a knife? Unjust persecution of one's husband was much more acceptable. If only he'd leave her alone, then she could be angry on her own, but he wouldn't, would he? He'd never leave her alone. Edward had taken to walking beside Erin with outstretched arms at the ready, as if she were a toddler running mindlessly towards the edge of a cliff.

'I think we should buy some Babygros,' Edward blurted out, grabbing Erin's elbow. 'It's four weeks until the baby is born. We have nothing.'

Erin filled with molten rage. She couldn't even see, she felt so mad. She didn't want to buy anything to do with babies. Nothing. Ever since discovering she was pregnant, she hadn't bought anything specifically for the baby, only a couple of maternity outfits ordered online with minimum fuss. She hadn't dared even to look inside the boutiques in Brighton's Lanes, refused hand-me-downs and gifts. Now Edward was being all cavalier about buying baby clothes, as if nothing had ever happened.

'We agreed that we wouldn't buy anything until a few days before the C-section,' she stated coldly.

'I don't care what we agreed,' said Edward in a stern voice. 'I want to buy some Babygros. This is my baby, too. Where's that really nice baby-clothes shop we saw?'

They stood on North Road and Erin's gaze landed on Mamissima, a baby boutique that sold gorgeous baby items you'd find on the pages of *Elle* or *Vogue*. Edward followed her eye-line and began walking towards the shop.

'Are you coming?' he asked, turning back briefly. 'Or not?'

Erin shook her head but didn't say a word. Edward was never this bold with her. How dare he go against her wishes? What was he thinking of, marching into the shop as if everything were perfectly normal? Erin stared on helplessly as Edward elbowed a pregnant woman out of the way so he could get past. What must the sales assistant think? She tried not to watch him through the glass shop window as he furiously picked up some Babygros from a rail and held them up in the air to inspect, but once she'd seen the brightly coloured, tiny outfits, she was drawn into the shop as if spellbound. Once inside, welcomed by smiling salespeople, she felt as if she'd entered a warm, comforting dream.

'What are you *doing*?' she said to Edward, her voice quivering as her eyes darted over the rails of baby clothes and shelves of toys. Edward, calm now, but with tears in his eyes, smiled warmly.

'I like this one,' he said, choking on his words. He held out a chocolate-brown sleepsuit. 'I'm going to get it. Erin, tell me you like it. The baby can wear it to come home from hospital.'

He picked up a white cashmere blanket. 'We should get this too,' he said, brushing it against his face. 'It's so soft, it'll be perfect to wrap the baby in to carry it to the car. Erin?'

Edward was shaking slightly, his eyes alight. Erin's heart melted. She was reminded of when they first met. He had been desperately keen to impress her, offering to take her to restaurants and bars in Norwich, and even – and this had been the clincher – learning how to tango. Despite being so stiff emotionally and socially, he was a natural dancer, elegant and smooth. Now, clutching the baby items, he was looking at her with all the hope in the world. Fearing she might cry, Erin nodded.

'Yes,' she said softly. 'They're perfect.'

She said nothing while she watched Edward choose another two sleepsuits, then pay. Her heart was aching too much to speak. When they left the shop, she felt the baby kicking hard inside, giving a stamp of approval.

'I'm sorry,' she said. 'Edward, I'm sorry. I should have gone for coffee. I shouldn't have been so mad.'

Edward wrapped his arms around her and held her tight. They stood there, for a moment, blocking the pavement, while Erin felt hope course through her veins and fill her with a giddying sense of joy.

Chapter Twelve

What a bitch, thought Katy as she walked back towards her office after tea. Why would Lexi throw that in her face? She must be incredibly insecure to want to try and score a point so pathetically. Katy decided never to mention it to Alan. What did it matter that he had had a 'fling' with Lexi years ago? He had dated many women in the past, and that's where those women stayed – in the past. He never mentioned any of them. He certainly hadn't talked about Lexi. But then he probably felt embarrassed. She wasn't exactly his type was she? Fat and loud with bright yellow hair? What a disaster area. And now she was having a child on her own; wasn't she, ultimately, a sad, lonely woman? No wonder Alan hadn't mentioned her.

'Hi,' she said, pressing the buzzer on the office door. 'It's Katy.'

The receptionist buzzed her in, and she walked past the vase of flowers on the reception desk and up the few stairs to her office, glancing at their recent clients popping up on a screen mounted on the wall. They had hundreds of properties on their books now, and repeat custom from some high-profile companies. She smiled at the familiar sense of pride it gave her to think that she and Anita had done this all themselves. Opening the door to her office, she gasped when she saw Anita sitting behind her computer.

'Good evening, Katy,' Anita said, her blonde, dead-straight hair gleaming like a sheet of velvet in the sunlight, her bright red lips contrasting against it.

'Come off it, I haven't been that long,' Katy sighed, putting down her bag. 'What are you doing in here?'

Anita didn't look up, but continued to tap at the keyboard with one finger. She couldn't touch-type, claiming never to have learned, since she had no intention of being someone's secretary. That little anecdote had impressed Katy when they first became colleagues, but now it just seemed to add to Anita's bitchy persona.

'Working,' she said. 'Someone has to sort out the Boots party before they walk away and refuse us their business. They need a location for their summer party and, since you're the one supposedly working on their account, I'm pretending to be you and doing your job. Telling their director that you're at antenatal class just won't wash, you know? And, by the way, Katy, I looked in your online history, and babycentre kept turning up and – what's the other one – mumsnet? Come on! Don't go all soft on me just because you're pregnant.'

Katy's mouth fell open. She felt wrong-footed on every level. Desperately wanting to justify herself on every single handful of mud Anita had thrown in her face, she found herself stammering hopelessly in reply. Anita took a moment to look up from the keyboard and gave her a patronizing smile.

'Don't get in a dither. I just don't want you to take your eye off the ball, darling,' she said. 'You know how Jake is snapping at your heels now he knows you'll be taking all that maternity leave.'

'All that maternity leave?' Katy said, gathering herself. 'I'm taking three months, and in that time I'll be checking my emails and available for meetings. Most women are on maternity leave when they're this pregnant. I'm hardly taking my eye off the ball!'

Anita, standing now, gave Katy a disbelieving look.

'I don't have kids,' said Anita, 'because I've seen what it does to women. You think you'll be coming to meetings a week after the baby is born? You won't. I wouldn't bother even trying to be involved for those three months. Have the baby, do what you need to do, then get yourself good childcare. That way, you can put your all into the business and we won't have to promote anyone else.'

Anita moved across the room, towards the door. Katy kept her lips shut tight, but she felt furious. Sitting in her office chair and moving around to make herself more comfortable, she picked up the phone and dialled Alan's number, deciding she would bloody well ask him about Lexi. She had a right to know if they had history. A tension headache tightened her forehead, but she didn't want to take painkillers, especially not after Lexi's little dig. Alan picked up immediately.

'Hey,' said Alan. 'How did your coffee go?'

Katy detected something in his voice. Hesitancy. She narrowed her eyes. It had to be Lexi. She opened her mouth to speak, but stopped herself just in time. She closed her eyes for a moment and sighed. Maybe she did need to stop working so hard before the birth. Maybe Alan and her midwife were right. But, no. She straightened up. She couldn't. She wouldn't give Anita the satisfaction. She wanted to be the woman who did it all.

'Katy?' Alan asked. 'I went to the chemist, and I got Calpol, baby monitors, burp cloths, baby scissors, a breast pump and a digital thermometer. I think our baby boy's medicine cabinet is all set.'

'Good,' Katy said, swallowing hard. 'That's great.' From out of nowhere, she felt the heat of tears coming into her throat and eyes. She had never, ever cried at work. Astonished by her own emotions, she took a deep breath, suddenly feeling more vulnerable than at any other point in her life. She said a hurried goodbye to Alan and put her palms flat on the desk, taking deep, regular breaths. She waited for the feeling of panic to pass. When it had, she wiped her eyes, had a sip of water and got on with the list of jobs before her.

On the other side of town, Mel was in a meeting with her boss and a colleague who would be taking on her workload when she went on maternity leave. They were talking about the branding of a new organic breakfast cereal which Mel was supposed to design before she left.

'The managing director wants to get the message across that the cereal is from farm to fork,' said her boss. 'Or farm to spoon, in this case. Have a look at what the competitors are doing, then do something completely different. You've got free rein on this, Mel, so you can finish up here with a really exciting project. Retailers they're aiming for include Selfridges Food Hall, Waitrose and Fresh & Wild. We need to see some ideas by tomorrow afternoon, so if you can sketch out a few today we can review them in the morning—'

Mel wasn't really listening. She was thinking about Leo. She was missing him badly and desperately wanted to talk to him. Having been to two antenatal classes without him, the reality of having the baby alone was hitting home. This made her sad. She wanted Leo to come home and for everything to go back to normal.

'Thanks, Mel,' her boss finished up. 'We're going to miss you.'

Her boss and colleague were standing up, ready to leave the room. She managed to smile.

'I'll be back,' she said. 'So don't even think about replacing me.'

She followed and returned to her desk, ate a couple of crackers and made herself concentrate. Sketching a few rough ideas on a piece of paper, envisaging a psychedelic Fillmore West style, before she knew it she was gazing out of the window at the clouds speeding over Brighton. Her office was high up and she had a view of rooftops, a view she loved. She sighed and chewed on her pencil. Opening her email, she checked her inbox to see if Leo had contacted her.

'Nothing,' Mel said, when his name didn't pop up. 'Not a thing.'

It was bizarre not getting emails from Leo. On a normal day, they'd email one another several times. Just banter, or a link to a gig Leo wanted to buy tickets for, or a satirical article from *The Onion* or a YouTube clip. Low-level contact, but contact all the same. They'd talk, too. Every lunchtime they'd speak to one another on the phone, deciding what to do that evening after work, whether to meet friends for drinks, or see a film, or walk by the sea. But since last week, there had been nothing. Neither of them were on Facebook or Twitter, so she couldn't check up on him that way, and she still hadn't told their friends what had happened. It was all a mystery. Finding babycentre.co.uk in her history, Mel logged on. She checked her boss was out of sight and typed a new subject into the discussion forum. *My boyfriend has left me and I'm nearly 8 months pregnant! What shall I do?*

While she was sitting there, replies pinged up on the forum site. Most were quick to condemn Leo as a bastard who couldn't be trusted and was better off gone. One or two were more understanding, recommending she talk to Leo and ask him to be completely honest, to find out exactly what was upsetting him. Someone wrote, *You might not like what you hear, though, so prepare yourself for the worst.*

Mel frowned. She wasn't sure what the worst was. Up until now, she hadn't contacted Leo. She was aware that it wasn't very mature of her to play the martyr, but wasn't it preferable to calling him endlessly? She knew she was going to see him again at some point – they were having a child together, for God's sake. It wasn't as if he could completely disappear. But perhaps she was being juvenile. Perhaps *she* needed to be the one to make the first move and attempt to find a peaceful resolution. Beginning an email, she couldn't find the right words and hated the thought that he could take hours, even days, to reply. With shaking hands, she dialled his number. It rang only once before he picked it up.

'Mel,' he said. 'Are you okay? Is the baby okay? I've missed you.'

She couldn't help but instinctively smile when she heard his voice. She swallowed hard.

'Yes,' she said. 'Leo, I miss you, too. I want you to talk to me, really talk to me. I need to know what all this is about.'

'I want to talk to you, too,' Leo said, sounding relieved. 'I thought you hated me. I've had things on my mind that I need to discuss with you. When are you free?'

'Whenever's good for you,' she said. 'I'm working now, but I'll be at home later.'

'I'll be there,' he said. 'Mel?'

'Yes,' she said.

'Thanks for phoning,' he said. 'I kept wanting to call you, but couldn't find the words. I know you must hate me.'

'No, Leo,' she said. 'I don't hate you.' She took a deep breath and blinked away tears. Be brave, she told herself. 'I love you,' she said. 'You know I do.'

'So,' said Mel, later that night. She was sitting next to Leo on the sofa, but there was so much space between them it felt like they were strangers. 'This is weird.'

Leo was perched on the edge of his seat as if he might bolt for the door at any given moment. Music was playing. Mel had set out a bowl of olives and opened a bottle of red wine, but he hadn't yet touched his glass. His coat was draped over his lap, which made him seem like an awkward guest in his own flat. He had dark crescents under his eyes and his stubble was overgrown. He looked like a man overloaded with problems, not at all an overjoyed expectant dad.

'Yes, it is,' he said, rubbing his chin. 'I'm sorry, Mel, for what I said outside the antenatal class last week. I should be publicly flogged for saying that. How's the baby?'

Mel felt her shoulders relax just a tiny bit. This was exactly what she had hoped for – an apology. But Leo still looked miserable as hell. He leaned back into the sofa and turned his head to face her. He extended his hand and held hers lightly. The warmth of his hand made her want to move into him, to wrap his arms around her, but she stayed still.

'Baby's energetic. Baby's fine, but Leo, I'm not fine. Is this about me?' Mel said, swallowing hard. 'What I mean is, have you fallen out of love? It happens. I know it happens. Your love just runs out and you can't work out why. Better you tell me now so I can get on with getting over you—'

Leo put his head in his hands. 'No,' he said. 'I haven't fallen out of love with you. It's—'

He looked up and back at Mel, his expression so downcast she felt a flash of dread. If it wasn't that he didn't love her, and he regretted saying he didn't want the baby, what the fuck was he going to say? She dredged her mind for the worst thing she could think of. Was he dying?

'Then what is it?' she asked quietly. 'You can tell me, Leo. Really. Are you sick?'

She was pretending to be strong, but would have said practically anything to get the truth out of him. This was like pulling teeth. She just wanted to get to the bottom of it.

'Come on,' she said. 'I'm prepared for anything. Are you going to prison? Have you killed someone? Masterminded a major drug deal?'

Leo managed a smile, but shook his head. 'I feel like I've been lying to you. All this time, I've been going along with it all, listening to everything you've said about what you want life to be like when the baby is born, but I'm having a nightmare, because I don't know if I can do it—'

'Of course you can do it,' said Mel.

Leo threw his hands angrily up in the air.

'If I—' he started. 'If I was being honest, I . . . oh shit, I don't know how to say this. It's just our lives will be changed for ever, Mel, and I'm worried about what will happen to our relationship. I'm fearful for us. I think you're going to be disappointed in me.'

Mel felt confused and let down, but struggled on with the conversation, trying to see Leo's side.

'What?' she said. 'So you don't think our relationship is strong enough to cope with having a baby?'

'I don't know,' he said. 'We've only been together for five minutes, and there are things that I wish I could do differently. As much as I love you, I wanted a few more years of just the two of us. To give me more time to sort myself out.'

Wow, thought Mel. Leo really *didn't* want the baby. She felt as if the rug had been pulled out from under her. She resisted the temptation to tell him he sounded like a selfish twat. Feeling her heart closing and herself withdrawing from him, she moved her hand away from his.

'Leo, we will have to cope, and I think our relationship could get even stronger,' she said. '*We* are not the priority now. The baby is the priority, isn't it?'

Leo looked angry again. His face paled. 'Yes,' he said. 'But there are other things in life. It's not just about this baby.'

'Well, *this* baby is all I'm interested in,' Mel said. 'It's the biggest thing ever to happen to me.'

'I know,' he said. 'I know that, but what about everything else? Us? Your job? Your ambitions? You started saying you didn't care about work any more and that you only wanted to look after the baby. Mel, you're at the top of that design agency. You're the star. I don't want you to give it all up and devote everything to the baby. And what about – oh, God, I don't know what I'm saying—'

Mel looked at him. His cheeks were pink and his lips were trembling. He was venting more than she'd ever seen him vent, but he didn't seem to be saying anything clearly. She felt like he was just coming out with confusing statement after confusing statement.

'Leo,' she said. 'I can't reassure you about anything, because I don't know what it's going to be like either. Being heavily pregnant like this, it's difficult to think about anything else because the birth is so near and I've got to squeeze a massive baby out of my fanny. You know? I don't know why I said that about my job. I do care about it, but I don't think it's the only thing I want to do with my life. You know how important a family is to me, and I can only think of a baby in a positive light. We can still have time together, of course we can. We could have had the whole of the last week together if you hadn't walked out on me.'

Mel's throat ached with the need to cry. She felt so tired, her eyelids were heavy. She needed Leo to be supporting *her*, not the other way around. He took a deep breath.

'It's fear, I think,' he said. 'I've never been so frightened before, because I think you're going to be disappointed in me when you find out what I'm like—'

'No I'm not!' said Mel. 'Stop being so cryptic and down on

yourself. Seriously, Leo, it's terrifying enough without you adding all this. If we talk about everything and are honest about how we're feeling, we'll be all right, won't we?'

She thought of Ginny's words of advice: talk to each other. Whatever you do, don't stop talking.

'Yes,' he said. 'If you're sure you're not going to hate me, for being honest?'

Mel didn't know how to answer that. Half of her felt angry with him for even questioning their decision to have the baby. The other half was relieved he was finally being honest – if he *was* being honest. Leo was an intelligent human being. He had been thinking too much. He always thought too much. They sat there in silence for a while. Mel hoped the baby couldn't hear Leo questioning their decision to have him or her.

'I guess I needed time out to prove a few things to myself,' he said. 'I'm sorry.'

Mel came to the conclusion that she was at a crossroads. She could tell Leo he was a selfish fool and that he needed to man up. Or be the bigger person and listen to him drivelling on about his fears and insecurities. He'd always listened to her in the past. Everything she'd ever felt about her dad's death, she'd told him and he had listened. Did she owe him this? She looked at Leo, who was staring at her, looking so lost and hopeless something in her snapped. She had to look after her baby. She made a decision.

Chapter Thirteen

Lenny came back to the flat just before three a.m. Rebecca was trying to be fast asleep but, really, she had fitfully snoozed, waiting for him to return before she could let herself properly relax. Her notepad was on the floor next to the bed, with several sheets torn out, words written and scribbled over them, the pages screwed up into rough balls. The letter to her mum hadn't gone at all well. Up until this point, it had been relatively easy to justify not seeing or contacting her parents since she'd arrived in Brighton. She'd taken to lying in bed and composing letters to her mum, but when she started to write they never came out as she wanted.

She'd had a strained telephone call with her mum and dad, and now Rebecca wanted to prove to her family that she could no longer be controlled, that she was a free spirit, as she'd always wanted to be. It was revenge, in a way, to give them a taste of their own medicine. Now that her due date was near, though, she felt differently. The thought of having to be responsible for another person made her look at her parents differently. She couldn't blame them for everything any more. Weren't they just doing their best at being parents? It wasn't as if they had ever been particularly mean to her. In fact, they'd given her a very privileged upbringing, compared to Lenny's. She was angry that her parents had controlled her with an iron grip. They'd insisted she did everything by their book: be a high achiever at school, go to university and then follow in the family's medical footsteps. Her older brother, Eddie, had done just that. But Rebecca wanted to walk – make that run – in the opposite direction at such a speed she sometimes wondered if she was actually their daughter, or if she'd been left by a group of travellers as a baby on their doorstep and they'd pitied her and adopted her.

'Hi,' she said huskily, opening her eyes a crack to see Lenny. 'Good night?'

Lenny took off all of his clothes and draped them over the white Lusty Loom wicker chair Rebecca had found at the tip. He drank a cup of cold water that had been on the set of drawers since earlier, then climbed into bed and lay down next to her under the duvet. He was so slim you'd never think he ate anything, yet he had the appetite of a mountaineer. He must have walked home in just his shirt and waistcoat, because his skin was cold and the sensation it gave her of ice cubes running down her legs woke Rebecca up further. She propped her head up on her elbow and they lay, tummy to tummy, their arms draped over each other's waists. In the full-length mirror behind Lenny, which was propped up against the wall and adorned with felt-flower fairy lights, she glanced at the reflection of his sharp shoulder blades, pleased to have him home. He smiled at her and kissed her mouth, then kissed her pregnant belly. He tasted of cigarettes and alcohol. Rebecca had once loved that taste, because it tasted of everything her parents disapproved of, but, now, it made her feel a little nauseous.

'There was a lock-in at the pub,' he said. 'I shouldn't have stayed, but there were people there who wanted to book us and, once I start drinking, I can't say no. Anyway, I've been talking about you and Elvis.'

'Have you?' Rebecca asked, surprised.

'Yeah,' he said. 'Just thinking about what it's going to be like when the baby is out and you're looking after him full time. I guess I'm worried you're going to be lonely while I'm out at gigs, and there's a chance we might go on tour soon.'

Lenny said the last few words so quickly, Rebecca had to play the sentence back in her head to take in the meaning.

'On tour?' said Rebecca, fully awake now. 'When?'

Lenny kissed her cheek and her forehead, placating her. She blinked at the print on the wall, a framed Pernod ad from the seventies which read 'Free the Spirit'.

'Nothing's been decided yet, babe,' he said. 'But it's been thrown out there. We'd only go round the UK on a few dates to begin with, then maybe Europe, possibly the States. I know we'll miss each other and stuff and I'll miss out on the baby for a few weeks, but you wouldn't want me to sacrifice the band, would you?'

Rebecca's heart sank. She'd planned to go with him if this ever happened. But now? Their son was about to be born. She had a horrible, cynical thought that this might be why he had proposed to her. Dismissing it as ridiculous, she turned on to her back, but it was way too uncomfortable and left her feeling breathless so she heaved herself back on to her side, but facing away from Lenny.

'Becs,' he said, leaning over her to see her face. 'What's up? I'm not talking about before the little guy's born, you know? Are you okay with it?'

'I guess,' she started. 'But, Lenny?'

'Yes?' he said.

'You know how I said I'd told my parents about you and me and the baby? Well, that wasn't entirely true. I haven't told them about you at all, but I've decided I need to be honest and I want to see them.'

Lenny digested the information and looked at her admiringly.

'You're a dark horse,' said Lenny. 'Why don't you invite them down? They could stay in our bed and we could sleep on the sofa.'

Rebecca imagined her mum and dad in their smart leisure clothes in the small flat stacked with records and books and recycled furniture and potted plants, their eyes running over Lenny as if he were a different species. They'd make their minds up about him the instant he told them he was a musician.

'They won't like you, Lenny,' Rebecca said, her cheeks burning. 'They don't like alternative people.'

'I'll win them over,' he said, unaffected.

'They won't like that I'm pregnant,' she said.

'The baby will win them over,' he said, his eyes closing. 'If he's mine, he'll be cool.'

'What do you mean "if"?' she asked.

'Joking, babe,' he said, kissing her shoulder. 'Where's your sense of humour?'

'It's gone on tour,' she said, but Lenny was already snoring.

Chapter Fourteen

'Sarah's here to show you all the breastfeeding basics,' Ginny said, beaming. 'Welcome, Sarah, and two-month-old baby, Meg.'

Nestled in a comfortable chair at the front of the classroom, the rain hammering against the window behind her head, Meg suckled at Sarah's breast, twisting tiny fingers in her mother's fine blonde hair as the antenatal group watched. Erin couldn't take her eyes off the baby. She was absolutely perfect. Pink, plump, smooth and perfect. She made adorable little snuffling noises as she tugged at her mother's breast, her feet moving rhythmically inside her pale pink sleepsuit. Erin, along with the other women, couldn't stop smiling.

'No one tells you but, to begin with, breastfeeding can be horrible,' said Sarah, looking up at the group. 'It hurt me like hell, even more than labour in some ways. My nipples bled, my back ached, I had mastitis and I got so fed up with it I almost gave up. But a woman from the La Leche League came to see me and showed me how the baby *should* latch on. I had been given so much conflicting advice in hospital and wasn't doing it right at all. After practising a little more and getting more advice, it didn't hurt at all and felt perfectly natural. I'm here because I want to show you that it can work out, even if it hurts like hell at the beginning. Are you all planning to breastfeed?'

Erin, her cheeks blooming with pleasure at the thought that, in just a few weeks' time, her own baby might be breast-feeding, nodded. All of the women said yes, they were planning to breastfeed.

'I'm only going to do it for a few weeks, though,' said Katy. 'I'm going back to work when the baby's three months, so Alan will need to give the baby a bottle.'

'I don't have the right equipment to breastfeed,' said Alan, flashing them all one of his best smiles. 'Shame, really.'

'I'm worried that I won't be able to do it,' said Lexi. 'Won't I smother the baby, being on the large side?'

Lenny sniggered and Rebecca smacked him.

'No!' said Ginny. 'Of course not, you just need to get the position right. And Katy, you could express your milk, so that the baby still gets the goodness when you go back to work.'

'Yes,' said Katy. 'But I want to get the baby into a routine. I've read the books that advocate a strict routine, and I'm going to try to feed the baby every four hours from when it's a few weeks old.'

Erin inwardly rolled her eyes. All those women she'd known in Norwich had stuck to various strict plans and, in some cases, they really had worked. But, to her, it all seemed at odds with instinctive parenting. Whenever she voiced her opinion, debate grew heated. Sometimes she thought that certain baby manuals were written purely to get new mothers arguing the minute their babies were born – as if they didn't have enough on their plates.

'Isn't that a bit like treating your baby as if it were a pet?' she said with feeling. 'I don't agree with regimes where you're not allowed to make eye contact with your baby at night. For God's sake! And all that controlled crying would leave me in pieces. I couldn't do it.'

'But I want to go back to work, you see,' replied Katy instantly. 'As much as I want this baby, I also want to work. And Alan and I hope to keep our lives as they are. If I don't get enough sleep, I'll be hopeless the next day. I need to be organized.'

'I think parents do get desperate,' said Ginny with a shrug of her shoulders. 'And it's worth remembering that all babies are different. For some, a routine might work; for others, definitely not. It's your call. But you might as well prepare now for the fact that the first few weeks will be sleepless and, at the start, midwives believe that a baby needs to be fed on demand, sometimes almost every hour. You'll be exhausted, and so your partner, or support system, will be invaluable at this time.'

'Would you recommend sleeping with the baby to make breastfeeding easier?' Mel asked.

'I think co-sleeping is fine, as long as you haven't been drinking alcohol or smoking and you don't have pillows or duvets that could get over the baby's airways,' answered Ginny. 'The World Health Organisation recommends that you have your baby in your room with you for at least the first six months, and having the baby in a Moses basket by the bed makes breastfeeding throughout the night much easier. In my opinion I think you need to have ten full days in bed after labour. With your baby in the basket next to you, you'll have time to focus on getting breastfeeding right and recover from labour.'

Laughter rippled through the room.

'Ten days!' said Katy, glancing at Alan. 'There's no way I could stay in bed for ten days.'

'Katy will probably be running a half-marathon by then,' laughed Alan. 'She's not very good at relaxing.'

'It's not really a matter of relaxing,' said Ginny. 'It's necessity. Giving birth is very tiring; then, the lack of sleep in those early days can leave you feeling exhausted physically and emotionally. Of course, exercise is really good for you, but if you can rest in bed for those few days, you'll recover from the whole experience much more quickly.'

Ginny's voice was soothing. Outside the window, a magpie hopped on to the windowsill and stared in. He was so blatant the way he walked back and forth, he might as well have been doing the cancan. Erin cursed the magpie and the bad luck associated with it. She closed her eyes briefly and drifted away from the conversation, allowing herself to imagine what feeding the baby might feel like. She knew it would be tiring in those first few weeks, waking up several times a night to feed, but she knew she wouldn't care. She'd stay awake all night if she had to. Once the baby was in her arms, she would do *anything* for him or her. Opening her eyes, she saw that the breastfeeding baby was now asleep and that Ginny was handing out dolls for them to hold in position, as if they were breastfeeding. Feeling a sudden pressure in her abdomen, Erin felt she needed the toilet.

'I'll be back in a minute,' she said to Edward. 'Just need the bathroom. Excuse me.'

Letting the door of the classroom close behind her, Erin walked to the toilets and went into the cubicle. She pulled down her underwear and sat on the toilet seat. Bloody magpie. *One for sorrow, two for joy, three for a girl, four for a boy.* She vowed to have a look for a second bird when she returned to the window. That would make her feel better. There usually was one somewhere nearby if you searched long and hard enough. Irritated with herself for having silly, super-stitious thoughts, she shook her head. Never used to be like this, did I? Absent-mindedly, she glanced at her underwear and saw a spot of red on the cotton. Blood. Oh, God. Blood. Blood.

'There's blood,' she said, suddenly desperately alert. 'Fuck. Blood.'

Twisting round, she looked into the toilet basin. There were a couple of drops of blood in the water and a tiny bit on the tissue too. Her heart pounded in her chest, she went from boiling hot to freezing cold and thought she might be sick.

'Oh no, oh shit, on please God no,' she said, gripping her throat, her voice rising higher. 'Please God, no. Please keep the baby alive. Please don't let the baby die.'

Without returning to the classroom or picking up her coat, Erin moved through reception and half ran, half walked across the car park through pouring rain towards the Accident and Emergency department of the hospital. *Please, God. Please don't let this happen.* With tears blurring her eyes, she stepped in front of a car, which slammed on its brakes to avoid her, its wheels gripping the wet road. The driver sounded the horn.

Erin didn't notice. Running into the hospital, she went straight to the reception desk.

'I'm thirty-seven weeks,' she said, when it was her turn to speak. 'I'm due to have a C-section in two weeks. I'm bleeding.'

'Okay,' said the lady. 'Let me get you seen to immediately. Take a seat.'

But Erin couldn't sit down. The room was spinning. Her head was floating. Her legs were liquid. Images of blood burst into her mind. She wished and prayed and made deals with God for the baby to be safe. She leaned over the reception desk.

'I've already lost one baby,' she said to the receptionist. 'I can't lose this one. Please.'

The receptionist was clearly concerned, but she was also trying to get attention for other patients, one of whom was screaming in pain and another who appeared to have lost consciousness.

'Okay, my love,' the woman said. 'Don't worry. We'll get a foetal monitor on you asap.'

Don't worry, thought Erin, how could she not worry! With shaking hands, she called Edward. He didn't pick up. She didn't leave a message. She phoned Katy, who she knew would have her phone on her lap. Sure enough, Katy picked up after one ring.

'Katy Tyler speaking,' she said. 'How can I help?'

In the background, Erin heard the sounds of the other women in the class chatting, the sound of Meg crying.

'It's Erin here,' she said with false calm. 'Edward's not answering his phone. I'm in A&E. I just went to the toilet and I'm bleeding.' Her voice wobbled and she swallowed. 'Can you ask him to come, please?' she finished.

'Yes,' said Katy calmly. 'Of course, Erin. Don't worry.'

Erin put down the phone without saying goodbye. She found a seat. With her head in her hands, she focused on the baby, pleading with it to be okay. She'd only been there for two minutes, but it felt like for ever.

'Erin,' said Edward, his hand suddenly on her back. 'What's happening?'

'I'm bleeding,' she said, feeling panic finger her spine. 'I'm waiting to see someone.'

'Is it labour?' he asked, but she shook her head.

'No,' she said. 'It's bright red blood and I can't feel the baby moving.'

Edward's face was ashen. He bit his lip and looked wildly about the A&E department, which was teeming with people. Erin watched him walk to the reception desk and speak to the receptionist.

'We lost our first baby,' he said. 'And now my wife is bleeding and she can't feel the baby moving. She needs to be seen right away.'

'The doctor is coming,' she said. 'He knows your situation.'

Erin watched Edward push his hands through his hair. She saw his jaw tighten and clench and his hands bunch into fists. Erin stood and moved towards him, holding her breath. She held out her arms towards him.

'WE NEED TO SEE A FUCKING DOCTOR,' Edward shouted at the top of his voice. 'NOW!'

Chapter Fifteen

Outside Erin's house, high-ceilinged and Victorian, with decorative stained-glass windows above the front door and flowers neatly bordering a square of grass, the antenatal group patiently waited, a quiet camaraderie between them, their umbrellas dripping with rain. Ringing the ting-a-ling-ling doorbell, a throwback to a different era when a maid in a frilly white hat and apron would have scuttled to the door to answer, the group fell into silence.

'Big house,' said Lexi, not knowing what to say.

It was the kind of house she'd imagined for herself during her years as a teenager, when, in retrospect, she had been at her most delusional. At that time in her life, squished into a two-bedroom terrace with her depressed mum and two stinking gerbils who wouldn't die whatever she fed them, Lexi had dreamed of a man on a white horse taking her away from the pebble-dashed estate she lived on, charging into her house through the bay window in the living room and whisking her off to a big house and frequent holidays in paradise. Ha! One failed relationship with a bloke who spent all his free time watching Robson Green's *Extreme Fishing* and eating peanuts had stapled open her eyes about that particular dream. That was when she realized she was going to have to get serious about sorting out her own life. She needed a vocation. Falling in love with her job made more sense. What she hadn't counted on was a) meeting Alan who, for one night only, seemed every bit the man on the white charger and b) owning a biological clock that ticked louder than Big Ben.

'Very,' said Rebecca. 'My flat is about as big as the storm porch.'

It was two days after the breastfeeding class (which had staggered on while Erin was in hospital). Under her umbrella, Lexi clutched a bunch of sunflowers that crinkled in their cellophane, and stood next to Mel, who had a box of chocolates balanced on top of her overflowing bag, and Rebecca, who carried a box of homemade brownies. Just behind them was Katy, who had brought an ostentatious fruit basket. That irritated Lexi, but she didn't let it show. Now wasn't the time for pettiness. She wanted and needed to make amends for her comments in the teashop.

'Do you think she minds us coming over?' said Mel. 'Her text was a bit strange.'

'She seems like a very private person to me,' said Katy. 'The last thing she probably wants is for us all to turn up on her doorstep like some kind of pregnant girl-band.'

'Ha!' said Lexi, smiling over-zealously at Katy. 'That's funny. Short-lived career, though. Look, I think she'll be pleased to see us. People need to see friends when they've had a shock, don't they? We're all going through the same thing. So, here goes.'

Lexi pressed the bell again, and the women stopped speaking. After a long pause, Erin opened the door, dressed in pale pink pyjamas and a dressing gown. She looked ethereal, her hair twisted in a plait and pinned at the top of her head. It was the first time Lexi had seen her without makeup and, though she was as white as snowdrops, she was naturally very beautiful.

'We brought you a few things,' said Lexi. 'Can we come in for a few minutes?'

Erin looked so startled, despite the fact she had known they were coming over, that Lexi wanted to hug her. Erin took steps backwards, which Lexi interpreted as an invitation, so she stepped over the threshold, the other women following close behind. They waited in the hallway, on the black-and-white-tiled floor, each smiling awkwardly at one another, not quite knowing what to do.

'How are you, Erin?' Katy asked. 'Is everything okay with the baby?'

Time seemed to stand still as Erin briefly closed her eyes, sighed and smiled a small, cautious smile. 'Yes,' she said. 'Thank God. Come through.'

She gestured towards the living room, so the women moved on in, murmuring appreciatively about Erin's splendid home. Erin waited by the door, pulling her dressing gown tighter across her bump. Her skin flushed pink.

'Are you feeling all right?' Rebecca asked. 'Sounds like you had a horrible shock. Edward texted us to say you had to spend the night in hospital. Ginny sends her regards. She said she'd see you at the next class.'

'Thank you,' said Erin, smiling warily. 'Yes, I'm all right

152

now. The bleeding stopped quite quickly, but it was . . . it was—'

Erin's hand shot to her throat. She pinched at the skin just under her chin and closed her eyes for a long moment.

'I'm sorry,' she said, opening them again, blinking away tears. 'It was pretty scary. I . . . I don't really want to go into—'

'Sit down, Erin,' Mel said. 'Please, you don't have to say anything. We just wanted you to know that we're thinking about you and, well, we're all in this together now, aren't we—'

'I—' Erin interrupted. 'I can't really explain . . . it was all because of . . . before . . . I had—'

Lexi saw that Erin was shaking violently. She stood up from her chair and gave her a hug then led her to the sofa and gestured for her to sit down.

'If you'd rather we left,' said Katy. 'We can do.'

But Erin shook her head. 'No,' she said. 'I'd like to tell you. I need to tell you.'

Chapter Sixteen

'Three years ago I was pregnant,' started Erin, slowly. She rolled the belt of her dressing gown between her fingertips, looked up at the ceiling and sighed.

'The baby was a boy, and I was so excited about having him,' she whispered, before clearing her throat. She looked around at the women's expectant faces. 'We'd tried for more than two years to conceive, you see. We thought we weren't going to be able to have a baby, and when I got pregnant with him we called him our miracle baby.'

She paused and drew her fingertips along underneath her eyes. Lexi gave her a warm, sympathetic smile.

'I spoke to him all the time in the womb,' Erin continued. 'I played him my favourite music and read him poems. I bought nursery furniture and a whole wardrobe of sleepsuits for him. I was a dance teacher at the time, and all my students were fascinated by my pregnancy – constantly asking me questions, which I was delighted to answer. I used to let them feel him kick. Josiah was the most exciting thing ever to happen to me.'

Smiling at the memory, she sat forward in her chair and looked at the carpet. The room was silent.

'But, when I was thirty-nine weeks pregnant, days away from my due date,' she continued, 'I realized the baby's movements had slowed down a little. I just thought Josiah was getting into position and getting ready to be born, rooting down for birth, but I went to the hospital to get checked out anyway, because I'd read that you should.'

Everyone was completely silent, but Erin didn't notice.

'My obstetrician listened for Josiah's heartbeat and kept on moving the monitor around my bump. But there was nothing. There was no heartbeat. I remember looking at the doctor, who was avoiding my eyes. He went completely pale and asked me to call Edward to the hospital. I kept asking "Is Josiah all right?" But he wouldn't give me a straight answer.'

Erin shook her head and let her hair fall in front of her eyes. After a few moments, she pushed it away and took a deep breath.

'While I was waiting for Edward to arrive,' she went on, her mouth contorting as she struggled not to cry, 'two more doctors checked me over. Their faces said it all, but I still asked them if the baby was all right. I still hung on to that hope. He was snug and warm inside me, ready to be born. What could go wrong? Finally, when Ed arrived, the doctor told us that Josiah had died in the womb. Even though I knew that was what he was going to say, hearing the words out loud almost killed me. That was my baby. He should have been alive. I was all ready for him. I had a little white polar bear in his cot and an elephant mobile hanging from the ceiling for him to look at. I felt as if my life had stopped, there and then.'

Tears were tumbling down Erin's cheeks now, and she pushed them away with her palms.

'Oh, Erin,' said Lexi, shaking her head. 'That's terrible.'

'I'm so sorry,' said Mel.

Rebecca's hand was over her mouth, and Katy's eyes were big and round and glassy.

'He told me that the baby had died in the womb but that I should give birth to him naturally,' said Erin, her voice breaking. 'So, the following morning I was injected with a hormone to begin contractions and, after a long, exhausting labour, Josiah was born. He was pink and warm and perfect. He looked alive. I knew he was dead, but the midwife handed him to me to hold and I wondered if they had it all wrong, because it felt as if he was alive, just sleeping. When I looked at him, I felt this immense rush of love. I loved him with everything I had, because I had only those few minutes with my baby. I phoned my mother and explained that Josiah had been born sleeping. Oh, God, she was trying so hard not to break down and be strong for me. I could hear my father in the background asking whether I'd had a boy or a girl and him crying out when she whispered what had happened. My mother spoke so lovingly to me, I was bowled over. For some reason, I'd expected her to be disappointed. I loved her more than ever that day. I remember her words exactly. She said, "He's your sweet child, darling, you hold him close, you love him and kiss him and talk to him. He's your son, no one can take that away from you, he's your baby. Enjoy these moments, my darling, and relish them. They are yours, together." Simple words, but, my gosh, it chokes me to tell you that.'

Mel, who had tears running down her cheeks, moved off the sofa to sit by Erin. She put her hand on her Erin's back and rubbed it slightly. Erin smiled at her gratefully.

'Edward took a photograph of me cradling Josiah, because he didn't look dead, he really didn't,' said Erin. 'It sounds macabre, but I let myself imagine he was alive. I dressed him and bathed him and the midwives gave us some time together as a family. I remember, it was a beautiful sunny day and Edward opened the window so I could sit near it holding Josiah to let the sun fall on his face. He needed to feel the sun on his skin. Of course I knew he couldn't, but it meant something to me. Edward sat with us, but then I asked him if I could have a few moments with Josiah on my own. I wanted to look at him and capture him in my heart. I wanted to be a mother. It was so quiet in that hospital room, and I held him and rocked him and I sang him the lullaby my mother used to sing to me. I did not cry, because I was holding my baby. I was holding my baby boy, my Josiah, my sweet boy, and I loved him more than I can possibly say.'

Erin, drained, stopped speaking and wiped her eyes with a tissue then covered her face with her hands. Rebecca stood and moved over to her, sat on the carpet near her feet and put one hand on her knee.

'Erin,' she said, 'did Josiah look like you? Did he have red hair?'

Erin looked up and smiled a little smile. She sniffed and laughed a small, sad laugh.

'Yes,' she said. 'He had lots of hair and had a small

strawberry birthmark at the bottom of his hairline. There was an autopsy, but nothing came out of that, so there was no one to blame, only myself.'

'Don't say that, Erin,' Rebecca said. 'This could happen to any of us.'

'Oh no,' said Katy. 'You can't possibly blame yourself.'

'No!' said Lexi. 'These things are totally random.'

'Give yourself a break, Erin,' said Mel. 'You can't possibly blame yourself.'

'I know it's irrational,' said Erin, 'but I did blame myself. I worried it was because of all the standing up I did as a dance teacher, or whether I'd done too much exercise early on, or, most profoundly, whether I could have saved him if I'd noticed his activity had reduced in the hours running up to the hospital visit.'

'You did everything you could have done,' said Lexi.

'How did you cope afterwards?' asked Mel softly.

'It was horrible,' she said. 'Leaving the hospital without my baby almost killed me. My breasts filled and were very painful. In a way, I liked the physical pain, because it was tangible. But the pain in my heart and my head was indescribable. My friends tried to help me, but I couldn't face their babies, couldn't face them pretending not to be in love with their own newborns. Only one friend got it right. She encouraged me to hold her baby and tell her about Josiah. But, most of the time, I sat at our home in Norwich, listening for his cry. Though I knew it would never come, I strained to hear it. Sometimes I even thought I had heard it and, as mad as this sounds, I'd check the cot to see if he was there. Then, after another eighteen months had passed, we gave up trying for a baby completely and – surprise, surprise – that's when I fell pregnant. It was then we decided to start afresh, move to Brighton, make new friends and put the past behind us. Of course, that's easier said than done.'

'I can't believe you've been through all that,' Mel croaked.

'No, me neither,' said Rebecca. 'Why didn't you say anything?'

'I don't know,' said Erin. 'I just wanted to be like everyone else and not be known for being the woman who lost her baby. No one knows what to say to a woman who has lost her baby. It's not the most cheerful subject.'

Lexi reached out for Erin's hand and held her fingers. 'We can imagine how you must have felt,' she said. 'We want you to know that you can always talk to us about Josiah. Honestly, whenever you want to talk about him, we'll listen, won't we, ladies?'

'Of course we will,' said Mel. 'And we should meet up outside the classes. If you've only just moved to Brighton, I can show you around. I have the most amazing landlady, who has lived here for ever and knows all the best places to go.'

Erin smiled and nodded. 'That would be great,' she said. 'Thank you. I'm sorry to bring you down—'

'Don't apologize,' said Rebecca. 'You're amazingly strong. So, in the antenatal class the other day, when you had spotting, I guess you were worried history was going to repeat itself?'

'Yes,' said Erin. 'I've been terrified this entire pregnancy, and when I saw blood I completely panicked.'

'And what was the blood?' said Katy. 'Was it all quite normal?'

'Apparently it was nothing to worry about,' said Erin. 'I just have a minor yeast infection that irritated the cervix. Nothing else wrong, so I'm still on course for the caesarean at thirty-nine weeks.'

'Well,' said Lexi. 'That is great news. Everything's going to be fine, Erin. Nothing like that can happen twice.'

'Didn't you want to find out what sex you were having?' asked Rebecca.

'No,' said Erin. 'I didn't want to bond too much with this baby. I've become incredibly superstitious. Stupidly! I don't have a name, a blanket or a nappy. Edward bought some sleep-suits but that's all we have. But, look, you're all being lovely and I don't want to alarm you. What happened to me with Josiah is very rare. It won't happen to you.'

'I don't know how you coped,' said Rebecca. 'You must be really strong.'

'You just *have* to cope,' said Erin.

The women nodded knowingly.

'That's the thing about being female,' said Lexi, 'you just have to cope. And women invariably do. That's why they give birth – they're the stronger sex.'

'I'd second that,' said Edward, appearing at the door then walking over to Erin and resting a hand on her shoulder. She held on to his fingers loosely. 'My wife is an amazingly strong woman. I'm sure I drive her up the wall with my un-macho ways. I'm so lucky to have her. Anyway, ladies, I don't want to interrupt, but can I get you all a nice cup of tea and a slice of chocolate cake?'

Chapter Seventeen

After listening to Erin's story, Katy felt frustratingly emotional. Humbled. Frightened. She fought the urge to cry, and told herself to get a grip. Mel and Rebecca might have soggy tissues in their hands, but she wasn't going to join them. Yes, Erin's story was tragic, completely awful, but it had all happened three years ago. You can't go delving into a troubled past like that. It was a fool's game. What was that quote Alan was always repeating?

"'If you don't look forward,'" she remembered, "'you're always in the same place.'"

Yes. That was it. Katy poured herself another cup of tea from the pot that Edward had brought into the living room, while she took in a framed photograph of Erin dressed in a red ballgown, caught off guard applying mascara in front of a mirror in a dressing room somewhere, blurry people in the background. She looked incredible. Before Katy had come to Erin's home, she'd pigeonholed Erin as a well-dressed but stand-offish housewife. It turned out that Erin was a glamorous professional dancer who had run her own studio back in

Norwich before losing her baby boy. Got that wrong, hadn't she? Glancing at the other women, she wondered what else she had missed. Life would be much easier if people came with a list of their life experiences with a short personal profile attached, a kind of life CV. Katy thought about hers: *From a deprived background, Katy wanted to make it big to prove to everyone she could escape her roots. She succeeded.*

'Whose phone is that?' Mel was asking her suddenly. 'Is it yours, Katy?'

Katy paused from drinking to listen and heard her mobile ringing from the pocket of her coat, which she'd left in the hallway, draped over the banister. Checking her wristwatch, she swore under her breath.

'I need to get to work,' she said, clattering her teacup on to the table of cakes and chocolates, which she had been careful to avoid eating. She left the room, picked up the phone and checked the caller ID. Anita. Returning to the living room, she saw that she had six missed calls and a text that read CRISIS followed by six exclamation marks.

'Six exclamation marks?' she said. 'I ask you, is that ever necessary? There's a crisis at work. Apparently. It's not like someone's died!'

As soon as she said the words, she felt terrible. Her hand shot to her mouth. Erin's eyes dropped to the floor.

'Oh, God, I'm so sorry,' she said, her cheeks burning, and hoped Erin would forgive her. 'That was incredibly stupid of me.'

'Don't worry,' said Erin with a kind smile. 'We all do that sort of thing.'

Not knowing quite how to leave, Katy, embarrassed and

flustered, gathered up her things and kissed Erin on both cheeks. She promised to see them all next week, though she did wonder briefly if any of them actually really liked her. She knew Lexi didn't – but, anyway, what did it matter?

'Can you meet up before the next group?' said Mel. 'Some girls at work are giving me a baby shower, and I'd love it if you came. I need support, because none of them are pregnant and they'll probably want to go clubbing. Can you imagine me in a nightclub? I'd probably get arrested. Worse, I might bang into Leo with a gorgeous model on his arm.'

'Have you seen him?' asked Erin. 'Is everything still difficult between you?'

'Don't ask,' said Mel, sighing. 'I've decided to put him out of my mind for now. Actually, I told him where to go last time I saw him, because he was being too vague about us—' She looked decidedly miserable.

'Good on you for taking control,' said Katy. 'And, yes, let me know the details of your baby shower and I'll try to make it.'

Outside, Katy hurried towards the bus stop, the baby somersaulting inside her. That's right, she told the baby, keep moving. Shaking the thought of Erin's story from her mind – she really didn't want to think about that – she dialled and listened to the voicemail Anita had left earlier. She must have called from her mobile while she was walking outside, because the sound of traffic and static buzzed over her words. Katy pressed the phone to her ear and heard the following: —*Really can't fucking run this business on my fucking own, Katy. You better have a bloody good reason for leaving me with the pitch for July, I've had enough of you going AWOL like this and*—

Katy didn't listen to the rest. A bus pulled in at the stop and she climbed on, throwing her phone into her bag. Accepting a seat from a young woman, she rubbed her temples and closed her eyes. On the backs of her eyelids she saw Erin's face, wet with tears. The sadness in her expression made Katy shudder. Her phone rang. She opened her eyes and looked at it. It was Anita, again. A strange, prickling sensation passed over her scalp and Katy felt her heart beating in her ears. Anita was turning into a bully and Katy didn't know what to do about it. They had been such good friends, but ever since Anita had caught her husband having an affair with a woman he worked with, she had got angry and stayed angry. Katy hadn't understood her decision to take her husband back. She knew that, if Alan ever strayed, she would have to tell him to leave. Not that he *would* stray. He just wasn't like that. Anita had insisted that forgiving her cheating husband showed strength, but at what price? She was clearly unhappy. Sighing, Katy picked up the phone. Sometimes, even to her, the world did not make sense.

'Anita,' said Katy. 'I'm coming in. What's the problem?'

'Where the fuck have you been?' Anita yelled down the phone. Katy held the phone away from her ear and widened her eyes.

'Anita,' she hissed into her phone. 'I've been talking to a woman whose baby died. Please, have some patience.'

'I don't give a fuck who died!' Anita said. 'We have a business to run and I can't do it all on my own. I can't give big clients like this to Jake or Heidi. They're too inexperienced. Have some sense, Katy! I don't care about this stupid woman! We all have our own problems.'

There were some days when Katy could put up with Anita and hold imaginary hands over her ears to block out her rants and raves. But today was not one of them. All she could think of was Erin.

'That's your problem, Anita,' she said. 'You don't give a toss about anyone but yourself and, at the moment, you are one miserable piece of work. Why are you so angry with me? I'm working as hard as I can, I love the agency, yet you treat me like I couldn't care less about it!' Katy felt her face flushing red and loosened her scarf. The woman next to her was glancing at her, concerned.

'I care about the business,' Anita said. 'You used to care, until you got bloody pregnant. Now, your brain has turned to sponge.'

That was completely unfair. Katy had worked her heart out from the moment she knew she was pregnant. She shook her head and closed her eyes. In her mind's eye, she could see Erin's face as she told the story about her baby, the way Mel had moved to rub her back, the kind look in Mel's eyes when she invited Katy to her baby shower. The two worlds – antenatal-group mums-to-be and her working life – seemed to be polar opposites.

'What is this really about?' she asked Anita. 'I don't believe you're this angry about something that isn't true. You know how hard I work.'

There was silence.

'Hello?' Katy said, thinking Anita had hung up.

Then Katy heard Anita snuffling down the phone. She paused and took a deep breath. 'It's Giovanni,' she said. 'He's had another affair. This time, I've got to leave him.'

Katy shook her head. All of a sudden she felt incredibly hot. 'Okaaay,' she said. 'Well, I'm sorry, but I think you're right about leaving him. What are you getting from your marriage apart from stress? Hard decision, but the right one. You can stay with me, if you like, while you sort it out.'

'It's not only that,' Anita said in a small voice.

'What is it then?'

'Oh it's—' Anita said. 'I can't talk about it.'

'Come on!' Katy said. 'How long have we known each other? I don't have *any* secrets from you.'

Apart from maybe one, thought Katy. But when Giovanni had made a pass at her when he and Anita had first got together, Katy had decided to give Giovanni a chance to prove himself to Anita, rather than tell her straight away. Maybe she *should* have told her. Then it wouldn't have gone on so long.

'Oh, Katy,' she said. 'I can't believe it. The worst possible thing has happened. I'm pregnant, and I *really* don't want to have a baby.'

Katy was taken aback. Giovanni had had a vasectomy when he and Anita had first married. Neither of them had wanted children and had been one hundred per cent certain about it. Katy leaned back into her seat, watching houses and cars blur past out of the window.

'You're pregnant?' she said, pushing her hair away from her forehead. 'Wow, I don't know what to say. I thought Giovanni had had a vasectomy.'

As she said the words, she thought about the lingering, leering looks Jake was always throwing at Anita. The way he always worked late when she did. How he made sure he sat next to her when the office team went for a drink after work. She pulled a face.

'He did,' said Anita. 'The baby's not his. It's Jake's. He's twenty-one years old. What the hell am I going to do?'

The bus came to a sudden halt at Katy's stop, in Brighton town centre on Station Road. Katy stood to get off the bus and grabbed hold of the handrail.

'Give me ten minutes,' she said, 'and I'll be in the office. We can talk.'

She leaned over to pick up her bag from the floor. And that's when her waters broke.

Chapter Eighteen

Every time she pushed open the heavy black door of the studio that Lenny and his band practised in, Rebecca felt a tremor of pride. It wasn't every girl who had a well-known musician for a partner. It wasn't every girl, she had convinced herself in bed over the past few nights, who would soon be able to say that her partner was going 'on tour'. But, today, even though the rest of his band – Tom, Mack and Little Dave – were sitting around waiting for him, their heads together over a magazine, in a halo of long hair and beards, Lenny wasn't there.

'How are you, Tom?' Rebecca asked.

'Depressed,' he said, shrugging. 'Where's the big man?'

'I was going to ask you the same thing,' she said. 'Except I don't call him the big man.'

'Small, is he?' said Mack, with a snigger. Rebecca rolled her eyes.

'Shut up, Mack,' said Lenny, bursting in the door. 'I heard that. Hey, Rebecca. Was that Mel outside?'

After hearing Erin's story, Rebecca had felt an urge to be

with Lenny and tell him how much she loved him and to hear that he loved her, too. Also, she realized, the desire to contact her parents, and specifically her mother, was stronger than before. The letter she'd eventually painstakingly written one sleepless night was in her bag. All she needed was to put a stamp on the envelope, and then, the next day, her mother would know everything about Lenny and the baby. No more secrets. She knew the words in the letter off by heart.

I'm pregnant, due in two weeks, I'm happy about this and I want you to be happy too. Lenny, my boyfriend, has proposed. He's a musician and going on tour around Europe. I'd like me and the baby to go, too, but I'm not sure if that will be possible. I know it was my choice not to see you, but I miss you, especially now I'm going to find out what it means to be a mother. I can see life isn't so straightforward.

'Yes,' she said. 'We're going for a walk along the seafront. But I just wanted to see you, Lenny. I'm going to post my letter to my mum. Where were you, anyway?'

Lenny had thrown his coat over a chair and was sitting opposite Rebecca, perched on the edge of a table, in dark-red jeans and a blue fisherman's jumper. He pushed his hair back from his face, swung his legs and grinned at her.

'Oh, you know,' he said. 'Doing stuff.'

'Oh yeah,' said Mack, raising his eyebrows.

'What's that mean?' Rebecca said, frowning. Mack often made barbed comments like this, which unsettled her, but Lenny usually laughed them off. Mack picked up his guitar and began to strum, facing away from the group and out of the window.

'Who knows?' said Lenny. 'Nothing. Mack, you're a prick.'

'Thanks, man,' Mack said. 'So are you.'

Lenny smiled and winked at Rebecca and ran his hand through his hair. She was again struck by his piercing good looks. She suffered a moment of self-doubt. Was Lenny going to love her when she'd had the baby and hadn't got her figure back? She sighed and bit at the inside of her cheek, telling herself she was being stupid. There was nothing more unattractive than insecurity. Lenny had told her the same thing.

'What's up?' he said, dropping off the table and cupping her face in his hands.

'Nothing,' she said, giving him a small smile. 'I'm in a strange mood. I've been talking to Erin, you know, the older lady in the antenatal group? She lost her last baby. He died in her womb. I guess it's scared me. I don't want anything to go wrong.'

Mack stopped playing for a moment and turned towards Lenny, frowning.

'Come on, Len, mate,' said Mack from the other side of the room. 'I thought we were rehearsing?'

'Nothing will go wrong,' Lenny said, kissing her nose. He turned to face Mack. 'Okay, mate!'

Mack plugged his guitar into his amp and started to play incredibly loudly. The baby kicked. Lenny moved over to the microphone and picked it up.

'I'd better get back to Mel,' Rebecca said. 'See you later.'

Lenny blew her a kiss, but wasn't really looking at her. Rebecca sighed, picked up her bag and left.

*

The sea was fish-skin silver. The beach was empty apart from a woman walking her dog. Rebecca and Mel walked along the road at the back of the beach, talking about possible baby names for a while, then more about how Erin must have felt after losing Josiah. When they reached a postbox, Rebecca pulled out the letter.

'Wish me luck,' she said to Mel.

'Good luck,' Mel said. 'Who's it to?'

'My mum,' Rebecca said. 'I've finally written to tell her the truth about Lenny and the baby.'

'Well done,' said Mel. 'That's brilliant.'

Rebecca smiled gratefully at her. She held the letter at the letter slit and closed her eyes. She said a silent prayer to the universe, and let it drop in among the other letters. Walking away, Mel started speaking, but Rebecca could only think about her mother's expression when she picked up the letter from the doormat. She'd be smart in her work suit, her hair neatly pinned up. A tremor of panic ran through Rebecca when she imagined her opening it. Why did Rebecca think she would accept this news? From everything she knew of her mother, this news would make her ashamed and disappointed. Christ, she'd probably have a heart attack.

'Rebecca?' said Mel. 'Are you listening? I was just saying that for ten minutes after I told Leo to leave the other night I felt better. More in control, you know? I said to him, if you can't be positive and supportive about this major event in our lives, then I don't want you in my life. I asked him to leave, and only come back if he was prepared to give it all his best shot. I know he's terrified, but, fuck, so am I.'

Mel gave Rebecca an exasperated smile and they both

stopped to watch the sun fall on to the sea through a break in the clouds, like a theatre spotlight moving around a stage.

'Now I'm wishing I hadn't told him to go,' she said quietly. 'I miss him really badly. Especially after everything Erin told us. Makes you think, doesn't it?'

'Yes, it really does. But you were strong. You did the right thing with Leo, because he'll have to decide what he really wants. I'm not so sure I have . . . maybe writing was the coward's way out.'

'You have done the right thing,' said Mel. 'You definitely have, and writing is best because it will give your parents time to think about where you're at. Don't worry too much. I'm sure they'll be pleased for you. Maybe this will be the thing to bring you closer.'

'Yeah,' said Rebecca. 'I hope so.'

The women linked arms and carried on walking, keeping their eyes on the setting sun, both wondering what on earth was going to happen next.

Chapter Nineteen

Finding her Evian water-spray bottle in her washbag on the table beside the hospital bed, Katy clutched it in her fist but paused as she felt a contraction coming. She decided the contractions made her feel as if she had a cheese wire around her middle which someone was tightening with pliers. She leaned over the side of the bed, raising her bottom in the air and stuffing her face in the mattress to groan, quietly thanking Alan's sister for making her such a gorgeous birth costume. Already she knew the whole labour process was going to be pretty unsightly for Alan.

'Well done,' said Alan, rubbing her back briefly until the pain relented. 'Shall we have some music now?'

As she quietened, he moved across the room to turn on the CD player. Track one of *Benedictine Monks Gregorian Chants: Volume One* burst into the room.

'Turn those fucking monks off!' Katy hissed. 'And you don't need to congratulate me every time I have a contraction. We could be here for days. It feels like we *have* been here for days.'

Alan held his hands up in the air, as if asking for mercy. 'Fine,' he said. 'No problem.'

'But thank you,' said Katy, through gritted teeth. 'Thank you.'

Since her waters had broken on the bus, much to the irritation of the bus driver, who threw a few paper towels down on to the floor while she clambered off on to the pavement, Katy's contractions had been erratic. At first, there was nothing, and the midwives at her hospital check had advised her that if the baby hadn't been born within twenty-four hours the labour would have to be induced to reduce the risk of infection. There had been a room free in the labour suite, so Katy and Alan had stayed in hospital, but after hours of irregular contractions, Katy was only two centimetres dilated and she'd been given a gel pessary to help. Except it wasn't helping. In her birth plan, Katy had been against being induced. She wanted to do the whole thing naturally and to feel in control. But all this waiting in the labour ward with nothing much happening was – well, it was awful. Despite giving herself a stern talking-to, she was becoming demoralized and beginning to feel as if she didn't have any idea what her body was doing. From other rooms, she heard cries coming from women who were in the final throes of birth and, though she'd been in pain on and off for hours, her pain was clearly nothing like theirs. She'd been checked by a midwife, but wasn't dilating any further. The midwife had given her the option of going home and returning in the morning, but it hardly seemed worth it. And, actually, because it wasn't going to plan – and the minutes in between contractions stretched out hopelessly and ineffectually – the whole process had become slightly terrifying. Thankfully, since she had Erin's story in the back of her mind, the baby's heartbeat on the foetal monitor was strong and steady and Katy's blood pressure only very slightly raised.

'It will all kick off properly in a bit,' said Alan happily, trying not to yawn in the pink vinyl chair he was reclining in, his legs stretched out and his ankles crossed. 'You should try to get some rest while you can. Everything's going to work out just fine, angel.'

Katy nodded. She smiled over at Alan from the side of the bed, his calm instructions reminding her of a holiday they'd been on to Tobago a few years back, where they'd stayed in an incredible hotel with an infinity pool overlooking the ocean. It was meant to be a dream trip, but she had caught tropical flu on the plane over and had been the most poorly she had ever been, not leaving the bedroom the entire ten days. Alan had been a hero, bringing her little bowls of ice cream to soothe her throat, resting wet flannels on her forehead, flinging open the window shutters and asking people in the pool to keep the noise down. She'd hated feeling so vulnerable and mortal – but something about this situation gave her a similar sensation, which was dreadful, since she was having a baby, supposedly the most natural and empowering thing on the planet.

'I'm so tired,' she said. 'My feet are swollen, my back aches and I'm nauseous.'

Even though she'd read every book there was about labour, the information seemed to have fallen out of her head. Her brain was muddled. She couldn't remember how long each stage of labour was supposed to last. It now seemed as though

Ginny's advice had been no help at all. Katy sighed. She knew that if she was going to be able to carry on she needed to sleep. Lifting herself up on to the bed, she asked Alan to come and lie with her. He stood, stretched and dimmed the lights. Perching on the very edge of the bed, he wrapped his body around hers, kissed her neck and gently massaged her shoulders. She felt his breath on her skin and closed her eyes.

'I love you, Katy,' he said, as she felt sleep wash over her. He kissed her again and closed his eyes. Within minutes, they were both asleep.

The sleep didn't last for long. Less than an hour later, Katy's contractions started up again. This time she understood what they meant by contracting. They were so unbearably painful, and she was so incredibly tired that, when she discovered she was only three centimetres dilated after hours of sucking in gas and air, which made her sick, she begged for an epidural. Alan didn't even question her on the decision, for which she was grateful. When the contractions slowed again, she was given an induction drug via a drip. Attached to the drip, a foetal heart monitor strapped around her belly and unable to feel her lower body, Katy couldn't move. Though she tried to keep her spirits up, she felt trapped. She had retreated within herself, more frightened than at any other time in her life. Alan was doing all the talking, keeping a flow of information from the midwife's mouth into her ears. He was her umbilical cord, but even though she could see his mouth moving, she wasn't wholly absorbing the meaning of his words. *Fluctuating heartbeat. Labour not progressing. Baby in distress. Failure to progress.* Surely this couldn't be happening to her?

When more people flooded into the room, offering up their opinions, Katy began to panic.

'What's going on?' she asked, in tears when, on the foetal heartbeat monitor, she heard the baby's heart racing, then slumping, racing, then slumping. 'That can't be right?'

Midwives offered placatory words. Doctors looked concerned. She was checked and checked again, but nobody actually seemed to be talking to *her*. What seemed like hours was probably only a matter of minutes. Gripping Alan's hand, she listened to the baby's heartbeat until it appeared to stop completely. She gasped. She held her breath. The baby had died. But the heartbeat started again.

'Oh, God,' she said, breathing hard. 'Oh no, oh God, please no. GET THE BABY OUT!'

'Katy, the baby's distressed,' a doctor said, holding her hand while she wept. 'We need to get you down to theatre for an emergency C-section.'

A form was shoved under her nose. She signed it, retching. At the same time, another midwife cut off her labour outfit (there was no time to waste) with scissors, shaved off her pubic hair with a razor and removed the nail varnish from her toes. If she'd been able to move, she would have curled up into a ball. She sucked her thumb. Her entire body shook. She didn't care any more. She wanted the baby out. She knew one of them was going to die – would it be her or the baby? *Let it be me*, she said in a silent prayer. *Let the baby live.*

'Could you put these on, please, if you'd like to come into theatre?' the midwife asked Alan, handing him blue scrubs, a hairnet and covers for his shoes.

'There's no way I'm not coming,' he said, pulling off his

jumper. Then his T-shirt. And his trousers. Standing in his underpants, the midwife shook her head.

'You put them on over your clothes,' she said, widening her eyes at Katy.

Alan cracked up laughing, and Katy wondered how he possibly could. She reeled, confused by how ludicrous he suddenly seemed. Rich, successful, effective, Alan was stripped down to his pants and laughing with the midwife while she was contemplating the possible death of her baby or herself. Were they in parallel universes? Alan scrabbled to put his trousers back on, then, seconds later, she was being pushed through corridors in her bed, knocking against walls as they rushed towards theatre. Alan caught up and was by her side, ridiculous in his blue hat.

Failure to progress. There it was. *Failure.* The worst word.

'You're going to be fine, Katy,' Alan said. So did other people, who she didn't know. They were just words. 'Fine' was easy to say, but nothing was further than the truth. This was hell. This had all gone horribly wrong. She racked her brains for all the things she had done wrong in her life and wondered if she was being punished for them. In the operating theatre, incredibly bright lights hurt her eyes. She covered her face. This was all wrong. Alan sat by her side, holding her hand. He looked ever so pale, despite his constant tan. There were so many people in the room, all scrubbed up, prepared. She felt as if they'd been down there waiting for her, knowing that she'd never do it properly, that she'd fail. One of the doctors proudly announced that she was his sixth emergency C-section that evening. She gleaned that he was trying to reassure her he knew what he was doing. She said thank you, though it was hard to speak. Her body was shaking so violently now her teeth were audibly chattering.

'Let's get this baby born,' the doctor said urgently, before raising a green sheet between her eyes and whatever they were doing with their scalpels. She lay back and felt a few tugging sensations before one of the surgeons spoke.

'Katy,' he said, in a quiet, serious voice. 'You have a baby boy.'

At the same moment, he lifted the baby up above the green sheet so she could see him. Dangling there in the air, for just a second, his arms outstretched and his face in an angry, squashed-up frown, was her baby. He was bigger than she imagined and more screwed up. His eyes were closed. He looked too floppy. The image imprinted itself on her memory in a snapshot. Katy found herself crying, but the cry sounded odd in the operating theatre with everyone going about their business in each corner of the room. Shouldn't her baby boy be crying by now? She heard a squeak. Was that a cry? Alan leaned over and kissed her, but now the midwife was by her side. Katy couldn't see the baby.

'We normally let you hold the baby immediately, but your little boy needs attention,' she said, as another person rushed into the room. Katy had one thought that wouldn't go away: shouldn't the baby be crying by now? Alan moved over to the baby and she saw his body moving very slightly, in a way that she knew was him trying not to cry. Was the baby dead? She was so tired her eyes were closing. The surgeons were still working on her abdomen, talking her through what was happening, but their words weren't making any sense. Alan was no longer by her side. She was aware of the baby being pushed out of the hospital room in a glass box – an incubator? Alan glanced at her with wide eyes, looking utterly helpless.

'I'll look after him,' Alan said. 'I'll find out what's going on.'

Katy swallowed. Her heart broke. She hadn't heard her baby cry. She willed herself to speak. Is he dead? Katy mouthed silently at him, tears dripping down her face.

He rushed over to her side and kissed her cheeks and head and held her arms.

'Of course not,' he said, tears on his cheeks. 'Of course not. He's alive and he's beautiful. He's here. He's just had a difficult birth, but you did it, angel. You did it.'

Katy stopped feeling anything. I didn't do it, she thought. I might as well have not even been here for all I actually did. She had been passive, immobile, paralysed. For a moment, while the surgeons continued to work, she stared at the ceiling, straining to remember the baby's face which had appeared above the green sheet. He was alive? What if they mixed him up with another baby boy? Would she be able to recognize him? She began to panic, and somebody in the room mentioned that her blood pressure was pretty high on the monitor.

'It's okay, Katy,' a midwife said. 'You're okay now.'

She nodded. Alan would look after the baby. Alan wouldn't allow anything to happen. She tried so hard to keep her eyes open, but she was so incredibly tired.

'Well done,' the midwife said, smiling sympathetically down at her. 'That was an ordeal. You coped well. I know this was far removed from the birth you wanted.'

'Can I see him? Katy asked. 'Can I see my baby now?'

She needed to see him. But she was so very tired.

'Soon,' said the midwife. 'Yes, soon.'

She hadn't slept more than an hour in thirty-six. The drugs she'd had were affecting her. Her eyes wouldn't stay open. She told herself that the baby had been born, that he was alive. Alive and safe with Alan. Her eyes closed, and she fell into a black, dreamless sleep.

Chapter Twenty

'Mum!' exclaimed Mel, opening the door of her building to find her mum standing on the doorstep. 'You're a day early!'

Mel's mum, Bella, put down her suitcase, let her handbag slip off her shoulder and on to the floor and held her arms outstretched towards Mel. In her long, cream, belted trench coat, pressed within an inch of its life, her soft silvery hair pushed up in tortoiseshell combs, cheekbones dusted with pink blusher and smiling lips painted a delicate plum colour, she was everything that represented home for Mel.

'Come here, my love,' Bella said, pulling Mel into her chest. 'Let me hug you.'

At the sight and feel of her mum, a lump formed in the back of Mel's throat. A hundred memories rushed into her mind: all those times in her life when life had thrown her a curveball and she'd needed someone, her mother was *always* there. She felt her shoulders drop a couple of inches and let out a little cry.

'I know, love,' Bella said, hugging her tight. 'I know.'

'Sorry,' Mel squeaked. 'It's seeing you, Mum. I've tried to be really strong, but I'm nearly due now and I'm exhausted and scared and—'

'Of course you are, love,' Bella said. 'But I'm here now. I'm going to help. I hope you don't mind me being early. I couldn't stand to stay with your aunt any longer, with all those stinking cats on the table licking the butter straight from the tub. And I've been desperate to see you and find out how you really are. You're almost ready to drop, aren't you, love? Aren't you going to let me in?'

Mel swallowed. She felt she'd been so strong so far, apart from her waterworks display at the first antenatal class, but seeing her mum made her feel floppy and incapable. Even getting up the stairs and explaining what was going on felt almost impossible. Did this feeling of being a child in your parent's company *ever* stop?

'Of course,' Mel said, taking her mum's suitcase and smiling a watery smile. 'It's so good to see you. I miss you.'

'Me, too,' said her mum, taking the suitcase back. 'I'll get that. So are you coping?'

'I'm trying, Mum, but I'm beginning to think Leo's never coming back and, if he did, I don't know if I'd have him now . . .' Mel said. 'And, upstairs, I'm in the middle of having a baby shower. They do it in America, apparently. There are a few people here. Some of the girls from work and my antenatal class came round to give me a little send-off. I don't think they'll be here too long. Then we can talk.'

'A baby shower?' asked Bella, with mock horror. 'I hope not *literally*.'

Mel smiled and gestured for her mum to follow her upstairs.

At the front door, she removed her ankle boots and took off her trench coat. Underneath the coat, she wore a chocolate-brown dress with a belt around the middle and a colourful scarf around her neck. She chatted about an art exhibition she'd seen with Mel's aunt before glancing at herself in the mirror and following Mel through into the living room, where Rebecca, Erin, Lexi and two girls from Mel's work were sitting on the sofas, chairs and floor, drinking non-alcoholic/alcoholic cocktails out of baby bottles. A Fleet Foxes album was playing and one of the windows was open slightly, because Mel had burned the pizzas and they'd had to order a takeaway instead.

'Ladies,' said Mel. 'This is my mum, Bella. She's going to be staying for a few days and, maybe, though we haven't talked about it yet, be my birth partner since Leo is—'

She stopped talking to prevent the tears coming and gave a heartfelt smile instead. Bella put her arm around her daughter and gave her a big hug.

'Hello, everyone,' she said. 'I hope you don't mind an oldie like me crashing your party.'

'Not at all,' said Lexi. 'We can't exactly be wild and reckless, though I think Mel's colleagues have other plans for later. I'm Lexi – it's lovely to meet you. Would you like one of these drinks?'

Mel's eyes darted around the flat, quickly summing up exactly how disappointed her mum was going to be in her powers of domesticity. Her gaze landed on the great pile of washing which towered in the entrance to the kitchen, near the washing machine but not in it, and the knitting projects she was halfway through exploding from the side of the sofa like a work of modern art. Even though Bella had a busy life running two jobs, as a nutritionist and a piano tutor, alongside the cycling club and tennis club and being an active member of the Green Party and the over-sixties folk club, her house was the stuff of lifestyle magazines.

'I bet you'd prefer a tea, wouldn't you, Mum?' Mel asked. 'Darjeeling? I've bought a new pack.'

'No, thank you,' Bella said, screwing up her nose. 'I want one of these cocktails, thank you, Lexi. What a great name, by the way.'

'Thanks,' said Lexi with a smile. 'I wish I could say it was my idea. It was probably the only good decision my mum ever made.'

Mel moved into the kitchen and emptied more bags of crisps into bowls, alongside a bowl of olives and artichoke hearts. Pouring water into a jug, she paused when she heard Bella laugh her tinkling laugh. Then she heard the conversation turn to Leo.

'If I could get my hands on him,' she heard Bella say, 'I'd wring his scrawny little neck, I really would. Where's his sense of loyalty, for heaven's sake—'

Mel stood still as she heard one of her colleagues, Bronya, speaking in a low voice. Bella began speaking again, but she couldn't hear what else her mum was saying. Suddenly, the girls burst into applause. Mel banged a cup down on the sideboard and felt the baby kick really hard. Lifting up her top, she watched the middle of her stomach protrude bizarrely, into a dome, almost as if the baby was going to burst out of her belly button. Minutes later, Lexi came into the kitchen with an empty bottle, which she put into the sink.

Amy Bratley

'Your mum's a live wire,' Lexi said. 'She's laying into Leo like nothing else.'

'Yeah,' said Mel. 'And it's pissing me off. She's only been here for a minute, and she doesn't know the whole story!'

'Ah,' said Lexi. 'She means well. She's only defending you. We'll be the same one day when our babies have grown up.'

'I guess so,' said Mel with a big sigh. 'I'm just kind of embarrassed that this is happening, you know? That I chose such a crap boyfriend? I really didn't think he was crap before now. I was completely in love. Ha!'

Mel tossed the burned pizza into the dustbin. Walking back into the living room, she caught the end of the conversation, where words like 'Leo' and 'bastard' were being tossed around so flamboyantly it was as if the women were actually having fun dissecting Mel's partner. But, thought Mel, it wasn't fair. Leo would absolutely hate being talked about like this, even if he did deserve it. She forced herself to smile, but Bella pulled a sad face at her.

'Come and sit down, love,' she said. 'Tell us what *you* think.'

Mel sat down on the sofa and tucked her legs up to reduce the swelling. She rubbed her eyes and pushed her hand through her fringe. 'I think he's a bastard,' she said with a smile. 'But I wanted to be the one to say it.'

Everyone laughed, and Mel leaned back, pointing at her navel, which was rippling as the baby moved. Bella rested her hand on Mel's belly and squealed with delight.

'No,' Mel said. 'I don't mean that about Leo. He's going through something. I'm not sure what because he won't tell me. I've told him not to bother coming back unless he can be supportive and, guess what, he's not here—'

'Can you ever really trust someone who can walk out like that at such an important time?' said Erica, one of Mel's colleagues.

Mel stayed quiet then let out a sigh. She banged her palms down on the armchair. 'I don't know!' she said. 'I really don't.'

'It'll all become clear, love,' said Bella. 'Everything always does. Nothing stays muddled for ever. Personally, I would like his guts for garters. He needs a good kick up the backside and someone to tell him what an immature little prick he's being—'

'Oh, Mum,' said Mel, feeling annoyingly protective of Leo. 'Don't say that.'

'Thought so,' said Bella, looking smug.

'What do you mean, "thought so?"' Mel asked.

'You love him,' Bella said. 'You still love him, despite his last-minute nerves.'

Mel felt annoyed. 'And?'

'And so you need to take the bull by the horns and sort it all out. Be the brave one. Take back what you said to him and try again to find out what's really going on with him. You love him and you need to take control.'

No shit, Sherlock, thought Mel, but she didn't say anything. She loved her mum, but, she remembered, she always thought she knew everything. What would she be like during the labour if she was Mel's birth partner? She'd be bossing everyone around. The doorbell went and Lexi went to answer it. Mel supposed it was the takeaway pizza they'd ordered, though now she was more tired than hungry. At the door, Mel's ears pricked up when she heard a familiar voice.

'I thought I could hear the unmistakable sounds of an all-girl party,' said Mrs Lelani, arriving in the room and clasping her hands together in pleasure. 'Any room for a little old one?'

At eleven p.m., Lexi was waiting outside Mel's flat for Gary to pick her up. It was a clear, cold night and the stars shone like white eyeballs in the sky. She pulled her coat a little closer to her and smiled when she saw the headlights of Gary's car flashing at her in the dark. She was pleased to see him, and waved. Since they'd met a couple of weeks ago, Lexi had started calling him her chauffeur, a title he seemed to have taken on with pride. Pulling up beside her, Gary leapt out the door of his Renault to open the door for her. She laughed when she saw he was wearing a chauffeur's hat.

'What's this?' she said, pulling at it.

Gary grinned, his gold tooth glinting. 'I'm simply taking my role in your life very seriously,' he said. 'Plus, I find myself intensely funny.'

Lexi let out a laugh and headed into the back of the cab.

'So,' Gary said, 'how was your night?'

'Good, thanks,' answered Lexi, as she moved uncomfortably in her seat, trying to pull the seatbelt over and plug it in. Being this pregnant was not easy, especially because she was carrying so much extra weight. The midwife had told her not to worry, as long as her blood pressure was fine, which it was. It was the heartburn, though, that she hated most of all. Avoiding spicy food and not eating late at night hadn't really helped. The only time she felt relieved of her weight and comfortable enough to relax was in a warm bath, with candles all around the bathroom, Café del Mar playing on the stereo, emptying her head of work and family stresses. Now, with swollen feet after sitting upright all evening, that's all she craved.

'I'd love a bath,' she said vaguely, at which Gary twisted to look at her and grinned as if she'd invited him in with her.

'Why the suggestive look?' she asked, laughing. 'I don't think there'd be room for us both.'

Gary laughed. This low-level flirting was how they talked; their conversation had never ventured beyond the silly and superficial. Lexi reflected that she related to most men like this – in a cheeky, witty manner. She found that was the easiest way: to make men laugh, not to divulge any personal information. That way, she could become their mate. If they weren't laughing, she started to panic and – it sounded terrible – would often end up sleeping with them. What was the psychology behind that? I can't make you laugh, but I'll make you orgasm. Whatever the relationship, she usually kept the upper hand. Apart from with Alan. There was always an exception to the rule, waiting to trip you up.

'Counting down the days now?' said Gary. 'Is your other half going to be at the birth with you?'

'Er,' she said. 'Erm.'

Lexi prepared herself to answer. This man was obsessed with her other half. Though she'd been in the cab four times since they'd met, she hadn't yet told him the truth. She'd spent the evening talking to the girls about sperm donation and felt exhausted by all the attention she'd got as a result. Sometimes, she wished she'd never told anyone. But what else would she say, and why should she hide the truth? She wasn't ashamed. Gary turned on his Guns N' Roses album and waited for her to answer. The music annoyed her, and she gestured for him to turn it down. He did as she asked, but not quite as low as she would have liked. Then he turned on the engine and started to drive. Lexi was relieved to be setting off home.

'Gotta to be able to hear my music, Lexi,' he said. 'It's the theme tune to my life.'

'Jesus,' said Lexi. 'Do you listen to the same album the whole time? What's wrong with *The Sound of Music*?'

'Are you serious?' asked Gary, laughing.

'No,' said Lexi. 'Talking of theme tunes, how's the script coming along?'

Gary's face was blank. 'Yeah,' he said, suddenly remembering what he'd told her. 'Storming. Sure to be a blockbuster. So, what were you going to say? About your other half?'

Lexi tipped her head back against the seat. The window had steamed up, so she rubbed a circle with the back of her hand. She leaned her cheek against the glass.

'Oh, for heaven's sake, I don't have an other half!' she said to Gary. 'I'm on my own. I'm having the baby alone. Why do you care so much? '

Gary looked forward as he waited at the lights, saying nothing. She watched his fingers clench the steering wheel. He turned down his music further and cleared his throat. 'I was hoping you'd say that,' he said quietly.

'Pardon?' Lexi answered, irritated, watching buildings blur by as he sped up and turned into her street. Pulling up outside her house, he turned off his engine and twisted round to face her, his leather jacket squeaking as he did so.

'Lexi,' he said, 'this might sound strange, because I know you're about to have a baby, but I can't stop thinking about you. When you call my heart leaps about like a frog in my chest. I drive up and down this street like a moron hoping you'll come out and I can offer you a lift somewhere. I've cancelled other customers, even feigned illness, so I can pick up you. It's the strangest thing, but I'm . . '

Lexi's cheeks were burning and her pulse racing. Her brain scrambled as she attempted to think of a fitting wisecrack, but nothing came. Pregnancy was making her a little bit slow. In the past, that kind of come-on would have been enough for her to invite Gary in, drink too much booze, end up having sex and wake up full of regret. With one hand on the handle of the car door, she opened her mouth to speak.

'Lexi,' he said giving her a winsome grin, 'I have a crush on you, something bad. I'd love it if we could be—'

Lexi held up her hand, gesturing for him to stop speaking. He did. He sat there in the dark, blinking, reduced suddenly from heavy-metal-loving alpha male to a harvest mouse, quivering in the moonlight. Lexi's heart softened. 'Before you say anything else,' she said with a sigh, 'I might as well point out some harsh truths. You may have noticed that I'm about to give birth. There are ten days until my due date. It's all rather complicated, because the baby is a baby by donor sperm, so I'm a single mother by choice. I know that sounds a bit like the title of a Beyoncé song, but I so wanted a baby and I looked for a partner, but every relationship I've ever had has ended in disaster. In my job, I can see where people go wrong. In my own life, I can't. There's something about me that doesn't equate with being in a steady relationship. Invariably, it's me who ruins it, by losing the plot and acting insanely. I think it's got something to do with my childhood. My mother was very depressed and my father not really around, so I spent years waiting for someone to take me away from it all, waiting for everything to change. I spent years waiting for a miracle. When it didn't come, I took control of my life and, from then on in, I've never really allowed myself to get close to people. I push them away. I've even made up lies in the past, to push people away. And, at the bottom of me, I'm never sure whether I want to push them away because they're wrong for me or because I'm wrong for them. Plus, I've got a ridiculous crush on someone that I had a one-night stand with and believed he was my soulmate. Basically, Gary, in a nutshell, I'm a no-go area. Off limits. Nightmare.'

Lexi exhaled. Why was she gabbling so much tonight? Ouch! A sudden cramping sensation burned in her abdomen. She wondered if she needed the loo. Her head fuzzed, too, and she blinked a few times, regretting the cocktail she'd had at Mel's. Gary's radio buzzed rudely into the cab, making her jump. He swore at it and turned down the volume.

'But what do you actually believe, though, Lexi?' asked Gary. 'Do you think true love exists?'

As nice as Gary was, Lexi was tired. She didn't feel like having a philosophical discussion with him about love when, really, she wanted to be in the bath, or in her bed, trying to snatch sleep from the tirade of broken nights that was late pregnancy. She was about to tell him so, then saw a pleading expression in his eyes. She sighed.

'I used to believe that there was one person for you,' said Lexi. 'But then I set out on this path of looking and I got kind of . . . of . . . of—'

There was another sharp pain. Lexi breathed deeply, realizing that she did definitely need the loo.

'—lost?' said Gary. 'Because our stories sound very similar.'

'Do they?' asked Lexi, frowning, thinking she hadn't even told her story yet.

'Yes,' said Gary. 'I grew up in foster homes and, though my foster parents loved me, I didn't really believe they wanted me, so I went through the first part of my adult life not believing I was good enough to love.'

'Oh my God,' said Lexi, closing her eyes.

'What?' said Gary. 'I haven't even got to the good bit yet! It's not a sob story, I promise. Hear me out?'

Lexi pulled open the car door and put one foot on the pavement.

'Maybe this was too much,' Gary was saying as he moved around to her door. 'I should have held back, but I can't! It's not in me to hold back. I'm half Italian!'

As he held her hand to help her up and out of the car, Lexi gripped on to his leather jacket and bent over as she felt another pain coming.

'No, it's because I think I need the toilet,' she said. 'Something's happening.'

Gripping on to Gary's arm, she waddled to her flat and unlocked the door.

'I feel like I've got a stick up my arse,' she said. 'Sorry. Not very ladylike.'

Flicking on the lights, she left Gary by the front door and pushed it to on his face without realizing, as she was bent over with more pain. She made it to the bathroom and pulled her trousers down to sit on the toilet. There, she had the 'show' – a lumpy glob of red snot.

'Fuck,' she said, feeling terrified but also incredibly excited.

She looked at her reflection and gave herself a little grin. *This is it*, she thought. The baby is coming early.

Standing, she pulled up her trousers and looked at her watch, waiting for another pain to come. After six minutes, another came. Stronger this time. Leaning on the back of the toilet, she closed her eyes and tried to breathe through it. From outside the toilet door, Gary cleared his throat.

'Are you still here?' she said, when the pain subsided.

'Yep,' he said. 'Are you . . . is it . . . Can I do anything?'

For all the antenatal classes and books she'd read and all the advice she'd listened to, now that she suspected labour was beginning, Lexi couldn't get her head straight. She had been going to call her best friend, Catherine, but now that it was happening, she didn't really want to. Catherine was amazing, but something in her wanted to be alone. Force of habit. Well, almost alone. She'd quite like to be at the hospital, surrounded by midwives. She'd quite like to be with Ginny, her big bag of Maltesers in hand, a warm smile on her face.

'Gary!' she said, pushing open the bathroom door to find him standing there with his sleeves pushed up as if he was about to deliver a calf. 'I'm going to need a chauffeur, not a vet.'

For Lexi, everything happened very, very quickly. Too quickly, she decided afterwards. One minute the baby was safe and warm inside her and a couple of hours later, her baby was in her arms, taking her first few breaths, blinking in the bedroom light. There had been no time to squirt her face with the water spritzer she'd bought in Boots, no time to eat an energy bar or put on her playlist of Dolly Parton favourites. There'd barely been time to take her trousers off! After the bloody show, the contractions had become so powerful and frequent she knew she couldn't travel in the car after all. She was having her baby at home.

'I'm having this baby at home,' she'd told Gary, wild-eyed.

With Gary blinking like a rabbit in headlights and holding her arm, she made it to her bedroom and, after half an hour of overwhelmingly painful contractions, her waters broke all over her duvet and she felt the urge to push. Gary, on the phone to a midwife at the labour unit, his high, quivery voice betraying his calm demeanour, repeated instructions to Lexi not to push yet, while they sent midwives to her address. He spoke to her in a quiet voice and held a cup of water under her lips when she was thirsty. He put towels down under her legs, without being asked. She felt strangely safe in his company and, frankly, didn't care a jot what he thought of her birthing positions. She was doing what her body dictated and was in awe of her instinct. While she focused on the increasingly intense contractions, he let the midwives in through the front door and waited in the kitchen while they encouraged her through the final pushes, cheering as if she were in the final leg of a marathon, before the baby shot out into the midwife's arms.

'You have a baby girl,' the midwife exclaimed, handing her immediately to Lexi, while another midwife cut the cord. 'Baby was born at 12.33 a.m.'

'A girl?' Lexi said, amazed. 'I was certain I was going to have a boy!'

She held her baby girl in her arms while the midwives worked around her and helped her deliver the placenta. Lexi hardly dared move, the baby was so tiny and new. With a wise and serious expression on her face, she fixed Lexi with a soulful stare that reached the very centre of Lexi's heart and squeezed it tight.

'Oh, baby,' she whispered into her deep, marble-dark eyes. Look at you! Here in my arms! You're delicate as a petal and lovelier than I ever expected. I'm your mummy and—' The donor came into Lexi's mind for a nanosecond, his DNA in her hands, but then became bizarrely immaterial. She didn't think of him again. The midwives left her alone for a few moments, and Lexi felt a sense of quiet peace and enormous relief, for she was now, at last, a mother. A mother who would defend and comfort her daughter no matter what. A mother whose eyes would light up with joy when her daughter came into the room. A mother who would never cry on to her daughter's small shoulders. A mother completely unlike her own.

'I will do my best for you,' Lexi whispered. 'I will love you and feed you and keep you safe and dry. I will show you kindness and patience and love and encourage you in your heart's desires. I will make you laugh and be your friend in loneliness, and teach you to be strong, whatever life lays at your feet. I will not let you down.'

Happy tears rolled down Lexi's face, dropping on to her baby's head. She kissed the tears away and stared into her daughter's eyes, never wanting to look away. *I will not let you down.*

You, baby girl, will never be alone.

Chapter Twenty-one

Four days passed before Katy could hold her baby boy, Rufus Alexander, for the first time. She had managed, with great difficulty, to express the colostrum to be fed to the baby through the feeding tube and had been able to poke a finger in the side of the incubator to stroke the baby's skin, but that was all. While Rufus lay in the baby observation unit, Katy had spent the first couple of days mostly lying in her bed on the ward, attached to an antibiotic drip and a catheter, waiting for her painkillers to kick in, listening to and watching new mothers around her bonding with their newborns. People had come in to visit her, brought her balloons, flowers and chocolates and baby clothes, but didn't know quite how to act. The baby wasn't there for them to see or to hold, and Katy was too shocked and disappointed about the birth to talk about it for long. Every time she sneezed or moved, she feared the C-section stitches would tear and, though she wanted to walk, she could shuffle down the corridor only a few steps before she felt dizzy and exhausted.

'It wasn't quite what I was expecting,' she'd said as chirpily as she could when Erin and Mel, still heavily pregnant, had come in to see her. Seeing something – perhaps fear – stretch across their faces as she briefly recounted her labour, Katy had done her best to hide the horror she felt. But, after fifteen minutes, she'd had to ask them to leave, pretending that she wanted to sleep. She'd seen the way they'd looked at one another as they left the ward, as if they felt sorry for her, but she told herself not to care. There was plenty of time to win back their admiration, to prove herself. She might not have had the birth she'd planned for, so she couldn't enjoy telling them all about the perfect birth, but there was plenty of time for them to see what a great job she would do as a mother. Besides, she hadn't told them how she was really feeling. She hadn't told them how awful she felt physically. Even though she'd had a C-section, there was still so much blood. When she stood up for the first time, a great pool of blood poured out of her and on to the floor, which made her want to faint. She had to wear tight medical stockings to prevent her blood from clotting, which were impossible to get on without Alan's help. And every time she went to the bathroom to change her sanitary towels, dragging her drip with her, the sight and smell of blood and amniotic fluid made her queasy. It was also impossible to wash thoroughly. Sitting on a plastic chair in the hospital shower, she was terrified her C-section scar would become infected. Everyone that visited (with the notable exception of Anita) encouraged her to 'get some rest' while the baby was on the neonatal ward, so that she would make a quick recovery after the C-section. But sleeping was almost impossible. The babies on the ward were constantly crying and Katy had a gnawing sense of dread snapping at her ankles which kept her awake. She was careful not to tell anyone how she felt and managed to hold it together for Alan's visits, but, inside, she felt like screaming.

'Does it feel good?' asked Alan, when Katy held Rufus properly for the first time and, after a stressful twenty minutes, eventually managed to get him to latch on to her breast. Katy blinked away the tears in her eyes, while Alan smiled fondly at her, relieved, she thought, that Katy was at last showing emotion. But the tears were not tears of joy. The tears were out of fear. No, she thought. It doesn't feel good. It feels like nothing. I feel nothing. She stared at Rufus, desperate for the sight of his tiny fingers and toes to inspire a rush of love, desperate for his little, dark eyes to trigger the maternal instinct. But it didn't happen. The thought that perhaps this wasn't even her son, that there had been a mix-up on the neonatal ward, had crossed her mind more than once. She felt nothing.

'Yes,' she mumbled at Alan, who put his arm over her shoulder and lovingly kissed her cheek.

'You're amazing,' Alan said, his eyes glassy. 'You've been through an awful trauma, but you're so together. Rufus is lucky to have a mum like you. Other women would not be able to cope, Katy. Well done. My folks are so proud of you. I thought we could Skype them when we get home.'

It was the worst thing he could have said. Now she was going to have to carry on the pretence. Perhaps she'd feel better when she got home, she told herself, if she went along with everything that Alan was saying. He seemed to be in control.

She tried to imagine herself in her kitchen at home, sitting at the oak table, holding Rufus on her chest as other mothers on the ward seemed to do, with Alan's family watching her over the Internet. She didn't want anyone to look at her. Alan's mother (a mother of four children) would know right away she was a fake. Right now, Katy wanted to hide. Perhaps it was the hospital environment that was making her feel so detached. The coming and going of the midwives, the fact that she could barely move on her own, the feeling of powerlessness, the other mothers looking pale and exhausted. Maybe the drugs weren't helping either. Those painkillers with codeine in them spun her out.

'I just want to get home,' she told Alan. 'I think we'll be better off at home.'

Eventually, Katy and Rufus had been given the green light to go home.

'Is anyone ever going to sign the discharge form?' she asked Alan as she sat on her bed, all her bags packed and ready to go, waiting for her drugs to be dispensed.

'I'll go and find out,' he said, marching off to the reception desk, where a couple of midwives in blue uniforms were writing on whiteboards. Finally, someone came, and Katy limped out of the hospital, an enormous sanitary towel stuffed in her pants, her breasts aching with milk and exhaustion pressing against her forehead.

'So,' said Alan cheerily, carefully carrying Rufus in the car seat. 'At last we can welcome Rufus to our home.'

'Slow down,' said Katy as they made their way to the exit. 'Remember, I can't really walk.'

Passing by the hospital staff, Katy had a sense of her insignificance. Here, she was just another new mother, just another emergency C-section. There were hundreds just like her passing in and out of the main doors. Pushing open the door to the outside world, Katy felt utterly overcome. People bustled past, shouted, laughed and smoked on the streets. The sun shone so brightly she felt almost blinded. Holding on to a handrail for a second, she followed Alan across the car park to his BMW and steeled herself for the journey home. Alan opened the door for her and helped her in. Tears pricked her eyes. She felt like an invalid. She felt nothing like her normal self. Rufus began to cry, wanting to be fed.

'Do you want to do it now?' Alan said. 'Before we leave?'

'It might take forty minutes or more, though,' she said. 'What do you think?'

The sound of Rufus screaming was slicing into her head, right behind her eyes. Again, she felt she wanted to cry. She tried to turn to look at Rufus, but her scar was too painful and, besides, his car seat was facing away from her. Alan unclipped his belt.

'I'll get him out and you can feed him,' he said. 'Otherwise, it'll be a dreadful car journey home.'

Katy now realized she was wearing the wrong top for breast-feeding. She had on a dress that she had to wriggle out of, leaving her top half completely bare. Luckily, Alan's car had tinted-glass windows, so no one could see in unless they pressed their nose up against the glass.

'I'll need my feeding pillow,' she said. Alan handed it to her and, when she'd arranged it, he passed her Rufus, who was now incandescent with hungry rage.

'Okay,' Katy said. 'I need to make sure the whole nipple goes in.'

Attempting to latch Rufus on properly took too long, and each time she tried a different position he wailed some more.

'I'll just put up with the pain,' she said, when he began to feed in the wrong position. Even through the wall of painkillers for the C-section, her toes curled in pain as he drank. She knew she'd pay for it later, but, for the time being, she was relieved Rufus was quiet. Alan put on the radio then stroked Katy's shoulder, while she tried as hard as she could to control the impulse to scream at both of them to get the hell off her. She focused on a conversation she'd had with a midwife that morning.

'How long does it take?' she had asked in a desperate whisper. 'To fall in love with the baby?'

The midwife had sat down on the end of the bed and held Katy's hand. She had smiled so kindly Katy had almost blurted out the truth.

'It can take a little while,' she said. 'Don't punish yourself if it doesn't happen straight away. It will happen, I promise you that, but it can take time. Katy, if there's one piece of advice I can give you, it's that you mustn't suffer in silence. Talk to your husband, talk to your friends and other new mums, talk to your health visitor, or doctor. Many, many women find having a newborn overwhelmingly hard.'

'Thank you,' said Katy, smiling weakly, disappointed in the midwife's answer, knowing that talking about how she felt would get her nowhere. If she started talking, all the negative feelings she had would become even more real. If she admitted to feeling totally out of control, how would she ever regain control? No. There was only one option available. She would have to suffer in silence.

Chapter Twenty-two

'Come down and try this,' said Bella, holding out a dish filled with fresh pineapple. 'Apparently, if you eat enough of it, the enzymes in it might do something to your tummy and kick-start labour.'

Mel pulled down her black maternity top, which had ridden up and over her bump, revealing skin so stretched it looked like purple bicycle tracks in places. But that was the least of her worries. She carefully climbed down the stepladder, clutching a feather duster she was using to spring-clean the top of the bookshelves, something she could happily say she had never done before. But, in the last couple of days Mel had found that she was turning into her mother, cleaning and organizing and arranging her flat, almost obsessively. She was completely desperate for her baby to be born, especially since going to the fourth antenatal class, when Ginny had talked about the practicalities of coping with a newborn. Only Erin, herself and Rebecca were there, since Katy and Lexi had already given birth. They were so lucky! Mind you, seeing Katy had left Mel feeling like a bag of nerves. Even

Katy, who seemed like Ms Capable, had been visibly shaken by her labour. But it had been an emergency C-section. Poor Katy. Lexi, on the other hand, had texted her a picture of her little girl, Poppy, and said she had 'quite literally popped out'. Mel just felt annoyed almost the entire time now. She was fed up of learning about birth and babies, fed up of hearing about other people's births. She just wanted to get on with her own.

'All this nesting is a sign it's near,' Bella said, as Mel chewed on a pineapple chunk. 'I've never seen you take such an interest in cleaning. When you were a teenager your bedroom always looked like it had been ransacked.'

Mel looked around the flat. The balls of mohair wool previously strewn over one side of the sofa were neatly squashed into an old-fashioned washing basket. The books and magazines that seemed to slip off the shelves and lie on every surface were back where they should be and Leo's various leads for his guitars and amps, normally draped over the furniture, were neatly folded into a shoebox. Most amazingly, Mel's clothes, usually discarded in a heap on the bedroom or bathroom floor, exactly where she'd taken them off, were hanging in her wardrobe. It was true that this tidy behaviour was completely out of character, but, frankly, nothing in her life felt remotely normal now. Two days away from her due date, and Mel found herself living with her mother instead of Leo, and in a flat that was so clean she could eat off the floor. Tidying up was a welcome change from obsessing about labour. And Leo? Where was Leo? Gone in a puff of smoke.

'Rather pineapple chunks than Mrs Lelani's suggestion,' said Bella, raising her eyebrows. 'I looked blue cohosh up on the web, and it's not recommended *at all*. I know she means well, but *honestly*.'

Mel swallowed a chunk of pineapple. Oh, God, the wait was unbearable – and made worse by well-meaning friends phoning or texting every five minutes to ask if anything had happened. Mel wanted to stop answering, but when she did ignore a message, frantic voicemails ensued congratulating her or wishing her good luck in labour. Bella and Mrs Lelani had been coming up with all sorts of tips to bring it on, but nothing worked. In the back of her mind –though too silly a thought to vocalize – Mel thought the baby was waiting for Mel and Leo to sort out their problems before she or he entered the world. Not that that was looking likely.

'Ah, no, Mrs Lelani is lovely,' Mel said, taking another piece of pineapple. 'She knows lots about herbal remedies. I thought you got on really well.'

She moved over to the window and looked out at the street and the sea beyond. The sky had grown dark, so she clicked on the lamp that stood on the wide windowsill. It was a small green banker's lamp Leo had bid for on eBay. She remembered the way he had jokingly punched the air when he won it. She thought of him and what he would be doing right now. She looked at her wristwatch. Almost noon. It was the weekend, but he may well be at work, staring at his screen, sipping a coffee. Flat white, one sugar. Resting her hands on her bump, she felt the baby hiccup.

'I just think you should be careful telling pregnant women to take those herbs,' Bella said. 'But we did get on, yes. We were comparing lives as single sixty-something women. Sometimes I can't believe I'm sixty and I've got a grandchild coming. I remember when I was waiting for you to come. I was a week overdue and your dad took me for a walk in the countryside. When we were walking across a field, he shouted that there was a bull coming. I was wearing red and he said it was coming towards me. You should have seen me run to the fence! I almost broke my ankle. Your dad was in stitches when he told me it was a ploy to bring on labour.'

Both women laughed.

'And did it work?' Mel asked, turning to Bella.

Bella shook her head. 'Not for another four days,' she said. 'Silly bugger. Oh Mel, I do miss your dad at times like these. Even twenty years later I miss him. I wish he could be here to see your baby.'

She moved towards the window and Mel put her arm around her, leaning her head into her shoulder, breathing in the faint smell of her Neal's Yard rose face cream.

'What do you think he'd say about Leo?' Mel asked. 'Wouldn't be too impressed, would he?'

Bella shrugged and shook her head slightly, folding her arms across her chest. 'Your dad was the kind of man who could talk to anyone and get to the bottom of them straight away,' she said. 'He would have taken the bull by the horns and confronted Leo, I know he would.'

'Yes,' said Mel. 'I've been thinking about doing that, but every time I pick up the phone to call him, I fill with a mix of indignation and dread. If he doesn't even have the inclination to phone me when I'm literally about to give birth, why should I convince him to come back?'

'I know what you mean, love,' said Bella. 'I'd feel the same, but I don't know what's got into him.'

Mel picked up her phone and looked at the blank screen. She was just about to throw it on to the sofa when it began to ring. She checked the screen again and stared up at Bella, open-mouthed.

'It's him,' she said, flushing.

'Answer it then!' said Bella.

Mel answered it and took a deep breath.

'Hi, Leo,' she said, widening her eyes at Bella, who stayed where she was, her hands on her hips, listening in.

'Mel,' said Leo, 'I need to tell you something. It's big, and you're not going to like it, but I want to get this off my chest before the baby is born. It's only fair, to be honest. Meet me on the beach?'

Mel's knees weakened at Leo's words. She felt the blood drain from her face. 'Yes,' she said warily. 'In an hour?'

Putting down the phone, she walked into Bella's outstretched arms and leaned her head on her shoulder as best she could with her bump in the way.

'He says he's got something big to tell me,' she said. 'Something I won't like. I'm meeting him in an hour.'

Bella rubbed Mel's back and kissed her cheek. 'Don't worry,' she said. 'I'll be here for you when you get back.'

Mel saw Leo before he saw her. He was the only person on the beach, under a blue sky bloated with grey clouds. He stood facing the sea, rough and foamy, the wind whipping his hair and scarf away from his head and his grey overcoat and trousers against his legs. His hands were shoved into his pockets, his collar pulled up. She thought he was watching the kite-surfer who was doing crazy tricks in the sea, but he bent down to pick up a stone and tossed it into the water with absolutely no vigour. Mel pulled her hat down over her ears, squinting in the March sunlight. Trudging towards him across the pebbles, even though the waves were crashing, she couldn't possibly take him by surprise. Hearing her struggle across the stones, he turned. She lifted her hand in greeting and saw a brief but genuine smile pass over his face.

'Hi, Leo,' she said, holding her hair back from her face with both hands. 'Shall we walk?'

'Yes,' he said, his expression tense. 'How are you?'

It was miserable trying to talk and walk along the beach when she could hardly walk now anyway, so Leo suggested they stop and sit down for a moment. That was pretty difficult, too, and while he stared into her face and, apparently, soundlessly communicated his feelings Mel began to feel irritated. She was exhausted, cold, uncomfortable and had no idea what this was about. What could possibly be so difficult to tell her?

'Leo,' she said, as the first drop of rain hit her cheek. 'This is your chance to tell me what's going on. I'm days away from my due date and the baby could come at any moment. It would be nice to know, before it turns up, what the fuck is going on. I'm kind of over this mysterious act you're pulling.'

'You're annoyed,' said Leo solemnly.

'Of course I'm bloody annoyed,' she said. 'This is supposed to be one of the most exciting times of my life – of our lives – and you're off sulking at your brother's house about something "big" I'm not going to like. You say you still love me, but I have to doubt that, Leo. I can't sleep, I can't eat, I'm constantly in tears, I don't know what's going to happen when I give birth, or how it's going to—'

Leo had gone very pale. He held up his hand, gesturing for her to stop, so, with a sigh, she did as he asked. Leo put his hand into his pocket and pulled out a photograph, which he handed to her. She frowned.

'Why are you showing me a photograph of you when you were a kid?' she asked, staring at the photograph of Leo in a pair of trousers and yellow T-shirt, holding a white teddy bear. Leo was almost touching her, and she could feel that he was trembling. 'What's going on?'

'It's not me,' he said. 'This is Jacques.' He paused and looked out to sea, then back at Mel.

'Who's Jacques?' asked Mel, fearing that deep down she already knew the answer. This was the "big" deal. A person. He had a son.

'This is a big thing I'm about to tell you. But Jacques . . . Jacques is . . . he's my son,' Leo said in a quiet voice, his mouth contorted as he struggled not to cry. 'He's nine years old and, up until a few weeks ago, he lived in France. His mother, Coco, and I met when I was eighteen and living with a family there for three months to learn the language before I went to university. Coco was only sixteen and I got her pregnant. Her family were Catholic and wouldn't entertain the idea of abortion, so she went ahead and had the baby. Her parents hated me, said I'd ruined her life. I felt terribly ashamed and had no idea what to do. They wouldn't let me see Coco and, though I tried to write a few letters, I soon gave up. After Jacques was born, Coco sent me a picture and a short letter and has done every year, on his birthday, to keep me updated. But I've had nothing to do with him at all. I stayed out of his life completely, but he's still in here.'

Leo pointed to his head and then his heart. Mel stayed silent, too shocked to react.

'Every day and every night, he's been in my thoughts,' he said. 'When you told me you were pregnant, I had all these feelings of guilt and shame. How could I be a dad to our child, when I already had a son that I totally ignored? Worse still, I'd never even told *you* about Jacques. I always knew I should and promised myself I would before our relationship got any more serious than it already was, but you got pregnant before I had the chance.'

Mel shook her head. She couldn't believe what she was hearing and tried sounding it out in her head to make it seem more real. Leo had a son. Leo was already a dad. Two years of getting to know him, and she didn't know this. Pretty fundamental fact about a person, no?

'A part of me thought I'd tell you once the baby was born,' he went on. 'But it felt wrong. I needed to sort it out before the baby came, so, about six weeks ago I contacted Coco and told her about you and our baby. It coincided with her having moved to London. I've met up with her and Jacques once, and she's staying in Brighton for a few days, because I wanted you to meet her, just to clear the air. I'm sorry. I should have been upfront with you from the start. I know how this looks—'

Mel was speechless. Trying to digest the information, she gulped. Leo used his thumb and first finger to wipe away tears that were welling up in his eyes. He sniffed loudly and puffed out, as if he'd been holding his breath.

'So she's here now?' Mel said, her stomach churning and her forehead creased. 'So you're playing happy families with your ex and your *child* in Brighton, while I'm going through hell on my own? Leo, I'm completely shocked.'

Her head was swimming. It was too much to take in. All those nights lying in bed together in the dark, sharing their most intimate dreams, and Leo had withheld this? And now, he was with *her*? They were spending time together while she was all alone, about to give birth?

'We're not playing happy families!' said Leo. 'On the contrary. I've only seen them once while they've been in Brighton, but she wanted us all to meet, to kind of clear the air. I told her that I had walked out on you and she was horrified. I don't know why I walked out – I think I was scared of what you'd say, or what kind of man this all makes me. I've been stalling because I didn't know what to do for the best.'

He shook his head and choked on his tears.

'I'm sorry, Mel,' he said. 'I love you, but I had all this to tell you. I didn't know what to do. I know this is terrible timing—'

This time, he was properly crying, and the sight of him choked Mel. She couldn't watch him suffer. She put her arms around his neck and pushed his head into her chest.

'Do you have any feelings for Coco?' Mel asked, still in shock. 'Now that you've seen her again?'

Leo pulled away from her and shook his head. 'I hardly know her,' he said. 'When we met, she was sixteen, French and quite pretty. She taught me how to smoke and got me drunk on red wine. It sounds awful, but she was just the first girl to take an interest in me, and I was grateful. I was an idiot teenager. I lost my virginity with her and look what happened. Now, she may as well be a complete stranger, but Jacques is different. I feel a bond with him. I am so sorry. I didn't know what to do.'

'So you keep saying,' said Mel, closing her eyes and blinking away her own tears.

'You must need time for this to sink in,' Leo said, before holding both her arms in a firm grasp. 'Mel, I love you. I want this baby, our baby. I want to come home, I want it all to be all right again, but I'm not sure you're going to want me to be its dad after everything I've told you. I'm sorry.'

Mel felt like she was caught in a bad dream. She opened her mouth to respond, but didn't know what to say. 'And what about Coco?' she asked despondently. 'How long is she staying here? Does she want you back?'

Leo shook his head. 'No, of course not,' he said. 'She's got a place in London. She came down here wanting to meet us all. She was shocked to hear that I'd walked out on you. She wants to meet you. She's over there in the car. Would you be willing? Then it's all done with and we can move on—'

'I don't want to meet her!' Mel said, starting to walk away from Leo, feeling too angry with him even to look at him. 'I want nothing to do with her. Or you.'

'I love you, Mel—' Leo started, his voice shaking, but Mel cut him off.

'Just fuck off, Leo,' she said, striding away from him. 'Just leave me alone—'

'I don't know what else to say,' he said, aghast. 'I'm sorry.'

Mel carried on walking away, instructing herself not to cry. 'I don't care,' she said, holding her bump protectively. 'Just go away.'

Mel glanced back and saw Leo put his head in his hands

and rub his eyes. Dropping his arms down to his side, he looked up at the sky and stared after her.

'Mel!' he shouted after her, but she didn't turn round. She didn't want him to see her tears. 'Come back!'

Chapter Twenty-three

Rebecca stared longingly at the photograph of the Bridge of the Immortals in China which her friend Ella had posted on Facebook. It was the world's highest bridge, and the thought of it made Rebecca breathless. Imagine the freedom. So close to the clouds, far away from home. For a moment, she imagined it was she who had taken the photographs, she who was standing in the mountains even higher than clouds, following in the footsteps of Taoist immortals. Then she had another contraction.

'What time will the midwives get here?' asked Lenny, interrupting her breathing. He was pacing the front room, his arms folded, checking the road outside the window every other second.

'Later,' she said. Now the contraction was over she was laying out the polka-dot plastic shower curtains she'd bought to protect the landlord's cream living-room carpet. They were cheaper than the plastic sheeting recommended for home water births, though she hadn't had the heart to tell the shopkeeper at the pound shop what they were actually for when he was showing her various patterns.

'I wish they'd just get here,' he said.

'Lenny, stop fretting!' she said, standing for a moment to massage her lower back as it throbbed with a dull ache. She had already attached the TENS machine, which buzzed ineffectively, and had taken a couple of paracetamol. Lenny flopped down on a chair which they'd pushed to the edge of the living room to make space. Music was playing; something folksy Lenny had chosen, and the fairy lights Rebecca had draped around the bookshelves were twinkling in the low light of the morning. There was a silver birthing ball, and blankets, too, colourful crocheted patchwork ones she'd bought from a charity shop for if she felt cold, though the heating was up high enough for a reptile enclosure. Briefly, she thought about Katy and the glamorous red labour outfit she'd had designed especially for labour. She'd probably had a team of interior designers making over the hospital room before she entered, wore full make-up and those feathered mule slippers old movie stars wore. Rebecca smiled at the thought. Unlike me, she thought, in my black, oversized T-shirt bearing the slogan of Lenny's band and my slipper socks. Mustn't forget to take those off. Rebecca looked around the room. Who needed glamour? This was beginning to feel exactly like a nest.

'We'll be all right,' she said. 'Millions of women have babies every year, don't they? I'm sure their partners get through it just fine. Don't start panicking, or you'll get me all wound up, too.'

The fact that 130 million babies were born worldwide each year helped Rebecca relax. If 130 million women could deliver babies, then surely she could be one of them.

'I'm not panicking!' he said. 'I just mean, we don't want to do this alone, do we? You know I'll faint if I have to see the blood. Oh, God, just the thought makes me feel dizzy. You know what I'm like when I cut my finger, but the umbilical cord? Don't make me cut it, Becs, please.'

A memory of a baby that was found abandoned by a paperboy in a basket outside a pub in the village where her parents lived flashed into her mind. The baby's mother, thought to be fifteen or sixteen years old, was never found. The baby was wrapped in a blood-stained T-shirt, which must have belonged to the mother. The village had become obsessed with finding out her identity for the sake of the foundling, and Rebecca's own parents had been outraged, but Rebecca had always felt strangely protective of the girl's anonymity. She could never get the thought of her giving birth on her own out of her head. What had she been through, to end up dumping her baby outside a pub? Where had she gone to have the baby? To the woods, in the middle of the night? How had she cut the cord? What must that girl feel now, three years later? Rebecca shivered.

'Lenny, stop!' she said. 'I'm the one actually having the baby! You're supposed to be making me feel more relaxed. Not the other way around.' Her lip wobbled.

'And I'm the one watching!' he said. 'It's hard on me, too, babe.'

Lenny picked up a white muslin square off the pile Rebecca had prepared and blew his nose on it. She pulled a face.

'They're not handkerchiefs,' she sighed. 'Oh, Lenny, do you think you should take a Natracalm? I've got some in the bathroom cabinet.'

Lenny stood up again and looked out of the window, leaning

against a tower of towels and buckets they'd stacked, ready for the labour. A seagull landed on the windowsill, opened its beak and screeched at the top of its lungs. Lenny knocked on the window to scare it away, but it didn't move.

'Those horse pills are not going to help,' Lenny said pitifully. 'I need proper drugs. Actually, I might go and smoke a spliff to calm my nerves. When did you say the midwives are coming again?'

Rebecca sighed more deeply. Ever since her waters had broken in a trickle during the night and she'd been checked out at hospital and it was confirmed that labour was beginning, she'd spent time preparing for the birth. The enormity of what was about to happen was in turn exciting and terrifying. The baby was coming. One question repeated itself in her head: could she be a good mother? Would she be in the same situation she was in with her own mother in twenty years? Not speaking. Opening a letter from her child, shocked by its handwritten revelations? No. She wouldn't be like that. They would be friends. They would talk. Rebecca wouldn't suffocate her child, no matter how wild they wanted to be. Would she?

'We have to call them when the contractions are strong and steady,' said Rebecca. 'They're not even bad yet. Pass me that yellow bag, will you? And, Lenny, you can't smoke weed with the baby around. It's absolutely not allowed.'

'What's going to happen to the baby if I smoke a spliff out the window?' he said. 'Jesus, Becs, don't go all God-fearing on me.'

'"God-fearing"?' said Rebecca, years of childhood church attendance flashing through her mind. 'What are you talking about? You're not allowed to be near the baby after you've smoked. It says in my pregnancy book.'

'But the baby's not even been born yet!' he said. 'Give me a break!'

'Give *me* a break!' she said.

Lenny exhaled noisily and turned away from the window. He dragged the yellow bag, the size of a rubbish-bin sack, which a midwife had dropped off a couple of weeks before, to Rebecca. She opened it and peered inside to find disposable mats, metal instruments wrapped in airtight clear packaging, sterile gloves and other mysterious objects. Lenny peered over her shoulder, his hair tickling her cheek, whistling in mock horror through his teeth. Rebecca elbowed him gently, and he gently elbowed her back. He caught her hand and kissed it. Rebecca turned and they grinned at one another.

'What do you think the baby's going to be like?' Lenny asked, suddenly softening. 'We're going to meet him soon. I hope he's like you.'

He stroked Rebecca's stretched belly, and seconds later she had another contraction. She leaned into him and let him support her weight. His hands rubbed her lower back, and he kissed her forehead. From that wordless connection, Rebecca felt oxytocin flood through her body. She kissed Lenny full on the mouth then, slowly, they parted and Lenny mounted the birthing ball and bounced over to where the birth pool was, collapsed and deflated in a heap.

'Shall I start blowing up the pool if I can't smoke?' he said, pushing his hair back. 'Is it too soon? Maybe we could have a go with my remote-control boat.'

'Lenny,' Rebecca said, noticing the seagull fly away from the windowsill, 'you're insane.'

Half a mile away, the same seagull landed on the roof of the hospital, where, in Labour Suite 3, Erin, after a final scan, was changing into her hospital gown and surgical stockings, ready for her caesarean.

'How many *more* hospital staff do you think will come and talk to us?' she asked Edward with a smile, squeezing his hand. 'I've never had so much attention.'

The consultant looking after Erin, the anaesthetist and various midwives had spoken to her and Edward, reassuring them about the impending operation. Soon, she would be in theatre.

'It's comforting, though, isn't it?' asked Edward. 'Not long now, then we can get on with being parents.'

Erin smiled and gazed out of the window. Thoughts of Josiah kept popping into her mind, but she tried to think about her new baby and what it would feel like to hold him or her against her chest.

Everything is going to be fine, she repeated to herself. *Everything is going to be fine.*

Once in theatre, with Edward dressed in scrubs, the consultant surgeon talked her through what was going to happen. Up on the bed, she felt nothing as the anaesthetist performed a spinal injection. As the midwife and Edward chatted happily, she tried to relax as the anaesthetic started to work.

'Okay, Erin,' said the surgeon, while a screen was erected across her middle. 'In ten minutes, you will meet your baby.'

Though the people in the room continued to talk to her, distracting her from the odd noises she could hear coming from beyond the screen, Erin said nothing at all. With all her might she willed her baby to be alive and well. *This time*, she thought, I will have my baby.

'I can see the head,' said the consultant calmly, and Erin held her breath. 'And now we have your baby. You have a girl.'

Erin broke into sobs. Edward covered her with kisses. The baby cried, a forceful cry, and was held briefly above the screen for Erin to see. Then she was quickly checked over and given to Edward, who held her right next to Erin's face. Her sobs turned into choked laughter. She felt elated. Utterly joyous.

'She's so beautiful,' she whispered, taking her.

'Congratulations,' said the consultant. 'I'm very pleased for you.'

Erin stared at her baby. Edward was grinning from ear to ear. 'Erin,' said Edward. 'It's our daughter, she's here! I love you. I love you so much.'

Erin recognized the elation in his voice. He had acted valiantly throughout the pregnancy, standing firm and tall, like an oak tree. He was going to be a brilliant father. She felt so happy, holding their baby, watching her breathe and blink and whimper. Erin glanced at the door, where suddenly a couple of student doctors had appeared, but they were turned away by one of the midwives.

'Sorry about that, Erin,' she said. 'This is a teaching hospital, so students are everywhere. I explained that you needed a little privacy right now.'

Erin nodded, not caring who else was in the room. She

thought about how everyday life carried on all around you, despite what enormous events are going on in your own. On the day Josiah was born, nothing else seemed to stop but his heartbeat. She distinctly remembered how appalled she felt when someone offered her a cup of tea. How could people drink tea when her baby was dead? Staring at her baby daughter, she put the thought from her mind.

'Erin,' said the midwife, waving a hand in front of her face. 'Everything is fine. Your baby girl is healthy.'

Erin held her daughter and looked up at the midwife, allowing relief to wash over her.

'She's beautiful,' said the midwife, wiping a tear from her own cheek. 'I'm so pleased for you both.'

Edward, beaming from ear to ear, hugged the midwife and lifted her feet off the floor. She let out a little screech.

'Put her down, Edward!' Erin laughed. She'd rarely seen him so demonstrative. Her heart leapt inside her chest. 'I'm just so happy,' he said. 'This is our family. This is what life is all about.'

'I know,' she said. 'I know.'

Edward kissed Erin again and again, all the time holding their baby daughter. Their lips touched and stayed together for a few moments.

'What will you call her?' asked the midwife, sweetly.

Erin and Edward looked at one another, smiling.

'Hope,' said Erin. 'We're going to call her Hope.'

In between contractions, which were now one minute apart, Rebecca felt utterly disorientated. In the flat, there were two midwives and Lenny sitting with her while her labour went on and on and on. Lenny was telling a story about when he was a toddler and pointed to a bottle of whiskey and said, 'Daddy's milk'. His dad, apparently, liked the booze. In her mind's eye, Rebecca was with her friend in China, walking across the Bridge of the Immortals.

'Like father, like son,' he said, taking a gulp from his glass of red wine.

The midwives laughed and bantered with him. She was astounded at how laid-back the women were, but then reminded herself of the 130 million births each year. To midwives, this happened every day. To them, she was just another woman having a baby. But weren't they *too* relaxed? Maybe it was the gas and air, but Rebecca felt detached, as if she was floating up high in the corner of the room, looking at herself from the ceiling. As her cervix dilated to ten centimetres and the baby crowned, she felt confused by her own life. How had she got into this position? Who were these people watching a baby come out of her body? Why was she not in contact with anyone she knew before she moved to Brighton? How could she be a good mother when she couldn't maintain a civil relationship with her own mother? Did she even know Lenny well enough to have a baby with him? Agreeing to marry him was one thing, but having his baby was another. Hadn't she, unequivocally, given herself to him? Didn't she want, more than anything, to go travelling round the world – and not with a baby hanging off her! Oh shit, she thought, as she felt the baby's head emerging from her body. Maybe this wasn't such a great idea after all.

'Are you still with me, babe?' Lenny said, stroking her head. All she could do was nod. The contractions were too painful for her to be able to communicate properly and, though she was with three other people, she felt more alone than she ever had. She could only think of one thing: she was never, ever, doing this again. Whatever Lenny said to her in the future, she wasn't even going to have sex again.

'Do you want to see the baby's head, Lenny?' asked one of the midwives. 'It's crowning. Won't be long before you meet the baby now, Rebecca.'

Lenny looked at Rebecca and, though, in her birth plan, she'd wanted him to stay at the head end, she couldn't care now what he saw or where he stood.

'Climb in, why don't you?' she muttered, giving him a vague smile. Then, she closed her eyes in pain for a contraction that seemed to last for ever.

'Okay,' said Lenny doubtfully, moving down to look at the baby's head in the water of the birthing pool. He was quiet for a while, and she glanced at him anxiously. Why wasn't he saying anything? Was the baby okay? Lenny stood with his hand on his chest, as his eyes seemed to roll back in his head.

'Christ,' he said. 'I wish I hadn't done that.'

He fainted.

'Oh, for fuck's sake,' Rebecca said, wanting to kill him. Her irritation was cut short by a contraction that nearly ripped her in half. Though she remained virtually silent outwardly, inside, Rebecca let out a blood-curdling scream that delivered the baby into the water just as Lenny came round again. Panting heavily, she let out a sob. The baby was out. Lenny, white as a ghost, warbled something unworldly. Then he gave her a tight squeeze.

'It's a boy,' said the midwife, cutting the cord then handing

Rebecca the baby. 'Congratulations. That was one big baby. Well done. We just have to deliver the placenta now.'

As the midwife injected her with a drug to speed up the third stage of delivery, Rebecca took the baby as if someone had just handed her a ticking bomb. She kissed his cheek and smelled him. For a moment, she thought about handing him back, grabbing her rucksack and getting a taxi to Gatwick, but as she stared at her baby, something shifted inside her heart. She melted. She fell in love. In a heartbeat, she knew for a fact that she belonged to the baby and the baby belonged to her. Nothing else mattered. This was it. This was the reason for everything. Her *meaning*. She thought of her own mother holding her in the same way on the day she was born, the photograph that she had framed by her bed which Rebecca had gazed at as a child, wondering what it felt like to hold a baby. Now she knew. Her baby was so soft and warm and fragile, she hardly dared to move. Rebecca lifted her head up to see Lenny coming towards her, holding two big glasses of red wine.

'You did it, babe,' he said, kissing her on the lips. He held her close and she smelled the wine on his breath. She took a sip from his glass and felt her body begin to relax, the relief sinking in. 'What do we do now?'

'This is where the parenting bit starts,' said one of the midwives. 'You're on your own now.'

Rebecca and Lenny looked at one another, and Lenny mouthed, Yikes. They both burst out laughing.

'I can't believe that it's like that,' Rebecca said, her eyes wide. 'It's so painful . . . and at the end, that feeling, it's like nothing else, it's—'

'Like doing a poo,' said the midwife. 'Isn't it?'

'Not one that I've ever done,' said Rebecca. 'But I know what you mean.'

Rebecca stared at her baby, checking his tiny features, counting his tiny fingers and toes. 'He's amazing,' she said, grinning.

Just then, Rebecca's phone started to ring. Lenny stood to move towards it, knocking the open bottle of wine all over the patch of cream carpet the shower curtains hadn't covered. Rebecca burst out laughing and couldn't stop. Lenny grinned at her before answering her phone. Listening to whoever it was, his expression sobered. He held his hand over the phone's mouthpiece.

'It's your mum,' he said. 'She wants to talk to you. Do you want to speak to her?'

Rebecca blinked. She looked at the baby boy in her arms and knew she had to be brave now. Not brave in the rebellious way she thought she was by not telling her family the truth about her pregnancy. Instead, brave in a way that meant she had to build bridges, forgive and ask to be forgiven. She held out her hand for the phone and nodded at Lenny, suddenly absolutely desperate to hear her mother's voice.

'Yes,' she said, tears bulging in her eyes. 'Yes, I do want to speak to her.'

In the hospital ward, when Edward had gone home high as the moon with a list of relatives and friends to phone, a midwife helped lift Hope out of her cot and get her into the right position to breastfeed. Although Erin had a drip and a catheter attached, she felt more elated and more content than at any time in her life, and here, in the warm ward, with a midwife on call if Hope so much as whimpered, Erin felt incredibly safe, as if she, too, were in a kind of womb, from which she was yet to emerge. She had particularly enjoyed the rounds of check-ups the doctors and midwives had done on Hope. Yes, her eyes were fine. Yes, her hearing was fine. Yes, her joints were fine. Yes, she was feeding well. Hope was one hundred per cent perfect. 'Hope,' Erin said in a whisper, 'I will love you for ever more. You are safe with me. I am devoted to you.' She checked her over completely, memorizing every little crease in her skin, even those between her toes. The midwives told Erin to rest, but she couldn't sleep, despite being exhausted. All she could do was stare at Hope, drinking in her tiny, perfect features, watching the rise and fall of her chest, grateful to hear her lungs working with her occasional cry. Erin couldn't take her eyes away from her baby.

As the night became dawn and Erin eventually slept, she understood, for the first time, what it meant to sleep with one eye open. And while she half slept, half listened for any changes in Hope's breathing, she continued to hold her little baby against her chest, for as long as she could. She never wanted to let go. She lay holding her and loving her. Loving Hope.

Chapter Twenty-four

Heart hammering and stomach churning, Mel felt sick. She lugged her weight up the stairs to her flat. She tucked her bob behind her ears, wiped the sweat from her brow and tried to feel calm, although that seemed like an impossible task. What the hell was she supposed to do now? Days away from giving birth, Leo had revealed something she'd never even contemplated. He had a son already – and not only that, but his ex-girlfriend and son were in town! She burst through the front door, flopped on to the sofa and burst into tears.

'Was it that bad?' Bella asked, throwing an arm around Mel's shoulders and pulling her close. 'What did he say?'

Mel sniffed and sobbed, eventually managing to croak out Leo's news. 'He's got a nine-year-old son!' she said, angrily wiping the tears from her eyes. 'He had a son when he was eighteen with a French girl he met on an exchange trip. He's never told me, so a few weeks ago he decided he needed to find his ex and see his son, before he could have a child with me.'

Bella gasped and put a hand to her mouth.

'The bloody French girl and his son are here, in Brighton,' said Mel, furiously blinking. 'He wants me to meet them!'

There was a creak as the front door was pushed open. Mel and Bella turned around to see Leo standing there, looking pale and exhausted.

'Mel,' he said. 'They came to visit Brighton, that's all. She wanted to meet you, so I thought, now or never. I wanted you to meet my son, too. I wanted to make everything all right before we had our child. I promise that's the truth. I'm not involved with Coco, I swear.'

Mel stood up, gripping her bump. She moved towards him and, just as she did so, a woman wearing sunglasses knocked on the door and walked in, cautiously, behind Leo.

'He's telling the truth,' she said with a French accent. 'I'm so sorry. This must be awful for you, but I came to tell you that Leo has been trying to do the right thing. He wanted to sort things out, and we thought, if we all just met up, you'd know everything and there would be no more secrets.'

Coco floated into the room past Leo and approached Mel. Slowly, she removed her sunglasses.

'Jacques is waiting with the lady downstairs,' she said. 'I have to apologize. We didn't come here to upset you. We came here to meet Leo, after all these years, and to help him tell you the truth. I didn't know until we met in Brighton that he had walked away from you. I must say I was mad with him, as you must be—'

Mel was speechless. When Coco had removed her enormous sunglasses, like a Bond girl, she had revealed that she was more than 'quite pretty'. She was pin-up exquisite, Olive-skinned, with dark, lustrous hair and piercing blue eyes. If

Coco was 'quite pretty', there was no point in the rest of the female population even owning a flannel. For a few moments, nobody said a word.

'Would anyone like a cup of tea?' Bella asked, but Coco shook her head.

'No, thank you,' she said. 'I should go. I have upset you enough, Mel.'

At this point Leo walked across the room and put his arm around Mel's shoulders. She couldn't find any words. She looked from Coco to Leo and found herself picturing the pair as they must have been, all those years ago. Free, wild and innocent, in her mind's eye they were together in swimwear on a beach in the south of France, Coco's hair flowing under a straw sunhat, chasing each other into the waves and knee-high in the foam, clinging together in an embrace. Their world seemed so different to Mel's world now, which was frightening and confusing and out of control. She wondered if she was going to cry, but let out a laugh instead. When was she going to learn to control her emotional urges? Covering her mouth, she turned the laugh into a spluttering cough.

'Leo wrote to me to say he was expecting a child with you,' said Coco, frowning, and finally taking a seat, 'but that he had never told you the truth about Jacques. I have never told Jacques the truth about Leo either and, as things have changed in my life, I felt this was a good time to start being honest with everyone involved. We moved to London a couple of months ago, so that's why we came here.'

Mel stared at Leo. Why hadn't he told her the truth before now? Did he think so little of her, he thought she wouldn't listen and attempt to understand his past?

'Up until this point I have believed it to be better that Jacques doesn't know the truth, but now, I know I am wrong,' Coco continued. 'When he picks up his guitar and his stepfather cannot even sing a single note in tune and insists on rugby practice, though Jacques hates ball games, I can see that Jacques senses that something doesn't click in their relationship. He is so like Leo. I would like to tell him about Leo and about your baby, if you approve.'

Mel let Coco's words sink into her head. So this woman wanted her son to be pals with Mel's unborn baby and, it seemed, Leo.

'I don't understand why you didn't tell me,' she said to Leo, but he just shook his head and shrugged hopelessly.

'I could never find the right time,' he said. 'And I didn't know what I had to tell you, because I didn't know whether I would ever meet Jacques again. I should have done all this ages ago.'

'We are only in London,' said Coco, 'so maybe we could all be friends.' Coco gabbled the last sentence and smiled for the first time since they'd met.

Mel raised her palms. 'Wait a minute,' she said. 'It's one thing to come here and tell me you have a child by my boyfriend when I'm literally about to give birth. It's another to say you want to move in and play happy families.'

Coco shook her head and blew out gently.

'She didn't say they were moving in, Mel,' said Bella, chipping in, with her head cocked to one side and an expression of forced calm on her face that Mel knew well. 'London is a good distance away. I think you're going to have to be really mature about this situation and try to keep yourself calm. It's not great timing, Leo, I have to say.'

'Point taken,' said Leo. 'I completely agree. I've handled this so badly.'

Mel shook her head. More than anything, she wanted to be left alone. She wanted to be left alone to think about Coco and Jacques and Leo, but, before all that, she wanted to be left alone to think about her baby. She felt angry that her baby, about to be born, was being outshone by all this . . . crap! A sudden pain ripped through the bottom of her back, like the baby was kicking her coccyx. She took a sharp intake of breath.

'I don't feel awfully calm,' she said, pulling away from Leo. 'I feel sick.'

'Don't be mad with Leo,' said Coco. 'This is not his fault. I think he was trying to do the right thing. From what I see, he's so excited to have your baby, but he felt guilty—'

'Thank you, Coco,' said Leo, holding up his hand. 'But I can speak for myself. I know you think I'm a shit, Mel, but I'm not. I love you. I'm sorry. Please forgive me for not being honest with you from the start.'

Mel shook her head and sighed, before exhaling. She sat down again on the sofa, feeling utterly confused. She jumped when her phone started to ring and vibrate. She didn't recognize the number, but automatically picked it up.

'What?' snapped Mel, rubbing a finger along her eyebrow.

'It's Alan,' said an exhausted-sounding voice. 'Do you have a moment? I wanted to talk to you about Katy. I'm worried about her.'

Chapter Twenty-five

The phone was ringing. Again! Crikey, thought Lexi, I've traded social work for a job in a call centre. So far that morning, with Poppy in her arms, Lexi had spoken to Rebecca about cracked nipples and Erin had called to tell Lexi she was having problems climbing the stairs, thanks to her stitches. Lexi had listened intently as each woman talked matter-of-factly about their dilating cervixes, contracting uteruses and sore breasts. Lexi had added her own sordid tale of constipation and fibregel to the mix. At least they'd had a good laugh. Funny how quickly she had become close to the other women, sharing intimate details that even Catherine, her best friend, didn't know – and wouldn't want to know. It was as if having a baby put you in a new, private club where each understood the other on a whole different level. It was brilliant, actually, having the other mums. Probably, in normal life, she would have taken one look at each one and decided they weren't her type. But she would have been wrong. All of them – with the possible exception of Katy – were lovely. She'd also had a missed call from Alan, but he'd left a message, reminding

Lexi that she and the others were supposed to be going over to Katy and Alan's house that morning. She listened to his smooth voice rumble on in the message three times before deleting. Well, he had a deeply sexy voice.

'Who is it this time, Poppy?' she said to Poppy, locating the phone under a cushion. She glanced at the number. Uh oh. Mum. She answered the call, knowing that, if she didn't, her mother would spend the remainder of the day trying to hunt her down.

'Mum,' she sighed.

'Why are you ignoring me?' her mother said in a flat voice. 'Why do you never ring me? Are you hoping that I will just *go away*? You're all I've got, Lex, you know that—'

'I do ring you!' Lexi said. 'But I've just had Poppy, and I'm not ringing anyone.'

'That's not true,' her mother said immediately. 'You've been engaged *all* morning.'

'That's other people calling me,' said Lexi. 'My *friends* calling me.'

'Friends?' said her mother. 'You never had any friends at school, because you weren't very sociable. I hope Poppy isn't like that, but I suppose we don't know much about what her personality will be like, do we? I can't get my head around the fact that you don't actually even know the father, that you've not even met him. Don't you think it's the most bizarre way to bring a child into the world? I wish it hadn't come to this Lexi, I really do—'

Lexi stared up at the ceiling, stuck her tongue out as if she were being asphyxiated and put the phone down on the table. What a short memory her mother had! Lexi hardly knew her own father, because, when given an ultimatum to choose between families, he'd rejected Northampton with Lexi and gone with the wife and child in Weymouth. He'd always liked arcade machines. So, what was so different, really? Lexi sighed again. With the tinny, tiny sound of her mother's shrill voice bemoaning the world in the background, she carried Poppy to the other side of the room to look out of the window. Her mother could go on talking for hours, leaking her poisonous negativity into Lexi's ear, Lexi thought, watching a robin hop about in the garden. Gazing at Poppy, though, she felt suddenly guilty, returned to the phone and picked it up. Her mother was still going on.

'—and so I think you should give WeightWatchers some thought, Lexi,' she was saying. 'I've never really known why you didn't do that in the first place. Might have been easier than all this.'

'WeightWatchers?' Lexi said. 'What are you on about?'

'Lexi!' wept her mother. 'Haven't you been listening to a word I've said? For God's sake, I'm going now. I've had enough of this. I can't cope with you—'

And then she was gone, and there was nothing but the dialling tone. Lexi felt her stomach burn with a rush of acid. She rubbed her left eye and sighed. Poppy began to cry.

'Are you hungry again?' asked Lexi, as Poppy started to whimper and she felt the responsive tingling of the 'let down' of milk in her breasts. Pressing her hands to her chest briefly, to stop the milk leaking, she carefully put the tip of her little finger in Poppy's mouth and felt her clamp down with her hard little gums with the force of a staple gun.

'I'll take that as a yes,' she said. It had only been two hours since the last feed, and when had it been before that? Maybe less than two hours. And the night had seemed like one long feeding session, with a few snatched minutes of blank sleep in between. Though she'd tried to keep a record of the times she was feeding Poppy during the night, holding a pen and paper and reading the clock were two ambitions too many. But wasn't Poppy supposed to be feeding less often? What was it that parenting book said? At first, a newborn baby would feed every two and a half to three hours on average. If it was feeding more often than that, the baby was 'snacking', and snacking was apparently not good because the baby would miss out on the richer, creamier, 'hind' milk. The term made Lexi feel like a dairy cow. She sighed and blinked, trying to clear the fog in her head.

'Let's feed you then, Poppy,' she said, unclipping her feeding bra and removing a breast pad, which she discarded on to the floor. She aimed her spraying nipple at Poppy's open mouth, wincing slightly as the staple gun latched on. Moving around a bit, Lexi settled when the now-familiar dragging sensation of Poppy's feeding didn't hurt and actually felt quite relaxing. She laughed a little laugh. The whole thing was such a performance it felt completely bizarre.

'Oh, Poppy,' she said, her eyes flitting about her living room, 'look at this place.'

In the bewildering, exhausting twelve days since Poppy had been born, it was as though a team of burglars had ransacked Lexi's home, turning out every drawer and cupboard, leaving muslins, nappies, breast pads, sleepsuits and rogue baby socks absolutely everywhere. Then there was all the stuff from visitors: well-meaning friends had brought helium balloons, flowers, baby massage cream, a large tin of chocolates and baby shoes, all of which were still scattered on the carpet in amongst the wrapping paper. They'd used every cup and plate in the flat, too, munching on cake as if it were somebody's birthday. Lexi told herself not to care about the chaos. Poppy had been born hungry, and her appetite had rendered Lexi powerless to do anything remotely domestic. Even taking a shower felt as luxurious as having a spa day. Lexi glanced down at Poppy's perfect little elfin face as she sucked, then heard the most awful explosive noise coming from her bottom.

'Uh oh,' said Lexi. 'That didn't sound too good.'

She screwed up her face as she watched bright orange liquid ooze out of the nappy and soak into the white sleepsuit Poppy was wearing. Poppy, seemingly unaware, carried on feeding. Lexi popped her little finger into the side of Poppy's mouth to detach her from her breast. Poppy, unsurprisingly, began to cry.

'Sorry, baby,' she said, 'but I need to change your nappy.'

Dressed in pyjama bottoms and dressing gown, with her feeding bra, which was flapping open *most* attractively, underneath, Lexi quickly found the changing mat, nappies, cotton-wool balls, a cup of clean water and a box of industrially scented nappy sacks. Warnings about babies suffocating on nappy sacks rushed into her head, so she moved the box well out of reach. So far out of reach, in fact, she had to get up to reach one.

'Sshh, shhh, shhh,' she said, like a train, as she unbuttoned Poppy's sleepsuit and surveyed the damage. 'Arrgh, I think we're going to have to give you a bath.'

Carefully putting a new nappy on her daughter and

disposing of the old one, Lexi picked up Poppy and cradled her against her chest. She moved to the sofa to feed again and turned on the TV. Thirsty herself now, since she hadn't had a drink since when – yesterday? – Lexi reached for her glass of water, but realized she had sat a little bit too far away. Sighing, she rested her head against the back of the chair in exasperation, when the doorbell sounded and the phone rang at exactly the same moment. Lexi picked up the phone first, knowing it would be her mother.

'What are you doing all day now you're not at work?' came her mother's accusatory voice. 'I can hear the TV. You were always on at me to turn off the telly. Now you're watching it! Tables turn, don't they? You were so rude earlier I need you to apologize before I can do anything else—'

'Oh, Mum—' said Lexi, wishing she could tell her mother what she really thought of her. 'I wasn't rude . . . I don't know what to say to you when you're in this mood.'

'You could try an apology,' her mother said. 'For being so mean to me.'

Lexi squeezed her eyes shut, utterly exasperated. This was classic Lorna Mason: she'd attack from all sides, with completely opposing points of view from one minute to the next. Trying to have a sensible conversation was hopeless. The doorbell rang again, for longer this time. Lorna began weeping down the phone. Lexi felt her entire body flush.

'That's the door,' she said calmly to her mother. 'Got to go. Don't cry. I'm sorry. Speak soon.'

Putting the phone back down on the carpet, hissing swear words at her mother, the doorbell rang for a third time, and Lexi exhaled.

'Christ!' she said, imagining irrationally that it was the donor at the door. 'Give me a bloody chance!'

Not having the heart to detach Poppy from her feed, she carefully stood up, keeping Poppy on the breast, and staggered slowly towards the door. The TV carried on talking to the empty room behind her.

'Hello?' Lexi called, irritated, to the shadow of person outside the front door. 'Who is it?'

'Lexi,' said Gary, bending down and speaking through the letterbox, 'I've come to pick you up. You rang yesterday and said you wanted a lift this morning, didn't you? To Katy's house? When you didn't open the door straight away, I thought you might be in trouble.'

'Trouble?' she said. 'Of course I'm not in trouble.'

'Well, it's just that I noticed the other night that your smoke alarms are out of batteries,' he said, producing a packet from his pocket and pushing them into the flat. 'I thought I could replace them for you.'

Lexi's mouth fell open, and she nodded numbly. The world had gone completely mad. Or else, she was even more sleep deprived than she thought.

'Thanks,' she said, unlocking the door. 'Hi, Gary. I completely forgot I called you. Sorry. I literally don't know what day it is at the moment.'

'That's fine,' he said quickly. 'The batteries were a crap excuse. I wanted to see you.'

Lexi blushed. It was cold outside compared to the hot fug of Lexi's flat and, at that moment, probably alarmed by the cool air, Poppy broke off Lexi's breast and Lexi's nipple was exposed for Gary and half of Brighton to view. Bar a narrow pavement, Lexi's front door was directly on the roadside and, when a bus drove past, everyone on board was apparently facing in her direction. A driver in the car behind the bus, who had seen it all, honked his horn. Gary turned round to give the driver the finger and swear at the car at the top of his voice.

'Oh my God!' she said, pulling her dressing gown around her with her one available arm and closing her eyes in embarrassment. Opening one eye, she cringed. 'I can't believe this. Gary, stop shouting!'

Poppy started to cry. She wanted to feed again. Lexi lifted her up, supporting her tiny head with her hands.

'Oh, sorry, baby girl,' she said, cuddling her. 'We'll go back inside.'

'Sorry,' he said. 'Did you see those spoilers on that guy's car? Meathead. So, can I come in? I feel like I should be selling chamois leathers standing here like this.'

Lexi shook her head and gestured for Gary to go into the living room, then re-found her position, draped herself with muslin squares to protect her vanity and popped Poppy on the breast. Her phone started to ring again. 'Mum' flashed up as the caller ID.

'I can't stand it,' she said. 'My mum is hounding me. I've spoken to her twice already, and she's being so horrible about the whole sperm-donor thing.'

Gary looked completely blank. His expression made Lexi laugh. The phone stopped ringing. Seconds later, it started again. Lexi moved to pick it up, but Gary got there first. He gave Lexi an imploring look and raised his eyebrows.

'May I?' he said. Lexi shrugged, intrigued. She watched him lift the phone to his ear.

'Good morning,' he said. 'Battersea Dogs Home. Do you have a hound to re-home?'

Lexi burst out laughing and Gary grinned, listening to Lorna's reply.

'No, madam,' said Gary, 'this is Battersea Dogs Home. You must have the wrong number. We have an Airedale by the name of Lexi, but no humans at all.'

He put the phone down and Lexi smiled.

'Airedale?' she said. 'Is that a reflection on my hairstyle? My mum's been a bit crazily angry with me since I decided to have a baby on my own, but then she's happiest when there's something to be upset about. Sometimes I wish I could divorce her, then I feel guilty and wish I could be more patient. She's the one person in my life who has all this power over me. Anyway. How are you, Gary?'

'I think you should tell your mum to back off,' said Gary. 'It's not like you're a kid any more. You're both adults, with your own lives. She's no right to dump all that stuff on your shoulders, especially now. She should be protecting you, with your gorgeous baby girl, not bullying you. She sounds like a witch.'

Lexi widened her eyes and nodded. 'Wow,' she said. 'Don't hold back, Gary.'

He lifted his hands up, as if to ask for mercy. 'Sorry,' he said. 'But that's my view. It seems to me that, right now, you need all the support you can get. So that's why I made these for you.'

Opening up his carrier bag, he pulled out a home-made lasagne and a home-made apple crumble. He held them up in their brown earthenware dishes with a lopsided grin on his face. 'Not exactly cordon bleu,' he said, 'but I thought you probably don't get much time to cook. I'm quite handy in the kitchen, actually.'

He stood there, looking awkward, and Lexi pointed towards the kitchen. Poppy had fallen asleep, so she did up her feeding top and rested her on her chest, gently rubbing her back with small circles.

'That's so sweet of you,' she said. 'The fridge is on the left.' Feeling touched, she heard him open it. A few moments later, he closed it.

'Are you even eating?' he asked, poking his head back in the living room. 'There's a head of celery and a jar of jam in that fridge. Let me get you some shopping in. You can write a list and I'll bring it over for you, or when I drop you off at your friend's house, I'll get it for you then. How does that sound? You must be knackered.'

Lexi didn't say anything. She *was* knackered – completely, utterly, mind-numbingly shattered – and hungry for some-thing that wasn't toast, cake or takeaway. She had *tried* to stay in bed, as Ginny had recommended, but it was almost impos-sible. The visitors had come thick and fast, and Poppy was awake every ninety minutes. Less even. She refused to start complaining, though. Having Poppy was a miracle. She could cope with the tiredness.

'I *am* tired,' she said, appalled to find herself welling up. 'But that's all. God, I don't know what this is all about.'

Gary came and sat on the sofa next to her. He held out his arms, offering to take Poppy. 'Can I hold her, while you have a shower? I'll call you if she wakes up.'

'Thanks. Since having Poppy I haven't been able to do anything at all. I can't even seem to be able to go to the toilet without waking her or—'

'Go on!' Gary said again. 'Have a shower.'

Lexi hardly dared breathe in the shower she was so preoccupied with listening out for Poppy's cry. But there was nothing, just the occasional reassuring comment from Gary: 'She's opened her eyes! . . . She's closed them again! . . . She's moved her left arm! . . . She's looking at her hand!' Towelling herself down, she noticed one of Poppy's socks in the corner of the bathroom and, at the same time, heard her gurgling in the living room. She looked at her reflection and felt an enormous sense of pride. Finally, after years of thinking about having a baby, she'd got Poppy, the daughter she'd dreamed of. But there was a slight niggle in her head. Maybe, if she'd pushed for Alan, she would now 'have it all'. Quickly getting dressed in the bedroom in a grey woollen maternity dress from Gap, she dismissed her thoughts as ludicrous and a result of hormonal imbalance. She towel-dried her hair and moved through to the living room to Gary and Poppy, who was now back in her Moses basket.

'Doesn't she look like you?' he said, and Lexi impulsively wanted to hug him. In truth, she thought Poppy looked a lot like the sperm donor. Reading the extended profiles and looking at pictures of possible donors, Lexi had expected to feel some kind of connection with one of them, but she hadn't. Just as in life, she hadn't found 'The One' on a website. So, she'd chosen someone who had similar colouring to her – blond hair, pale skin, blue-grey eyes – and who had a high IQ. Now Poppy was here, Lexi felt no connection with the donor at all. It was as though Poppy belonged entirely to her, but still, she could see the donor in Poppy's features, which, she had to be honest, took her by surprise from time to time.

'Yes,' Lexi said. 'I hope so.'

'If I was a woman,' said Gary suddenly. 'I would have done the same thing as you. I'd like a baby of my own, but it's a bit difficult when you haven't got a womb.'

Lexi was surprised. She hadn't bothered to think about it from the single male's point of view. Her heart softened to Gary once again.

'There's still time for you, isn't there?' said Lexi. 'You could meet the girl of your dreams this week and have a family with her.'

Gary pulled on his jacket and pushed his hands in the pockets.

'Yeah,' said Gary, his face falling. 'You're right.'

Lexi suddenly remembered what he'd said on the night of Poppy's birth, about having a crush on her. She felt embarrassed. As though she should set him straight. But she'd already done that, hadn't she? He knew she had too many other things going on. Besides, Gary was kind of nice to have around. No other man she'd ever met had made her lasagne or apple crumble. Alan's mushroom omelette was looking decidedly paltry in comparison. And no other man had dared take on Lorna on her behalf.

'Maybe I could set you up with someone at work?' she said, trying to be helpful but immediately regretting her words. Why would she want someone at work to have Gary?

'Ah, no, I'm not interested,' he said curtly.

Then, visibly rallying, he said in a theatrical voice, 'My heart is stone, Lexi. My heart is stone.'

With a laugh, he picked up her bags for her while she put Poppy in the car seat and opened the front door, switching off the lights behind her.

'So,' Gary said, opening the car door for her, 'where are we going?'

'That's a big question,' she said, smiling.

'It is,' he said. 'But you seem like a woman who knows the answers. A woman who knows where she's going and what she wants from life.'

He grinned at Lexi and her face broke into a wide smile. She couldn't remember being given a better compliment.

Chapter Twenty-six

Upstairs in the master bedroom, Katy sat at the bay window, looking out over the street and holding her knees. She was wearing her work clothes: a black wraparound dress, black tights and a cardigan appliquéd with a sequinned heart. She'd been up since dawn, when she'd woken from a nightmare damp with sweat. From downstairs, she could hear the sound of Rufus crying and Alan singing a lullaby – something about the sunshine – to him, and pacing up and down the kitchen in his clip-clop designer shoes. A smell of coffee and toast drifted up the stairs, Alan's attempt to lure her down. Katy knew Rufus was crying for her – specifically, for her breast milk – but she didn't want to move, wasn't able to move, from her spot. Not that she was content where she was. Watching her neighbour opposite leaving for work, holding her briefcase in one hand, her mobile phone in the other, Katy felt a pang of jealousy. She wished she could get up and go to work, be the successful person she was *before*. Since Rufus had been born, Katy could think only about those three words she'd heard the doctor say in hushed tones: *Failure to progress*. And she felt the same condemnation applied to her now. She was failing to progress. She couldn't breastfeed properly without it hurting so much she was reduced to tears, and without Rufus fussing. She couldn't get him to stop crying or to fall asleep. She couldn't change his nappy without him screaming until he was red in the face. She couldn't hold him without thinking she was going to drop him. She couldn't even get the fiddly sleepsuits buttoned up properly. Nor could she walk up and down the stairs without pain from her C-section scar reminding her that now she was an invalid – unable to drive, unable to exercise. In other words, she was what the doctor had said: a failure.

'There you are,' said Alan from the doorway, holding a quiet Rufus against his chest. 'I think Rufus is hungry. Do you want me to try him with a bottle?'

His tone was gentle, hesitant, and Katy knew he didn't know how to handle her mood. But she couldn't reassure him with a breezy apology. *She* didn't know how to handle her mood. It was as if a giant bird had grabbed her by the shoulders with its claws and carried her away to a distant, dark land where she recognized nothing and nobody. Katy didn't turn around but kept watching the people outside moving quickly in the morning rush.

'Yeah,' she said, 'I think that would be a good idea. I'm not getting on too well with the breastfeeding, am I? I don't think he likes me.'

Alan moved across the room and sat down next to her at the bay window. He had one hand on Rufus's back and neck to support him, but with the other, he found Katy's hand and grasped it tight. She turned her head towards him, her eyes downcast.

'Of course he likes you,' he said passionately. 'He loves and adores you. You're his mother! There's nobody more important to him than you. Surely you know that? When he was crying out in the night, he would only stop when you went to him. What does that tell you?'

Katy thought about the night and the sense of dread she felt when the lamp went out. Though she was desperately tired, she was always aware that, very soon, she'd have to be awake again, trying to breastfeed without crying out in pain. Yes, Rufus was quiet when she picked him up, but that thought didn't help Katy. Instead, it made her even more aware of her responsibility. She knew what Alan was doing, trying to rouse her by showing her that Rufus had expectations of her that she must meet. He was using managerial tactics. She nodded, to placate him, but felt peculiarly numb. Alan looked worried. He had never known her to be like this, but then she had never known herself to be like this. All she knew was that she couldn't look after Rufus. She wasn't up to the job. She was much better off at work, talking to clients and promoting the company.

'Remember that your friends are coming over this morning?' he said. 'Erin, Mel, Lexi and Rebecca? Then the health visitor is coming again this afternoon.'

Katy thought about the health visitor, a frumpy woman who thought she was being helpful by showing Katy a questionnaire about postnatal depression. 'Do you find yourself crying all the time?' was one of the questions. Who on earth, Katy had wondered, would tell the truth? It was a hell of a lot easier to lie and tick 'No', to let the issue be forgotten.

'Why are you talking to me as if I'm a child?' Katy said to

Alan, feeling suddenly irritated. 'You're treating me like I've had a lobotomy since Rufus was born.'

Alan was aghast. Katy never spoke to him like that. His jaw set.

'I'm not,' he said calmly. 'I'm reminding you that you have appointments because, Katy, you seem so spaced out. Don't you want to hold your son?'

Katy heard desperation in his voice. She sighed and put her head in her hands.

'You're doing a fine job without me,' she said. 'Just give me a few minutes and I'll be down to feed him. I'll try one more time and, if it doesn't work, then we'll do the bottle.'

When Alan left the room, Katy lay down on the bed and put her hands over her face. She heard Rufus begin crying again downstairs and Alan's voice calling her name. He sounded cross. Closing her eyes tight, she refused to let herself cry. Gathering all the strength she had left in her body, she left the bedroom and walked down the stairs. In her mind, as she took Rufus in her arms and walked to the chair she used for feeding him, she heard only one word repeating itself, like a heartbeat: failure, failure, failure.

'Here goes,' she said as happily as she could, as she tried to push her breast in the direction of Rufus's mouth. Her voice sounded unreal to her own ears. He couldn't latch on because her breasts were so solid and painful with milk. After ten minutes of trying, he was clammy and over-hungry. Tears were rolling down Katy's cheeks, and Alan took control.

'Let me take him,' he said, taking Rufus. 'I'm going to try him on a bottle. I've made one up for him.'

Thank God.

'Thank you,' Katy said, as she wiped her eyes and moved out of the chair. She took a seat at the dining-room table and watched Rufus take the bottle immediately. She'd read that babies usually rejected the bottle after the breast – not so with her boy. He was obviously ravenous. Katy gulped.

'Katy,' said Alan, fixing her with a stare while he held the bottle to Rufus's mouth. 'Are you okay? Because, if you're not, you can tell me.'

Katy looked at Alan. He was the perfect husband. Charming, optimistic, supportive, now he was feeding Rufus like a natural. He was a better dad than she would ever be a good mother. How could she tell him the truth? How could she tell him she couldn't sleep because when she closed her eyes she relived the horrible birth? How could she tell him that when she looked at Rufus and held him she didn't feel any over-whelming love? How could she tell him that she thought Rufus may have been a big mistake? That when Alan left the house, even to go to the shops, she stood at the window waiting for him to return, terrified that she wouldn't be able to look after Rufus on her own.

'I'll be all right,' she forced herself to say. 'I think I probably need to go back to work sooner rather than later. I'm sure Anita could do with the help.'

Alan tried to conceal his shock.

'But you've been so excited about your maternity leave,' he said. 'You've agreed to having three months off with Anita, and that's how long you should take. You're not thinking of going back before then, are you? He's days old, sweetheart.'

'I thought I could go into the office this afternoon,' she said numbly. 'I'll make a few calls and then come home. How does that sound?'

Katy knew that she sounded crazy and that Alan was furious, but she needed normality, she needed to feel back to her old self. In one part of her brain, she knew what she was saying was irrational, but, in another part, it made perfect sense. Alan was much better at looking after Rufus. She was much better at being at work. Yes, it was early days. But what did it matter?

'It sounds like a terrible idea,' he said steadily. 'I know this is hard, Katy, especially the breastfeeding, but you're going to be a brilliant mum. You already are. You carried Rufus around for nine months and looked after yourself better than anyone. Maybe seeing your friends will make you feel more relaxed.'

He glanced at his wristwatch.

'They'll be here in ten minutes,' he said. 'Why don't you put some music on and make some fresh coffee? I'll change Rufus and put him down after this feed. It's all going to be good, I promise you. These early days are bound to be strange, especially after your C-section. That's a major op.'

Katy nodded, lifted herself out of her chair and walked into the kitchen. She filled the kettle with water, turned it on and opened the fridge to find the fresh coffee. Seeing the formula scoop on the side and the packaging from the bottle Alan was using, she held her breath. She felt her entire body heat up and prickle with panic. Rushing through to the room where Alan was feeding Rufus, she snatched the bottle away from his lips. Rufus screamed at the top of his lungs. Alan's mouth fell open.

'You didn't sterilize it!' she cried. 'You forgot to sterilize the bottle! He'll get ill! He'll die!'

Alan stood up and laid Rufus down in his Moses basket, where he lay crying, arms flailing, wanting the rest of his feed. He took the bottle from Katy's hands and rested it on the table then took Katy in his arms and held her tight.

'I did sterilize it,' he said, while she cried into his chest. 'Of course I did. Oh, Katy, don't worry. Of course I did.'

'Sorry,' she sobbed, clutching at his jumper, squeezing her eyes closed. 'I'm so sorry.'

Erin was the happiest woman in the world. It had been only twelve days since Hope had been born, but she was a perfect baby. Cute as could be, she fed like a dream and slept in between her feeds like a dream. In fact, everything was so dream-like Erin had to pinch herself to make sure she *wasn't* dreaming. Though she couldn't walk too fast or lift very much, her scar was healing well, and she'd made the short journey to Katy's house feeling as if she were presenting a rare, precious jewel to the world. It was difficult, when passing strangers, not to ask them to stop and look inside the pram so they could appreciate how precious and beautiful Hope really was. Passing blossoming trees and gardens bursting with daffodils, she hummed in pleasure as she felt the spring sunshine on her face. Standing still for a second to pause for a rest, she closed her eyes and tipped her chin up to the sun. It was warm. Blissfully warm. She opened her eyes. Was Hope too warm? This was the first time she'd taken her out for more than a walk round the garden, and she thought maybe she'd underestimated the strength of the sun and dressed her in too many clothes. Feeling the warmth of Hope's skin by placing a fingertip underneath her top, she checked that she wasn't clammy in her pale pink matinee jacket and hat.

'I think you're fine, aren't you, Hope?' she said, smiling at her, letting her red hair tickle Hope's hands. 'Shall we go and see Rufus?'

Erin hadn't spoken to Katy since the day she had visited her in hospital, but that morning Alan had phoned to make sure she was still coming over. He'd sounded tired. But that was normal for new dads. Poor, bemused things. All this was hard on them, too. On the one night that Hope hadn't slept at all, Edward had stayed up an entire night, tuning the radio so it emitted a soothing white noise to help her fall asleep. Darling Edward. He had been a brick during the labour and, since Hope had been home, he had devoted himself to her one hundred per cent. The two of them couldn't take their eyes off Hope and, though they knew she should be put in her basket occasionally, most of the time they carried her in their arms or let her sleep on their chests, just to be close. It was the most perfect bubble of love. Of course, Erin had thought about Josiah a lot, wondering how he would have reacted to his baby sister and whether the two of them shared any features, but though she had compared photographs of them just born, the sight of Josiah had rocked her and she didn't want Hope to begin her days with shadows of grief falling over her, so Erin had done her best to think only of Hope.

'Here we are,' she said, opening Katy's wrought-iron gate, which squeaked as she pushed it. 'Let's go and introduce you.'

Dressed in a yellow-and-white spotted dress that fitted over her still-swollen tummy, Erin straightened up and put a smile on her face. Ringing the doorbell, she felt elated. Here she was, having tea with another new mother. This was the start of the next phase in her life, which she had been looking forward to for years. She felt none of the cynicism about staying at home with her baby that other women she knew felt, and who complained bitterly about the glittery lives they'd sacrificed to care for their babies. No, this wasn't sacrifice, this was brilliant. Absolutely the best thing to happen.

'Hello,' she said, as the door was opened by a tear-streaked Katy dressed in black work clothes, paler than Erin had ever seen her.

'Sorry, I'm, I'm—' began Katy. 'I'm—'

Erin recognized a sadness in Katy and it struck a chord in her heart. She felt a compulsion to hug her and tell her that everything would be all right. Alan walked to the door behind Katy, carrying Rufus in his arms. He wore a smile on his face, but he looked strained. Erin's feeling of joy faded and her mood sobered. She bit her lip, feeling sorry for them both.

'Is this a bad time?' she said softly. 'Or shall we come in?'

Chapter Twenty-seven

'I think Lenny is shell-shocked,' laughed Rebecca to the group sitting in Katy's sleek, minimalist living room. 'On the first night, Elvis wouldn't stop crying and Lenny started pacing like a tiger around the flat complaining that the baby was going to ruin our lives. I was sitting there in bed, with Elvis in my arms crying and Lenny with his head in his hands, thinking, Shit! Help me, someone! What do I do now? I mean, everyone assumes that, just because you're female, you'll automatically know what to do, but I felt clueless. I still do. I worry I'm going to drop him or something and, every time I change him, he screams so loud I can't get him to stop!'

Lexi and Erin nodded to show that they understood. Erin had propped Hope up on a moleskin cushion and was dangling a silk scarf gently over her, occasionally brushing it against her cheek, then smiling encouragingly. Lexi was feeding Poppy, and Rebecca was hoping Elvis would stay asleep for a while. Mel, still pregnant, looked a little terrified.

'Apparently, it helps if you tell the baby what you're going to do,' said Erin, not looking away from Hope. 'Like, if you're going to get him changed, you explain what you're going to do. I don't know whether there's truth in that, but I guess it's a logical approach.'

'Yeah, I've been doing that, too,' said Rebecca. 'But it feels bizarre talking into the empty room like that. All Elvis does is sleep and eat and cry and poo, and there's me telling him about the record Lenny has put on, or what I'd love to eat – if I had the time or energy to cook anything, which I don't. It's a strange thing talking to someone who doesn't talk back, but I'm trying to get used to it.'

Conversation was stilted and the atmosphere tense, because Katy hadn't said a word, nor was she even acknowledging their presence in her living room. She simply sat on the thick cream carpet with Rufus in front of her, quietly blinking in his designer bouncer chair, which was on the 'vibrate' setting to lull him to sleep. Rebecca scanned the walls, looking at various black-and-white pictures of Katy and Alan on holiday. They made a dynamic duo on skis in snow, on board a yacht in the ocean, in a Land Rover on an animal safari. Her beaming, gleaming self in the photographs couldn't be more different to how she seemed now. No one said anything for a moment, concentrating on the babies instead. A bus rumbled past, and Rebecca wished she was on it.

'It takes me ages to change Poppy's nappy,' said Lexi, breaking the silence. 'Locating the changing mat, filling up a bowl of warm water, finding the cotton-wool balls and then gingerly opening the thing to find that unbelievable explosion of mustard seeds inside! My advice to you all is: don't have curry. I had one the night before last and have regretted it ever since. Although, for you, Mel, a curry might help get things started.'

The women groaned, grateful to laugh. Katy sighed and wiped at the tiny beads of sweat which, Rebecca had noticed, had formed on her top lip.

'I've tried curry,' Mel said, shrugging. 'Nothing happened, obviously. Maybe I'll have to drink a litre of castor oil.'

'Nice,' said Lexi. 'That'll do you good!'

Mel and Lexi shared smiles but then lapsed into silence again, their eyes flicking to Katy, who wasn't reacting or responding to any of the conversation. Rebecca checked her watch. She'd been there for fifteen minutes. In another ten, she'd make an excuse and go.

'Are you using disposable nappies?' said Erin, clearly trying to help the conversation flow. 'Because I am, even though I said I'd try real ones. I must have got through a hundred already.'

Elvis started to wake up, so Rebecca lifted him up on to her chest and patted his back while he snuffled into her. His trousers were much too big for him and came up to just under his armpits.

'I'm using real nappies,' said Rebecca. 'And I'm not convinced they're so much better for the environment. The number of washes I have to do in a day and the amount of detergent I use that gets flushed down the drains is probably just as bad as a sackful of disposable nappies. Still, I'm going to stick with it, as it's a lot cheaper and the landfill is reduced. How about you, Katy?'

It was the first time any of them had addressed Katy directly, and there was a sudden hush in the room as they waited for her to answer. She smiled a watery smile and answered in a bored, quiet voice.

'Disposables,' she said. 'Pampers.'

The room fell silent, except for the snuffling sounds of the babies and everyone shared concerned glances, once again.

'How's your buggy, Katy?' said Lexi, smiling at her. 'Don't you have a Bugaboo? I was thinking of using my sling until the baby gets a bit bigger, then I've got a Maclaren my friend gave me, but it's a bit knackered. I might splash out on a new one. Are Bugaboos as cool as they look?'

Katy sighed and rubbed her eyes with her palms. Rufus started to cry. She didn't pick him up but turned up the vibration setting on the bouncer chair. Rebecca started to feel impatient with her. Why had she invited them all over, if she didn't want them there?

'You'll have to ask Alan about that,' she said. 'I haven't been able to go out yet with my scar. The doctor told me it's the same injury as having a car crash. That's exactly how I feel, like I've been in a car crash.'

'Oh dear,' said Erin. 'I don't feel like that after my caesarean, but I know it was different for you—'

'Yes,' snapped Katy. 'It bloody well was.'

Everyone held their breath. Lexi pulled her lips back in an apologetic smile, apparently regretting that she'd asked the question.

'Sorry,' Lexi said. 'It can't be easy for you. How long before you're back to normal?'

'Six weeks,' said Katy automatically. 'So that's another three or four weeks.'

'It's six weeks until you can resume all your normal activities, like exercise classes and more strenuous things,' said

Erin. 'But look at us, Katy, we're already doing most things just fine, aren't we? I don't feel too bad at all. I was up and about after three days.'

'Well, I'm not waiting any longer anyway,' said Katy.

For what? Rebecca had the thought but dared not ask. She and Mel were eyeballing one another. Rebecca pulled an exasperated face and Mel widened her eyes.

'It's six weeks for everything, isn't it?' Mel said. 'Six weeks for a C-section scar to heal. Six weeks before you can have sex again.'

Rebecca didn't say that Lenny had already requested sex but had been firmly sent away with his tail between his legs, which he hadn't liked at all. But, honestly, what did he expect? She was exhausted beyond belief and still nowhere near back to normal down below. One day, she'd told him, generously. But not yet.

'Six weeks seems far too soon,' said Mel. 'Anyway, I don't think I'm going to have sex *ever* again, now or after the baby is born. Leo has set it upon himself to bang big nails into that particular coffin.'

Her eyes filled with tears, but she blinked them away, rubbing her pregnant bump rhythmically. Rebecca made a mental note to go over to Mel's flat on her own, to cheer her up.

'You won't believe what's happened,' she continued. 'I found out a couple of days ago, and I'm still in shock. I don't know how to feel about it, I'm just sort of numb.'

All eyes were on Mel.

'Why?' Rebecca asked. 'What has Leo done?'

Rebecca listened open-mouthed as Mel told her about Leo's child with Coco and about her coming to the flat.

'Wow,' said Rebecca, shaking her head. 'You must feel *so* pissed off.'

Mel looked at her as if to say, *That's an understatement.* Rebecca smiled apologetically.

'I think,' finished Mel, smiling, 'that, after hearing all that, my baby doesn't want to come out of the womb, where it's all warm and safe. I don't blame it.'

'Jesus!' said Lexi. 'That's a massive thing to have to deal with right now. You must be furious with Leo for not telling you sooner.'

'Sure am,' said Mel, shifting uncomfortably. 'I'm fucking crazy mad with him. I didn't want him to be a cliché, but looks like he is. Anyway, enough about me. I'm trying to be as cold as I can about it so I don't get stressed out and upset the baby. Rebecca, did you speak to your mum?'

Rebecca nodded. She thought back to the conversation. Her mother had gone from being shocked and clipped about the baby to suddenly being really emotional and actually crying down the phone, begging to visit. Rebecca had been blown away.

'She wants to meet Lenny and Elvis,' Rebecca said. 'I'm not sure what to expect. It'll probably be a nightmare. I haven't actually told her that I've called the baby Elvis yet. She'll think I'm insane. Do you think we are?'

The women didn't reply for a long moment, which made Rebecca laugh.

'Yes, then,' she laughed, lifting up Elvis for a feed. 'Poor little man! Everyone's going to laugh at you!'

Katy stood up and, without saying where she was going, abruptly left the room, leaving Rufus on his chair, moving his limbs like a crab on his back. Rebecca, Mel and Lexi shared a worried look, and Lexi shrugged, moving closer to Rufus, who began to cry.

'What's wrong with Katy?' Mel asked in a low voice. 'Has she spoken to any of you?'

Before anyone answered, from the kitchen came a loud bang, like a cup being slammed down on the table. The women exchanged concerned glances, hearing Katy and Alan talking urgently. Alan raised his voice. Though the words were indecipherable, he was definitely angry. Rebecca and the others started to pack up their changing bags and gather together their things. Rufus began to grizzle, and Lexi gave the now sleeping Poppy to Mel, so she could pick him up. She stood up and bobbed him up and down by bending and straightening her legs. Not wanting Katy and Alan to think they were listening, Rebecca started to chat.

'Do you think you can forgive Leo, Mel?' she asked quietly. 'For the sake of the baby?'

All of the women were watching Lexi trying to calm Rufus down. He began crying more loudly.

'I'm not sure,' said Mel. 'There's too much going on to work out how I really feel. I'm just so angry with him. His timing has been awful. You know, I would have been completely understanding about him having a son if he'd just told me at the beginning of our relationship. But to leave it until now and bring the bloody child and his mother to our flat, it's just stupidity—'

Mel's words trailed off, as she heard the front door slam shut.

'Do you think we should go now?' she asked the others.

Amy Bratley

Just then, Alan appeared at the door to the living room, sweeping his hair back with one hand, his expression bleak. It looked as if he were deciding whether or not to collapse. He moved towards Lexi, holding out his arms to take Rufus, who emitted a small posset of sick on to his navy jumper and then stopped crying. Alan looked completely defeated. Lexi, reaching for a pack of wipes, cleaned it away . He smiled gratefully, and Lexi blushed.

'Katy's had to pop out,' he said with a sad smile. 'I'm sorry.'

Outside, Katy passed determinedly by the bay window, looking straight ahead. Rebecca caught Mel's eye, and they both nodded at Alan, as if they understood.

'We should go,' said Lexi, clipping Poppy into her sling and collecting together her bag.

'How is Katy feeling?' asked Erin, but Alan didn't immediately answer. He looked dismayed, all out of energy, and sat down on the sofa, leaning back into the moleskin cushions.

'I don't know,' he said. 'I really don't know.'

'Do you know where she's gone?' asked Mel.

He opened his eyes and looked at her. 'She says she's going to the office,' he said, shaking his head in disbelief, 'but she needs to be here, with Rufus. It's like she's gone into this state of denial that she's actually had a baby at all. It's so unlike Katy. She's the most capable person I know, and she was so looking forward to having a baby.'

'Do you think it was the shock of the birth?' Rebecca asked. 'It must have been pretty stressful when the heartbeat almost stopped. Awful! Or the baby blues? I know I've had them. Three days after Elvis was born, I cried all day.'

'It *was* stressful,' said Alan. 'But the baby's here now, and

262

the birth is over. I don't understand *what* she feels. She doesn't cry. When I bring it up, she says that she wants to get back to normal.'

'Perhaps she needs to sleep,' said Lexi. 'She's probably not getting much. I know what sleep deprivation can do to your mind.'

Rebecca watched Alan and Lexi exchange some kind of meaningful look and wondered if Lexi knew something about Katy that the rest of them didn't.

'She's getting sleep,' Alan said. 'I'm taking Rufus most of the time, so she can sleep. You, Lexi, on the other hand, you're doing this all alone, which is amazing.'

'Yes,' said Rebecca, agreeing with Alan. 'You are amazing, Lexi.'

But Lexi shrugged off the compliment. 'Don't say that to Katy, for God's sake,' she said. 'And I'm not amazing. It's probably easier for me in some ways. I don't have the added stress of a partner. No offence, Alan! But I can just get on with it – *have* to just get on with it. I'm sure Katy will improve in a few days. Sometimes the baby blues can last a bit longer. Just go easy on her, and if you want some company to go for a walk with the baby and give Katy some time alone to have a bath or sleep or whatever, give me a call. We could meet on the seafront.'

'Yes,' said Rebecca, not knowing whether she was invited. 'Good idea. Let's meet the same time next week on the seafront. We should do a baby-massage class as well. There's one at the centre I work at which is really great. Cheap, too. Plus, I need to talk to you all about this wedding on a shoestring I'm supposed to be arranging. Lenny still wants to have it at the end of summer, which gives me a few months to slim down again. I thought, after the baby came out, I'd deflate.'

'No such luck,' said Lexi, pointing to her own body. 'Apparently, breastfeeding helps, though.'

By now, the women were all packed up, feeling awkward and ready to leave. Alan was just standing, wearily, to show them to the door when they heard the front door open and bang shut, followed by the sound of footsteps climbing the stairs to the bedroom. Alan sighed.

'Do you want me to go and see her?' asked Lexi, but he shook his head.

'I'll talk to her,' he said gently. 'You go. Thanks for coming over. Sorry it was a little . . . strained.'

The women and babies were all ushered out of the house, and let out a collective sigh of relief as soon as the front door closed behind them. They all looked at one another, bemused.

'That was awful,' said Lexi, voicing everyone's exact thought. 'I think Katy needs some help. We'll have to do something, but I'm not sure what.'

'We just need to be there for her,' said Erin. 'Even if she doesn't seem to want us, she needs to know we're here.'

Chapter Twenty-eight

Mel hadn't meant to break Leo's fingers. But, seven centimetres dilated and in the labour ward on the bed on all fours, sucking the life out of the gas and air canister, Bella calling out instructions on panting techniques – and demonstrating them – Mel decided enough was enough. She told Bella to 'for God's sake, shut up' and decided that Leo should be there to witness this incredible, indescribable agony first hand.

'Where the hell is Leo?' she'd roared at the midwives, and Bella, who calmly responded by telling her that, previously, she hadn't wanted to see Leo until after the birth.

'Fuck that,' she said, suddenly furious with the entire world, but especially with Bella. 'If he's with Coco, I'll kill him! Get him here now!'

When Leo eventually skidded into the room, his Adidas pumps squeaking on the vinyl flooring, breathless and pale, carrying a ridiculous, wilted bunch of yellow flowers bought from the hospital shop, she was relieved, but growled at him and gripped hold of his fingers. As each contraction came, she couldn't believe how unbelievably painful it was. She'd had a shot of pethidine early on, but that had long since worn off. She had never before imagined such pain, and wondered why on earth, in a world where you could practically fly to the moon on a weekend break, women were still going through this white-hot pain in order to reproduce.

'Are you okay?' asked Leo, clearly and loudly, as if speaking to someone who couldn't understand his language. 'Do you need an epidural?'

'Too late, I'm afraid,' said the midwife. Mel sucked even harder on the gas and air. It barely touched the sides.

While Leo looked sheepish, Bella told her to push and the midwives cheered from the sidelines, from somewhere deep inside Mel there came a realization that it was her, and her alone, who had to endure the pain and get her baby out of her body. She felt herself mentally curl up into an intensely personal place and cope as best she could. At every contraction, she squeezed Leo's fingers with the strength of Atlas. He let out a strange, strangled sob, but made no other complaint, gritting his teeth and beaming at Mel in encouragement, even when she shouted obscenities at him for getting her pregnant and generally being an absolute arsehole. It was only afterwards, when baby Mabel had been born and Leo and Mel had burst into tears in a rush of love and emotion and hugged one another, Mel rashly forgiving him everything, apologizing for shouting at him, apologizing to the midwives for being rude, instantly forgetting the pain, that he showed her his swollen index finger.

'I think it's broken,' he said, trying to wiggle it. 'I can't move it.'

Nobody seemed to care, really. Mel did feel terrible, but

not so bad she could tear her eyes away from Mabel for longer than a couple of seconds. Mabel looked like a delicate, tiny version of Leo. She had a shock of dark hair, gorgeous lips and a small, pointed chin that made Mel think of a forest imp. She felt and smelled like a warm loaf, straight out of the oven. On her wrist she had on the identity band which the midwife had immediately put on her, with 'Baby Holden' and the date written on it.

'This is the happiest day of my life,' said Bella from the side of the room. Mel had almost forgotten she was there. Mascara was running in rivulets down her lined face. 'Your father would have been so proud.'

Mel beckoned for her mum to come over, and they hugged, three generations of females together.

'Please forgive me,' said Leo, as Mel was wheeled under bright lights to the ward with Mabel in her arms, wrapped in a blanket and wearing a little hat, 'for everything wrong I have done. I want to be a good father and partner. I want to get it right with you, Mel. Please forgive me. Let me back. I want to get it right. I love you.'

Mel didn't know how she was going to feel later – the last few days, she had been so angry with Leo she hadn't wanted to see him – but, right now, streaking along the hospital corridor in a wheelchair, dressed in a none too fetching hospital gown and not much else, clutching her new baby, more relieved than she'd ever known it was possible to be, she wanted Leo with her. Bella followed on behind, carrying pillows, bags and the wilting flowers, wearing a beatific smile. What was the point in blighting Mabel's first moments with negative emotions about Leo's past? Now, Mel thought, as she settled in to the

Amy Bratley

ward bed and breathed in the warm bakery smell of Mabel's newly born skin, the whole issue seemed far less important. The four of them together huddled behind the blue-and-grey checked hospital curtain was what mattered, whatever the hurdles they had to leap over in life. This was the beginning of their new life as a family. Who said it should be easy? Family life wasn't meant to be easy. Mel concentrated on committing these first few moments in the hot hospital ward, the faint sounds of women chattering in the ward all around her, her knot of family looped around the bed, to her memory. Her baby had been born healthy. Seven pounds seven ounces. She'd scored top marks in the APGAR assessment. Everything was good. Those who loved her and Mabel were there. Mel was ecstatically happy. She channelled positive feelings into her baby, visualizing the tiny girl's future filled with love and achievement and sunshine and fun. Mabel began to cry. Mel stared at her, confused. Why was she crying? Everything was great, wasn't it?

'You need to feed your baby,' said a stern midwife, suddenly sweeping back the curtain and leaving a bundle of menus on the bed. 'Before she dehydrates.'

When Mrs Lelani and Rebecca visited later, Leo held his bandaged broken finger up in the air for the women to inspect.

'I can't get over that,' Mrs Lelani croaked when she'd finished creasing up at the sight of Leo's finger. 'I've never known anyone to break their partner's finger during labour. That's hysterical.'

Leo managed a smile, but obviously wasn't sharing Mrs Lelani's hysteria. Mel smiled. Anyone could say anything, and still she would smile. In her overtired, floaty, relieved, exhausted mind-set, she couldn't have been more serene – apart from the feeding. That hurt like mad. It was only after five minutes of pain that she could cope with it, then her head and heart seemed to fill with stars and feathers and flowers.

'Are you taking any medication?' asked Mrs Lelani, concerned. 'You seem a little spaced out.'

'No wonder,' said Bella, protectively. 'She's only just given birth. Can't you remember what that feels like?'

'Not really,' Mrs Lelani said. 'It was about one hundred years ago when I gave birth. I think I blocked it out the moment I'd done it. So, you're fine then, are you, lovey? What a gorgeous baby you have.'

Mel nodded and beamed. Leo sat on a low armchair, his head level with hers. Occasionally, because Mel's arms were holding Mabel up as she fed, he swept her hair out of her eyes when it fell. It wasn't altogether necessary, but Mel was happy he felt needed.

'So, I bought you green-cabbage leaves,' said Mrs Lelani, pulling out the head-shaped leaves from her carrier bag and laying them on the bottom of the bed. 'Put them in your bra in between feeds and they'll keep your bosoms cool.'

'That's right,' said Bella, putting a bunch of Sweet Williams Rebecca had brought into a vase. 'They do actually work.'

'I tried them,' said Rebecca, who was sitting at the foot of the bed smiling. 'And I can vouch for them, too.'

Mel asked Leo to pop another chocolate into her mouth. She smiled at her visitors, her mouth full of chocolate while Leo then poured everyone a glass of champagne and handed them around, again pleased that he had a job. He held his glass in the air.

'I'd like to raise a toast,' he said. 'To my wonderful Mel and my beautiful new daughter, who I already love so much it hurts. I promise to love you and look after you both. And I'm sorry, Mel, for everything I've put you through.'

His eyes filled with tears, which made everyone else well up. He kissed Mel. Tears rolled down Mel's cheeks, and Bella wiped them away with a tissue. Everyone sat smiling at one another.

'I feel like the Queen of Sheba,' Mel said. 'Or some kind of empress. I just seem to sit here, and lovely people in smocks bring me food, then my lovely friends bring me gifts.'

'And cabbage leaves,' said Mrs Lelani. 'Don't forget those.'

'Yes,' said Mel. 'And cabbage leaves. Actually, Ginny did mention them.'

'I've no idea who Ginny is,' said Mrs Lelani. 'But I like the sound of her.'

Half an hour later, with Mabel asleep in the hospital cot, her head turned at a weirdly sharp ninety-degree angle which meant that side of her face was completely concealed against the sheet, her arms up above her head as if she were silently cheering she was so happy to have been born, Mel pulled the sheet over her bare legs and up to her waist. Despite the pain from the small tear she had, she felt great.

'What are those cabbage leaves for again?' Leo asked, looking puzzled, as Mrs Lelani stood to leave.

'They're to help with soreness,' Mel replied.

'For the split?' he asked.

'It's called a tear!' Mel said, exasperated. 'For God's sake, Leo! And, no, they're for breastfeeding pain, to go in my bra.'

'Sorry,' he said. 'This is all just a bit new to me.'

'Not that new,' Mrs Lelani muttered into her handbag. Mel stared at her, widening her eyes. Leo blushed crimson red and gulped down another glass of champagne.

'Yes, well,' said Leo, 'we can't all be perfect.'

'Oh, Leo,' said Mrs Lelani affectionately, 'I'm far from perfect. You should see how much money I owe to Ladbrokes.'

'Mrs Lelani,' Mel said, her sides aching with laughing, 'you are something else.'

Chapter Twenty-nine

Lexi opened the text message: Lexi, I'm near your house, can I pop in? I'm with Rufus. Ax

Alan. She hadn't expected this. Not a *home visit*.

'Oh, Christ!' she exclaimed. 'This is just what I don't need.'

In her flat, sitting at the kitchen table eating toast and dropping crumbs on Poppy, she took a deep breath. She narrowed her eyes, trying, through her sleep-deprived haze, to think straight. What shall I do? Ignore him? Answer him but pretend to be out? He might try to meet me somewhere. She found herself typing, quickly replying, 'Yep', then stuffed her fist into her mouth and bit down on her knuckles. Shit. What did I do that for? Lexi looked about the kitchen, her eyes frantically sweeping the cluttered kitchen surfaces. She muttered instructions at herself to tidy up. Glancing down at her outfit, she took a sharp intake of breath. Am I still wearing these maternity trousers? Am I still wearing that black nursing top with stains all over the shoulders? How long have my breasts been flapping around outside my top like this?

'Gross,' she said, popping them back inside her bra. 'Have I even changed clothes since you were born, Poppy?'

It was as if she were facing an inspection from Alan. She feared he might come over with his clipboard and mark her out of ten on how she was doing on her own. Devotion to breastfeeding: 9. Nappy changing: 8. Personal hygiene: 4. Domestic ability: 0. She stood up, holding Poppy, wondering where to begin.

'Why's he coming anyway?' she asked Poppy, who answered with a shriek.

Perhaps he wanted to remind himself of what Lexi was like. He'd probably thought he'd never see her again. Moving into her bedroom, the duvet was hanging off the bed, left over from Lexi having literally rolled out of bed during the night to crawl across the room to tend to Poppy, too tired to stand. She stood by her dressing table and looked at her reflection. Almost grey with tiredness, her skin and eyelids were drooping. She opened her eyes wide and smiled at herself, trying to inject energy into her features. Propping Poppy up on a pillow on the bed, she located her make-up bag and unzipped it, staring at the now unfamiliar objects inside. Make-up seemed a thing of the past, relegated to those days when there was time to care about superficial matters such as her appearance. So *not* a priority any more. Squirting a blob of Touche Éclat on to her fingers, she smeared a little around her panda eyes but was interrupted by Poppy crying before she could blend it in properly.

'Oh Poppy,' she said, wiping her fingers on her top, then picking her up. 'What's wrong, baby girl?'

Having forgotten about her make-up, once Poppy was calm

she rested her on the bed again and pulled off her dirty black top to change into a clean one. Pulling open a drawer and retrieving a white nursing top from a pile of crumpled clothes, she was sitting in her bra when she glanced up at the door to see Alan standing there, his hand raised, as if he were about to knock. Though she registered it was him, she let out a scream, which made Poppy scream, too. Alan started furiously shaking his head, flapping his hands around and lifting his finger to his lips to silence her. She clapped her hand over her mouth.

'What the hell?' she said. 'Alan, for God's sake! *Normal* people use the doorbell.'

Lexi lifted a towel from the floor and clutched it against her half-dressed self, then picked up Poppy, too.

'I'm sorry, I've just got Rufus to sleep,' he shout-whispered, holding his hands over his eyes. 'The door was open, and I didn't want to ring the bell or knock because he wakes up if I even breathe too loud. I texted you to tell you I was outside. Did you get it? Sorry if I shocked you. I thought you'd be able to hear me walking across the floorboards. Lexi, you look like you've seen a ghost.'

Yes, she thought. A ghost! That's exactly how it felt having him in her bedroom again. Like seeing a ghost. She silently shooed him away towards the living room, then quickly pulled on the clean top and, carrying Poppy, followed him into the living room, where he was sitting on an armchair. He was wearing a black jumper that fitted perfectly over his broad shoulders and dark jeans that clung to his thighs, and his jacket was casually strewn over the back of the chair. There was just something overtly *male* about Alan.

'Sorry, Lexi,' he said again, leaning forward on to his knees. 'Didn't mean to frighten you.'

Lexi had a flashback to the last time he had been in the flat. Once through the door, they'd been at one another like wild beasts. Now, Lexi felt awkward and uncomfortably self-aware. No one wants to see their significant ex when they look like a pile of crap.

'You have something white around your eyes,' said Alan, frowning. 'I'm not sure what it is.'

Lexi rubbed at the make-up and reddened. Here we go. First box on the clipboard form completed. Appearance: 0.

'Ok,' said Lexi, slightly aggressively. 'So what's up? Why are you here?'

Alan rubbed his forehead. He sighed and shook his head a little. For a moment, his eyes seemed to glass over. Lexi thought of Katy. 'How's it going with Rufus?' she said, more gently.

Alan smiled. 'I love Rufus,' he said. 'When I hold him in my arms, the world feels right. I knew I wanted children and I couldn't be happier with him. It's Katy I'm worried about. She's my world, but something is happening to her. I'm with her all the time, but she's not the Katy I married right now and – you know what? I really miss her.'

Right, thought Lexi, her heart sinking. So that's why you're here. You need to talk to me about Katy. This is because, when we met, those years ago, you saw me as someone who would listen to you all night long – the 24/7 social worker, ever the listener, ever the sympathizer. Lexi sat down opposite Alan, still holding Poppy, and suddenly didn't care what she looked like. Alan didn't care, so why should she? Alan was looking right through her, his thoughts clearly on Katy. But why wouldn't they be? She was his wife. But Lexi had thought that, just maybe, he would be coming over to say that seeing her again had made him feel something – *anything*. Ha. What a joke. Blushing, she saw with absolute clarity that her crush on Alan was exactly that, a pure case of unrequited love. She had deluded herself into thinking that something special had passed between them, but it hadn't. Just as she'd lived in a fantasy world to escape reality as a child, she'd done the same as an adult. Her childhood fantasies of what life should be like had regularly crumbled around her ears. There was a theme developing here. Fantasy was easier than real life.

'Is Katy unwell?' she asked, concealing the confused emotions tumbling around in her heart.

Alan looked out of the window for a moment, his expression grave. He linked his fingers together behind his head, which opened up his chest wide enough to beat on, then dropped them down again, his torso deflating like bagpipes.

'I just don't know what's going on,' he said. 'She won't talk to me about it, but I feel like she's shut down. I feel that she's wary of Rufus, almost scared of him, and she's become obsessive about hygiene. One day she's saying she wants to go to work, another day she stays in bed all day.'

Lexi wondered why she played this role in so many people's lives. Why did people turn to her? Why had Alan turned to her? Was it because she posed no threat? Or was it her own fault? Had she spent her life getting private information from people in order to get close to them, in order to justify her role in their life? Or maybe it was practice. An image of her as a young girl sitting on the edge of her mother's bed trying to say something useful while her mother sobbed and complained about her life popped into her head.

'Do you mind me talking to you like this?' Alan asked, as if reading her mind. 'It's just you're so easy to talk to. You're such a nice person.'

Aha! thought Lexi. I'm a nice person. Damned by faint praise!

'Of course I don't mind,' Lexi said. 'Katy's probably completely exhausted. I know I've never known tiredness like this ever before. I think it twists your brain, you know? The crying, the sleepless nights, the realization that your life has changed beyond recognition. If I don't nap when Poppy does, I often suddenly burst out crying for no specific reason. I think we all feel a little out of control right now and, if I'm right in saying Katy likes being in control, I can imagine she finds this hard, too. As well as being really happy to have Rufus, of course.'

Alan nodded, but he still looked miserable. He leaned back in his chair and his eyelids looked heavy. 'I know,' he said. 'But it seems like more than that. I know you work in health, and I was wondering whether it might be postnatal depression. Do you think it could be?'

Poor Alan, his eyes all big and sad. Lexi felt sorry for him.

'I think it's too early to say at the moment,' she said. 'Rufus is only a few weeks old. Give Katy time. We're all struggling in one way or another, and perhaps she needs more support than she lets on.'

Poppy had started to cry and, deftly, Lexi attached her to her breast, not making eye contact with Alan. Years ago, her breasts had taken a very different role in this flat. How times change.

'She's usually so in control,' he said. 'I've never seen her like this. I feel like, though she's in the room and going through the motions with Rufus, she's not really there. It's not really how I imagined it to be. I don't know why, but I let myself think we'd be taking trips to the beach, smiling a lot and cuddling Rufus together—'

His eyes misted over. He swallowed and exhaled. 'Sorry, Lexi,' he said, lifting up his hand by way of apology. 'Last thing you need is this, but the first person I wanted to talk to about this was you. You're about the only person I've ever spoken to about anything personal.'

He looked at her and their eyes locked. Lexi's cheeks burned.

'That night we spent together,' he said, 'it was so long ago, but I still remember all our conversations. I had never been so frank with anyone before that night. All that stuff I told you about my brother, I'd not told anyone.'

Lexi nodded, remembering the sad story. His brother had run away from the family when he was fifteen because, he wrote in his letters, he couldn't stand being in Alan's shadow any longer. He had never come home. Alan had hired private detectives to find him and, eight months later, they did, working on a farm, fruit picking. He'd refused to be reunited with his family, refused money from Alan and even refused to read a letter Alan had written explaining that he had never, ever, intentionally tried to put him in the shade. The experience was painful for Alan because he had been unaware of Ben's suffering and, when his brother left, had felt guilty on a multitude of layers. That was part of the reason he had emigrated: he had wanted to give Ben the opportunity to go home.

'You haven't heard from him since, have you?' she said.

'No,' Alan said. 'Though my mother has seen him once, which is a great thing. Anyway, listen, I shouldn't be round here, dumping all this on your shoulders, when you're all on your own, dealing with a newborn.'

All on your own. The words made Lexi flinch.

'How are you doing?' he said. 'Are you all right?'

Lexi nodded and smiled, but said nothing. She wasn't even going to begin trying to explain how she felt: the heart-racing tiredness, the unending joy, the fear that she loved Poppy too much, the darkness of the bedroom walls at night. There were no words, really.

'I admire you, Lexi,' he said. 'I hardly know you but, from what I get from you, you're incredibly strong. A bit like Katy, really – different, but the same. Look, it's been great to talk. Thanks for listening. I'd better get back before Rufus wakes up and wants a feed. I've come out without the formula.'

He put down his cup on the table, stood up. They smiled at one another, and there was a sudden spark between them. Her heart beat wildly in her chest. Poppy had fallen asleep at the breast, so Lexi detached her and lay her in the Moses basket. She stood up and folded her arms across herself.

'I think you should speak to the health visitor about Katy,' she suggested. 'They're usually really helpful. If she seems worse, then make an appointment with the GP. In the meantime, maybe me and the antenatal-group girls can arrange to meet up and support her more.'

They moved towards the front door, and Lexi focused on Rufus, whose little lips were making sucking motions in his sleep.

'He's adorable,' said Lexi, stroking his hand.

Alan put his hand around Lexi's shoulder and squeezed. She didn't look up because, if she had done, his mouth would have been too close to hers. She laughed, not really knowing what to do, blood rushing in her ears. Alan kissed the top of her head and then let go of her, briefly rubbing the top of her back. She tensed her shoulders.

'Thank you, Lexi,' he said. 'I appreciate that. You're a good friend. It's strange how we met again like this. Out of all people, I'm in your antenatal class.'

'Yes, it's weird,' she said, the words burning on her lips. 'Alan, listen, I just need to know something. I've always wanted to know what you felt after that night—'

She paused to find her words, Alan's eyes burning into her face. Lexi shook her head, thoroughly confused. What was it she wanted to ask him? What did it matter how he felt? She reminded herself of the reason Alan had come over. She reminded herself of their situations. Cocking her head, she heard Poppy wake up again and begin crying in the living room.

'Oh, it doesn't matter,' she said. 'I'm not making any sense.'

She opened the front door and ushered Alan out. He bumped the pushchair down the steps and waited on the pavement. He smiled a smile tinged with sadness.

'I guess I felt torn,' he said thoughtfully. 'I clicked with you in a soulful way, but I'd just met Katy and knew she was for keeps. Life's not black and white, is it?'

And with that horribly unsatisfactory answer, the sound of a car horn burst into their bubble. Lexi and Alan turned to look out. Gary was there, waving. He climbed out and opened the back door.

'Did you call a cab earlier?' said Lexi. Alan nodded then looked at Gary.

'Alan Nicholson?' Gary said, his eyes moving slowly from Alan to Lexi and back again. His face fell. 'Your chariot awaits.'

It was three a.m. and, despite being more tired than she'd ever been in her entire life, Mel couldn't sleep. It was amazing, she thought, sitting up in bed and peering into the Moses basket by her side, how a baby who was not even as big as a handbag could completely change your life. When they'd arrived home with Mabel earlier that night, Mel and Leo had had plans to eat the chilli Bella had cooked for them to celebrate their homecoming. Leo had started to talk about Coco and Jacques, but Mel had refused to join in. She felt she'd spent far too much time in the last month worrying about Leo and what was going on with him. All she'd wanted to do that evening was stare at Mabel as she lay in the Moses basket, tucked in with cream knitted blankets, tiny and helpless in the living room Mel now worried was too cold, too draughty and probably too noisy, since Mrs Lelani's TV was blaring away downstairs. Mel had so many questions: When should she feed her again? What should she be dressed in to sleep? Should the contents of Mabel's nappy be that *yellow*? What were those white spots around her nose? Should they trim her fingernails? Leo drank filter coffee to help him pay attention, holding the mug with his good hand as he turned the pages of the baby manuals like flick books, searching for the answers.

'Are you breathing, Mabel?' whispered Mel into the night,

worried now that she had somehow managed to suffocate her with a blanket.

Leo was snoring gently beside her, and the light of the street lamp fell over their wardrobe, which was open and spewing clothes into the room. She was amazed that Leo could sleep after all that coffee, but she was glad he was there. She didn't like to think how she'd feel if he hadn't come back home, if he had actually gone off with Coco. She was too anxious to relax, and felt that she would be eternally awake now that she had a baby. Holding her own breath to listen for Mabel's, she slowly rested her hand on her tiny chest, to feel it rise and fall. Immediately, Mabel started to scream at the top of her lungs.

'Oh my God!' Mel said, clapping her hands over her mouth and falling back into her pillow in fright. 'I woke her up!'

Leo sat bolt upright, eyes wide as saucers, then stumbled out of bed, his hand scrabbling across the wall in search of the light switch.

'No,' Mel hissed, half out of bed. 'Don't turn the light on. She'll never go back to sleep if you turn the light on.'

Bleary-eyed, Leo paused, then staggered round the bed to Mabel's Moses basket. 'Shall I pick her up?' said he asked, hovering near the basket. 'What time is it?'

They both peered down at Mabel, whose little face was scrunched up and getting pinker by the second.

'Just wait a minute,' said Mel. 'See if she stops on her own. It's half three.'

'In the morning half three?' asked Leo, blinking.

'Yes, of course in the morning!'

Mabel's cry grew louder. Mel and Leo sat together in the dark for a few seconds, looking worriedly at each other.

'Do you think she needs a feed?' Leo asked. Mel shook her head.

'I only gave her one fifty minutes ago, and it's so bloody sore,' she said. 'Better pick her up, otherwise the neighbours will complain. Maybe I put her nappy on the wrong way.'

Gently lifting Mabel out of the basket, Leo knocked his head against the musical mobile they had installed just above. 'Twinkle, Twinkle, Little Star' burst into the room, turned up to the highest, daytime volume. Mel grabbed at it and turned it off, while Leo held Mabel upright against his chest and rubbed her back, doing energetic, rhythmic knee bends at the same time. The baby calmed down a little but started to noodle against Leo's shoulder, looking for Mel's breast. After a moment's quiet, she started to cry again.

'How about a nappy change?' Leo said, sniffing deeply and still doing the knee bends. 'No, don't think so.'

Mabel did a tiny hiccup. 'Maybe she's got wind,' Mel said. 'Do you think? Don't they get colic sometimes? Or is that horses?'

Leo shrugged and shook his head at the same time. Mel sighed. She felt deranged with lack of sleep. She could not believe how impossible it was to know what was wrong with Mabel. She'd expected to feel some kind of instinctive knowledge enter her brain when she was born, but she felt completely clueless, especially in the middle of the night.

'I need an instruction manual,' she said. 'I can't work out what cry means what.'

'What did that book I read earlier say?' Leo said, his brow crinkling. 'There was a checklist. Hungry, nappy change, tired

'. . . hot? Yes, that was it. Is the baby too hot? Or too cold, maybe. The window's open, did you know?'

'Oh, God,' said Mel, moving over to close it. 'Who opened it? Did I? We'll have to be careful with that. She might fall out.'

'Yes,' said Leo. 'I'll get some locks at the weekend. Or shutters. We could get shutters.'

Moving over to the shelves, Mel checked the room thermometer, but the batteries had died. She shook it, and some numbers flicked on to the screen then disappeared.

'Bloody thing. Maybe that Grobag's too hot,' she said. 'Is it the right tog? I think it's 1.5 for this time of year but – hang on, maybe she's too small to be in one? Can you read the label and check again? I'll just take her if you like, but, when I do, she's going to want to feed.'

Leo lay Mabel on the bed and unzipped the sleeping bag. She started to cry again. This time, Mel picked her up and started to walk back and forth to calm her, repeating a 'sshhhh' noise into her ear. Leo stood there, his hands on his hips, also making the 'sshhh' noise. The crying got louder.

'Is this normal?' Mel said. 'For her to cry like this? Do you think something is wrong?'

'Should we check for a rash?' Leo said. 'Maybe she's not well.'

Leaning over Mabel, who was on the bed again now, they took off her sleepsuit. Mel fished around in the brown envelope full of information the hospital had given her, searching for the leaflet about rashes.

'I can't see her skin properly,' said Leo. 'It's too dark.'

'Better put the main light on then,' said Mel. 'I'll get the thermometer.'

Under the bright glare of the main light, they checked Mabel's skin, comparing it to the pictures in the leaflet. It seemed fine. Mel pressed a thermometer strip against Mabel's forehead and declared that her temperature was also fine. Mabel's hands were curled up into little fists as she continued to cry.

'Looks like she's about to deck us,' said Leo with a quick grin. 'Don't blame her. We're a bit hopeless, aren't we?'

Leo turned to look at Mel and gave her a slightly guilty glance, which she ignored.

'Shall I just feed her again?' said Mel. 'I'm just so tired, and it bloody hurts.'

'Why don't you sleep with her next to you in bed?' Leo suggested. 'Then you can doze as she feeds.'

'You try dozing with razors round your nipples!' said Mel. 'But, yes, I'd like to lie down.'

'Maybe we should change to bottle-feeding,' said Leo. 'Then I could do it, too.'

'Yes. I'm already thinking that might be a good idea.'

Mel climbed into bed and lay down on her side, with Mabel next to her. She immediately started to feed and Mel screwed up her face until the pain subsided.

'I'll fall asleep in a minute,' she said, her eyelids drooping. 'I know I will. You'll have to stay awake, Leo, and watch us, in case I roll on her.'

'I'll watch you,' he replied. 'I'll turn the light out.'

Checking the clock again, it was 4.20 a.m. when Leo lay down next to them, holding his eyelids open with his fingers, desperately trying not to go back to sleep.

'It must make you think more about Jacques,' said Mel sleepily. 'This is what you missed out on with him.'

Leo turned on to his back and faced the ceiling, still holding his eyes open.

'There's not really time to think about Jacques, and it's completely different because I wasn't *with* Coco,' he said. 'I'm sorry about not telling you the truth. It's a tough one, because I never knew whether I'd ever see him again. In a way, I grieved for him long ago, but I had to find out once and for all what he meant to me, and whether he would ever be in my life. The important thing is that we make this work. I promise to be entirely honest with you from now on.'

Mel looked at the clock again. The sky was lightening and the birds were starting to sing. 'Let's just get a few hours of sleep,' she said, feeling like she'd been drugged. 'She seems to have nodded off. Can you put her back in her basket for me?'

Leo lifted baby Mabel into the basket and Mel shifted down the bed, pulling the duvet up to her chin. A second later, she was asleep – only to be woken ninety minutes later by the doorbell ringing in two long bursts. Mabel woke up, too.

'I'll get it,' Leo said, groaning. His eyes were bright-red slits. He staggered like a drunk towards the front door in just his pants, and Mel heard him say 'Thank you', then a rustling noise as he walked into the bedroom clutching a big bunch of roses.

'They're probably from work,' she said, pulling off the envelope and opening it. Glancing at the card, she saw Coco's name under a message, which she didn't read, before grabbing the flowers and dumping them in the bin in the corner of the room. Leo was back in the bed, leaning over to smile at Mabel.

'Don't fucking believe it,' she said.

'Who are they from?' Leo said.

'Coco,' she said. 'I'm not even reading the message. Silly cow. Doesn't she know when to leave it?'

Leo sat up, not knowing whether to be pleased or angry.

'Really?' he said. 'Well, I guess she's trying to be friendly because she feels bad for upsetting you.'

Mel got them out of the bin, opened the window and threw the flowers outside to the bins below. A cat screeched. She slammed the window shut.

'I have had two minutes' sleep,' she said in a stone-cold voice. 'I do not want flowers from your ex, with whom you already have a child. Okay? I wish she didn't even exist.'

She burst into tears. Leo was out of bed again, pulling on his T-shirt and jeans.

'I'll take Mabel out for a walk in the pram. You can have a nap.'

'I'm so tired,' she said, 'I can't function. My nipples hurt.'

'I'll buy you lots of chocolate,' he said. 'Keep you going. I'm sorry about Coco's flowers.'

'What about the changing bag?' she said. 'You need to take all that stuff with you, and it's half empty. Nappies, wipes, changing mat, change of clothes, cotton wool. Shall I fill it up before you—'

'No,' Leo interrupted. 'I'll sort that out. We'll just walk down to the beach and sit there for a while. I'll buy some formula, too, so we can try her on a bottle.'

'But it's windy out there,' Mel said. 'What if she—'

'What if she what?' said Leo. 'Stops breathing because of the wind?'

'Yes!' Mel said, bursting into tears again. 'What if she dies?'

Leo put his arms around Mel and held her. He pressed his face into her hair and kissed her head. 'I'll make sure she's exactly the right warmth,' he said. 'Now get into bed and sleep.'

Suddenly, with the doors closed, the flat was silent. Mel closed her eyes, only to be woken up again by the sound of drilling coming from next door. With her hands over her ears, she laughed, half hysterically. Out the corner of her eye, she saw Coco's card, which had fallen from the flowers. She picked it up and read it. It was written in a florist's hand, dictated, perhaps, over the phone.

'Leo, I hope Mel is well. Congratulations on your second baby. I'm in London. Call me sometime. Coco.' Under her name was her new address in London and her number.

What's that supposed to mean? Mel thought. *I'm in London. Call me.* Why does she want Leo to call her?'

Mel walked through to the kitchen and turned on the cooker. She held the card in the flame and watched the corner burn and curl in the flame. But, at the last second, she had an idea. Blowing out the flame, she cooled the card and pushed it inside her diary. She had a thought: I might need that. One day.

Chapter Thirty

'We need toilet roll,' said Lenny, as he shoved his house keys into his pocket and picked up his guitar. He moved towards the front door and put his hand on the latch. 'Can you pick some up? I'll probably be rehearsing most of the day.'

Rebecca eyed up the yellow-and-brown Moroccan jug Lenny's mum had given her as a gift and considered throwing it at Lenny. It was heavy enough to knock him out. His hair was wet from the shower, and he'd put on a flannel red-and-green checked shirt and jeans. Unlike Rebecca, he looked fresh as a daisy. Like a boy. Unlike Rebecca, who felt like a haggard old witch, he seemed to be able to sleep through Elvis's night crying. Though she used to sleep well, now she woke up at Elvis's every sniff.

'Great,' she muttered. 'That's something to look forward to.'

Lenny let his hand fall. He moved towards her and put his guitar down on the floor.

'What's up, babe?' he said, running his eyes over her face worriedly, reaching out and putting an arm around her waist. 'Becs?'

Rebecca felt suddenly desperate, but made herself keep those feelings inside. *What about me?* she wanted to shout out. *What about me?* Behind Lenny's head, there was a big wall mirror. Rebecca looked in it and saw how dreadful she looked. Her hair was scraped back and unwashed, her skin was pale and the skin under her eyes was grey and sunken. Dressed in mismatched pyjamas, there were baby-sick stains and milk spills all over them. She'd seen how her friends looked at her with a mixture of pity and disgust when they came round to see Elvis. But there wasn't any time for anything any more.

'You're with Elvis,' he said, gesturing towards the bedroom, where Elvis slept, the door open. 'You'll be fine.'

'But I need sleep, Lenny,' she said, her throat hurting with the need to cry. 'It's been nearly a month, and I haven't slept for longer than two hours in a row. And I need to eat something that isn't peanut butter on toast. And I'm so thirsty.'

'Look, babe,' he said, 'you know I'll do anything for you. But I've got to rehearse today. I can't let the band down. Get some sleep when he sleeps, and I'll be home to give him a bath and we'll get a takeaway.'

Rebecca didn't say anything. She swallowed. She knew she was going to cry, and she didn't want Lenny to see her cry. She didn't want to make him feel guilty for rehearsing. He had every right to. He needed it. I don't even know why I want to cry, she thought. I love Elvis. I love feeding him and cuddling him and talking to him . . . It was just, she'd never imagined feeling so exhausted, and there was so much to do. The nappies needed washing and drying, the dishes weren't done, there was all the food shopping and cooking, she wanted a shower and to wash her hair, she needed to buy cream for

Elvis's bottom. She wanted to call the others, to see how they were. She wanted to see her friends and talk about music and parties and travelling.

They needed toilet roll.

'Don't forget,' Lenny said, giving her a kiss, then making a move to leave. 'We need toilet roll.'

She picked up the jug, but he'd closed the door by the time she threw it. Mercifully, her throw was poor and it landed on the mattress Lenny had dragged into the living room to ensure he got a decent night's sleep. She went to the window to watch him walk off down the road. She folded her arms and looked over at Elvis, who was rousing from his sleep. The sight of him, his little starfish hands waving around, lifted her spirits. His eyes were open and she grinned at him.

'Shall we go and get some fresh air?' she said, gently lifting him out. 'Buy some toilet roll?'

Pulling shut the window with one hand, she glanced out of it again, watching people bustling up and down the street. She noticed Katy, dressed in a heavy work suit, getting out of a cab and walking in the direction of Rebecca's flat while speaking into her phone.

'Katy!' Rebecca called out of the window, and Katy looked up, startled but distant.

'Where's Rufus?' Rebecca muttered to herself, but waved and gestured that Katy should come in for a cup of tea, which Katy seemed to think about for a few minutes, before shaking her head and pointing down the street, as if she needed to be somewhere.

'Wait!' Rebecca said. 'I'll come down.'

She put on a polka-dot jersey dress that wasn't too tight

anywhere and put Elvis into his sling. Grabbing the changing bag, she pushed her feet into her ballet pumps and walked quickly down the staircase, passing two people who said 'Hello' and 'How's the baby?', great big smiles on their faces. Pushing open the heavy main door, she walked out into the communal front garden, where two boys were playing football. Patting Elvis's back, Rebecca smiled, feeling instantly happier to be out in the bright day. Brighton seemed to sparkle in the sun.

'Katy?' she said, frowning as she scanned the street. But there was no sign. She had gone.

It was instinctive, this need to be at work, thought Katy, walking as quickly as her slowly healing scar would allow. Some women found their meaning when they had a baby. Katy's meaning in life, she decided, was work.

'Stay at home and be with Rufus and me,' Alan had said that morning when Katy had told him about her decision to go into work for a few hours. 'Anita says she doesn't need you.'

But Katy wasn't going to abandon what she loved. She wasn't going to be made to feel ashamed about wanting to work despite only just having had Rufus, and had ignored Alan and Anita. She'd known this was what was wrong all along. She was just missing work, wasn't she? Being in control was what she was best at. As she walked through the bustling town, her legs felt like jelly and, when a police car sped past with its siren blaring, she nearly jumped out of her skin. She pulled her jacket round her and tried to remember if she'd emailed that production company who'd called, looking for an old-fashioned swimming pool in a garden, before Rufus was born.

She'd thought of one near Haywards Heath that would be perfect and was determined to make sure the deal went ahead. She'd have to explain to Rebecca at some point. Arriving at the office, Katy began to feel tired. She was met by the receptionist, who said Anita would not be in until the afternoon. She gave her a meaningful stare, which Katy didn't understand.

'I think she has an appointment,' she said, pulling a face.

'What?' said Katy. 'An interview?'

The receptionist shook her head. 'No,' she said. 'Sorry, it's not my place to say. But, you know, this is a small office, and everyone knows. Must be horrible for her, knowing you've had your new baby, but, well, you know, we're all entitled to make our own decisions.'

Appointment? Katy frowned. Own decision?

'I see,' she said, realizing. Anita was having an abortion. She waited for the news to affect her, but she felt only numb. She nodded knowingly at the receptionist and excused herself. Anita had never wanted a baby; Katy was unsurprised.

'I'll just be a few hours,' she said. 'Then Alan wants me home.'

'Ahhh,' she said. 'You shouldn't have come in at all. Rufus is what? Three or four weeks old? He'll miss you!'

Katy forced herself to smile then went into her office, where she turned on the computer and scrolled down her emails until she found the client she wanted to contact. Images of what Anita must be going through flashed into her mind, interspersed with the sounds of Rufus's cry ringing out in her head. Whatever she did, she couldn't shake the images of his birth from her memory. The panic she had felt when the consultant explained that Rufus was in distress had been profound. Now, sitting at her desk in her small, sun-baked office, something was happening to Katy, but she wasn't sure what. She rested her hand against her chest. She was palpitating. Sweat formed on her brow and, though she was hot, she began to tremble as if she were freezing. There was a ringing in her ears and a feeling of dread in the pit of her stomach. An email popped into her inbox from the swimming-pool client. She opened it and read that Anita had sorted out the swimming pool weeks ago. Closing her eyes, Katy tried to breathe but felt as if someone had their hands around her neck, deliberately trying to choke her. I should be with Rufus, she thought, her hands shaking violently now as she dialled Alan's number. I want to be with Rufus. I should be with Rufus. I want someone to help me. Alan's phone rang out four times before he picked up. She opened her mouth to speak, but he got in there first.

'Lexi?' he said. 'Sorry, I had to ring off because Rufus puked on me. So, what's up?'

Katy held the phone away from her ear, too shocked to speak. Lexi? Alan and Lexi? How had this happened? Don't jump to conclusions, she told herself. Without saying a word, she put the phone down again and rested her head on the keyboard of her computer. On the back of her eyelids she saw images of Alan and Lexi, then Rufus, minutes after he was born. She hadn't known if he was alive or dead. She hadn't been able to hold him for four days. She rocked her head from side to side, pressing her face into the keys, aware of the sharpness of their edges on her skin. Why was she feeling like this? What was wrong with her? She should be with Rufus. He needed her. Why was Alan speaking to Lexi? She wanted to hold her baby in her arms, but would he ever forgive her for not loving him as much as she thought she would? Her mobile began to ring – it was Alan calling – but she covered her ears and closed her eyes, blocking out light and sound.

Chapter Thirty-one

'Oh,' said Mel wistfully, putting her coffee cup down. 'Look at that blissful scene.'

Lexi and Rebecca turned their heads to see what Mel was pointing at. There, on the table next to theirs in the café, were a couple of women in their early twenties talking over a cooked breakfast, a pile of papers on the table waiting to be devoured, nothing and nobody to hurry them. All three women sighed.

'Those were the days,' said Rebecca. 'Have you seen that lot over there? That'll be us soon enough.'

Lexi and Mel turned their gaze to the other side of the café, where three mums and their toddlers and newborns were sitting, attempting to have a coffee. One of the toddlers had thrown the sugar packets all over the floor, another was opening them and tipping sugar into her mouth and the third was having an enormous lie-down tantrum on the floor. Their mothers, also trying to juggle newborns, looked knackered: haphazard hairstyles, jogging bottoms, plates piled with choco-late cake.

'Wow,' said Mel. 'It's hard work, isn't it? No one actually tells you it's going to be quite this hard, do they? They sort of laugh and say "Enjoy your last days of freedom," or something equally ambiguous. I can't believe what breastfeeding was like. I'm so relieved I've gone on to bottles. Now I can share the load with Leo and he can prove his worth, plus, my nipples can recover.'

'How are things with Leo?' asked Rebecca.

'I'm still pissed off with him,' replied Mel. 'Because of the timing more than anything, but I'm trying to be adult about it and understand his side of it.'

Lexi and Rebecca shook their heads.

'It's not been easy for you,' said Lexi. 'That was one hell of a surprise.'

'Hmm,' said Mel. 'It certainly was.'

'How are you finding it, Lexi?' asked Rebecca. 'Must be tough not having a man to be completely unreasonable to in the middle of the night! Lenny is getting it in the neck at the moment. I can't help but take out my tiredness on him, especially because I found a pair of earplugs under his pillow. The arse has been sleeping through Elvis waking but not telling me he's been wearing earplugs!'

'My God!' said Mel. 'Grounds for divorce! What are these men like?'

'Maybe I'm better off without one,' Lexi said. 'Actually, I'm okay – though, obviously, completely knackered.'

The three women had met so that Mel could talk to Rebecca about the design of her wedding invites but also so they could decide what to do about Katy. So far, Rebecca had come up with the idea of a massage, Mel had thought she could do an exercise class with her and Lexi thought professional help might be the way forward.

'You know what?' said Rebecca, standing. 'I'm going to have to change Elvis in a minute, and there's no baby-changing room here and the toilet's locked today for some reason. I think I'll have to head off.'

'Yeah,' said Lexi, with a sigh. 'I need to get Poppy off to sleep, and I suppose I should put a wash on if I want to wear anything clean ever again.'

'My flat needs sorting out,' said Mel drearily. 'Plus, I should hoover. How completely dull.'

At that moment, Poppy started to cry and Lexi lifted her out of the buggy and put her in the sling instead, then began to do knee bends. Mel glanced around the café at the other women there: shoppers with bags, workers with their laptops, women chatting – women who seemed so completely free without their buggies and babies and changing bags around their necks, tethering them to the home. Mel sighed and looked at her watch. It was almost noon.

'How about a spritzer by the beach?' she said, lifting her eyebrows. 'There's a café bar there with baby-changing. Go on, just this once.'

Rebecca's and Lexi's eyes lit up.

'Yes!' Lexi said. 'What a great idea. Did you ask Erin and Katy today?'

Mel nodded. 'Katy said she had to go into work,' she said. 'And Erin was taking Hope to see a friend in Norwich. Why don't we call Katy again and see if she can come down for a quick break? Something tells me we'll have to be quite persistent with her.'

The women started to walk along through the Lanes.

'Do you think she's ill?' said Mel.

'Alan came to see me,' said Lexi, 'and said she wasn't doing very well at all, so yeah, I think she could be.'

The other women nodded and sighed.

By the time they had reached the café on the beach, the babies were asleep after the walk. The sun came out and they ordered three white-wine spritzers.

'I guess all we can do is encourage her to get some help,' said Lexi distractedly. 'I think it's taking its toll on Alan.'

'I think it takes its toll on everyone to some degree,' said Mel. 'Don't you?'

Lexi widened her eyes and took a sip of her drink. She leaned back in her chair and lifted up her sunglasses.

'It's the lack of sleep that gets you,' she said. 'But I've wanted Poppy for so long, I'd probably not care if I never slept again.'

Rebecca and Mel smiled.

'I love Elvis so much,' Rebecca said, 'but I miss my old life. Definitely. I miss the way Lenny and I used to be together. Now it's all – obviously – about Elvis. And Lenny seems to think that, because I'm at home with Elvis, while he's *slogging his guts out* at the vintage-clothes shop, I'm not really doing anything. He comes home and says, "What's for dinner, babe? Did you have a relaxed day?" I mean, he has *no* idea. But on the whole, I'm pretty much blissed out. How about you, Mel?'

Mel leaned into the buggy to check on Poppy. She looked up and smiled.

'It's good when she's asleep,' she said, before cracking up laughing. She opened her mouth to speak again, but Rebecca got in first.

'I know what you're going to say,' she said. 'You're going to say you don't mean it and you love her to bits. I think we can be honest with each other. Yes, we love our babies – but it's bloody tough sometimes! At least we all understand.'

'Let's drink to that,' said Lexi, and the three women clinked glasses. 'At least we all understand.'

Chapter Thirty-two

'Do you think this will be enough?' asked Erin, laying out dozens of wooden skewers lined with bright chunks of red, green and yellow pepper, courgette, mushrooms and onions. They smelled fresh, like sunshine. She was in the kitchen preparing food for the barbecue she'd invited all the ante-natal-group mums and their partners to. Though she'd planned to wait until the babies were a bit older, the weather forecast had been so good for this weekend she'd organized a last-minute get-together.

'Maybe I should do more salad,' she said, scanning the kitchen surfaces, on which stood an enormous salad of endives, walnuts and blue cheese, a bowl of green and black olives glistening in chilli oil, a plate of avocado and tomato sliced up together, a beetroot and carrot salad, and a massive fruit salad for pudding, plus a meringue, which she had yet to stuff with fresh cream and berries. Then there was the salmon and chicken marinating in the fridge, and sausages to serve in buns.

'Oh, isn't this exciting?' she said, sipping a small glass of rosé as she worked and turning up the volume on the radio a little better to hear Haydn's Symphony No. 4 on Classic FM. 'A party for you gorgeous babies! I'm beginning to feel like my old self all over again.'

Lying in a pink bouncer seat dressed in a Katvig sleepsuit with a red apple on the front and kicking her little feet, Hope tried out one of her new smiles. Erin smiled, laughed and clapped all at once. Hope'd been an early smiler, starting at five weeks. Edward had at first insisted it was wind, but Erin knew better. Hope was full of joy at being alive and couldn't wait to smile. Could there be anything more wonderful than the first smiles of a tiny baby? Sky-high happy, that's how Erin felt when she looked into Hope's perfect face. She bent down and stroked her cheek.

'Look at you,' she sighed. 'You are the most beautiful little girl, with the whole of life ahead of you.'

Hope started to cry a little bit, so Erin dried her hands on her apron and unclipped her from the seat. She picked her up and stood at the open French doors of the kitchen, smelling the roses which clung to the fence just outside. Their scent was amazing, almost ambrosial. She looked up at the clear blue sky, watching a seagull flapping his big wings as he flew. A gentle breeze blew on their faces and Hope blinked her eyes in response. Erin stepped outside and walked her around the garden. She kissed Hope's cheek.

'It's just the breeze, Hope,' she said. 'Let me sing you a song.'

She began singing 'Summertime' and, as she sang, she felt tears filling her eyes.

'One of these mornings,' she sang, 'you're going to rise up

singing. And you'll spread your wings and you'll take to the sky—'

Just then, Edward walked outside into the garden and put his hand on her shoulder. 'Why are you crying?' he asked.

'It's those words in the song,' she spluttered. 'I can't bear the thought of Hope taking off and leaving home.'

It was true. Erin didn't want to let Hope out of her sight. She was the most precious package ever to exist. And Erin knew she would get even more beautiful as she grew. Those tiny strawberry-pink lips would get sweeter still and, when she was grown, every man would want a taste. That shock of blonde hair would grow long and tumble beautifully around her features, causing people to turn and stare. She was going to be star-quality beautiful, Erin just knew it. Talented, too. Yes, Hope would be a dancer, just as she had been, but far more successful, far more bold.

'I want us to live together for ever and I want to lock all the doors,' she said.

Edward tried not to, but he couldn't help himself. He burst out laughing, holding his stomach he was laughing so hard. He threw his arms around Erin and held her tight. 'You're unbelievable,' he said. 'You won't be saying that when she's a moody teenager, slamming the bedroom door in our faces.'

'I will,' she said, acting hurt. 'Of course I will. This is love at its most unconditional. I would, quite literally, do anything for this girl.'

Edward kissed Erin on the lips then checked his watch. They moved back into the kitchen, where the symphony was still playing on the radio. Erin placed a sleepy Hope back into the chair and kneeled on the kitchen floor to rock her. Edward looked around at all of the food. He rubbed the back of his neck, and Erin realized he was nervous. It had been a long time since they'd entertained friends, she reflected. In Norwich, they often had people over for dinner, or had parties in the garden, with music and dancing and alcohol. Since Josiah had died, years of their lives had passed by without them entertaining at all. But this was the start of something new. Erin liked the women she'd met. She was worried about Katy, and that was part of the reason for having this get-together. She wanted to make sure Katy was okay, and for them all to be better friends. Finally, her and Edward's new life in Brighton was getting off the ground. All those promises she'd made to herself about getting her old self back were coming good.

'You know they'll be here in a couple of hours,' Edward said, pushing bottles of white wine, rosé and beer into the fridge. 'I'd better do something manly with the barbecue.'

Erin glanced at Hope, who had now fallen asleep in her bouncy chair. She pulled a blanket over her and tucked it in around her legs to keep her warm. She watched Edward's back moving under his white shirt as he worked and hummed along to Classic FM.

'Why don't you do something manly with me first?' said Erin, pulling him towards her. It was the first time she'd initiated sex in months. The first time since she'd found out that she was pregnant for the second time. The first time she'd actually felt like making love with her husband in over a year.

'Where?' he said quietly, his lips trembling. In the background, the symphony was reaching a climax, the first violin soaring ever higher.

and began to climb out. 'Don't say that,' she said. 'He'll refuse to go in it at all if you tell him it's a prison.'

Alan turned off the engine and pulled the keys out of the ignition. He bunched them into his palm and got out of the car. Over the roof, he spoke to Katy. 'I don't think he knows what a prison is yet,' he said with a deathly serious face. Then, much more quietly, 'Although I'm beginning to get an understanding.'

'What does that mean?' she snapped, slamming the passenger door and opening Rufus's. 'You think you're in prison being married to me?'

Katy looked at Alan. Dapper, in dark trousers and shirt, his sleeves were loosely rolled up to his elbows, showing tanned forearms. She remembered the call to Lexi. She hadn't yet mentioned it to Alan, because she wanted to trust that he was the good man she married – but was he? Perhaps he'd got fed up with her. She wiped tears from Rufus's bright pink cheeks, unclipped his belt and picked him up. She held him against her chest and walked towards Erin's house, not waiting for Alan's answer. Glancing back, she saw him leaning against the car, his hands linked on the top of his head in exasperation.

'What do you want me to do, Katy?' he called out, his voice breaking slightly. 'Because I don't bloody well know any more!'

Ah, Katy thought. I've pressed his button. He's had enough. He's seen through me. He's going to tell me I've failed him now, as well as Rufus. He'll probably leave. She braced herself, ready for him to hurl abuse at her, which she probably deserved, when the door opened and Erin greeted her, in a beautiful pale lemon lace dress, and wearing bright red lipstick that contrasted wonderfully with her hair, which was gathered up.

Katy looked down at her own black clothes and frowned. Why hadn't she changed?

'Hello, Katy. Hello, gorgeous boy,' Erin said, opening her arms wide and hugging Katy and Rufus in one go. 'How are you both?'

Katy opened her mouth to speak, but no sound came out. Alan, immediately by her side, took over, complimenting Erin on how wonderful she looked. It was as if a different person had been born with Hope. Erin was stunning. Alan guided Katy into the house, his hand on the small of her back.

Sorry, he mouthed, when Erin wasn't looking. Katy smiled at him gratefully and he put his arm protectively over her shoulders, which were shaking, despite her being too warm.

'Yes, we're good,' he said. 'Tired, maybe. How about you?'

Katy, carrying Rufus as if he were made of porcelain, followed Erin as she moved through her house with the posture and grace of the dancer she was. In the kitchen, she felt a glass being thrust into her hand. Moving into the garden, she was aware of Erin's voice, so light and happy and bright, telling her about Hope. Katy was nodding, but couldn't really hear her words because she was too focused on holding Rufus properly. He felt awkward in the position he was in and his skin was getting sweaty against hers, so she tried to move him, but he cried out, crossly.

'Oh,' said Erin kindly, stroking his cheek. 'What's wrong, little man?'

Voices filled Katy's head. She imagined Rufus answering Erin: *My mummy doesn't love me properly. My mummy's scared of me. My mummy cries on my head in the night when she holds me. She thinks I can't hear her thoughts, but I know every-thing.*

'Oh,' Katy said, the words sticking in her throat. 'He's just hungry, I think. Alan, do you want to take him? I need to use the bathroom quickly, then I'll prepare his bottle.'

Erin smiled at Katy and offered to show her where to go. They walked side by side through the hallway, their shoes clipping on the hard stone tiles, to the downstairs bathroom.

'Is everything okay?' Erin asked, resting a hand on Katy's arm. 'You don't seem yourself.'

Katy forced herself to laugh. 'I'm knackered!' she said. 'That's all.'

Erin smiled a small smile, as if she didn't believe her, then Katy locked the bathroom door and leaned against the sink, her hands gripping each side. She breathed deeply but felt a familiar feeling of dread wash over her. She deliberately avoided the mirror, and turned on the tap, watching the water swirl down the plughole. Swallowing, she tried to tell herself that she would be fine in a few moments, that the trembling would stop and the sensation that she was choking would fade. She closed her eyes and saw the same image of Rufus on the backs of her eyelids, the image of him when he was born. She hadn't known if he was dead or alive, she wasn't even allowed to hold him. She had *failed to progress.* Was anything going on with Alan and Lexi? She glanced at her reflection now and hardly recognized the woman who stared back. I've failed. I'm cracking up, she thought. Tears dripped down her cheeks and she sank down on to her knees, leaning against the cold stem of the bathroom sink.

*

'And this one,' Erin was saying, as she scrolled through pictures of Hope on her iPad, 'was when we went down to the seafront. I'm sure she's aware of the sea, because she instantly calms down when we go to the beach.'

Rebecca and Lenny (holding Elvis) were standing beside Erin at her kitchen table. They exchanged a comical look, their eyes sweeping to a happily sleeping Hope in the baby-bouncer seat.

'Hope seems pretty chilled out as it is,' said Lenny, helping himself to a cracker heaped with cream cheese and smoked salmon. 'But, yeah, maybe it's the sea.'

Erin turned to him, smiling, her eyebrows raised. 'Are you making fun of me Lenny?' she said. 'I know I can go on a bit. I've posted two hundred pictures of Hope on Facebook and I think my friends are getting bored! But look at our babies. They are so adorable. Oh, I've had an idea. Let's line up the babies on a rug outside and take a photo of them! We can send it to Ginny. Let me find a rug.'

Erin went into another room, so Rebecca and Lenny moved into the garden, where they heard Edward talking Leo through the flowers that had come into bloom. Lexi, who had come with Gary, was standing with him, and Alan, too.

'Look at the body language there,' whispered Rebecca to Lenny, gesturing at Gary and Alan. 'I'm guessing Gary doesn't rate Alan for some reason.'

Rebecca giggled, but the tension between Gary and Alan was almost tangible. Gary's face was set in a cold stare and he wasn't saying anything, just sipping on a cold beer, while Alan and Lexi talked flirtatiously about their various adventures going out and about with the babies.

'Have you heard from your mum again?' asked Erin, sweeping past with a rug and throwing it down on to the lawn. 'You said she was going to visit after the letter you sent?'

Rebecca took a deep breath, laughed nervously and looked at Lenny. He stuck his tongue out, turned Elvis round and lifted him up so he could talk directly to his face.

'Lady Granny Dragon-face is coming to see you this week, Elvis,' he said. 'So you've got to be on your best behaviour. No farting, burping, throwing up or shitting yourself in her company. She will be appalled.'

Erin laughed, and Alan, who had moved away from Lexi and Gary, was now listening in.

'Is she that bad?' he asked, creasing his eyes at Rebecca. 'You seem too nice to be the daughter of a dragon.'

'No,' Rebecca said. 'She's not a dragon, but we parted on pretty bad terms. She's a GP, and very well respected in the village I grew up in. I had a strict upbringing of shiny polished shoes, Sunday school, Girl Guides and studying. I longed to be in the woods on my bike, smoking with the boys. I felt completely trapped as a teenager and was never allowed to do anything I wanted, which probably explains why I want to go travelling so much now. I don't know what to expect of her visit. My dad is coming too but he's always kept himself to himself.'

'Yes,' said Alan. 'I guess we're all products of our childhoods. Apparently, everything that happens before you're seven years old moulds your personality type for the rest of your life. Scary, huh?'

'I don't stand a chance then,' said Lenny. 'My parents were nuts. All I remember from my early years is moving from place to place with my dad's band, helping him unload the van like a mini-roadie. Saw them all doing drugs and drinking too much, so I've done the exact same thing. Basically, I'm screwed!'

Everyone laughed, Rebecca a little nervously. Erin looked about the garden.

'Where's Katy?' she said. 'Not back from the bathroom?'

'No,' Alan frowned. 'She never came back. I'll go and check on her.'

'I hope she's all right,' Mel said to Rebecca, so only she could hear. 'She seems to get a good hand from Alan. Leo could do with a lesson from him.'

'I know,' whispered Rebecca. 'I've had to tell Lenny to help more, because, as far as I can tell his life hasn't really changed at all and mine completely has. I need him to know we're in this together, you know?'

'Yeah,' said Mel. 'You need to know it's a shared thing, don't you? It's hard not to argue about what you're both doing. Leo and I had a pointless row about who was doing more house-work yesterday. I mean, Jesus, what's that all about? Thank God for my mum staying down here for a few weeks, though. Without her, we'd be in even more of a zombie-like state.'

'Have you had sex yet?' asked Rebecca. 'Lenny keeps pestering me.'

'God, no!' said Mel. 'I couldn't cope with anyone else pawing me right now. Maybe next week.'

'Yeah,' said Rebecca. 'Maybe next week.'

They stopped talking when Erin stood up and clapped her hands together. At the same moment, Alan came back into the garden with his arm around a very pale Katy. She sat down heavily on a garden chair, shaking Rufus's bottle of milk in her hand.

'Everyone,' said Erin. 'This is a photo-opportunity. I thought we could line up all the babies in a row. What do you think?'

They lay the babies on the rug while Edward took some pictures and talked about their varying sizes.

'Rufus is the clear winner!' said Erin, grinning. 'He's such a lovely, chunky baby. Followed by Mabel.'

'That's what bottle-feeding does, isn't it?' said Lexi. 'I mean, babies normally put on weight more quickly when they have formula.'

'Mabel seems massive!' said Mel, giggling. 'But I'm not sure she wouldn't be exactly the same if I'd carried on breastfeeding!'

'Yeah, well, I couldn't breastfeed,' said Katy, speaking up for the first time and handing Alan the bottle of milk so he could feed Rufus. 'Whatever those women from La Leche League think, I'm afraid the pain just was not worth it.'

'It's harder for some people than others, isn't it?' said Lexi kindly. 'Some women can do it easily, others have to persevere, and others—'

'I did persevere,' said Katy defensively. 'So don't criticize, okay?'

'I wasn't saying you didn't, Katy,' said Lexi. 'I was going to say that breastfeeding isn't for everyone. Some women just can't do it at all. Mel said she found it impossible after those first few days—'

Katy's face was white. Her lips were trembling and her hands, down by her side, were clenched into tight fists.

'Thank you, Lexi,' she snapped. 'For pointing out that I am one of those women who can't do it *at all*. Just like

312

I couldn't do natural birth and just like I can't do being a good mother—'

'Oh, Katy,' said Lexi. 'You know I didn't mean that.'

'Didn't you?' Katy spat, her eyes shining. Everyone else was silent. No one knew where to look. Alan put his hand on Katy's arm.

'Calm down, sweetheart,' he said. 'Lexi didn't mean anything by it.'

'You would say that,' Katy said, bending swiftly down to pick up Rufus and clutch him to her chest. 'Because you're screwing each other!'

There was a sharp intake of breath, and Katy stormed out of the garden and into the house then out of the front door, slamming it behind her. Rebecca watched Alan and Lexi, who were ashen-faced. Alan, still holding the bottle of milk, rested his hand on Erin's shoulder, made a brusque apology and followed Katy. Everyone else was silent. They looked at Lexi, waiting for an explanation.

'Before you think anything,' said Lexi to the group, 'what Katy said is completely untrue. Alan and I had a one-night stand, a few years ago, before he got together properly with Katy. Nothing else has happened since. I need to speak to Katy. Do you think I should go now, or let them be together?'

Still no one said anything, then a voice came from the edge of the garden.

'Let them be together,' said Gary, stubbing out his cigarette. Rebecca had forgotten he was still there. Everyone looked at him. He was staring at Lexi, a grim expression on his face. 'You don't belong with him,' he said sharply.

'I don't belong with anyone,' said Lexi, deliberately turning her back on Gary to talk to Rebecca. He stood up, thanked Edward for the drink and left. Rebecca smiled doubtfully at Lexi.

'I cope alone,' she muttered.

'Are you all right?' Rebecca said. She'd never seen Lexi looking stressed before.

'What a nightmare,' Lexi said, dropping her gaze to the ground.

'What was all that about with Katy?' said Mel. 'You kept that close to your chest, didn't you?'

'But what was there to say?' said Leo, clearly defending the right to remain silent about big life issues. 'Why should she announce to everyone that something happened in ancient history?'

'Well, you would say that,' said Mel.

Erin tried to jolly the dwindling numbers along with proclamations about the food that was on its way: Sausages! Salmon! Salad! Rebecca watched her tip back her head and finish the contents of her glass.

'So, let's talk about something fun,' said Erin cheerfully. 'What about your wedding? I was wondering if you wanted me to teach you and Lenny a dance?'

Rebecca looked at Lenny, who laughed so hard that wine shot out of his nose. Mel, Leo and Lexi were pleased to laugh after the previous tension.

'That sounds like a great idea,' said Leo. 'What sort of dance? I can see Lenny doing a Bavarian waltz.'

Lenny laughed and slapped his thigh theatrically. 'Actually, I'd like that,' he said. 'Wouldn't you, Becs?'

'Um,' she said, pulling a face. 'I'm not sure.'

'Think about it,' he said. 'I think we could pull it out of the bag. So, you're really good, are you, Erin?'

'I haven't danced since before Josiah was born, but I was once very good,' she answered. 'I miss it, I really do.'

Edward went into the kitchen and, seconds later, music burst out of the speakers that were on the patio. He strode towards Erin, his back straight and head held high. Rebecca shared looks with Mel, who was giggling.

'Care to dance?' Edward said, holding his hand out to Erin. Rebecca and Mel slow-clapped their hands together in anticipation. Erin took hold of Edward's hand and grinned.

Watching Erin and Edward dance blew Lexi away. They moved so beautifully together, as if their limbs had been hand-stitched together. Lexi felt hungry for something she realized she had never found, not even with Alan, the man she had put on a pedestal as being The One Who Got Away. Placing her glass on the wooden garden table, she lifted a rose from a vase and held it under her nose. Love. Why was it so elusive for her? Why had she placed so much at Alan's feet when she barely knew him? Was it some kind of defence mechanism set in place to keep herself from becoming involved? Had she known, in her heart, that what she felt for Alan was fantasy and would never actually materialize into anything? Is that why she had chosen to focus on him? She shook her head. I'm more like my mother than I like to admit, she thought. Fucked up. Thinking of her mother sent a shiver across her neck. She looked at Poppy, whose eyes were droopy.

'I need to see Katy,' Lexi told Rebecca and Mel. 'I'm going

to walk around to her house and get Poppy off to sleep on the way.'

Thanking Erin and Edward, she put Poppy into her pram and left the house, moving up the street, past houses and gardens, their lights flicking on one after another in the dusk, like a flame catching. Poppy quickly fell asleep and Lexi paused to tuck her in. Walking down Katy's road, she watched the outline of people moving inside their houses, weaving stories from room to room. Everyone had a story, didn't they? There was one house that was still in darkness, though: Katy and Alan's house. For a moment, Lexi thought they weren't there, but Alan's BMW was parked outside and the windows were open. She approached the house and knocked, not wanting to wake Rufus with the bell.

'Do you mind if we talk?' she asked Katy, when the door opened. Katy didn't reply but silently showed her in. Lexi wheeled Poppy into the hallway and left her sleeping in the pram before following Katy through to the living room, which stretched from the front to the back of the house. She saw, through the French doors, that Alan was on the phone, walking back and forth, his arm wrapped around his chest. She felt herself blush. She barely knew him really, did she?

'He's speaking to his family,' Katy said. 'Pretending everything is great. Rufus is asleep. Today wore him out. What was it you wanted to talk about?'

Katy's eyes were dull, her blonde curls flattened and, when she flopped on to the sofa, her slim frame seemed stick-thin underneath the black dress she wore.

'After what you said at Erin's house, I wanted to assure you there's nothing going on with Alan and me,' said Lexi, speaking in a low, calm voice. 'I admit that we had a one-night stand years ago, as you know, but that was before you were together. I got a bit excited when I saw him again, but he's never been interested in me. Not remotely. I'm not exactly his type, am I? I don't think so. Seriously, Katy, nothing happened, nothing ever would happen.'

Katy looked up to the ceiling and blinked. 'Oh, I know,' she said, in a resigned voice. 'I never really thought anything was going on between you. I trust Alan, and he's been really good since Rufus was born. I just wanted to lash out. I'm sorry.'

Lexi lifted her hands as if to acknowledge the apology. 'But, look, I'm not here to talk about him,' she said.

'What then?' asked Katy, looking blank.

Lexi looked at her hands and suddenly felt like a thir-teen-year-old girl, sitting in the living room alongside her mother in one of her episodes of depression, willing herself to tell her mother to get up off the sofa and get help. To take control and be the grown-up. To listen. But, though she sat up in her bedroom with a script written in her diary rehearsing exactly what she would say, when they were face to face her tongue felt like a useless stump in her mouth. The heaviness of the atmosphere that hung around her mother when she was in this distant, lonely, private state of depression suffo-cated Lexi like a hand slapped over her mouth. Swallowing hard, she took a deep breath and reminded herself of why she was here.

'I think you need help,' she said, sitting forward in her chair. 'I think you should go to the doctor and tell him or her exactly how you're feeling.'

Katy picked at a thread that was loose on the hem of her

dress. 'I don't need help,' she said in a flat voice, not looking at Lexi. 'Who are you to tell me that?'

'Professionally, I'm a social worker, and I've worked with new mothers,' she said. 'Have you considered that you might have a mild form of postnatal depression? I know the symptoms very well, and I think you are displaying them. Has the health visitor done one of those questionnaires with you?'

'I haven't seen the health visitor since that first check,' Katy said. 'But, no, I don't think I have postnatal depression and I certainly don't need any help. I've never needed help.'

Katy was crying now, wiping at the tears falling down her cheeks with a tissue. In the background, she saw Alan clock her but stay outside, his hands pushed into his trouser pockets.

'We all need help sometimes,' said Lexi with a kind smile. 'My help came in the form of a Danish wanker.'

Katy met Lexi's eye and smiled.

'And Katy,' said Lexi with a sigh, 'my mother had depression that went undiagnosed for my entire childhood. It was not a good environment for me to grow up in, and she could so easily have taken responsibility and got herself to the doctor. He might have been able to help her. Instead, she refused to do anything about it and I really, really, resent her for that. You owe it to Rufus.'

Katy's eyes flashed. She wrapped her cardigan tightly around her body. 'I'm so frightened,' she said in a tiny voice. 'I don't know why I feel like this. I'm frightened that I can't look after Rufus and that I don't love him enough. There must be something wrong with me if I'm not woman enough to love my baby.'

'No,' said Lexi. 'We have to learn to be good parents, and

318

you have to learn to love your baby. I really believe that. You had a horrible, stressful birth, and you might need counselling for that. Perhaps the post-traumatic stress has triggered post-natal depression.'

'I've never needed counselling,' said Katy. 'The whole idea of it makes me feel that I've failed.'

'Not admitting you have a problem would be a failure,' said Lexi. 'If you get help – counselling, treatment, medication, whatever works – that's success.'

Lexi strained to listen as she heard Poppy stir in the hallway. She got up from her seat. 'I'll leave you now and go home and feed Poppy,' she said, moving towards the door. 'Don't get up. I'll be in touch, and maybe we could try helping each other out. Or not. Don't worry, I'm not going to force myself upon you.'

She closed the door behind her and pushed the pram, with Poppy waking now, towards her flat. The houses towered into the early evening sky. She was pleased with herself. She'd done the right thing. She hoped that Katy would, too. Later, when she climbed into bed, exhausted, with Poppy asleep in the basket beside the bed, her mobile phone beeped. Thinking it would probably be Gary, she picked up the phone, feeling guilty for not calling him earlier. It wasn't him. There was a text from Alan. In the darkness, she read his words: Lexi. You worked some magic. Thank you for being great. Alan x

A moment's hesitation before she deleted his message. A sense of relief washed over her. Goodbye, Alan.

Chapter Thirty-three

'What's the weather like, Len?' Rebecca asked as Lenny lifted up the edge of the blind to reveal bright blue sky. She was sitting up in bed after a sleepless night worrying, giving Elvis his morning feed.

'Gorgeous,' he said, pulling up the blind completely. 'Postcard perfect.'

Relief swept over Rebecca. She's been anxious all night that, if it rained, she'd have to go to a café or stay in the flat while her mum and dad were visiting, and Elvis hated staying inside or even being still. Now, though, on a day like this, they could walk down to the seafront and Elvis could be in the pushchair or sling and nap.

'Are you worried?' Rebecca asked. 'About meeting my parents?'

Lenny shook his head but continued to look out of the window. Rebecca frowned. He'd been really distant the last few days, as if he had something on his mind. But when she asked, he shrugged it off.

'Not at all,' he said. 'They either like me or they don't. It's no big deal.'

'So, if you're not bothered about my parents' visit,' she continued, 'what are you thinking about? You've been really quiet recently.'

Pressing her breast to see if it was empty, she swapped Elvis over to the other side, where he latched on and started to drink, pulling strands of her hair with his tiny hands while he did so.

Lenny looked at his shoes, gave her a sideways glance and a reassuring grin. He grabbed a towel and moved towards the shower.

'Do you still want to get married?' Rebecca asked, as he walked away. 'Because I don't mind putting it off and waiting, or whatever.'

'Of course I want to,' he said. 'Don't start saying you can wait. Jesus babe, look at me. I'm a great catch. You should be chasing me up the aisle.' He put his arms out by his side and rotated his hips, making his penis swing round and round in circles. Rebecca cracked up laughing.

'Don't do that when my mum and dad get here,' she said. 'They're coming in two hours.'

'Oh no, really? I was planning just to be naked when they're here,' he said sarcastically. 'I'll sit on the armchair naked, maybe with a strategic leaf over this monster and act like I'm fully clothed. Maybe I'll even sing a song to your mum. That'd be funny.'

'My mum wouldn't be laughing,' Rebecca said. 'She's not into nudity. In fact, I don't think I've ever seen her naked. She's a very private person.'

'Really?' said Lenny. 'Wow, my folks walk around naked the entire time. Even now! Last time I went home my dad was doing some gardening in the nude, just to piss off the neighbours. Fuck, I've just had a thought – they're not going to get on too well at the wedding, are they?'

'So, Lenny,' said Harriet, sitting neatly on the sofa in the living room where Elvis had been born ten weeks before, 'what is it that you do?'

Rebecca had been struck by her mother's appearance when she arrived. Though they looked very similar, sharing soft, dark eyes, pale pink lips and lustrous black hair, Harriet had lost quite a lot of weight. Despite the fact that she looked lovely in her rust-coloured dress, with lace detail on the arms and collar and dangly earrings in a matching tone, she looked worn out. Her dad, too, unassuming in a blue shirt tucked into his jeans, seemed less intimidating than usual. When they'd embraced, Harriet had squeezed her so tight, Rebecca fought for air.

'I'm a musician,' said Lenny. 'I'm in a band and we're making an album.'

Rebecca held her breath, waiting for her mother's reaction. Even though she'd convinced herself she didn't care what her mother thought of her life in Brighton, really, she desperately wanted her to approve and to understand. She was acutely aware that this life was nothing like the one her mother had wanted for her – a university education, a respectable, well-paid career in medicine. But would she be able to see how much happier Rebecca was, and that she was able to be herself here?

'That's very interesting,' Harriet said. 'And can you support your family on the money from that?'

Lenny shifted uncomfortably in his seat. He earned a pittance, but that wasn't the point of his music. He opened his mouth to speak, but Rebecca interrupted.

'We're not materialistic, Mum,' she said. 'Money isn't what matters to us.'

'I know that,' said Harriet. 'But you've still got to live, haven't you? This flat won't be big enough for all of you for much longer. Elvis is going to need his own room.'

Lenny pushed his hand through his hair.

'Lenny earns enough,' said Rebecca. 'And I'm doing massage at a health centre in Kemptown, which pays well. We can manage just fine. Elvis sleeps with us at the moment. That suits us.'

She felt full of rage. She couldn't believe how just a few words from her mother's mouth could put her back up so much.

'Don't take what your mother is asking the wrong way,' said Thomas, her dad. 'We were talking in the car about offering to give you some money if you needed it. That's all. Please don't take offence.'

Lenny's lips tightened. He shook his head. Rebecca tutted.

'That's very generous,' Lenny said. 'But we're fine. We're doing okay. We've even managed to save our pennies for the wedding. Do you think you'll be able to come? My friend is going to do it for us.'

'Your friend?' said Harriet.

'Yes. I've got this pal who's a total eccentric and a poet. He knows both of us, and I think he'll be the best celebrant there could be. We'll have a registrar there, so it's official, but he's going to run the whole gig for us.'

'We're having a humanist wedding,' said Rebecca. 'On the beach.'

Harriet nodded slowly. Rebecca felt annoyed. Her mother seemed completely distracted and kept glancing at Thomas, as if she wanted to run from the room.

'I'm sure you don't approve of that either,' said Rebecca coldly. 'But it's what we want.'

Harriet looked up in surprise. Thomas cleared his throat.

'It sounds very good, and of course I approve,' said Harriet. 'Listen, Rebecca, I know you have me down as some kind of monster, but I'm really not. Could I trouble you for a glass of water, please? I need to take a paracetamol.'

Rebecca felt embarrassed, as if she was acting like a teenager. Lenny jumped up and poured Harriet a glass of water. At the same time, Elvis had started to fuss. Rebecca picked him up, grateful for the distraction.

'Lenny,' she said, 'do you mind if I take Elvis for a walk with my parents? I think we could all do with the fresh air.'

Lenny virtually threw Rebecca the sling, which she placed Elvis inside and clicked up together like a professional. While Harriet swallowed her pill then pulled on her jacket and collected her bag, Thomas moved over to Lenny and patted him on the shoulder.

'I'm not sure when I'll see you again,' he said. 'But good luck with your music. It's been good to meet you. Hopefully, we'll make the wedding.'

Lenny smiled awkwardly. For the first time since Rebecca had known him, he didn't seem to know what to say. Rebecca couldn't get outside fast enough but, once they were on the streets, walking side by side, her parents in silence and occasionally exchanging worried glances, she wondered why she had ever agreed to this visit in the first place. Though she was trying to be calm, she suddenly stopped dead in the street and exploded.

'Why are you so quiet?' she asked. 'Why are you so disapproving of me and everything I do? Can't you just appreciate the fact I have found Lenny and had Elvis? I love them both! Isn't that the most important thing in life? Will you ever, ever, be pleased with what I choose to do?'

Harriet put her hand on Rebecca's shoulder. 'We are pleased,' she said unconvincingly.

'No, you're not!' said Rebecca. 'You want me to be just like your darling son! You want me to be at uni, studying medicine. I'm probably an embarrassment to you. Why don't you just admit it! All I really want to do is love my boys and go travelling one day. I want to see India. I want to see where our family lived and where Grandpa was born. Just because I've had Elvis doesn't mean I'm suddenly going to give up on my dreams or not use my brain.'

Harriet and Thomas looked pale and upset. Rebecca hated herself for shouting at them, but why were they holding back so much? It felt so passive aggressive.

'We've always known you're a free spirit,' said Harriet quietly. 'I guess I haven't let you be what you want to be. I know how that feels. Honestly, I really do. I spent my entire life trying to please my father and, in a way, I envy your independence. Your father and I have had a bit of a wake-up call recently. We were wondering if you, Lenny and Elvis would agree to a week's holiday with us in a few months' time?'

'Here?' Erin said, pushing aside the bags on the kitchen table and laying down a blanket she'd found for the garden.

Their first kiss was tentative, embarrassed. The second was more relaxed. The third was passionate and uplifting, as Erin realized when her hands moved to Edward's zip, in more ways than one. While Erin and Edward leaned over the table together, two muted violins played on the radio and the spring breeze blew on to their naked skin. Hope slept peacefully. Life was beautiful.

Rufus didn't like his car seat. Even though it was the best money could buy, he bawled from the moment he was strapped in until the moment he was released.

'We should have walked,' said Katy, in a monotone, as Alan swung round the corner towards Erin's house. Rufus's cry filled the car.

He indicated and slowed down to park, behind Erin and Edward's Golf.

'You need to take it easy,' said Alan through clenched teeth. He was trying to be patient, but his voice was spiky with anger. Katy knew he was at breaking point and that soon he would not be able to hold his tongue. Though some distant voice warned her not to push him any further, because he was already overloaded – she knew that – something in her wanted him to break, so that she could see he was fallible, too, that he sometimes failed. Perhaps if he broke, she would be instantly mended.

'Don't cry, Rufus,' called Alan, craning his neck to see his son. 'We're here now. Let's get you out of that little prison.'

Katy tutted and shook her head. She opened the car door

Harriet's lips were trembling. Thomas had his arm around her, his expression grave. Rebecca almost laughed. Go on holiday with her parents after months of not speaking and years of being at loggerheads?

'On holiday?' she said, bemused. 'Why?'

Thomas and Harriet looked at one another. Thomas held her mother more tightly and nodded at her. Harriet picked up Rebecca's hand and held it.

'We didn't always fight,' she said. 'When you were little, you and I were incredibly close. I can remember you sleeping next to me when you were a toddler, holding my hand all through the night. I remember all your school plays and the sports matches you played in. We even used to paint our toenails together. I was so proud and, though I haven't always shown it – I am proud of you still. We both are.'

'Thank you,' said Rebecca, taken aback. 'But why a holiday? Isn't that a bit drastic?'

'Well, not really,' Harriet said flatly. 'Look, shall we just carry on walking?'

'No,' said Rebecca. 'Tell me what's going on.'

Harriet looked at Thomas, who gave her a kind smile.

'Your mother's not well,' he said.

'What do you mean?' asked Rebecca, her throat constricting.

'We don't know how long I have to live,' said Harriet, her eyes glassy.

Rebecca stood frozen to the spot. Her stomach turned over and her face flushed. Her mother was dying?

'What?' she said, her voice shaking. 'I don't understand. You can't just say that—'

She hadn't even got to know her mother properly and here

she was, saying she was going to die? Rebecca was taken aback. The idea of Harriet, strong-minded, proper, high-achieving, strict mum becoming frail and weak was too awful. She cursed herself for not being in contact these past few months.

'But you're a doctor,' said Rebecca lamely. 'I . . . I—'

'It's a brain tumour. I'm going to have radiotherapy, but I'm not sure how long I'll have,' sighed Harriet. 'So we want to give you a lasting memory that's positive. I've been far too controlling of you, but only because I loved you. Only because I wanted to give you the best chance in life. Since finding out about my condition, I've become very reflective, and my biggest regret is not listening to you properly. I knew in my heart you wanted different things to me and your dad, but I didn't give you the chance to get your voice heard. I'm sorry.'

Rebecca felt the tears rushing into her eyes. She pushed her head into her mother's shoulder and held on tight. Thomas put his arm around them both and held them.

'I'm sorry, darling,' said Harriet in a whisper. 'I'm glad you have Lenny and Elvis. I'm glad you have them both to love and to love you. I'm sorry I haven't been a good mother. I'm sorry.'

'No, Mum,' Rebecca said. '*I'm* sorry, I'm really sorry, Mum. Oh, Mum, I'm so sorry.'

Chapter Thirty-four

An accident. Yes. That's what it was. Just as she hadn't meant to break Leo's finger, Mel hadn't meant to open Leo's email. His Googlemail account was just there, open and tempting on the desktop of the computer. An invitation. He'd told her his password. There were no secrets between them. What was the big deal if her fingertips accidentally landed on the letters that spelled out his password?

'Mabel,' she said, placing her cup of coffee on the desk, her face flushing in vague embarrassment as she typed in Leo's password and waited for his emails to appear. 'I know this is a bit naughty, but, while Daddy's at work, I want to make sure Coco isn't sticking her nose where it's not wanted—'

While the computer made its unnerving whirring sound as it loaded, Mel twisted in her chair to check on her daughter, who was on a mat on the carpet, cooing and trying her damnedest to roll over. Surrounding the mat lay various squeaking and beeping toys Mrs Lelani had bought her; there was something new virtually every day, and they now had a collection that rendered their subtle wooden toy box useless.

She passed her eyes over the rest of the living room. It was a bright day, and the streaks of sunshine falling through the shutter slats were throwing spotlights on dustballs everywhere. Yikes. The corners of the room had balls of fur in them. What if Mabel was breathing all that in? Would she get asthma? Groaning and pledging to dust and tidy at some point in her life, Mel cocked her head apologetically towards Mabel.

'Shall we go swimming in a minute with Becs and Elvis, away from all this dust?' she said. 'Just let Mummy do this and we'll go.'

Beaming at her daughter then turning back to the computer, her eyes fell on the screen, which was slightly obscured by the leaves of the spider plant that sat on top. She blinked. Pushing it back so hard it fell down the back of the computer and on to the carpet, she gaped. Three emails down from the top was one from Coco. It was clearly part of an ongoing conversation.

'I don't believe this!' she said, opening the succession of emails, her heart banging and her mouth going dry.

Her eyes wide, she read their email conversation:

Hi, Leo. My address is 24 Honey Hill, Hampstead, London. Just call to arrange x

Then came Leo's answer:

I'll talk to Mel and see how she feels. Honey Hill – does Eeyore live there, too?

Then another one from Coco:

Just come on your own. I didn't tell you everything when we met— x

The reply from Leo:

I'll talk to Mel.

Then, finally, from Coco:

Seriously, we should talk. Things aren't quite as they seem in Honey Hill— x

Mel read the emails twice more before closing down the computer. Honey Hill? Was that some kind of joke? Only someone as beautiful as Coco could have an address like Honey Hill. Mel's blood boiled. How dare she try to lure Leo to Honey Hill? Mel tried to calm herself. *Seriously, we should talk. Things aren't as they seem in Honey Hill . . .* it sounded like the name of some dodgy porn flick. And Leo had made a joke about Eeyore! Did that count as flirtation? Mel stood up and put her hands on her hips. Staring at the computer, she kicked the office chair. *Serves you right for looking* came her mother's voice in her head. But did it serve her right? If Leo and Coco were conversing, didn't she have the right to know? Mel had never been the jealous type, but this situation was completely different. And, since having Mabel, Mel didn't feel quite as confident as her old self. No one could ignore the fact that Coco was so . . . so . . . incredibly beautiful! Only eight weeks after giving birth, sleep-deprived Mel felt hideously unattractive. With bags like aubergines under her eyes, her face looked drawn and defeated. Her maternity blouse was billowing and shapeless. And her trousers? She knew she was being ambitious putting them on. The seams were about to split. She sucked in her stomach and clenched her bottom, thinking of Coco and Leo together, smirking at how mumsy Mel had become already. Leo rarely complimented her these days, did he? And as for sex? That was a big no-go area. Maybe Leo didn't look at her in the same way since seeing Mabel emerge from the depths of her body? Stop, she told herself. You're being stupid, he'd never think that. Would he?

'Oh, God,' said Mel, her hands on the side of her head. 'What should I do?'

Mabel started to whimper and so Mel picked her up, kissing her head and cuddling her close then shaking a rattle in front of her. She took a deep breath. I will not cry, she instructed herself. I will not cry. I will not laugh. Feeling tears spring into her eyes, she closed her eyes and breathed. *Leo's not actually done anything wrong* came her mother's voice again. At last – a voice of reason! Her eyes pinged open.

What's happening to me? she thought, as if she could suddenly see herself like she was watching herself on television. I'm falling apart! I'm acting like a loon.

Dismayed, Mel stared at the soil from the pot of the plant that had scattered on the floor. I used to be the lead graphic designer at Yellow. I used to be the star of the agency. I used to get asked to take on the most important jobs. Deal with the biggest clients. I've won awards! I've endured labour, for God's sake! Now I'm behaving like a simpering idiot. What's got into me? Mabel was wriggling in her arms, restless, Mel sensed, to get out of the flat. Mel checked the clock. She was due to meet Rebecca in ten minutes.

'Okay, sweetheart,' she said, her hands clammy with anxious sweat. 'I'm sorry. Let's go swimming.'

Stuffing a bikini, too small and years old – her swimsuit had disappeared into the same place all her knickers, except for her massive, apple-gathering, post-birth ones, had gone – into a bag with a towel, nappies, wipes, a change of clothes for Mabel and a couple of swimming nappies, Coco's words ran on a loop in her head. *Things aren't as they seem in Honey Hill. Come on your own.* With Mabel in her arms, cursing Coco under her breath, she made her way out of the flat, locking the door and collecting the buggy from the top of the stairs. Gingerly carrying Mabel, the pushchair and two bags downstairs with her, images of them both tumbling to their deaths as she walked and chastising herself for not doing two journeys, she breathed a sigh of relief when she reached the bottom and opened the front door. Checking she had her wallet in her pocket, an idea flashed into her mind. A very bad idea. *I'll go and see Coco. She surprised me. Now it's my turn to surprise her.* No, she told herself. That's ludicrous. You can't possibly go. Striding up the street, pushing Mabel in the pushchair to meet Rebecca on the crossroads, the swimming bag dangling off one handle, the changing bag off the other and knocking against her knees, she repeated to herself that she couldn't possibly go. *Only forty-five minutes on the train.* Speak to Leo, that's what I should do. Wait. But then he'd know she was spying on his emails. Then he'd think she was crazy. Maybe she was. Pulling her phone out of her pocket, she dialled him. When he picked up, she didn't even say hello.

'Have you got anything to tell me?' she asked brusquely. 'Anything about Coco?'

A lump rose in her throat as she waited for his answer. She hated being like this, but couldn't help herself.

'What?' he said, sounding confused. 'Do you mean because I've heard from her? I said we'd visit her some time. Of course I've said not right now, but I would like to talk to Jacques properly and tell him who I am, in the future. I wanted to leave it until things had calmed down a bit.'

'How do you think her husband feels about that?' Mel asked.

Leo was silent for a while, then he answered. 'Do you know what?' he said. 'I get the feeling her husband isn't on the scene any more.'

'Right,' said Mel, as calmly as she could. Inwardly, she was screaming obscenities at Coco. Her mind was made up. 'Well, look, if I'm late tonight don't worry. I might go round to Rebecca's to talk about her wedding.'

Silence. She cringed, knowing that he must be guessing what she planned.

'Oh,' said Leo, disappointed. 'So you won't be there when I get home from work? I'm missing Mabel. And you.'

Incredible. Why were men so thick-skinned? It wasn't even occurring to Leo that she might be planning to go to see Coco. That's because he was sane. And she wasn't.

'No, but we'll talk later,' Mel said firmly before hanging up.

Waving at Rebecca, who was waiting on the corner, leaning against a red brick wall like a model in a trendy jeans advert, looking as if she might start street dancing at any moment if she hadn't been carrying Elvis in his sling, Mel felt her resolve grow stronger. One part of her brain told her she was being teenaged, another part told her she was being brave. A final part told her she just wanted to avoid putting on her bikini.

'Fancy a trip to London?' asked Mel. 'I'll get the tickets.'

Rebecca looked bemused, but smiled at the same time. There was a glint in her eyes.

'Err, yeah?' said Rebecca. 'But why? I thought we were going to Little Swimmers. I'd rather go to London, though.'

'I'll explain on the way,' she said. 'If we walk quickly we'll make the twelve o'clock.'

Smile, Katy told herself. Go on. Smile now. As she sat in the GP surgery's waiting room with Rufus in the car seat, asleep, a young mother, tall, with long, dark hair tumbling over her shoulders and dressed in a long, flowery dress and a mohair cardigan, holding her baby in her arms and pacing back and forth, smiled at Katy.

'Is your baby poorly?' said the woman, standing still but rocking from side to side to soothe her baby.

'No,' said Katy with a brief smile, though she felt like curling up into a ball. 'He's fine. How about yours?'

Katy really didn't want to listen to this woman. She needed these few minutes to psyche herself up. Speaking to a perfect Mother Earth type would only make matters worse. Make the fear swallow her up in one gulp. If I don't make eye contact, she thought, maybe I'll be left alone.

'Oh, she's fine,' said the woman. 'I'm the one with the problem. Since she's been born, I can't stop crying. I don't know what's wrong with me. I used to be so upbeat, and now I can barely drag myself out of bed in the morning.'

The woman let out a duck-like laugh. Katy felt surprised. She smiled at the woman sympathetically. Maybe she wasn't alone in the world.

'I know what you mean,' she said briefly.

'Do you?' said the woman. 'Because so many people I talk to don't. Sorry, I think I'm venting.'

'No,' said Katy hesitantly. 'No, you're not. Actually, well, I'm not too good either. I had a horrible birth and, well, it's scarred me, in more ways than one.'

There. She'd said it. Admitted to a perfect stranger that she had a problem. That wasn't so hard. No one laughed. No enormous arrow inscribed with 'failure' fell from the sky and pointed at her. She felt shaken but also buoyed up, ready to see her GP. But she knew her mood could change at any moment. Glancing at the electronic board, she willed her name to flash up next. It's unbelievable how nervous I feel, she thought. Christ, my hands and legs are shaking.

'I go to a brilliant group,' said the woman. 'It's for women who had a tough time in labour. I did, too. We don't all sit around analysing our births, but you can talk about it if you want to and it's just good to be with other women who understand. All my friends seem to have had ideal births and, though I'm glad for them, it can be a little galling when it's literally all they talk about. Here, have my card.'

The woman handed her a business card. Katy scanned it: Shereen Blake, Events Organizer. They'd probably come across each other professionally before now. Then the electronic board bleeped and Katy's name came up. Room number 3. She smiled at Shereen, picked up the sleeping Rufus and carried him down the corridor to Room 3. As she knocked cautiously on the door and entered the brightly lit room, her heart was beating too fast and too loudly. She felt light-headed. Christ, she thought, can I do this?

'Hello, Katy,' said Dr Wallace, a female doctor Katy had been to on the few occasions she'd had to see the GP during pregnancy. 'How can I help you?'

Sit down, she told herself. Take deep breaths. Closing her

eyes for a few moments, she took a long deep breath and did what she'd never had to do in her life. She asked for help.

'This has come as a surprise to me. I'm a successful businesswoman and director of a company. Everything in my life used to be ordered. My wardrobe is colour-coded, my books alphabetically shelved,' she said, choking on her words. 'I had a healthy pregnancy and really looked after myself. But, now that Rufus is here, my life feels like it's spiralling out of control. I'm not coping very well.'

She swallowed, blinking back the tears in her eyes. She thought of the way she'd spoken to Alan that morning. They'd argued so viciously – about what? The way he'd made the porridge, of all things! She blushed remembering how she'd shouted at Alan for using full-fat milk and not her organic skimmed milk. She'd refused to eat breakfast, pushed the bowl away and folded her arms like a moody teenager. Alan had shouted back and dumped the porridge in the sink. Rufus had started to cry, his face turning bright pink. In a vision of the future, Katy had been hit with a flash-forward of ten years: Rufus in his bedroom with his headphones jammed against his ears, door closed, to drown out Mum and Dad screeching at each other downstairs. Her blood had run cold and she'd picked up the phone to make an appointment at the surgery. Now or never.

'I think I need help,' she said. 'I'm not myself. At all.'

Dr Wallace was nodding at Katy knowingly, and smiling sympathetically.

'I understand,' she said. 'A lot of women feel like this, which may comfort you. If you could tell me more about your feel-

ings, I will try to help you. And, Katy, I've been there myself.
I know what you're going through.'

Katy's eyes grew wider. Dr Wallace was a smooth-skinned,
cool, lively young doctor she instinctively admired. She looked
as if she'd never had a problem of her own in her life. Katy
gave her a small nod, to acknowledge her sharing. She took
a deep breath and started at the beginning, when the nightmare began.

'The birth didn't go as I had planned,' she said, her eyes
on Rufus. 'I had an emergency C-section, but it wasn't the
C-section that was the problem. I could get my head around
not having a natural birth. No, it was the fact that I didn't
know, when he came out, if he was alive or—'

The journey to London was the length of Rebecca's breastfeed, much to the apparent distaste of a businessman sitting
opposite them. Mel was so angry at that moment, she didn't
give a fuck what he thought and, every time he looked at
Rebecca, she glared back at him, daring him to say a word.
If he says anything, she told herself, I will ask him why Rebecca's
breasts offend him and those on page three of his newspaper
don't. Perhaps it's because he thinks Rebecca's breasts should
be there for *him* to appreciate and not Elvis? I might even
suggest she squirt him in the eye with a jet of milk. That would
silence him. When he got bored with staring at Mel and
Rebecca, the man immersed himself in his newspaper and
Mel gazed out of the window at the changing landscape. The
Sussex Downs were so surprisingly green compared to
Brighton, and the sight of all those fields made her think of
her childhood. They'd lived in a small house that backed on

Amy Bratley

to the fields, so she'd spent many hours rambling across them alone or with pals. After her dad had died, Mel's perspective on the hills changed. They seemed empty and lonely, somewhere she didn't want to be when she grew up. She had quietly planned out the rest of her life. She would earn money from drawing pictures, because she was best in her class at art. When she was old enough, she would have a family with lots of children running around her house by the sea. There would be a happy ever after. There had to be. What of that happy ending now? Was Coco going to ruin it?

'So, the plan is,' Rebecca said nervously, from beside Mel, 'we go to Coco's house, or flat, or caravan, or whatever she lives in, and take her by surprise and tell her to stay out of Leo's life.'

'I don't think it's a caravan,' said Mel with a smile. 'From what I've witnessed of her, she probably lives in one of those amazing London town houses. Or a palace even.'

'Okay,' said Rebecca. 'So we'll storm the palace and take her by surprise! Good plan.'

Mel laughed. She didn't actually have a clue what the plan was. In fact, by the time the train pulled into London, the strong urge to kill Coco she had felt after reading her email conversation with Leo was fading slightly. And by the time they'd spent twenty minutes travelling on two different tube lines and sitting in a clump of warm, stringy, chewing gum (during which, the babies, mercifully, slept), her reason for coming almost eluded her. Walking in the direction of Honey Hill, Mel passed the lush green Hampstead Heath, but she was too absorbed in what she was about to do to notice her surroundings. What. Am. I. Doing. She chanted it in time

338

with her steps. Catching sight of herself in a car window, she was mildly horrified. What was that top all about? She looked as if she'd walked into a kite, or a banner that had fallen from a shopfront. And those trousers! Was it really possible to have been wearing size twelve jeans just a year ago?

'I can't go,' she said, stopping abruptly. 'This is ridiculous. What am I doing?'

Rebecca, probably wishing she'd never agreed to come, put her hand on Mel's arm.

'Just go and talk to her,' she said. 'You can always say we were in London for another reason and decided to look her up. At least if you talk you can get an idea of what she really wants. One thing I think now, since my mum told me about her illness, is that you have to tell the truth. Be open.'

Mel rubbed the back of her neck and checked on Mabel, who was still fast asleep. She was going to wake up screaming for food any minute.

'She's going to think I'm crazy, but you're right,' she replied. 'I can't read an email and freak out like this. Why do I feel so totally threatened by her? I'm sorry about your mum, Rebecca.'

Rebecca smiled in acknowledgement. 'It's probably because you've just had Mabel and everything is new and fragile and difficult, but underneath all that you've got a baby with the man you love and you don't want anything or anyone to threaten that. I understand that.'

Mel smiled at Rebecca and hugged her, avoiding Elvis, asleep in his sling.

'Thanks,' she said. 'Thanks for coming. You're the only one

I could have asked. Lexi, Katy and Erin would have stopped me.'

'They probably have more sense than me,' said Rebecca with a grin. 'Come on, let's just go and get it over with then sit on the heath and get an ice cream.'

Outside Coco's address, Mel and Rebecca stopped at the ornate iron railings and gawped. In the garden, pruning roses, the image of a breathtakingly pretty Catherine Zeta-Jones in *The Darling Buds of May*, her hair up in a loose bun, tendrils falling around her jaw, dressed in denim hotpants, wedges and a white blouse tied at the waist so her tanned midriff was visible, was Coco. On the grass nearby, a slim woman with short blonde hair dressed in a striped top and jeans sat with a young boy: Jacques. Adorable. Mel's legs almost gave way. He was the image of Leo. The woman lay on her back, reading, while Jacques played on some kind of computer game. Mel shook her head at Rebecca and pointed in the direction they'd come. Grabbing her by the elbow, she steered her away from the iron railings, wanting to run away as fast as her legs would carry her. But, at that moment, Mabel woke up and let out a piercing cry. Mabel's cry woke up Elvis, and he, too, began to cry. Coco, the woman and Jacques all looked towards the sound. Shit. Mel's stomach flipped.

'*Mon Dieu!*' said Coco, waving her pruning shears in the air. 'Mel? What are you doing here?'

Mel smiled a watery smile. She attempted to arrange her features in a 'Fancy that, you live here, do you?' type of expression. And failed miserably.

'Mel?' Coco said again, sashaying over the grass towards them then opening the garden gate and gesturing that they should enter. 'What are you doing here? Is Leo with you?'

Mel froze. No words came. She suddenly had no idea why she was there or what she wanted to say. Slowly, she walked in through the garden gate. She shook her head in answer to Coco's question. Jacques, Leo's boy, was staring at them and all Mel could think was that he and Mabel were half-brother and -sister. Staring at Coco, she thought she could still pass for seventeen, so fresh-faced and bright-eyed was she. Mel had never looked like that, not even when she was seventeen. A goth, she'd been. Hair dyed blue-black, black nail varnish, lashings of black eye make-up. They would never have been friends. Rebecca elbowed her in the ribs and Mel blinked.

'Go on,' she muttered. 'Tell her why you're here.'

Mel was inches away from Coco, whose expression was confused yet amiable. Mabel cried in her pushchair, so Mel unclipped her and lifted her out. She was hungry, and Mel needed to feed her. At least that was what the damp patches on her kite blouse were telling her.

'Oh!' said Coco, tickling Mabel's chin. 'I have never seen such a beautiful baby girl.'

Instantly, Mabel stopped crying and suddenly Coco was holding her, kissing Mel on both cheeks and shaking Rebecca's hand.

'Congratulations,' she said, holding Mabel up to look at her properly. 'You're so lucky to have her. She looks like Leo?'

When Mel didn't respond, Coco frowned. The slim woman with long legs on the rug stood up and brushed off her trousers, lolloping over to where they were standing. She rested her hand affectionately on Coco's shoulder.

'Is everything okay?' she said. She had an American accent

---

and delicate features. Coco patted the woman's hand and nodded.

'This is Mel,' she said. 'And her friend Rebecca. Mel is Leo's partner. This is Suki. Are you going to speak, Mel?'

Mel opened her mouth to answer and thought she began to speak, but her words trailed off. Rebecca, frantically bobbing Elvis up and down to stop him crying, gave her a hard stare.

'Go on, Mel,' she urged. 'Don't be shy now.'

'I . . . I . . .' she said, taking a deep breath. 'I want to know why you are emailing Leo and asking him to come and see you, alone, without me?'

Coco was frowning. She looked utterly bemused. Mel suddenly felt really, really silly.

'I emailed because I need to talk to him,' she said. 'But I didn't want to see him alone.'

'Do you want him back?' Mel asked. 'Because I'd really like to know if you're going to attempt to steal my boyfriend from under my nose, just so you can play families, nine years on.'

'Why don't you come in?' said Coco, looking suddenly tired, but Mel shook her head. Coco sighed.

'I should explain,' she said, glancing at Jacques, who was still showing no interest in the women. 'The reason I wanted to see Leo is because Suki and I are together. I realized I was in love with her three years ago. I had to break off my relationship with Peter, my husband, and he was very upset with me. That's why we moved to London, for a clean break. I wanted to speak to Leo, to let him know what was happening. I didn't feel it was right to tell him all this when we came down to Brighton, because he was so preoccupied with the fact he thought he was hurting you. I know that Jacques would probably appreciate a male in his life, if Leo would be happy to, occasionally, meet up with him. Peter wants nothing to do with us. I just wanted to give him all the information.'

Suki put her arm around Coco's shoulders. Mel gaped at them as if it was the first time she'd ever seen a lesbian couple. She felt so utterly foolish.

'Shit,' she said. 'I've made a fool of myself. I'm sorry.'

'No,' said Coco. 'I should have explained when we met. It is my fault. I'm sorry if I have caused you distress. That was never my intention. You must be really fed up with me. Please, come inside.'

Mel and Rebecca were quiet as they followed Coco and Suki inside the house and into the immaculate kitchen, where pale blue French doors opened out on to a small back garden bursting with bushes of pink peonies. Mel, carrying Mabel, felt ridiculous and embarrassed as Coco invited her to sit down at the oak kitchen table decorated with three small glass vases of lilac flowers. Suki offered seats and moved books and newspapers away from the table top, making space. Mel heard herself say thank you for the hundredth time. Jacques' footsteps could be heard jumping up the stairs.

'Jacques?' Suki called out of the kitchen door and up the stairs. 'Would you like a drink?'

There came a muffled 'no' response and Suki returned to the kitchen, smiling at the awkward assembled group.

'Can I make you both tea?' she said kindly. 'I'm sure you need to feed Mabel?'

Mabel was grizzling and did need feeding. Finding the

formula and mixing it with cooled boiled water, Mel gave Mabel her bottle, wishing she was invisible.

'Thank you,' she said, again, glancing nervously at Rebecca. 'Listen, I'm sorry, Coco. I feel really stupidly ridiculous about coming here today. I think it's the post-pregnancy hormones. I've lost the plot.'

Coco shook her head and laughed slightly. Rebecca smiled encouragingly at Mel and sat Elvis on her knee with her set of keys.

'How were you to know what was going on in my life?' said Coco. 'I have hardly known what is going on in my life! Never been certain of anything until I met Suki and knew I had to break up with Peter. I'm sure seeing me in Brighton was the last thing you needed—'

Suki put her arm around Coco and they shared a smile. Mel nodded, noting how incredibly attractive both Coco and Suki were. Her cheeks flushed.

'As I said, I got in touch with Leo by email because I know that Jacques is missing Peter,' she said. 'And Peter will have nothing to do with any of us—'

She looked suddenly very sad and shook her head, hopelessly. She looked up at the ceiling. 'What am I supposed to say to Jacques?' she continued. 'He thinks Peter is his dad and that there's no chance of seeing his genetic father. He needs to know that's not the case. I thought, since Leo contacted me, that it could be the time to tell the truth. I know that's not easy for him or you, Mel.'

Coco put a white teapot down on the table and poured a cup for Rebecca, then for Mel. She opened up a tin of biscuits, all delicately iced in sorbet colours, but, notably, didn't eat one herself.

'Thanks,' Mel said once more, taking a sip of her tea. 'I do understand where you are coming from. I grew up without my dad, and I know how empty that can leave you feeling. I think, if Leo's willing, it would be unfair to deny Jacques the chance to get to know him. To be honest, my frustration was more about your intentions with Leo . . . and now I can see that's not going to be an issue—'

'No,' said Suki drily. 'Absolutely not an issue.'

'Of course not,' said Coco. 'It is Jacques that I am thinking of. It is always of him I am thinking—'

From upstairs, there was the sound of a guitar being strummed. Jacques.

'And Jacques,' said Mel. 'What is Jacques really like?'

Coco pulled back her hair and smiled an enormous, infectious smile. Mel felt herself relax.

'From what I remember of Leo, when he was just sixteen, Jacques is so much like him,' said Coco. 'He can be shy, but is quietly determined. He loves music and art at school. He's thoughtful and sensitive, but pretty independent. Does that sound like Leo to you?'

'Pretty much,' said Mel. 'Those are his good traits. I don't think you knew him long enough to get past those—'

Everyone laughed.

'I think they will get on,' said Coco. 'But I know Leo has Mabel and you to concentrate on. You are a new family and I don't want to upset that. Perhaps, down the line, if you feel this is right for your family, Leo could consider meeting Jacques again, to get to know him.'

Mabel had fallen asleep after her feed and Mel lifted her up, holding her gently against her shoulder. Rebecca looked at Mel, waiting for her answer.

'I've always wanted a big family in whatever shape or form,' said Mel calmly, with a warm little shrug of her shoulders, 'With Jacques' best interests at heart, why don't we see how it goes?'

'Yes,' said Coco, moving over to Mel and giving her a hug. 'That sounds very wise. Let's see how it goes. Thank you.'

Later, at home in the flat, when Mabel was asleep, Leo brought Mel a large glass of red wine. That was one great perk about bottle-feeding. She could have a few glasses of wine whenever she felt like it. Wrapped in her dressing gown, she wiped London's dust from her skin with cleanser-soaked cotton-wool balls, collecting a small heap on the arm of the sofa before taking a deep slug of the wine. She thought about her afternoon with Coco and Suki.

'So,' he said, sitting next to her on the sofa and lifting her legs up on his own so he could massage her feet, 'how did the wedding stuff go? Is Rebecca all sorted?'

Mel wriggled her toes, looked at Leo and narrowed her eyes. Did he really have no inkling that she'd been to London to see Coco? How should she phrase it? Leo, his hair sticking out at the back from where he'd fallen asleep while putting Mabel to bed, seemed completely oblivious. While she had been in emotional turmoil, unveiling truths about his significant ex, he had been working on his computer, in his slightly stinky all-male office overlooking the back of the Churchill Square shopping centre, filing through the archives of code in his brain to bring another website design to life. Mel stuck her nose in her glass of wine and took another gulp.

'About earlier,' he started. 'I'm sorry if you were pissed off. I wanted to tell you that Coco has been in touch, but after all you've said and how paranoid you are about it, I guess I'm a little worried that you might be right. What if she does have a crush on me?'

'What?' Mel spluttered, laughing so hard wine shot through her nose. She slapped the arm of the chair and the cotton-wool balls flew off. 'Oh, Leo!'

'What?' he asked, wide-eyed. 'What's so funny?'

'Life,' said Mel. 'Life's funny.'

Chapter Thirty-five

It wasn't Goa. It wasn't Mauritius. It wasn't Bora Bora. But it *was* Brighton – where the sea-salty taste of the air, the sea-gulls circling discarded chips, the smooth, warm pebbles on the beach, the stragglers, deserters and smugglers wandering the streets alongside the organic lovers, vintage kids, the pea-shoot-munching folk, the queens with their kings – and it felt to Rebecca just like home. And what better place to get married than Brighton beach on a beautiful, blue-sky day in August? Rebecca had parked Lenny's VW Beetle, with Elvis strapped in the back, opposite the beach. If I believed in God, which I don't, she thought as she waited for the engine to cut out, I would thank the old man for this amazing weather.

'So, Elvis,' she said, her Fifties prom-style pale-yellow wedding dress bunching up over the bottom half of the steering wheel. 'I'm getting married today, to your daddy.'

From his car seat, Elvis gurgled.

'Is that funny?' asked Rebecca, turning round to watch him blow a gleeful raspberry.

Checking her reflection, she smoothed down her eyebrows

and checked that her yellow-rose hair clip was still in place behind her ear. Opening the driver door, she hummed the wedding march, before laughing at herself. Lifting a smiling, cooing Elvis, dressed in his finest gingham dungarees, out of his car seat, she strapped him into the pushchair, locked the car door and crossed the road to the beach, her vintage sling-backs clip-clopping on the pavement. Some might say it wasn't very glamorous, driving yourself to the beach, pushing your baby boy along, with a changing bag stuffed in the basket underneath. But, for Rebecca, it was perfect. She'd never been a horse-and-chariot sort of girl, just as she'd never wanted an academic life, or fit in to the claustrophobic village she'd grown up in. This, with the sun warm on her face, the glittering sea – and what was that in the distance? She squinted in the light. A naked man paddling in the shallows was being escorted away by a policeman. Ha! That was the beauty of Brighton. It was full of characters. Nothing was predictable. Walking just a little further, she lifted her hand over her eyes, looking for her crowd. Lenny was getting there early to decorate the white marquee they'd bought from Argos with Hawaiian flower strings and balloons. Ah, she thought, spotting everyone, all dressed up. Her heart flipped over. The only bad thing about today was that her mum was even more poorly. Over the last few weeks they'd spoken on the phone so many times she felt she was getting to know her mother as an equal, but in the last few days, Harriet had admitted to feeling worse. Rebecca took a deep breath, trying not to let herself think of it, but jumped as someone grabbed her arm.

'Becs!' said Lenny, suddenly there right in her face, sweaty from running, dressed in a pale-blue suit, flowery shirt and white shoes. 'I'm really sorry, but there's been a bit of a scene. My dad's been arrested. No, not arrested exactly. I told you how much he likes to get naked. He went for a swim and made a big deal of it, so a copper just came and asked him to put his kit on. He refused, so now he's talking to him in his panda car.'

He stopped gabbling for a moment and stood still, taking Rebecca in, his mouth open in amazement, admiring her.

'Wow, Becs,' he said. 'You look gorgeous. Incredible. You're dazzling, babe. Truly. Quick, let's get married before you change your mind! Yeah, but sorry about my dad. He goes his own way.'

Lenny pantomimed that his dad was a bit cuckoo, by circling his finger by the side of his head. Rebecca grinned and stopped to hug Lenny. 'I love you, Lenny, and I think your dad is great,' she said, linking arms with him. 'Let's go. Is my mum here yet? Did she see your dad get naked?'

'Yes,' Lenny said, leaning down to ruffle Elvis's shock of dark hair. 'She's here and, yes, she saw him. She looks well.'

Rebecca smiled warily, and sighed.

'Everything else okay?' said Rebecca.

'Yeah,' said Lenny, suddenly deflated. 'Except for Mack. He's really pissed off with me.'

Rebecca felt worried. 'Why, Len? What's up?'

Lenny sighed then shook his head, cheering up as they moved closer towards the marquee.

'Nothing to worry about,' he said, lifting the pushchair over the pebbles while they moved towards the group, who clapped to welcome them. Rebecca scanned her friends, excitedly saying hello to the antenatal-group mums, who all looked amazing, to her friends from college and work and her parents. Just seeing her mum and dad there, dressed up and standing slightly awkwardly together, made her heart beat too fast. She was overjoyed they'd come.

'Hi, Mum and Dad.' She smiled, kissing them briefly before lifting Elvis from his pushchair and holding him balanced on her hip. 'I'm so glad you came—'

Elvis waved his arms in the air, trying to dive-bomb out of Rebecca's arms. She bounced him up and down to distract him and, after a few seconds, handed him to her mum. He smiled and made a 'da, da, da' noise. Harriet instinctively beamed at his happy little face.

'Of course we've come,' she said. 'You're our only daughter and Elvis is our only grandson. Isn't he lovely, Thomas?'

Her father nodded, also smiling kindly at Elvis. Babies were good like that, made even the most serious people smile. Rebecca grabbed her parents a glass of sparkling wine each, kept cold in ice buckets they'd borrowed from the Pig and Whistle.

'I know,' she said, 'but it means a lot to me. Really it does. How are you, Mum?'

Harriet closed her eyes briefly and shook her head. 'I do not want to hear one word about my illness today, thank you very much,' she said. 'This is your wedding day and we're here to celebrate.'

Rebecca looked at her dad, who nodded to indicate that she should listen to Harriet's words.

'I'm not one to mope around,' she said. 'I'd rather we all got along with life as usual. I'm sure you know that.'

Rebecca took a deep breath and squeezed her mum's hands.

She noticed tears in Harriet's eyes, and that made her heart ache. Taking a deep breath, she gave her a big hug.

'You do know I love you, don't you, Mum? Having Elvis has changed the way I think about everything. I wish I'd told you I love you more often. And you, Dad.'

Harriet closed her eyes for a long moment and, when she opened them, they were sparkling with tears. 'We love you too, Rebecca,' she said. 'Really, from the bottom of our hearts. Don't we, Thomas?'

'Yes,' he agreed. 'Now do stop all this emotional wrangling. Elvis and me don't know what to do with ourselves.'

Rebecca laughed and gave him a hug. She looked around the group. 'So, what do you think, Dad?' she said, gesturing to the pimped up marquee, which was full of lots of Lenny's musician friends, who were hitting the booze already. 'Did Lenny say hello?'

'He certainly did, and introduced me to lots of the others,' he said. 'It's all very unusual really. You look lovely.'

Rebecca smiled at her dad, who couldn't look more like a small-town family GP if he were wearing fancy dress. Bushy white eyebrows, clipped white hair, white shirt and navy suit trousers, he had probably been born with a stethoscope around his neck. She felt suddenly and unusually protective about him. All this with her mum must be exhausting for him.

'Thanks, Dad,' she said. 'But do you mean it's unusual that I look lovely, or that the setting is unusual?'

'The setting,' he said. 'And Elvis seems very good indeed. I'm pleased for you, Rebecca, I really am. You know we hardly talk, but I think well of you. I want you to know that.'

Rebecca took a deep breath. *I think well of you.* That was

about as emotional as her dad got. Be grateful for small mercies, she told herself. Be grateful they're here at all. Elvis was wriggling now, so she took him back from Harriet.

'Thanks, Dad,' she said, kissing his cheek, determined that they would all enjoy the day.

They fell silent for a moment and, in the distance, she noticed Mack, set apart from the crowd, on the edge of the water throwing skimmers into the sea. She wondered what he could possibly be angry about today. Must be to do with the band. Perhaps Lenny hadn't liked his lyrics or something. Despite his acerbic wit, Mack was a sensitive soul. Or maybe he was secretly in love with Lenny and didn't want him to marry her? Come to think of it, she'd never seen him with a girlfriend.

'Lenny's father seems quite a character,' said Harriet from under her wide-brimmed hat, circling a finger around her plastic champagne flute. They all watched Alf get out of the police car parked on the road at the top of the beach and make his way, dressed in shorts, towards them, lifting his arms up in a silent cheer. 'Hopefully Lenny won't be quite the same.'

At that moment, Rebecca turned to see Lenny climb up on to one of the trestle tables, accidentally knocking off a small vase of freesias, which Leo caught before it hit the stones, and shaking up a bottle of champagne as if he were Jenson Button at Monaco, spraying the liquid everywhere. Elvis gurgled and began waving his arms around. He adored Lenny, who spent hours playing with him, making him chuckle and smile. Rebecca glanced at the expression on her mother's face and couldn't help laughing.

'I rather think he is, Mum,' she said. 'And that's why I'm marrying him.'

'They must be Rebecca's parents,' muttered Erin to Mel, Lexi and Edward, who had a crying baby Hope strapped to his chest in a BabyBjörn. Doesn't she look like her mum? Rebecca looks completely gorgeous, and this whole wedding is delightful.'

'Yes, she does look gorgeous,' said Lexi, following Erin's gaze and yawning an enormous yawn. 'Sorry. Poppy's not sleeping well at the moment. She's waking every hour or so. She's just started to roll but, when she gets on her front, she gets stuck and doesn't like it, so cries until I turn her back round.'

'Oh, no!' Erin said. 'What a nightmare! How do you cope with that?'

'I don't. I just put her in bed with me,' said Lexi. 'Probably a bad habit to get into, but I'm so tired, I don't know what else to do.'

Erin adjusted the strap of her green silk dress and nodded sympathetically. 'All you can do is get by. That's what I think.'

'Definitely,' said Mel. 'I'd never realized how tiring this was going to be. Those mums whose babies sleep eleven hours a night have no idea how lucky they are.'

'Mmm,' said Erin, feeling guilty and staying quiet. Hope normally slept for ten hours straight these days but, on the nights she didn't, Erin felt like a zombie the next day.

'By the way,' she said, quickly changing the subject before

anyone asked her how well Hope slept, 'you all look really lovely. I'm going to take some photographs in a minute.'

She scanned the wedding congregation. Katy and Alan were just arriving. Katy looked lovely in a red dress, but very thin. She'd obviously lost all her baby weight. And more. They both looked pretty harassed. Alan, carrying Rufus in his arms, bags over both shoulders and dressed in a suit, looked exhausted. Maybe he was doing the night feeds to help out Katy, who looked, it seemed to Erin, a little bit more healthy in her face though not as confident in her manner as she was when they'd first met at antenatal group. To her left was Lexi, yawning again, with Gary, who seemed to be around quite a lot these days, and, on her right, Mel and Leo, who were arguing about what factor suncream they should use on Mabel's bare arms and legs. None of the mums was paying Rebecca and Lenny a blind bit of notice! Babies ruled. Even if you tried to have your own life, in those early days, the baby came first. Erin reflected how having a baby was the ultimate equalizer among women. No matter how successful, or attractive, or well off you were – or, indeed, the opposite – babies cried and didn't sleep and needed endless attention, and whoever you were, whatever your circumstances, you had to try to learn to cope with that.

'Hey,' she said to the group, 'I've had an idea. Do you think one of us should offer to look after Rufus for the night, so Alan and Katy can have a proper rest together? It might give them both a lift to remember what life used to be like if they stayed in a hotel and had a few treats.'

Lexi looked a bit miffed, digging her toe into the pebbles.

Amy Bratley

'I wouldn't mind a night in a hotel. I'm bloody knackered. But, yeah, it's a sweet idea. We should do that.'

'I know you're tired, Lexi, I'm sorry,' said Erin. 'But I was just thinking that, because of how Katy has been and what she's been through, it might help.'

'Good idea,' said Mel, her eyes on Mabel, who was on the pebbles and had managed to grab one. She was about to put it in her mouth, before Mel snatched it out of the way, prompting tears. 'Oh, God. No, Mabel! Don't eat stones!'

Erin smiled at Alan and Katy and waved at them to join their group. At that moment, Lenny's friends cheered as he drank straight from the bottle he'd opened and sprayed everywhere. Gosh, she thought. Edward and Lenny were so different! Erin thought back to her own wedding, where Edward had been the archetypal restrained and traditional top-hat-and-tails groom. He would never, in a million years, have stood on a table top and drunk from a bottle. Her wedding had been held in a small village church near when she'd grown up. What a fiasco that day had been! Her father had driven her in his vintage car, choosing to go through a ford instead of over the bridge. Predictably, the car had broken down in the middle of the ford and she'd sat there in the back seat while the car bobbed up and down on the water and her dad stood, up to his knees in the stream, swearing and tinkering with the engine. Eventually, they'd abandoned the car to the AA and he'd carried her over his shoulder in a fireman's lift to safety. Her tiara had fallen off and drifted down the stream with the ducks and newts, probably ending up in a nest somewhere. Her memories were interrupted by a louder cry from Hope. She held on to Hope's hand.

356

'What's wrong, Hope?' she asked. 'Are you tired?'

Erin suppressed a yawn and saw Edward do the same. She widened her eyes at him, warning him not to say anything to the other mums. She felt too daft to admit why they were all so tired. They'd been up most of the night debating whether to take Hope to A&E because Edward had sprayed her room with fly spray after finding a mosquito bite on her ankle. It hadn't occurred to him to put a net over her cot, or to hunt down the culprit and squash him against the wall. A panic read of the mosquito-repellent instructions under a magnifying glass made it clear it should not be used around babies. It was even written in capitals! Calls to NHS Direct ensued, and they were reassured that Hope would be fine, although they should probably put her in a different room. But it wasn't enough. Josiah was never far from Erin's mind. The terror of loss never left her. If even the smallest thing threatened Hope's health in any way whatsoever, Erin could not rest. At two a.m., they went to A&E to get Hope checked over by a paediatrician, only to be sent home with his sympathetic smile and, just when the doctor had thought they were out of earshot, an exasperated sigh and muttered blasphemy. Erin had blushed from head to toe.

'Is it too bright for her here?' Edward asked, correcting Hope's hat. 'Maybe it's the breeze. I've noticed she doesn't really like the wind.'

Erin eyed Edward, dressed in a linen suit and straw fedora, jogging on the spot to pacify Hope. He then started swaying from side to side, so Hope's legs were swinging like pendulums. She burst out laughing.

'Doesn't like wind?' she laughed, incredulous. 'Don't be

ridiculous. Of course she likes wind. She likes nature in all its guises, don't you, sweet pea?'

'I don't think Mabel likes the wind either,' Mel said, lifting her up from the pebbles and turning her to face the group. 'She screws up her face so much it makes me laugh. How about Poppy?'

Erin and Mel waited for Lexi to answer, but she seemed preoccupied with staring over at Alan and Katy.

'Lexi?' said Erin. 'Does Poppy hate the wind?'

'What?' Lexi said. 'Wind? Yes, she has terrible wind.'

'Much like her mother,' muttered Gary.

'Hey!' said Lexi, nudging Gary.

'Actually,' said Mel smiling, 'I said does she like the wind?'

'Oh I see!' Lexi said, laughing. 'Gary, can you hold my glass for a second, please? I need to change Poppy. But do you know what? Poppy *hates* the wind.'

'That's all the babies agreed then,' said Leo with a grin, then he was distracted by the sound of a spoon banging against a glass. Erin followed his gaze to Lenny, who was still standing on the table, now clearing his throat. Erin smiled. He looked so young up there. She ran her eyes over his tanned face and golden locks. He looked dangerously handsome. A fleeting X-rated thought took her by surprise. She widened her eyes and shook her head. Took a gulp of her champagne. What was she thinking of?

'Hello, ladies and gentleman and babies,' said Lenny. 'Thank you for coming today. We're going to have the ceremony now, then you can get on with eating and drinking at the Pig and Whistle over the road. I'd just like to point out how lovely my wife-to-be looks. I'm so happy she's my bride, and thank you all for coming. We're gonna have a great party!'

Everyone cheered, and Erin glanced at Mabel, thinking the noise would probably frighten her. She liked wind, but not sudden loud noises. But under her pink, floral sunhat she had dropped fast asleep, her lips squished against the edge of the BabyBjörn into a cute heart shape. She'd passed the crying baton to Poppy, who needed a feed. Erin watched Lexi push a hand through her hair and take her glass back from Gary to take a swig. Poppy's cry got louder.

'Hello, everyone,' said Ted, Lenny's friend, and the celebrant of the ceremony. 'I'm here to talk to you about two people I love. Lenny and Rebecca—'

Poppy continued to cry and a few people turned to stare.

'Crap,' Lexi said, swallowing and moving away from the group. 'I need to feed her, now. I'll go and find somewhere.'

Lexi, with her sunglasses pushed on to the top of her head, sat on a rug away from the tent and rearranged her wrap-around dress until Poppy was happily feeding. She sucked in her tummy. In nearly six months, she hadn't lost much of her baby weight. Never mind. Being stick thin wasn't exactly a priority right now. Getting through each day being the best mum she could was her priority. Looking towards the sea, she watched the other people on the beach, most of them sunbathing or sitting around chatting, a few brave people in the sea. Most had given the wedding party a wide berth, but some had set their towels up near the small marquee so they could have a good stare at proceedings. The wedding group had quietened down, listening to Ted. She checked her watch. It was noon and, when the breeze stopped, pretty boiling. With the sun beating down on her head she longed to close her eyes and sleep. That rare commodity: sleep. In her pre-Poppy life, she'd had no idea how much of an indulgence sleeping in was. That feeling, when you woke up naturally and the light was streaming in through the curtains and the sounds of the traffic and people outside indicated it was probably almost lunchtime, felt like a dream. She didn't miss her old life, but to have one long lie-in, just once, would be fantastic. Bloody fantastic! Pulling down her sunglasses, she closed her eyes behind them, listening to the applause coming from the wedding tent. In spite of herself, Lexi felt glum. How many weddings had she been to in her life? Twenty? And she had always, or almost always, been on her own. Not that she was on her own any more. Poppy was here. Poppy was all she had ever wanted. Still, there was an ache in her heart when she watched Lenny and Rebecca hold one another close and kiss. Or Erin and Edward dance in the way they had that day. Why me? Why did I never meet Mr Right? Why had romantic love always been so elusive? And who was Mr Right anyway? Not Alan. That was very clear. All along she'd waited for someone to tick all the boxes, but did anyone ever do that?

'Hey,' said Gary, suddenly by her side. 'How are you doing? You missed the service.'

She opened her eyes, looked at him and smiled. He was a good guy. Funny, kind and thoughtful, they had become good friends over recent weeks and she'd been happy to ask him to come along to the wedding. But, even though he'd hinted he wanted to be more than friends, she wasn't going to entertain the idea of a relationship yet. I will just have to endure weddings and be happy for the lucky ones.

'I know, but I had to feed her,' she said. 'I heard some of Ted's words, from over here.'

Gary sat down on the pebbles next to her. Poppy had fallen asleep, so Lexi carefully put her in the buggy and pulled a parasol over her. 'Erin was just talking to me,' said Gary. 'She said she would take Poppy for a few hours and we could go out together, if you'd like that. *I* would, so I wondered if I could take you for dinner?'

Lexi smiled. 'She's sweet. But I don't know. I mean, Gary, I think you're brilliant. You've been a real friend to me over the last few weeks—'

'Not to mention chauffeur,' said Gary.

'Yes, and that. It's just that I'm reluctant to start seeing you in a different light. What I mean is, I really like you, a lot, but I don't need to complicate Poppy's life any more than I have already. I don't need to complicate my life. I'm hopeless at relationships. Always have been. I'm destined to be single for ever.'

'So,' said Gary, 'are you going to take a pledge of abstinence for the rest of her life just because things haven't worked out before? Or could we just try and enjoy a couple of nights out together? It might do you good.'

Lexi frowned. *Might do you good* made her feel like he was doing her a favour.

'I'm not an invalid!' she said. 'Just because I'm a single mother, please don't take pity on me and see me as an easy ride.'

Gary put his hands up in the air. 'I don't!' he said. 'Christ,

Lexi, you're hard work. All I'm suggesting is a night out. Dress up, eat a tasty dinner, wash it down with a glass of wine and then that's it. But I'm not going to force you into it! Is it because you still like that Alan bloke? Is he still sniffing around you?' His face darkened. He bit his bottom lip and narrowed his eyes at her.

'No!' said Lexi. 'Alan was a fantasy. He only wants to talk to me now about Katy, so we've had a few conversations about how he can help her out. Which is fine, of course. Actually, since meeting him again, I feel like I almost invented the entire thing.'

'Maybe you did. You decided to be in love with a man who you couldn't have, because it was easier than making a relationship work with someone you could have. That's what some people like you do. They find reasons to destroy every relationship they ever have. You're not even giving me a chance.'

Lexi shook her head and, though she smiled, tears pricked her eyes. 'What do you mean, "people like you"?' she said, her voice hoarse.

'I mean people who had a shitty childhood. People who didn't get enough love and attention from their parents and so didn't get the chance to form a loving, trusting relationship with them. People who protect their hearts at all costs. That's what I mean.'

Lexi swallowed. No one had ever spoken to her like this before. No one had probably cared enough to speak to her like this before. She tried to laugh him off, but couldn't.

'Enough pseudo-psychology, thanks, Gary,' she said, standing up now. 'You don't know what you're talking about. You hardly know me.'

'I do know you,' he said. 'I've seen how loving and devoted you are to Poppy. I've seen how much you care about the people you work with and I've seen your face fall when you talk about your childhood. I've seen how horrible your mum is to you. You care about everyone else and work to make them feel safe and secure, but you've never had that yourself. You deserve it, Lexi, and I want to be the man to give you that.'

Lexi's mouth hung open. Gary's words stung her, but they were laden with truth. 'I should get back to the others,' she whispered. 'I think we're all going to the pub now, aren't we?'

'Yeah,' said Gary, his eyes downcast but his face blazing. 'Look, I might head off home soon.'

'Oh,' said Lexi, the lump in her throat getting bigger by the second. 'Right. See you and – oh, it doesn't matter.'

Pulling the pushchair over the bumpy pebbles, she felt furious. What? So just because she wouldn't agree to a night out with him, Gary was going off in a sulk? Typical. He didn't get what he wanted, so he didn't want to stay around. Well, that was fine. He could go home. She wouldn't care if she never saw him again. She was off relationships, wasn't she? Sworn against them. And this was exactly why. Women were supposed to be fickle, but it was the men! Gary wasn't really interested in her, and nor did he know her as well as he claimed. If he did, there was no way he'd go home now. But, then again, she thought, clocking Alan striding towards her, holding two full glasses of champagne, what was there to stay for? Maybe he was right. Maybe she had deliberately decided to be in love with an unavailable man so she wouldn't have to be in a long-term relationship.

'Lexi,' said Alan, now in front of her, offering her a glass. She shook her head crossly.

'Oh,' he said. 'Like that, is it? So, I wanted to speak to you, quickly, before we head over to the pub. It's about Katy.'

Why don't you speak to Katy about Katy? Lexi thought. Why did he have to speak to her? Katy was the mum she knew least, because she'd come to very few of the meet-ups. Understandably.

'I'm really pleased to say that she went to see the doctor,' he said. 'And I think it's really helping. Katy told me that you said something that changed her mind. Something about your childhood.'

Bloody hell. Not again! Why was everyone talking about her childhood? Yes, it was true, her childhood was a cautionary tale for mothers, which she rarely put under the microscope, but she didn't want to think about it now. Though she was listening to Alan, her eyes were on Katy, who, on the other side of the tent, with her back to Alan and Lexi, was having an in-depth talk to Erin. All she'd done was give Katy a little bit of advice. Why was he making such a big deal out of it?

'And I just want to say thank you for sharing that with her, because none of her other friends told her what they thought,' said Alan, taking Lexi in his arms and hugging her tight. 'It's helped us both. Katy is such a successful, powerful woman, you know, and I can already feel some of her coming back.'

Lexi accepted the hug, expecting to feel something. But she didn't. All she felt was worried that Katy would turn around and see them and guilty that Gary would think she'd just lied to him.

'Alan,' she said, 'I don't think Katy would like you hugging me like this.'

'What?' he said, pulling back with a confused expression on his face. 'Oh, I've told her all about our one-night stand, just to reassure her. She knows it doesn't mean a thing any more. I'm sure she's had a few in her life. We all have, haven't we? With you, it wasn't about the sex, was it? It was the way we talked. Like now. We get on vocally.'

Alan's hand was on her shoulder and she longed to shake it off. She nodded at his words but felt her stomach folding and churning.

'Is everything all right, Lexi?' said Gary, suddenly by her side again. 'I think I will stay, just for a while, if you don't mind.' He gave Alan a hard stare but didn't say hello.

'Hello, Gary,' said Alan. 'How's life in the taxi?'

'Life's a journey,' said Gary. 'And I don't spend my whole life in the taxi.'

Alan burst out laughing and patted Gary on the back. 'Okay,' he said. 'Better get back to Katy. Thanks again, Lexi.'

'Bye,' said Gary and, when Alan walked away, he muttered 'Fuck off' under his breath. Lexi elbowed him in the ribs.

'Well,' he said. 'I can't stand him. And, besides, he made you miserable.'

'That was then,' she said, raising her face to look at Gary. She smiled.

'And this is now,' he said, leaning in to give her a surprisingly gentle, lingering kiss on her lips. Her body tingled, first with anxiety and then with delight.

Someone whistled, but she had no idea who. For a second, she pulled away and widened her eyes. Gary's face was frozen, probably thinking she was about to roast him alive for lunging in. She laughed.

'Go on,' he said. 'Live a little.'

Oh, what the hell! She kissed him back.

Over in the pub garden, the party became increasingly raucous as the hours rolled on. Lenny's dad played the guitar, while his mum passed around the delicious vegetarian food she'd prepared and a waitress from the pub made sure the alcohol flowed. Rebecca, tipsy now, was trying to retract her mobile phone from Elvis's mouth. Even though he had a rattle to chew on, it was her phone he liked the most.

'We'll have to start them on solids soon, won't we?' said Mel. 'We'll all be covered in pureed butternut squash.'

'That's something to look forward to!' said Erin. 'Rebecca, I need to tell you how lovely you look. Thank you for inviting us. We're having a lovely day.'

Rebecca grinned. 'I think I'm going to start telling you all how much I love you now,' she said. 'I don't know what I would have done without you all since having Elvis.'

Rebecca watched Mel and Erin's faces. They were smiling in return, both of them a little bit pissed.

'I feel the same,' said Mel. 'When I first met you all, I never thought we'd become friends like this. Actually, when we first met, I didn't even look at you because I was too busy crying into my sleeve!'

The women laughed, but quietened when Harriet approached them. 'Rebecca,' she said, looking slightly pale. 'I think your father and I are going to head off.' She rubbed her head and closed her eyes for a second.

'Are you all right, Mum?'

'Yes,' she said. 'Don't fret. Bye, Rebecca. Enjoy your day. Here's something for you. Wait until we've gone before you open it – and remember the holiday.'

Harriet handed Rebecca a white envelope, which felt as though it had a letter inside. She kissed her parents, and then they were gone. Sitting down on a chair, taking a moment to think about her mum, with Elvis on her knee and the party going on around them, she was about to open the envelope when Mack approached her. He was holding a pint of beer that was sloshing dangerously close to the top.

'Congratulations, Becs,' he said. 'You look beautiful.'

'Thanks,' she said, while Elvis tried to grab the envelope. 'Hey, what's up?'

Mack pulled up a seat next to her. 'Yes,' he said. 'I was being selfish. Lenny must think I'm a twat.'

'Why?' Rebecca said. 'He would never think that. You're his best friend. What happened?'

'When he told me this morning that he didn't want to do the tour I felt like he was taking away my chance at living the dream,' he said. 'But I get why he said no. Elvis is too little and he doesn't want to leave you on your own.'

Rebecca processed Mack's words, unable not to show how shocked she was.

'You did know about the tour, didn't you?' Mack said slowly. 'That he's turned it down?'

Rebecca shook her head.

'Shit,' he said. 'Sorry.'

'So,' she said, 'what was it going to be?'

'Six weeks around California,' he said. 'Supporting Tree

People. Would've done so much for our profile – not to mention my love life.'

'When was it?' she asked, thinking about Lenny's recent quiet moods.

'In about six weeks from now,' Mack said. 'You know, I even thought about getting a new lead man. But then I realized that Lenny is irreplaceable. I'm trying to forget about it. Lenny reckons we'll have a chance again in the future. So, what's this you've got, Elvis? Should he be eating that envelope, Becs?'

Rebecca glanced down at Elvis to see him sucking and chewing the edge of the white envelope. She pulled it out of his mouth and ripped open one end, all the time thinking of what Lenny had sacrificed, without even telling her. It made her love him all the more, but she also felt sad that he'd had to give up on a dream. She didn't want having a baby to mean either of them giving up on their dreams. If only she could go with him. Take Elvis, too. Six weeks in California sounded amazing. Maybe they could sell the Beetle. Would that be enough money? Opening the letter from her mum and dad and seeing what was in the envelope, she froze. Two return round-the-world-ticket vouchers. *Choose where you want to go*, her mother had written. *I'm sorry if we held you back. Life is too short not to follow your dreams.* She was wiping at the tears in her eyes when a plan sprang into her head.

'Can you hold Elvis for a second, Mack?' she asked, handing him her son. 'I need to find the microphone. I've got an announcement to make.'

*

Katy and Alan, Erin and Edward, Mel and Leo, Lexi and Gary were all sitting together around a large wooden picnic table in the pub garden with their plates of food and drinks. Their babies were either in their laps or asleep in pushchairs, muslin squares draped strategically over them to prevent the sun burning their skin. Initially, there had been several other people on the same table, but when the antenatal group began talking about the babies incessantly, those other people glazed over and drifted away from the table, rolling their eyes at one another as they did so.

'Bloody new parents,' Katy heard one woman say. 'They think everyone wants to hear about the colour of their baby's poo! I'll never be like that if I have kids.'

Katy smiled to herself. She bet the woman would be exactly like that. Even though she realized that her talking about Rufus was incredibly boring for most other people, she was still obsessed with everything he did, especially because, now, he did so much more than when he was first born. Born. She closed her eyes as a memory of the birth flashed into her head. Feeling a familiar prickle of sweat bead on her forehead, she gripped the edge of the table and thought about what her psychotherapist had suggested she did at these times. Take deep breaths. Mindfulness. Concentrate on breathing. Think only of your breathing. But it was too noisy, and Katy couldn't concentrate. What else had the psychotherapist said? Distract yourself from the moment. Talk to someone else. Let other people support you. She looked at her hands. They were shaking slightly. To her left, Alan was talking to Edward about New Zealand, and to her right Lexi and Gary were talking to each other. She lifted her glass of water to her lips and drank.

'Are you all right, Katy?' asked Lexi softly and kindly. No one else was listening. 'How are you feeling now?'

Katy smiled gratefully at her. But should she just launch in and say how she felt? Was it appropriate? Wouldn't Lexi think she was insane? Katy had never talked to others about things like that.

'You don't have to tell me,' said Lexi. 'But I hope you're okay.'

'I saw the doctor,' Katy said, her voice shaky. 'And she referred me to a psychotherapist. I've been diagnosed with post-traumatic-stress disorder.'

'Right,' said Lexi.

Katy thought about the diagnosis. The psychotherapist said it had prompted her feelings of detachment and depression. Rather than give her anti-depressants, she'd been referred to see a psychologist who specialized in PTSD. She'd been encouraged to talk about the birth and what it had meant to her, which had been a revelation.

'Not really wedding-party chat, is it?' Katy said, trying to make light of it, but her panic was passing.

'Oh, course it is,' Lexi replied. 'I'd rather we had an honest chat about how we felt than pretended everything was fine. I'm glad you're seeing a psychotherapist. Who is it? I know a few of them.'

'Dr Anthony Hill,' she said. 'He's a specialist. Honestly, anyone would think I'd been on the front line.'

'No,' Lexi said, with a small shake of her head. 'Don't put yourself down. You've had a seriously bad time.'

Katy swallowed a gulp of her water, feeling wobbly and

emotional. She turned to Lexi and grabbed her hand. She held it for a few moments, tears misting her eyes.

'Thank you for what you said,' she said. 'None of my so-called friends confronted me about how I was behaving, you know? Not even Anita, my business partner, who I've known for years and knows me inside out. Only you.'

Lexi smiled. 'I only said what you already knew. I'm really pleased you're getting support. But, look, it's here, too, around this table.'

Katy looked up. Suddenly, all the women were looking at Lexi and Katy, listening in, smiling eagerly, showing her their support.

'We all have our own issues, and we all have small babies to look after,' said Lexi. 'We'd love it if you came along to some more of the meet-ups we have. There's even been talk of exercising, hasn't there, Mel?'

'Yep,' Mel said. 'Yoga is the next one we thought we should try, if you're interested, Katy.'

Lexi squeezed Katy's hand briefly and the women smiled at one another. Then they both let go.

Moments later, Katy was holding Rufus's hand while he made gurgling noises. She was about to pick him up when she was interrupted by a noise from the microphone. Rebecca was testing it out.

'Hello, hello,' she said, tapping it. 'Can everyone hear me? I have something to say'. Lenny was sitting at a table nearby, with Elvis on his lap. He grinned at her appreciatively. Her hair had come loose from being pinned up and she looked even more breathtaking than earlier. Katy felt from nowhere a stab of jealousy. 'Something to say to Len, Rebecca continued.'

She couldn't stop smiling. She cleared her throat and waved two tickets at him.

'These are round-the-world tickets my parents gave us for a wedding present,' she said. 'Mack told me you were asked to tour with the Tree People in California, but you turned it down. I can't believe you did that! It's everything you've always wanted. So, I have an idea. We'll come, too! It can be the first leg of our round-the-world trip. What do you say, Len?'

Katy watched Lenny, whose expression was one of complete astonishment. Probably for the first time, he had been rendered speechless. His dad, Alf, stood up from his seat.

'He says yes!' he shouted. 'And if he doesn't, I'll come with you instead.'

Everyone laughed, muttering with excitement. Lenny stood up with Elvis and approached Rebecca. He said something in her ear and they kissed passionately, his free hand slipping to her bottom, which he squeezed, provoking a cheer and whistles from their guests. Then, Rebecca handed the microphone back to Alf, who in turn cleared his throat and called for attention.

'Okay, crowd,' he said. 'I think Len and Becs are going to take to the dance floor now. Apparently, thanks to their friend Erin, they've got a surprise in store.'

Everyone clapped and cheered. Lenny handed Elvis to his mum, then he and Rebecca, both laughing, took their position in the middle of the open space in the garden area. Rebecca stretched her left leg back and bent her right in between Lenny's legs. They took each other's hands and Rebecca threw back her head, her hair flowing down her back. Alf pressed a button on the DVD player and tango music began to play. Erin stood up on her chair, clapped and cheered wildly.

Argentine tango, she mouthed to the group, before turning back to Rebecca and Lenny and chanting, 'Walk, cross, figure eight, leg hook!'

For the length of the song, the crowd were mesmerized.

'Wow!' said Lexi, turning to Katy. 'Love's young dream, eh?'

'Yes,' said Katy. 'I guess that's the thing about life. It has its ups and its downs.'

'Bloody rollercoaster more like,' said Lexi. 'One minute you're going slowly uphill, the next thing you're cascading into a deep, dark hole, clinging on for dear life.'

Both women laughed and continued to stare at the dancing couple, transfixed by their happiness.

I'm not drunk. I can still walk in a straight line, Mel told herself, as she and Leo staggered down their road towards home. Worryingly, the street lamps appeared to be bending like giraffes eating leaves and the cracks between the pavement stones were moving like snakes in the grass. Gripping hold of Leo's arm, she paused to take off her heels and convince her head to stop swimming. Regretting the extra wine she'd had, after a day of dribs and drabs of booze, she groaned. The alcohol had hit her hard.

'I shouldn't have had anything to drink at all!' she said, suddenly maudlin. 'I'm a mother now! How irresponsible is that?'

'You're still allowed to enjoy yourself every now and then,'

Leo said, laughing. 'Just drink lots of water when we get home. God, I'm knackered. We're not used to this any more, are we?'

Mel shook her head but felt irrationally annoyed with herself. 'I know I'm allowed to enjoy myself,' she said, 'but everything's changed now, hasn't it? Before we had Mabel, it didn't matter if I was irresponsible. Now, if something happened to me, Mabel would be left alone, without her mother. She'd be one parent down, and I know exactly how it feels to not have—'

To not have . . . a dad. She knew what it felt like not to have a dad. She couldn't hold in the tears. Leo put his arm around her and pulled her in close. 'Don't cry,' he said. 'You're just feeling tired. We need to sleep.'

Mel sniffed. She thought about how much she missed her dad, and found herself thinking about Jacques in London with Coco and Suki. He needed Leo in his life.

'I've been thinking,' said Mel, trying to get the key in the lock of their front door. 'You should go and see Jacques. Take part in his life. He needs you, I'm sure.'

'Thanks,' Leo said. 'I'd like that. But why the change of heart?'

He slipped his hand around her waist and kissed the back of her neck. She pushed open the door and Mel flicked on the light. Leo carried the pushchair up the stairs and Mel staggered up after him. Inside the flat, they moved straight into the bedroom and Leo transferred Mabel from her buggy to her cot. They made amazed faces at each other when she sniffed but didn't wake up howling. Leo, in his clothes, lay on the bed. Mel unzipped her dress and let it fall on to the carpet where she was standing. She found a glass of water and drank it down in one.

'I went to see Coco,' said Mel in a loud whisper.

'Did you?' Leo said. 'Why?'

'I wanted to see if she was interested in you,' Mel said.

'And?' Leo said.

'She's gay,' Mel replied.

Leo sat up in the dark. 'Is she?' said Leo. 'Wow. I didn't see that coming.'

'Anyway,' said Mel, climbing on to the bed. 'I've been thinking. After today, I thought I'd ask . . . Would you like to . . . would you like to—'

'Have another baby?' said Leo. 'Not right yet, Mel, but one day. In a couple of years maybe?'

'No, I wasn't going to say that,' she said, yawning. 'I was going to say, would you like to get married? Would you marry me? I'd like to, I mean, I'd like to get married. To you. Be our own family.'

She lay down and Leo moved his body around hers so they lay on the cover in spoons. He held her tightly.

'Yes,' he said, into her hair. 'Yes. I'd love to.'

Mel said nothing. Leo lifted his head and leaned over to see her face. But she was fast asleep now. She didn't hear a thing when Leo carefully put the blanket over her, kissed her cheek and placed a fresh glass of water by her bedside. She didn't hear a whisper all night long, as the three of them slept softly, dreaming about one another, their breaths and lives and hearts so close and intertwined. It was the first night that Mabel slept through without waking.

Epilogue

'Is everyone ready to see Becs?' asked Erin, excitedly. 'It's all set up.'

It was Elvis and Hope's first birthday, and Erin had arranged a get-together for the antenatal group to mark a year since they'd all met. On the rainiest, windiest day that year, Lexi, Katy and Mel had blown through Erin's front door, fighting with beaten umbrellas and haywire hair, clutching their wide-eyed children. Once inside, Erin leaned hard on the door against the wind until it clicked shut.

'Did you hear that thunder?' she had exclaimed as she ushered the damp, windswept mums into the warmly lit kitchen with Hope balanced comfortably on her hip. 'Come in and get cosy. I've been baking.'

It wasn't as if the women hadn't seen each other recently. They had, but not all together for a while, so Erin had made a special effort, baking cakes and biscuits for them, loving every minute. It was hard to find days that suited everyone, especially now that Mel was setting up her own freelance design agency from home one day a week while Leo looked after

Mabel and Katy was working four days a week, and had been for some time. Lexi was due back at work part-time soon, and Erin was holding dance classes two evenings a week. Also, none of them had seen Rebecca since a month after her wedding, the previous August. They'd sold Lenny's VW Beetle, got back the deposit on their flat and emptied their bank of savings before heading to California, the first leg of their round-the-world trip. Now, five months later, they were in Sydney and, to raise cash, Rebecca was working part-time in a café during the day while Lenny did gigs at night, sharing the care of Elvis. Rebecca kept a blog and frequently posted on Facebook to keep in touch. Today, though, they had arranged to Skype her so they could all see her together. Erin had set up the computer on the kitchen table and arranged chairs in front for all to sit on. While the others chatted and the babies played with colourful building blocks on a mat she'd put down on the floor, Erin made hot drinks, glancing happily at her friends and their children, acutely aware of how lucky she was.

'Here you go,' said Erin, handing out mugs of hot chocolate to Lexi, Mel and Katy. 'I thought we needed warming up in this weather.'

'Lovely!' said Lexi, placing her mug on the table. 'Could I get a glass of water as well, please? I'm parched.'

'This is delicious,' Mel said, taking a sip, suddenly jumping up to disentangle Mabel's fingers from the flex of a lamp. 'Careful, Mabel! You find danger wherever you go!'

'Oh, they all do,' said Erin. 'You have to have eyes in the back of your head. I've completely baby-proofed this house, so the babies should be all right. *I* can't even get into some of the cupboards now! Anyway, shall I call Rebecca? I said I would about now.'

'Yes,' said Katy, sitting down with Rufus on her lap. 'Let's see her. Thanks for setting this up, Erin. I keep meaning to contact her, but work's so busy.'

Erin smiled at Katy. She understood that Katy wasn't complaining but that she was pleased work was busy. It was how she operated best, and keeping occupied was part of her coping strategy when anxiety struck. Mabel started to cry.

'Look,' Mel said, picking her up and straightening the lamp flex. 'We're going to see Rebecca on the screen.'

'Yes,' said Erin. 'Let me get on with this before the babies go wild.'

Erin clicked on the Call button, glancing over her shoulder at Hope, who was chewing the ear of a plastic rabbit. Rufus, who could now toddle, had wriggled down from Katy's lap and was enjoying knocking over anything Hope showed an interest in.

'That's boys for you,' said Katy apologetically. 'Rufus, darling, be gentle with Hope. Little girls don't like to be manhandled.'

Suddenly, the screen went black, there was the sound of a dial tone and then Rebecca's face appeared. Everyone cheered. With some of her hair braided over the top of her head and the rest of it fanned over her shoulders, her eyes huge and brown, she looked beautiful.

'Hello!' Erin said. 'Rebecca. We're all here!'

'Doesn't she look good?' said Lexi, to no one in particular, looking over Erin's shoulder. 'Rebecca, you look great. How are you?'

'Hey, girls,' Rebecca said, holding Elvis on her knee, dressed in a Hawaiian print shirt and blue shorts. 'I'm good. Great. Wow, look at you all! How are you?'

They each squinted, at Elvis, trying to focus on his face, but he was moving so much, his arms and legs circling like windmills, that Rebecca had to put him down.

'That was Elvis,' Rebecca said. 'He's quite an independent little man!'

'Well, he *has* already travelled the world,' said Mel. 'He's pretty rich in the life-experience department.'

Rebecca laughed then pulled a sad face. 'Oh, I miss you, girls,' she said. 'This is brilliant, being here, seeing these places I've dreamed of seeing, but, especially with having Elvis, I miss my original antenatal-group friends.'

'We miss you, too,' said Erin, sighing. 'How's Lenny?'

'Yes,' said Katy quietly. 'How is Lenny?'

For some reason, Erin felt herself blush when she asked about Lenny. And wasn't Katy blinking a little furiously? A certain stillness descended on the room as they waited for Rebecca to answer. Maybe he had the same effect on all women. She'd never dare ask.

'Oh, he's unbelievable,' said Rebecca. 'Lenny is becoming more and more like his dad. The other day when he was looking after Elvis while I was working at the café, he started busking with Elvis out on the beach. I nearly fainted when I saw them. They were collecting money in Elvis's sippy cup!'

The women laughed. Katy took a drink of her hot chocolate and murmured with pleasure.

'How about you guys?' she said. 'Any big news? How's life?'

No one said anything, waiting for the others to go first. Mel cleared her throat.

'You know I proposed,' said Mel. 'Well, I'm thinking of retracting it. Leo is driving me insane! He thinks that, just because I'm at home four days a week looking after Mabel, I should do all the housework. Honestly, we've had so many rows about it. He doesn't implicitly say I should do it, but it's all in the noises he makes. Home from work, he walks in the door and starts unpacking the dishwasher before he's even taken off his coat!'

Another big laugh from everyone, and then a lot of crying from Rebecca's end as Elvis fell over and bumped his nose on the floor. She tried to calm him down, but he was getting more upset.

'What about Jacques?' said Rebecca. 'Have you seen him? Any more impromptu visits to London?'

'Not me,' said Mel, tucking her black bob behind her ears. 'Leo has been up to see him twice more and to talk to Coco. He said Jacques was fairly suspicious of him, but he plans to take it slowly. You can't blame Jacques. Coco's going to bring him down here next month to meet me and Mabel, so I'll let you know how that goes.'

'You've been very understanding,' said Erin, gently patting Mel's back. They smiled at one another. On the screen, Rebecca bounced Elvis on her knee, but he was still grizzling.

'Is everything okay with Leo, though?' said Rebecca.

'Yes,' said Mel. 'Apart from the housework crap, he's actually a bit of a star when it comes to being a new dad. I don't know if he's making up for lost time or something, but he's so possessive of Mabel I can hardly get a hold of her at the weekend. Actually, I barely get any attention from him at all, but I'm glad, if you catch my drift.'

'I know what you mean.' Rebecca smiled. 'And how are things with you, Katy?'

'Yes,' said Katy. 'I'm a lot better, thanks, Rebecca. It's taken a while, but I'm getting there. Working helps, and knowing that Rufus is in good hands when I'm at work helps me relax. Alan's brilliant with him as well. I thought the novelty might wear off, but I guess he's the kind of person who excels in whatever he does. Does that sound annoying?'

'No,' said Rebecca, before laughing. 'Well, maybe a bit.'

Katy laughed and rolled her eyes. 'Anyway, how's your mum? Mel told me about her illness.'

Rebecca's face fell. She took a sip from a glass of water near her chair and gave a sad smile.

'We had a week's holiday with my parents,' she said, 'but I think we should have done it sooner. She was in quite a bad way. I just regret the time I didn't spend with her so much, I can't tell you. When I look back at how I was, I think I was so immature.'

Elvis screamed, and Rebecca stood, rocking him against her chest.

'You weren't,' said Mel. 'We all have to make a bid for freedom at some point. I guess this little lot will do, too, in the future. We'll have to stick together so we can help each other through when they leave home and refuse to talk to us!'

The women laughed, and the babies made their noises. Elvis's scream was getting louder.

'Sorry,' Rebecca said. 'I think I'll have to go. Elvis needs to sleep. I was going to put him to bed before we spoke but I wanted you all to see him. Let's do this again? Bye, ladies.'

They all said goodbye and Erin turned off the computer.

Taking seats around the table, they all pulled sad faces at each other.

'I miss her,' said Mel. 'I don't want to wish away her trip of a lifetime, but I can't wait until she comes back. She was really good to me at the start, when Leo decided to bugger off.'

'Why don't we eat?' said Erin, moving the computer out of the way. She handed plates to everyone, plastic ones for the babies, now in highchairs around the table. After a few minutes of trying to get food into the baby's mouths and a fragment into their own, all eyes were on Lexi, who had turned a pale shade of green and had gone completely silent. Her hot chocolate and plate of food was untouched in front of her, and she sat, both hands around her glass of water, sipping delicately, as if she had a horrendous hangover.

'Are you all right, Lexi?' asked Erin, frowning. 'You've barely said a word. Is everything all right with Gary?'

Lexi sighed and flushed pink. 'Yes,' she said. 'It's all good with Gary. I've been seeing him more, and he seems to have a shirt hanging in my wardrobe.'

Erin clapped and grinned. 'That's what I like to hear,' she said. 'But are you feeling well? You look ever so pale.'

'Er, sorry, I'm feeling a bit strange,' she answered, her eyes flicking up to the group. 'I'm . . . I'm . . . er, well. Actually, it's early days, but I can't sit here and not tell you.'

Katy stretched over the table to briefly place her hand on Lexi's. 'Tell us what? Has this anything to do with your mother?'

Lexi shook her head and screwed up her nose. 'No,' she said. 'It's . . . I'm . . . I'm pregnant. I'm only six weeks gone, so obviously there's a chance I could miscarry. But, yes. Believe it or not, I'm pregnant!'

They all gasped. Katy put her hand over her mouth.

'Congratulations!' Mel and Katy said in unison. Katy leaned over to hug Lexi.

Erin looked around at the other women. She knew they were dying to ask if this baby was by donor sperm or if Gary was the father. Erin opened her mouth to ask the question, but the moment passed when Mabel yanked at the tablecloth and managed to knock over three glasses of water.

'Oops!' said Mel, pushing back her chair, grabbing the glasses and unwrapping a roll of kitchen paper to soak up the water, by which time Erin had thrown a towel on to the table. 'Bloody hell. Sorry, Erin.'

'You're a dark horse,' said Katy to Lexi, next to her. 'You kept that quiet. How many times have I seen you in the last six weeks? Three times, and you haven't told me?'

'I only just found out,' she said. 'I only just did a test. I say "a" test but, actually I did nine tests. You know what it's like when you can't see if the line is there or not, and so many of them come in packs of two, it's a bargain really.'

The women laughed knowingly and Lexi put her hand on her tummy, unconsciously protective, before gingerly taking another sip of water.

'Round two,' said Mel with a laugh. 'You're a brave woman.'

Lexi smiled and pulled an anxious expression, running a hand through her short blonde hair.

'Another one of these mysterious beings coming into the world then,' Erin said, looking around the table at the four different babies wriggling in their highchairs. Mabel, with an

air of decadence, had her feet up on the tray, a chocolate biscuit smeared all over her face and feet; Poppy was turning her
pot of yoghurt upside down and hitting it like a drum, shriek-
ing in delight when the contents splattered out the sides; Rufus
was throwing chunks of cheese on the floor and gabbling in
what sounded like Russian; while Hope was aiming food at
her mouth and giggling hysterically when she missed.

'Yes,' said Lexi. 'I hope I can be a good mum to two children. One seems like a big job.'

'Of course you can,' said Mel. 'You'll be brilliant. You already
are. Much better than me.'

'Don't be mad,' said Lexi. 'I have my moments, but it's a
learning experience, isn't it? Some days I'm hopeless, and other
days it all goes to plan.'

'I think it's easier being at work,' said Katy. 'And don't let
anyone tell you otherwise, though the picking up and dropping off is much more stressful than you'd ever think.'

'Don't let Leo hear you say it's harder than going to work,'
said Mel. 'He'd try his hardest to prove that I've got it easier
by looking after Mabel for most of the week.'

'Fruitless activity,' said Katy. 'Motherhood is the hardest job
a woman will ever do, whatever choices she makes about going
back to work and when. Take it from me.'

'And the most rewarding,' said Erin. 'One hopes.'

Another laugh as Hope, on queue, threw her yoghurt pot
at Erin's head.

'Great comic timing,' said Lexi. 'Perhaps she'll be a com-
edienne.'

'Perhaps,' Erin said, looking doubtful. She leaned over to
wipe Hope's face and kiss her cheek, neon pink with teething.

What will you be, little girl? she thought to herself, as she pulled her out of the highchair and on to her lap for a cuddle. What will you dream of? Who will you love? Fleetingly, Erin thought of Josiah. She kissed Hope's head, never wanting to let her go out there into the big wide world. Glancing at Lexi, she noticed her yawning.

'Do you want a sleep, Lexi?' she asked. 'I remember that blanket tiredness you feel at the start. All those hormones going crazy.'

Lexi widened her eyes knowingly and grinned. 'Thanks, but I'm happy here. I don't want to miss out on anything you talk about.'

'I'm bound to say something profound,' said Erin with a peal of laughter.

'I need to ask your advice, actually,' said Mel, to everyone. She moved her eyes comically from side to side. 'It's about my sex life – or, should I say, my non-existent sex life—'

'See?' said Lexi. 'It's all about to get interesting.'

'Let me top up your hot chocolate first,' said Erin. 'We're all ears—'

And so, in the warmth of Erin's kitchen, while the rain streaked against the windows, they talked together, while the babies giggled and cried and crawled and Lexi's baby developed in her womb, now no bigger than a pea, with buds for arms and legs and a heart the size of a poppy seed. Another everyday miracle, already loved.

The Girls' Guide to Homemaking
AMY BRATLEY

Is home really where the heart is?

'What makes you happy? What do you want from life?'

I ran through a list of things that I supposed would make me sound cool. And then I told the truth.

'A home,' I said. 'A home with some people in it I love.'

On a mission to have the perfect home, with tweeting blue-birds and a white picket fence, Juliet hits a major stumbling block – reality. On the first night with her boyfriend in their new flat, Juliet discovers that Simon has been sleeping with her best friend. After growing up in a dysfunctional family with secrets that haunt her, there's no way she is prepared to build her nest on a broken branch.

Heartbroken and seeking an escape from her troubles, Juliet retreats into the comforting world of her grandmother's Fifties homemaking manuals, discovering tips like 'Put a ribbon in your hair to brighten your husband's day', and, though Juliet knows that won't get her anywhere, she discovers that craft and homemaking are back in style. Taking control of her life, Juliet is determined to get her home with a heart. But who will win hers?

ISBN: 978-0-330-51800-0

The Saturday Supper Club
AMY BRATLEY

A dinner date with destiny?

Wanted: four amateur cooks to compete
in a supper-club contest

Rules: four strangers, four weeks, four houses,
four dinner parties

You might win: a cash prize

You might lose: your heart

Eve had her world torn apart three years ago, when the love of her life, Ethan, disappeared – and she never found out why. But, now, her life is rosy. With a lovely new boyfriend, Joe, and a café opening on the cards, things finally seem to be falling into place.

. . . until she agrees to take part in a supper-club competition for a local newspaper. Eve is cooking the first dinner, and who should turn up on her doorstep expecting a three-course meal but her long-lost love, Ethan?

ISBN: 978-0-330-51968-7

extracts reading groups
competitions books new
discounts extracts extracts
competitions discounts
books new events reading groups
reading groups extracts discounts
new books
events extracts reading groups
new titles reading groups
interviews events new
reading groups events extracts extracts books
books new books events events interviews new books extracts
new books events events new

www.panmacmillan.com

discounts extracts discounts books
extracts events reading groups
competitions books extracts new